Escape

Escape

Who do you rely on

when the worst happens?

by

A M Newson

To Sofia
I hope you enjoy the story — I like Rosie the best — I hope you like her too!
A M Newson

Copyright © 2018

All rights reserved

ISBN-9798853745278

To friendship

Chapter One

Day 1: Friday - Police

One late Friday afternoon in March in the relevant police headquarters of a northern town, a message popped up in the Chief Superintendent's inbox. It was not marked urgent but he was organised and decisive so he sent a message to the relevant sergeant who spoke to the relevant constable and that was that. Except it wasn't.

Chapter 2

Day 2: Saturday - Jack

As his hand felt the scratchy, peeling paint on the wooden gate, Jack realised that this was not going to be any kind of adventure. He hadn't had a letter from Hogwarts, he hadn't got a contract from a sports academy or been cast as the next Dr Who, nor would he be saving the world from a mad scientist, and judging by the state of the cottage behind the gate, there would be no walking through wardrobes into another world.

"Jack, stop gawping and help!"

The car boot clunked open behind him. He sighed, took his hand from the gate and shuffled over to be handed a pile of loose bedding; a duvet with a cover picturing grimacing unicorns frolicking around some lurid rainbows and two matching pillows, along with an indeterminate furry toy called Unk.

"And this too," said his mother, pushing a pink rucksack with silver straps on top of the pile.

As he struggled to balance the pile in one hand and open the gate with the other, the rucksack fell into the bare hedge and a pillow fell onto the rutted track leading to the shack that he was now to call home. Immediately a shriek came from the car. Wailing, his sister (half-sister, spawn of Satan,) grabbed the pillow from the ground.

"Mine," she whined, pushing herself past him to grab the rucksack. "Mine, not Jack's!"

"Then you carry it," Jack said. He opened the gate and headed towards what seemed to be the front door.

"Mum!" wailed the girl.

"Carry your bag in, Lu, be a good girl today," Mum said, as she loaded her own arms with an assortment of bags and coats.

"No! Tired!"

For once Mum didn't help Lu, she didn't take the bag and pillow, she didn't try to placate her. As Jack looked back, waiting for her to come and unlock the door (a good kick would have opened it but he thought he'd better wait) he realised that Mum was tired and felt a bit guilty he didn't make more effort with Lu.

As Mum got to the door she dropped the bags in a heap and took a key from her pocket.

"Here we go," she said as she pushed the key into the lock and turned it. "New home." He heard the edge to her voice. Be a good boy, Jack. She didn't say it out loud but he heard it inside his head.

Yep, a shack. That's what it was. The hallway was dark, with faded, flowery wallpaper and thin, scuffed lino covering the floor. {*Lino? Ask someone really old.*} The doors on either side were painted green, and they didn't look very straight. Mum pushed one open. The bottom scraped the floor.

"The living room," she said, stating the obvious. She stared for a bit, probably trying to find something positive to say but she failed and turned to the door on the opposite side of the hall. It, too, scraped its way open.

"A bedroom," she said. Even Lu was quiet. What could you say, it was grim.

They all walked softly down the dim hallway, as if they were afraid they might wake someone up. There were three more doors. The first was a kitchen with a window looking out over a rambling garden. That's a plus, thought Jack, never had a garden before. The second was another bedroom also looking out over the garden. That's a negative, thought Jack, bunkbeds. The final room was a bathroom. It felt chilled and and damp - it smelt odd, he wasn't sure what of but just - odd.

"Well, that's us then, home," Mum said.

Lu tugged at Mum's arm. "Where's Lu's bed?"

Jack could sense a tsunami of a tantrum coming so he went back along the hallway and out into the front garden where there were some brown and green plants alongside the broken pathway and some droopy bushes around the edges of what might have once been a lawn. He began to transfer things from the car to the porch and hoped they'd actually brought what they needed in the rush to leave what had been home, and which he hoped they might be able to go back to. There were some boxes, many bags and numerous things packed in the car and which would take forever to carry separately to the porch.

"Well done, Jack," said Mum as she came out. "I'll carry these through if you can fetch more stuff."

"Lu wants Unk."

"Please," reminded Mum.

Lu threw herself on the floor and screamed. Jack and Mum ignored her and between them brought inside everything they now owned, ready to be unpacked. Mum moved the car off the track and parked it behind some bushes around the back of the cottage. {*It's home now so let's be generous and call it a cottage not a shack.*}

For three people, they didn't have much but the cottage had furniture and there was some stuff in the kitchen (saucepans and cutlery and so on) so they would be okay with what they had brought (clothes, toys and some food.) Mum set to cleaning some of the kitchen before unpacking their boxes and seeing what she had brought to make something to eat.

Jack took Lu's bedding and the sleeping bags into the right bedrooms and tried to make the beds. He struggled a bit but managed to get them ready to sleep in later. In his room, Lu was on the bottom bunk and he was on the top, which wasn't so bad when he found a shelf and a little cupboard above his bunk where he could store his things away from Lu. If he remembered to unhook the ladder and put it on top of the bunk, she wouldn't be able to get up there at all. He helped her put some of her things around her bunk, and put her toys in the bottom of a rickety chest-of-drawers. There was a brown wooden wardrobe, with a misty mirror set in the centre panel of the door. But it was creepy and it smelt musty when he opened the door, so he put their clothes on some shelves fixed to a wall. He got it done while Lu played with some of her ghastly toys sitting on her bunk. And, it didn't seem too bad when he looked around. It was better than the alternative.

"Well," said Mum as she sat down at the table in the kitchen, "There's enough food for a couple of days but we'll need to find a shop soon."

Jack's plate was brown with an orange pattern around the edge {*Very 1980's*} but the beans on toast were hot and steamy and he began eating quickly, suddenly realising he was very hungry. Lu looked at her plate and frowned.

"Lu wants ice cream," she stated as she pushed the plate away.

"There isn't any, Lu but …"

Lu shrieked and pushed the plate away but Jack caught it before it reached the edge of the table.

"Hey up Lu," he said as he shuffled his chair nearer to her. "Let's eat this shall we? Look." He swirled the beans and made a mountain in the middle of the toast. Then he squeezed sauce {*The brown stuff, you know the one, other makes available.*} around the beans so the beans looked like an island rising from a brown sea. "Lu's island, where Unk comes from, only Lu can eat it." He held the spoon towards her. Her expression was blank for a moment (a sign she was thinking) and then she took the spoon and began to eat, saying through a mouthful of beans, "Lu's dinner."

Mum smiled at Jack and for a while they ate in silence, peacefully and comfortably, feeling like a family is supposed to.

Later, when Lu was dreaming of whatever Lu dreamed of, when she was quiet and undemanding, Jack lay in the dark on his bunk and reached up and touched the ceiling above his head. That was weird, touching the ceiling. But no more weird than how they got here. Yesterday, he'd woken up at home, their real home in the flats, not this one, and had heard some noises from the living room …

Chapter Three

Day 1: Friday - Jack

Jack had woken up in the middle of the night. He'd listened for a bit, before he had reached out and tweaked the curtain to peer outside. There were lights on in the buildings and it was still dark. He'd slipped out of bed and opened his bedroom door as quietly as he could and listened. There was a clatter of something falling. He had crept along the hall, past Lu's room, past Mum's room and to the partly open living room door. A light was on. Were they being robbed? No point, they didn't have anything worth stealing. Very slowly, he had looked through the crack of the open door. The floor had been covered in bags and some boxes. So, they were being robbed then. Seemed a bit daft to steal Lu's toys but he supposed someone must be worse off than they were if they had to steal some old, chewed and dribbled on toys.

Then a hand had fallen on his shoulder. He had felt the whole of his insides crash into his stomach. "Jack, what are you doing up?"

How did they know his name? What would they do to him?

"Did I wake you up?"

Mum, it was Mum. Jack had looked around, his heart had been pounding in fear but he had tried to look as normal as he could manage.

"No, I just needed the bathroom."

Mum had looked at him for a moment before saying, "It's that way." And she had pointed down the hall, past his room - in the opposite direction to where he was now.

"Yes ... but ... I ... thought ... I ... saw the light on." He nodded towards the living room.

"Oh, did you? Well, I'm just doing some organising, I'll try not to be noisy. Get back to bed. See you in the morning."

And Jack had gone back to bed, had gone back to sleep and had woken again when the daylight was coming in through the curtains and it was time to get up.

When he had gone in to the living room clutching a bowl of cereal {*again, a brown one, chocolatey, other makes available*} he had seen that Mum had certainly been 'organising.' The floor was covered in piles of stuff. Some of it was boxed up, most of it was in carrier bags and some things were just gathered in heaps. He had picked his way across to the settee and rummaged for the clicker to turn on the TV. Then Mum had come in to tell him she was going out, wouldn't be long, Lu had had breakfast and don't open the door for anyone - anyone. A bit weird, she didn't usually go anywhere this early and she didn't usually leave Lu with him. He had stared at the TV for a while, not really taking in what was flashing across the screen. His bowl was empty. Mum wasn't here. He could sneak another bowl while she was out. He had been half way through his third bowl - and feeling a bit sick if he was honest - when Lu had whined until he changed channels so she could watch her cartoons. So he had washed up his bowl, cleaned his teeth, sort-of washed and then got dressed, looked out onto the estate for a bit to see if anyone was out and about he could meet up with, and - most of all - he had looked at the stuff Mum had been 'organising' during the night. There were some books, folders of papers, candles, leads and adaptors, a torch, batteries ... and in the kitchen some of the food was bagged up with a couple of saucepans, can opener, bread knife ... and in Mum's room some of her clothes were in bags with some jewellery and make-up. He might have thought she was having a de-clutter, clearing out unwanted things, taking stuff to the charity shop or recycling clothes bank. But food? And they bought things in the charity shops, they didn't donate to them. Were they moving? He had hoped not, he liked it here. He knew where everything was around and about. Holiday? Not likely, they hadn't been on holiday since … well, since Lu had arrived, it was just too difficult.

Lu had just realised Mum wasn't there and was about to reach full volume wailing when the front door had opened and Mum had come home, followed in by Stacey and Taz from two doors down.

"I'll put what needs to go by the door and you can carry it down," she had said to them, "I've done most of what can go now."

"Alright, Jack," said Taz, noticing Jack peering around the edge of his door.

They had set-to, collecting and taking out the boxes and bags. Only Stacey and Taz were carrying stuff out while Mum loaded it at the front door. It was a trek down six flights of stairs and out to their car parked in the area below, so it took ages to get everything that was needed out of the flat. While Lu had whined and got in the way, Jack had been given his school backpack and was told to put in anything he wanted to take, to keep, and only as much as the backpack would hold.

"But, what do I need? Where are we going?"

"Just pick out what you really want."

"But …"

"Fill the bag Jack, just what you really want. Like …" Mum picked up his tablet "… this and …" Mum picked up the charger "… this." She put them in the bag he was holding.

"But …"

"Just do it, Jack."

And while he had picked up some of his most important things to take wherever they were going, Mum had emptied his drawers of some clothes - not all, just the most clean and tidy. And then Mum had stripped his bed and dumped it all at the front door.

Mrs Jones, nosey Mrs Jones from four doors along, had walked by and stopped to stare at Mum as she was piling Lu's bedding just inside the open front door.

"Moonlight flit? Doing a runner Sal?"

Mum had laughed, the kind of laugh Jack knew she didn't really mean. "I wish, Vi. No, just doing a spring clean. You know, like people did back in the day. This lot's going down the launderette."

"Oh, a bit keen, Sal. Making me feel like I should blow the winter dust away. Might give it a go when I get back from the shops." And she had ambled off and Mum had looked relieved.

"Right, next?"

As Mum had looked around Stacey and Taz had come back for the umpteenth time, looking a bit frazzled and a lot less cheery than when they had started.

"How much more, Sal? The car's pretty much packed full," said Stacey.

"This and the kitchen stuff and …"

"Too much," said Taz. "Leave the bedding. It's too bulky. You need the food."

"But we need the bedding too and there's the towels and …"

"We've got a couple of sleeping bags, take Lu's bedding, it's smaller then yours, and you and Jack can have the sleeping bags. We might get some towels and food in if you do that."

Jack's head had been buzzing. So many questions. Sleeping bags? Torches? Camping? The trouble with being eleven was no one bothered to tell you anything, you didn't count, you just had to go along with whatever they decided. But when you are eleven you do notice when things are going on, you do want to know *what is going on.*

Jack had wandered around feeling lost and worried until Stacey and Taz had taken the last of the stuff and Mum had closed the front door. Lu had fallen asleep on the sofa, the flat was finally still.

Mum had looked at Jack.

"I can't explain Jack, but we're going away. I don't want to tell you too much in case … well, just in case … He's out, and he's looking for us."

And that had been enough for Jack.

Chapter Four

Day 2: Saturday - Police Constable Anstey

Constable Anstey knocked at the flat door for the fourth time and wearily turned and spoke into his radio. *{The police use radios. Like a phone but more reliable, especially in places where signals are weak.}* He looked up and down the row of flats for signs of neighbours. "There's no one here, Sarge."

He listened to the garbled instruction and sighed. "Righto, Sarge."

No one answered at any of the flat doors as he made his way along the row. She could be anywhere on a Saturday. At work. At the shops. At the cinema. On holiday in Crete. Probably not that last one but you never know.

An elderly lady came out from her flat onto the balcony, trundling a shopping trolley behind her.

"Madam," he began to walk towards her.

She turned her back and carefully closed the door and locked it.

"Madam," he said, "Could I ask …?"

"Vi - not madam."

"Er … Vi, could I ask you about Mrs Sinclair?"

"Stop mumbling. How am I supposed to hear when you're mumbling."

"I'm looking for Mrs Sinclair …"

"Never heard of her. Who is she?"

"Number 18, that one." He pointed back at the door he'd been knocking at to begin with.

"No, that's Sal. Not Sinclair."

"Are you sure?" He checked his notebook, definitely eighteen.

The woman trundled past him crossly, running his left foot over with her trolley. "Think I don't know my own neighbours. She's not Mrs Sinclair."

He stared after her, flexing his toes - grateful for the regulation boots he was wearing.

"Sarge," he spoke into his radio again. "Sarge, a neighbour says she doesn't live here. Is it the right address?"

The noises made him smile with relief. "Thanks Sarge, coming back now."

Chapter Five

Day 3: Sunday - Jack {*You need to keep track of the days so you know when it's happening and who to - so I'll put it here at the start of the chapter so you can keep a check.*}

When Jack woke up in the morning he didn't know where he was - so, he sat up. His head cracked on the ceiling. He rubbed the top of his head and waited for the buzzing to stop. The zip on the sleeping bag was stuck and it took a while to get it undone enough to wriggle out but he liked using it because no draughts got in during the night - and it was cold here, cold and damp. Lu wasn't in her bunk as he climbed past; her duvet was in a heap on the floor and her toys were spread all the way to the door. The floor was freezing to his bare feet as he walked out to find the kitchen.

"Morning. Up at last?"

Mum was sitting at the table with Lu who was annihilating some toast. Strawberry jam was smeared across her face and she smiled at him spraying crumbs down her pyjamas. She was in a good mood. It could be a good day.

"Toast?"

Jack nodded. He would have preferred cereal but he thought he had emptied the box yesterday and didn't want Mum to know how much he had eaten. His chair was wooden and felt hard against his bony body. What with banging his head, the cold floor, and uncomfortable chair -

and toast not cereal for breakfast - he was missing the cosy safety of the sleeping bag.

"So, exploring today?"

Explore what? Jack wondered. He didn't even know where he was.

Mum gave him a drink (in a glass with flamingos dancing around the rim) and some toast (on a brown and orange plate) and sat down to finish her cup of coffee.

"I need to do some more cleaning today, get the place tidied up a bit. You could have a look around the garden."

Jack's idea of a garden was a bit hazy. He wasn't interested in flowers - wasn't that what you had in a garden? Or lawns. Or bushes. He wasn't much interested in this toast either. He much preferred cereal. Did shops sell cereal here?

"There might be something interesting. Once you've finished that, go and get dressed and see what you can find. You'll need your coat, it's still a bit nippy."

While Jack finished the toast using his drink to help get it down, Lu was happily smearing her jammy fingers in a pattern on her plate. He really didn't hold out much hope for this place. Lu might be happy with some jam and a plate but he didn't think a garden was going to make him happy. However, as he'd never lived anywhere with one before he thought he might as well give it a try out.

He opened the front door and stepped outside. Mum was right (as she always was) and it was definitely a nippy morning. He shrugged his arms into his coat and put on the trainers he'd left in the hall last night. As he skirted the cottage he realised the garden wasn't just at the back - it was all around the actual building. And it was really big. He couldn't see any fences so he didn't know where it stopped and there were no signs of any neighbours. That was different. He'd always had people next door, sharing a building, with only a wall between each others' rooms.

There was no noise. Not a sound. No voices and no traffic. He stopped by the corner of the cottage, the corner where his room looked out onto the garden, straining to hear anything at all. Then, as he concentrated he realised he could hear things. Rustling. Not sure what it was that was rustling. Leaves? And some birds? And an aeroplane going over? And something else - a sort of humming, buzzing noise.

He set off across what looked like a lawn and headed towards the clump of bushes a few metres away. They were wet and dripped annoyingly as he ducked around them to see what was behind. He had to push his way through but there did seem to be a pathway or track leading past them to even more bushes, most of which were much taller than he was. They weren't trees like he knew from the park and rec at home. He ducked his way through, brushing the drips off his face, panicking a bit when a cobweb caught on his hair and stuck to his hand when he brushed it away. As he broke through the last of the shrubbery he slipped on the muddy ground and slid out from the shrubs, just about hanging on to a branch to save himself from falling over completely. Whoa! {*He didn't say 'whoa' but you get the idea.*}

So, Whoa! And there it was, a river. A real river. In the garden. Well, not **in** the garden but flowing along the end of the garden. He stood on the muddy river bank by some tall reeds and looked along as far as he could see in both directions, and then across to the other side as far as he could see. This was a definite plus. A river. An actual river. There were fields and hedges opposite and it looked like there were some buildings in the fields not too far away. Jack felt disorientated; not because he was now living somewhere he wasn't used to but because he was used to looking out of his bedroom window and seeing a very large part of his town spread out below. He could see his school, the rec, and he knew all the streets, roads, houses and flats around and about. Perhaps when Mum said to explore she meant he should go and find what was around here so he would feel more at home.

Making his way along to his right there were squelchy patches and he had to skirt around carefully so he didn't slip down into the river. It was clear that no one walked along this side of the river, not here anyway. In the park and on the school field the ground was level, the grass was short and it was easy to walk on but here he was struggling. He was just beginning to think he couldn't carry on when it cleared enough for him to push his way back through to the bushes to a more open area, still with bushes surrounding it but with some space to see that there was a shed-like building in front of him, sort of sticking out into the river. He wondered if this was in his garden, or had he walked into someone else's garden?

He walked over to the shed and looked at how it was shaped and how it sat so close to the water. It was nothing like anything he'd seen before. Checking again to make sure he was on his own, he gently pushed at the door. It didn't budge so he pulled instead and it scraped open just a little bit. Tugging hard he prised the door open enough to wriggle through. Well, this was different. An actual house for a boat. In the semi-darkness he could see a boat parked in the water and a walkway alongside it. *{He didn't know yet that the word for a boat being parked was moored.}* It had some doors at one end and a small platform at the other, with some hooks and shelves - and some boxes, a lamp, a flat bed and - a rolled up sleeping bag just like the one he'd used last night. He stepped back against the wooden wall and stayed as quiet as he could. He looked around carefully.

When he was sure no-one was there he went to look at the pile of belongings. Was someone living here? Homeless perhaps? Or just hiding out here? Or just camping here sometimes? There seemed to be some clothes in one of the boxes, but about the size he might wear. There was some food, just biscuits and crisps, so not what his mum called proper food. There was a comic and a book, both meant for someone his age. So, Jack decided that someone was hanging out in the shed, as a den of some sort. He hoped it was someone he could hang out with while he was here. It was going to be a nightmare spending all day with just Mum and Lu.

The boat bobbed a little on the water as he looked down at it. There were some oars wedged on the sides so, he guessed it was a rowing boat. The roof had strands of light flickering through some tiles but the doors at the end looked fairly solid. Who did it belong to? And why have a boathouse as big as this for a little rowing boat? You wouldn't have a garage just to park your bike, would you?

Having looked around as much as he needed to, Jack pushed himself back through the door into the weak sunlight and carefully pulled the door shut, hoping whoever used this boathouse wouldn't know he'd been there. He knew he wouldn't like someone poking about in his stuff.

Where to go next. He didn't want to go back along the river as it was too difficult to walk along but he could see a track through the bushes and he decided to follow that ... and before he knew it he was back at the cottage. Okay. That meant there was a quicker and easier way to get to the boathouse. And possibly meant it belonged to the cottage.

Jack decided to change his exploring plans. He knew gardens usually had fences and someone else's garden would be on the other side of the fence. So if he wanted to work out where the garden stopped he needed to find the neighbours' houses or cottages and find the fences that way. He stepped out into the lane they had parked in yesterday to unload the car. He looked in both directions. It wasn't a proper road, as it was narrow, and although it had some gravel covering most of its surface, it was very patchy, as if it wasn't important enough to be repaired. He headed along the way they had come in - and wandered along a bit more - and a bit more - and some more.

He'd soon lost sight of the cottage and there were some bends in the road so although he didn't think he'd gone far he felt almost lost. Through gaps in the hedgerows he could see fields on one side and not very much on the side on which the cottage sat. He'd never been so alone; even in the flat you could often hear the neighbours on either side - and above and below - and there were always dim sounds floating upwards from the streets around and about.

Just as he thought he should turn back he saw that the hedgerow was thinning on both sides and the road seemed to widen out. And then he reached another road, a wider one, with a proper surface. This must be one they had driven along to get to the cottage but he hadn't noticed when Mum must have turned left onto their road. He scrambled up a small bank on the far side and peered through the hedge only to see yet more fields. It was so flat here, no hills and definitely no mountains. He would have liked to live somewhere with something to look at in the distance.

What to do next? It wasn't much fun out here on his own. He decided to walk along this road for a bit, just to see what might be there and headed along as if he'd taken a left turn out of his road. And quite soon he reached a small stone bridge over a river. He stood on it peering down, watching the water swirl along gently. It was clear and he could see some weed and fish. Real fish. In the river. Was this his river? The one at the end of his garden? He hoped so. He stepped to the other side of the bridge and watched the water on that side. It flowed away into the distance and he could see that some hedgerows followed it along, marking the boundaries between the river and the fields. Well, this was different. He was living by a river in the middle of no where. He found a largish stone by the road and picked it up, weighing it in the palm of his hand. He leaned over the side of the bridge and dropped it into the water below. It plunked heavily, sending circular ripples across the water, breaking its flow and lapping at the weeds and edges. The ripples cast out further and further before they all disappeared and you would never know they'd been here.

There was a road sign on the other side of the bridge so he walked over and went around it to see if it told him where he was, you know the sort of thing, 'Welcome to ....' But it just had two arrows, one bigger than the other and each pointing in different ways - up and down. No idea what that was about. And as he was looking at it a car flew over the bridge and shot past. He felt his heart jump as he ducked down as the car whizzed by. If he'd been standing on the bridge he'd have been flattened. As he shakily stood and turned to look at the car, a greenish, muddy square shaped thing like you saw in army films, he saw a face peering back at him through the back window. A small face, wide-eyed as if they were surprised to see him there. Not as surprised as he was to see them. But then, this was a road and the cars did have right of way, so as he went back across the bridge and down the road he was careful to walk close to the hedgerow and to look before crossing over to his road.

As he walked back down to the cottage he thought about what he'd found out so far. They were living in a cottage by a river along a deserted road which came off a quiet road running through the middle of some fields - somewhere flat. Not much to go on.

"Mum," he said as soon as he got back inside, "Where are we?"

"Norfolk." Mum stopped scrubbing at the kitchen table and looked up.

He thought about that as he searched the cupboards for a glass so he could get a drink. He wasn't sure where Norfolk was. It had taken all night to get here so it must be a long way from home. "Why are we here? In Norfolk I mean. I know why we had to go somewhere but why here?"

Mum went back to her cleaning and he couldn't see her face properly. "It's out of the way."

He thought about that as he filled his glass from the tap. He stared at the water suspiciously. It wasn't from the river was it? He didn't fancy drinking bugs and slime. And did fish pee? In the river? But the water in the glass looked clear so he sipped it to check how it tasted before gulping it down.

"So, how long will we be here?"

Mum paused but kept her head down. "Not sure."

"What about school? How will I get to school? And what about Jas and Acky? When can I see them? And I left my bike in Sandy's lock-up…"

"Stop, Jack." Mum turned and stared at him. "I've got enough to think about without you whining about your bike. This is it for now. I don't know how long we'll be here okay? It's for a while, there's no school, you'll miss your mates but there will be other things to do. Just think of this more like a holiday."

"There's nothing here. There's no one here. A holiday is by the sea, in summer, with theme parks and … and …" Jack had never been on holiday but he knew this wasn't one.

"Think of this as an adventure, somewhere you haven't been before, somewhere where something might happen like in one of those books you're always reading." She resumed her scrubbing, as if to say end of conversation.

An adventure? Here?

Later, after Jack had walked down their road in the other direction and found nothing, not even another road or a bridge, as he wandered back to the cottage along the deserted road that went nowhere, he thought about the boathouse he'd found. Was that going to be the most exciting thing here? He hoped not. {*And you probably do too. You need a bit more in a story than a boathouse.*}

{*What? Who is this? Who's writing this bit? It's me. The writer. It gets a bit lonely tapping away at a keyboard on your own so I'll join in every so often, if you don't mind. Just sometimes.*}

Chapter Six

Day 5: Sunday Evening - Jack

That evening Jack began to realise just how tricky life was going to get when the electricity went off.

"Oh no! I forgot about the generator." And Mum dashed off leaving Jack and Lu sitting at the kitchen table in semi-darkness. No, thought Jack, we can't live somewhere with no lights, and no way to cook anything. And what about TV? He hadn't even looked in the living room since they arrived and couldn't imagine life without a TV to keep Lu quiet. And wi-fi? No wi-fi? Lu opened her mouth wide and began to wail. In the semi-darkness, he pulled the loaf of bread towards him and took out a slice.

"Here Lu. Let's make some soldiers."

Lu looked at the slice of bread he put on her plate and then at him. "Jam."

"Here's the jam. You can do it." He put a spoonful of jam onto the bread and gave Lu a knife.

She thought for a moment and began spreading the jam clumsily with the flat blade of the knife. *{A blunt one obviously, before someone starts going on about health and safety and irresponsible carers.}*

"That's it, well done," he said before helping her by holding the knife with her and cutting the bread into soldiers.

"Yum," said Lu and she began to eat.

Jack really didn't want jammy soldiers. They'd had baked beans on toast last night, toast for breakfast, a sandwich for lunch and now - jam and toast? Really? He needed something else to eat. Even vegetables, real ones not just tomato sauce. And as he was about to work his way through the food he really wanted to eat, the lights popped back on.

Mum came back in looking relieved. "Must remember to keep a check on that," she said and began to do her usual clattering and bustling while she cooked tea. "It's not like at home, we have to make sure the generator is set up, keep a check on it."

"What's a generator?"

"It makes electricity. There's one in the shed out back. We can't use too much at once or it seems to stop but we can get by."

"What if it goes off when you're not here?" Jack was thinking about being left in the dark.

"I'm going to be here."

"But what if you're not? What if you go to the shops and leave me here and it goes off and it's dark and Lu falls over and I can't see her and ..."

"Jack, I'll be here, but I'll show you so you know."

Jack sat waiting for his tea and thought about today. Somehow, a whole day (nearly, it was tea time so the day wasn't over yet) had passed and he hadn't been to school, or been out with his mates, or watched any TV. He'd walked through some bushes by a river bank, along a road, over a bridge, along another bit of road and then walked home. He'd helped Mum clean the furniture in this room and then he'd slouched on his bed, on the top bunk away from Lu, and read his book and played a game for a bit. And now it was tea time. Hardly a holiday and certainly not an adventure. He looked at the plate Mum put in front of him. Pizza and chips. Not too shabby.

Later, having discovered the TV sort of worked if you only wanted to watch two channels, which he didn't particularly but Lu did so that at least meant she was quiet, Jack sat at a dusty bookshelf (Mum hadn't started on the room yet) and looked at the dusty books. Some had hard covers like you got from the library, but they were old, with pages beginning to turn brown. Some had pictures on torn dust-jackets, and others had just titles and authors written in faded gold lettering on the plain cover. Some of the books had paperback covers, and were a bit torn and marked. And as only few of them looked like the kind of book someone his age might be interested in, he unexpectedly found himself reading a book about Norfolk that had been tucked under some way-out-of-date magazines. It looked old but he thought that some things couldn't have changed, like where it was, where the towns were and what sort of things were here, and therefore he spent a quiet hour reading while Lu watched some animal programme and the news and Mum dozed off in the one comfortable armchair.

Norfolk, the place where the 'north folk' once lived the book explained, seemed very different from home. It was a big county, with some seaside places, some big towns and lots of rivers and broads. He liked the photos of people in the old days, wearing so many clothes just to go onto the beaches they would probably get heat stroke. There were some old photos of fishermen and farmers, and some pictures of some of the towns then-and-now. A diagram showed how much of the land had been reclaimed from the sea and he wondered how climate change would affect all those little pockets of land surrounded by water. If the sea levels rose then all that land would be back under water. What would happen to the roads? And the houses? And the cows? He found a map page, which opened out to be four times the size of the book and spent some time following the rivers with his finger and checking where the towns were.

When Mum woke from her doze he asked where they were, the name of the place they were staying at. The cottage did have an address (otherwise how would they have put it into the satnav in order to be able to get here) but Jack couldn't find the village on the map. It was too small to be included so he asked where the nearest town was. Mum said it was Stavesey, that was where they would go to get shopping, there was a supermarket there. So Jack found Stavesey, small and isolated, surrounded by countryside and rivers. And their village must be around that area, and his river must be one of the blue lines. Which one? Probably one of the little ones, he thought, perhaps flowing into one of the Broads. Could he really take a boat and follow the rivers until he got to the sea? He was more and more sure that the boat did belong to the cottage as there was nothing else nearby but he didn't want to ask Mum because she might tell him it wasn't safe and to keep away. And it wasn't lying not to tell her. And if she didn't know she wouldn't worry.

And much later, when Jack was on his bunk with Lu snuffling on the bottom bunk beneath him, he thought of how they had got here …

So, Mum had said 'He' was looking for them. And that said it all to Jack. They'd been safe for four years, changing names and towns and schools, and not seeing anyone they once knew. And he'd got so used to being Jack Williamson he'd almost forgotten he was once Jake Sinclair. He liked the flat and the buildings around them - he was at home there. But he could remember what had happened and sometimes, on a bad night, he dreamt of it and woke up with his heart pounding and his skin wet with sweat. So when Mum had said 'He' was looking for them, he knew they had to run.

After Stacey and Taz had taken everything away, Mum had tidied up and they had left the flat late afternoon as if they were going out to the shops, but they had got on a bus and went across town, and then had got on another bus which took them to the retail park. There they had gone to have something to eat. Mum had keys to a car which Jack had never seen but which was loaded with their stuff, and they had got in and driven away.

It had been almost dark when they finally set off, perhaps late evening, and Jack knew he had fallen asleep for some of the time and that Lu had slept most of the time, and that they had come off the motorway and stopped at a service station when Lu had been sick. Then they had driven for another long time in the dark. He had had no idea where they going, north or south, round in circles or zigzagging across the country. He hadn't known if they were still in England or had gone into Wales or Scotland. And now he knew they were in Norfolk but it was still a long way from where they had been.

He started thinking about the way things had turned out. Just when he was happy with how his life was going, he was running away again. He lay awake, watching the stars on Lu's night lamp in the darkness. Was this how the rest of his life was going to be? Escaping the past?

Chapter Seven

Day 3: Sunday - Police - PC Anstey

"You were here before."

"Er - yes, looking for the family who lives here."

He turned back to the door and knocked and rang again.

"They're not in."

He turned again and looked down at the boy staring up at him. Get a grip, Anstey, you can deal with a kid. He took out his notebook and pen. He straightened himself up and stared back at the boy.

"And who are you?"

"Milo."

"Your full name."

"Why?"

"What?"

"Why? Why do you need to know?"

Because Sarge said to get people's names, wasn't the answer he felt he could give. "So I know it was you who told me."

"Told you what?"

"That they're not in. How do you know they're not in?"

"You knocked didn't you?"

Constable Anstey nodded.

"Did anyone answer?"

Constable Anstey shook his head.

Milo shrugged. "So …They're not in."

Milo began to walk away.

"Hold on, do you know them? Friends?"

Milo nodded. "Jack didn't come out today, I knocked earlier. They're still not back."

"Jack?"

Milo nodded. "Jack, my mate. School. And football. And cycling."

Constable Anstey checked his notebook. "Jack? Not Jake? Jake Sinclair?"

"No, Jack Williamson, that's who lives there. You got the wrong flat." And Milo walked off.

Constable Anstey wrote down Jack Williamson carefully and closed his notebook. Result. He had told Sarge it was the wrong address - now he could prove it. He headed back to the stairs - six flights - he hoped there were some biscuits left in the tea room when he got back.

Chapter Eight

Day 4: Monday Morning - Jack

As they drove along their lane Jack paid more attention than he had when they arrived. When they soon reached the junction to turn onto the bigger road with the bridge he realised that he hadn't really walked very far yesterday when he went exploring, although it had seemed a long way at the time. And as he was sitting in the car, in the front passenger seat, he could see a bit more as he was higher up than when he was walking. Mum turned left so he knew they would go over the stone bridge so he was ready to peer over to see where the river went - and as they drove along he cranked round to see if he could see the cottage or the boathouse. No, but he thought he could see the top of the boathouse at the water's edge. Probably? Possibly? He turned back to concentrate on where they were going. There was a turn-off a little way down the bridge road, with a road leading to what looked like some buildings in the distance. How far away they were he couldn't tell.

Stavesey had a sign to let you know that's where you were, a statement saying 'Here I am.' And it needed one; there wasn't much and if you sneezed as you drove through you really wouldn't know it was there. There were some houses, all different and straggling along each side of the road, and there were some shops: a greengrocer's, a post office which was a newsagent too, and ... nothing else, not even a fish and chip shop. But there was a church with a square tower and a graveyard. And a war memorial was tucked away at the side of the road on a little patch of grass. And there was a bus stop in front of a little brick open shelter with a tiled roof and a bench along the back wall.

The supermarket was, as Jack was now expecting, small. More the 'express' kind than anything but perhaps a little bigger. It was just off the main road and had a car park. Mum pulled into a space away from the other cars, leaving room to get Lu out and into her buggy.

"We won't be able to come and go like we did before, Jack, so we need to make sure we get everything we need each time we do come." She strapped Lu into her seat and pulled up the hood of her little red coat, pulling it forward and straightening out the fur. She rummaged in her purse for a coin which she gave to Jack, telling him to go and get a trolley.

"Here we go," she said, and Jack thought she was trying to be brave.

He pushed the coin into the slot and pulled the trolley towards him, swung it round in a semi-circle and headed for the door. He was used to this. Lu was a bit big now but it was easier if she was in her buggy and he pushed the trolley; she couldn't escape and she couldn't pull things off the shelves so easily. Supermarkets are basically the same anywhere you go and whichever brand you go to, so he knew where to wait for Mum out of the way of other customers and when to move towards her so she could put things in. He also knew when to stop Lu from grabbing things and how to distract her. He looked for things he might like and chose when to ask and when to make a mental note for next time. That way he knew he'd get some of the things he liked but which Mum wasn't so keen on him having, like chocolate cereal *{You know the one}* and biscuits *{Any with chocolate in or on or both}* and by the time they were half way round he'd wrangled enough for this trip and stopped before he pushed his luck. Then he began to look around, getting more of a feel for the place. And one man actually had a dog on a lead, in a supermarket, and it wasn't a guide dog. It didn't take long to get around as it was such a small shop and before he could get bored they were standing in the queue for the checkout (no self-service or scanning here).

It was while queueing here that Jack understood why Mum had looked a bit nervous when they came in. It was slow. Really slow. The man in front was slow, the person on the till was slow. They had a chat between scanning each item. It took forever for the man to look through his wallet and pay in cash and for the woman (her name badge read Queenie) to hand over the right change. And when it was their turn Queenie kept looking at Mum who was packing the shopping in bags, and then looking down at Lu who was quietly re-dressing a one legged doll, and then at Jack … just as he looked up from putting a bag into the trolley. She smiled at him but he didn't think it was a friendly smile, and he didn't smile back, just ducked his head and put another shopping bag in the trolley.

"So, local are you? Haven't seen you before."

Mum carried on packing her shopping but said quietly, "On holiday for a bit." She knew the lady behind was listening, and the man behind her too.

"Oh, that's nice. We don't usually get holiday makers this time of year, not until after Easter, when it's a bit warmer. Where you staying then? Somewhere in the village?"

"Cottage by the river." Jack noticed she didn't say the same of the village near where they were staying and there were lots of cottages and lots of rivers. He packed faster.

"Oh, that's nice. Just you is it?"

"Just us." Mum was packing quickly, taking things as soon as Queenie scanned them.

"You don't talk like us. One of them northern accents is it? Have you come far?"

"No, not too far."

Queenie scanned a few more items before continuing her interrogation. "Got some plans then? Places to go to? Lots to do here. There's a museum in Easterly, your boy there might like looking at the old things in there." Only four more things to be scanned. "It don't cost much to get in. And there's a railway museum at the old station near Halfbrook, that's a good one." Three. "My Albert - God rest his soul, he's been dead these past ten years, he used to help out with the engines when they had a bit of track working and people could ride between Westerbridge and Halfbrook." Two. "And that's gone now, no volunteers and it cost too much to repair the track." One. Mum got out her purse ready to pay. "And there's always the seaside. The little girl there would love it." All done. Jack picked up the last item and mum opened her purse. But Lu had heard 'little girl' and she knew someone was talking about her. And that's when she looked up, pushing her hood off her face and smiling her lopsided smile.

"Oh!" Queenie gasped. "Poor thing." The man behind them looked interested and tried to peer around Mum to see what Queenie had seen.

Mum had her blank face on, the one she used when she didn't want to react or to explain. When she didn't want pity or blame. "How much?" she asked.

"Er… £52.75. Cash or card? Such a pretty face too."

Mum handed over some notes and waited for her change.

"Perhaps she can have surgery when she's older. They can do such marvellous things, these days, can't they? That's £7.25 change. Hope you have a good holiday. See you again soon."

Mum pushed the buggy quickly past the trolley and headed for the doors. Jack followed with the trolley. Mum opened the boot and they unloaded quickly. While Mum put Lu into her car seat and put the buggy in the boot, Jack went to retrieve his coin by returning the trolley.

The lady who had stood behind them in the queue came out and she paused, looking over at Mum before saying to him, "Don't mind Queenie, she's always talking, she don't stop some days. And she don't stop to think. Just opens her mouth and out it comes. Your mum looks like she's doing a grand job of looking after you, that's all that matters, love." She slipped her shopping bag over her arm and slowly walked towards the main street.

Jack looked at his feet as he went back to the car. Sometimes he did that. It helped when he was thinking. He opened his door and climbed in.

He held the coin to Mum and she said, "You keep it, for helping." He pushed the coin into his pocket, closed the door and put on his seatbelt.

He was still thinking as Mum reversed and pulled away from the space. That went well. Really, it did. He'd been there before - when Mum had gone ballistic, full neutron bomb, when someone commented on Lu's face. She didn't want to tell a stranger what had happened, why Lu looked as she did. She didn't want sympathy or pity. And she really really really didn't want blame - and that was the occasion Jack remembered most, when he was seven. Mum was taking him to school and she heard some other mum at the school gate saying to someone that it had to be his mum's fault. Mum had dropped his hand and grabbed the woman by the hair, and she had pinned her to the fence and screamed in her face. He couldn't remember what she said, perhaps he was too young to have understood, but he knew she was angry, so angry that she was banging the woman's head against the metal railings and screeching so loudly that everyone stopped and watched. Then someone pulled her off and took them inside. He didn't go back to that school. That was when they moved to another town, and that was when he changed his name.

He felt relief when they pulled into the space down the side in the garden, as if they were safe again. Mum hadn't spoken all the way home. He helped carry some bags into the kitchen and, having found a bag of crisps and made himself and Lu a drink, went to his bunk and kept out of the way for a while. He was reading one of the books from the shelf in the living room. It was okay, not what he would usually choose but sometimes you need to try something different. He liked his bunk. It was small and cosy. He was out of the way and Lu couldn't climb up. He could be on his own and not have to worry about being pulled about or jumped on or made to play with her mutilated dolls. He stayed there until Mum called him for lunch.

Sausage sandwich. His favourite sandwich. Especially when the sausage was still hot and the butter melted and made the bread go all squishy.

"What are you going to do this afternoon?" Mum asked. "You can't stay in bed all day. You're not a teenager yet." She was washing up at the sink, overlooking the garden at the back.

Jack waited until he'd swallowed his mouthful before replying. "I might go back round the garden. It seems really big. I don't know where it starts and where it ends." Should he tell her about the boathouse? Not yet.

"There's a river down there, " he nodded down from the kitchen window, "behind some bushes."

"I know, it's not much more than a stream but keep away, it's not safe."

"I can swim," he reminded her.

"I know but swimming in the pool is different from swimming in a river. There's a current. And you can get tangled up in the plants and weeds."

He ate two more mouthfuls while he thought about that. He could find a shallow part and give it a try, but perhaps not yet.

"How much of it is our garden?" he asked.

"Not sure. There's no one else around, so just keep away from the river and the road and then you can explore the rest as much as you like."

Lu had finished eating and once Mum had cleaned her up she wandered off to play in their bedroom.

"Before you go, Jack, we need to talk." Mum sat down. Oh, he thought, one of those sitting-down talks - serious. "I know you remember all those times we had to move about after - you know - and before we ended up at the flat. I don't know how long we will be here. It may be for a few days but I think it might be longer. It's not much but it's away from everywhere and anyone we know. I don't think anyone can find us. But you remember what you have to do?"

He nodded. Yes, he remembered.

"Tell me."

"Run and hide. Don't come out until you tell me."

"Good. And now you have do two things. You have to find some hiding places here, not in the cottage but outside - not too far away but not close. And if you do have to hide, this time you have to take Lu with you."

Really? Lu?

"I know it won't be easy but she's better than she was, calmer. She doesn't make quite so much noise. And she likes it here. She hasn't played up since the first day, and that was because she was tired and confused. It could be a game."

He thought about it but he had to say yes, of course he'd take Lu. It was the last thing he wanted. It was bad enough before when he just had to think about himself but to have to look after Lu as well was too much to ask.

Chapter Nine

Day 4: Monday Afternoon - Jack

So, he went out in the weak spring sunshine and thought about hiding places. The boathouse was possible but it could be easily found and there weren't many hiding places inside. He'd think about that one. He turned to the side of the cottage where Mum had parked the car. He opened a door to a lean-to on the side of the kitchen wall. It had some machinery inside, probably the generator Mum had spoken about, and some tools on a shelf. He looked through the tools to see what might be useful and opened the lid to a wooden box on the floor. More tools, a bit rusty. Think about those later, too.

Round the back of the cottage he peered in through his bedroom window. Lu was playing on the floor. It would be easy to break in, and to climb in and out. He moved away before Lu saw him and wanted him to play with her and he headed off towards those bushes at the end of the lawn. Instead of pushing through the way he had done to get to the river, he moved over to the left and made his way across. The bushes were just as wet as they had been before and he was wary of catching himself in cobwebs again. He caught his coat on a prickly branch and had to untangle himself before he could move on, scratching his hand. Nature was all very well but he thought he preferred looking at it in the distance.

He soon came to the river bank again, as it curved round. He didn't want to fight his way along it as he'd done before so he backtracked and pushed through until he came into an overgrown clearing. In the middle was a wooden shed. All around it were brambles and weeds but he could see there had been a path leading to it from the direction he thought the cottage must be. The shed door was difficult to open and some of the undergrowth stopped him from pulling it outwards but he managed to open it enough to peer in. He could see some shelves with paint pots on, some containers of who-knew-what, and possibly something like a spade, and a push lawn mower. {*Ask someone ancient. They were really heavy and difficult to use but better than using sheep to keep your grass short.*} Garden stuff mostly. There may be somewhere to hide but he would need to be careful not to trample the brambles down too much and to keep the door jammed as much as possible so it looked like no one had gone in there for a long time. Possibly a hiding place.

He moved away from the shed and made his way to a wall running along towards the road. It was made of stones, covered in moss and yet more brambles, but it wasn't very high. He climbed on top and squatted there to see what was on the other side. There were mounds and mounds of brambles running along the wall and lots of trees. He jumped down, spiking his legs on the brambles, and followed the wall, turning four times until he got back to where he had started. There was no house or cottage, not even a shed. An orchard, that's what it was. Did it belong to the cottage? No one seemed to care for it; he was sure it shouldn't look so overgrown. Hiding places? He moved towards where he thought the centre might be and looked up at the trees. They were spaced apart and low growing, much shorter than the trees in the park. Not good for climbing and hiding in. And as it was only just coming up to spring they didn't have many leaves yet, just some small bright green ones popping out along the branches. Still, once they had some more leaves they were low enough to get Lu into and they might be able to hide in the branches of one; who would find them in one tree in so many? Possible hiding place?

He climbed over the wall back onto the road. How did you know where you were when it all looked the same? One hedgerow was just like another. He had an idea and crossed over to the fields on the other side and found himself looking at a wide space with lots of brown and some spots of green growing in the ridges. He had no idea what was starting to grow here and didn't really want to walk on it in case the farmer shot at him for trespassing (did they do that?) so he walked along the edge next to the road towards the cottage. There were some places he could dodge into and hide in if he had to leg it down the road. Lots of hiding places.

He had to cross a ditch and climb through a hedge into another field and follow the edge of that one before he got back to the cottage. He could have walked along the road but he was still hiding-place-spotting and he felt he needed to keep out of sight. It wasn't easy living in the country, he decided. Too much walking and none of it along a nice flat pavement. He wasn't sure what the time was or how long he'd been out so he headed back to the cottage hoping it was tea time.

Mum was cleaning the living room. Lu was in their bedroom. The contents of two kitchen cupboards were spread over the surfaces and table drying off, smelling vaguely like bleach. And it wasn't tea time, nowhere near. Not wishing to sit in the bathroom to be on his own, Jack helped himself to a handful of biscuits and set out again. He found the track leading more directly to the boat house and headed towards somewhere he thought he might be able to sit and think for a while.

He found it first time. He prised back the door so he could squeeze through and went in. It was gloomy in the dull afternoon light. He listened. No sounds of anyone there. He crept along the side by the boat towards the platform at the back. The things were still there. The owner wasn't. That was good. He went back along to the front of the boat, facing the doors. There was more light here as the doors were like gates and light came in the gaps between the planks. He eased himself down on the platform and sat down with his legs dangling over the edge. He sat watching the light sparkling on the water while eating a biscuit and thinking about what was happening to them.

He was scared. He admitted that. He knew kids at school, mainly boys but some of the girls too, who would never say they were scared. Even when they were. He knew what it was to be scared, really scared, with your heart thumping, your head pounding, your legs shaking. He knew what it was to be petrified, unable to move a centimetre let alone run for his life. There was nothing to be ashamed of in being scared. It was - is - a reaction, just the same as being happy and laughing. But he didn't want to be scared, not like before. This time, this time he would be ready. He would have hiding places. He would be on his guard. He would check around him everywhere he went …

"What are you doing in here?!"

Jack felt his heart crash in his chest as he leapt up - then fell off the platform into the pointed end of the boat. He grabbed at the side and clung on as the boat rocked and dipped, almost throwing him into the dark water. He felt his knees graze against the bottom of the boat and and he caught his chin on an oar as it slid off its perch and slammed into him.

He flailed his arms, trying to gain his balance, making the boat rock even more. He felt a rising panic. He might drown like Mum said - and she wouldn't know where he was or how to find him.

"Just stop moving, idiot."

What? Who was that?

"You're making it worse. Stay still!"

He shuffled round at the bottom of the boat and held still. It calmed down and stopped moving so much.

"Here. Grab hold."

A hand reached down. After a pause, he took it and someone hauled him up so he was half sitting on the seat in the boat. It rocked again but this time he waited until it had stopped before pulling himself onto the seat properly. The boat moved again and he felt very uneasy. He sat still, not daring to move. He raised his head slightly to see who was there. In the half light he could see someone about as big as he was, lying along the platform so they could reach down to him to help him off the bottom of the boat. They sat up now he was seated and swung their legs over the side of the platform.

"You have to balance your weight so it doesn't rock."

And how do I do that? he thought. And who are you? And what are *you* doing here?

He reached over and grabbed the platform with both hands. He held on tightly and hauled himself up. But his body weight pushed the boat away from the platform and the gap between the platform and the boat got wider and wider until his feet were so far from the platform he had made an arch of his body.

"Idiot! Sit down. You'll fall in!"

Desperately he scrabbled with his feet and pushed harder. The person grabbed his arms and struggled to pull him up. Somehow they got him half onto the platform. The wood scratched his hands - he flinched and almost let go - but he pushed down and hauled himself onto the platform. He lay looking up at the roof, exhausted and panting and scared.

"You alright?"

What a stupid question, he thought, of course I'm not alright, I nearly drowned. And it was your fault, you scared me. But he said, "I'm good. Thanks."

A face peered down at him. It was upside down but he could see they were worried. He pulled himself to sitting up and swivelled round to face them. It was the person he'd seen in that car on the bridge, he was sure even though it had only been a passing glimpse for for a few seconds.

"Oh, it's you. The boy on the bridge."

"And you were in the car."

They eyed each other for a few seconds. If they had been lions on the plains they would have been circling each other, working out who was the strongest, deciding who would win a battle to the death and wondering whether they should run away to fight another day. With people it's not really much different; we keep a distance and we look carefully, sometimes without really knowing we are doing it. We check out how big they are, look at what they are wearing, think about how they are standing, focus on their expression - and we decide how to behave towards them. Friendly or not friendly. It's a basic survival trait humans have learned over thousands of years. And Jack was very good at it. He had learned to check people carefully in the changes of homes and schools over the past four years. Who could be a friend and fun to hang around with? Who would be a bully and was best avoided? Who would be patient and not ask questions? And as he looked at this person he found it difficult to decide. There was something guarded behind their eyes.

"I'm Jack," he said.

"Rosie," she said.

He saw that she was indeed a girl. He hadn't been sure as her hat and clothes covered her up.

"Is that your stuff?" He nodded to the back wall at the pile of things he had found on the first day here.

She looked over and then frowned at him, "Yes, it's mine. Did you mess with it?"

"No, I just looked at it."

"Good, you don't touch it."

"I wouldn't. Don't worry."

For a minute or so they just sat, looking away from each other.

Jack asked. "Do you live round here?"

"Rowley's Farm."

There was very long pause. Jack finally shrugged his shoulders to let her know he had no idea where that was.

"Over there, up the fields." She pointed out towards the opposite bank of the river. Not a clue, thought Jack. It was much easier in a town. If you wanted to tell someone where you lived, you just said the name of the street, or 'next to the bike shop' or 'down the alley by the old church on the corner by the traffic lights in the high street.' Saying 'up the fields' was no use at all. Which fields? There were loads of them and they all looked the same. Perhaps you had to say 'third field down from the crossroads' or 'the fields growing cabbages' or 'the field with the big tree in the middle.'

"Past the bridge?" he asked.

She looked at him and frowned. "You talk funny. Where are you from?"

"Not far."

"You staying in Orchard Cottage?"

So that's what it's called, he thought. "Yes."

Another long pause.

"So, do you stay in here sometimes then?"

Rosie stood up and went to check the things she had stored on the back decking. "Sometimes." She opened a box and looked in, felt to the bottom and then closed it up. Apparently it was all in order. She lifted the sleeping bag and checked a couple of bags.

"Happy?" Jack asked. "I said I hadn't touched it."

She made a snorting noise which said, 'I don't believe you, why should I?' and took out a bag of crisps, opened it and began to munch.

"Whose boat is this? Does it belong to the cottage?" asked Jack.

Rosie went and sat on the platform next to him and looked at the boat. "I use it."

"Really?" Jack was impressed.

"Only on this stretch though, there's not too much current and I can get all the way to the village before I get too tired and have to turn back."

"Could you show me how to do it?"

"Show you how to do what?"

"How to row?"

"Probably."

"So would you - show me. Teach me."

Rosie ate another crisp before she answered. "Well, you could drown - so you have to listen and follow the rules."

"Yes."

"Can you swim? You have to be able to swim."

"Yes. The crawl, backstroke and breast stroke. And I've started the life-saving certificate. I've had lessons after school every Thursday."

Rosie ate another crisp and thought for a moment. "But I've only got one lifejacket. You have to have a lifejacket."

"But I can swim."

"Rules. You have to wear a lifejacket every time you go out on the water."

They sat thinking. Rosie peered into the bag before tipping the last few into her hand and putting them all into her mouth at once. {*Don't you hate that? When someone eats the whole lot and doesn't even offer you a crumb?*}

"What if I could get a lifejacket?"

"They sell them in Hubbards."

What was Hubbards? Where was Hubbards? Why did she think he knew where things were around here? He wished he was home, talking to Jas who made sense when she talked.

"And that would be…?"

"In town." She looked at him quizzically.

"Stavesey?"

"Marsham."

Jack sighed. He wished he was home, where he knew where everything was.

"Okay. If I can get a lifejacket will you teach me how to row?"

Rosie considered her position. "Well, I could but … it's hard taking a boat out. You could fall in and I'd have to rescue you. And you might be a really slow learner and it might take ages. And I do have other things to do, I can't just spend all my time on you - I don't even know you. And what do I get out of it?"

If Jack had been one of those lions out on the plains, he would have been pacing in a line in front of the other lion (Rosie) deciding how to conquer her. He wouldn't have gone for a kill, because he needed her, but he had to be the lead lion somehow, show her he was in charge so he could get what he wanted.

"Just thinking, if this shed belongs to the cottage, who lets you park your boat in it and who lets you stay here sometimes?"

Rosie's face went blank. Gotcha, thought Jack.

"I've been using it for ages. They don't mind … But, I suppose now you're living here I could help you out … only if you get a lifejacket though. That's a rule. An unbreakable rule."

Jack looked down at the boat as it swayed gently in the water. He was going to learn to row!

Later, after they had shut up the boathouse and Rosie had cycled off home, Jack followed the track back to the cottage, thinking that today had been an okay day. When he had got out of the car and stood at the gate on that first day, he didn't think it was going to be a good place to live, even for a little while. The cottage was small and lonely and tired. They had arrived after a long and boring journey and he didn't know where he was. But today, he had found something interesting to do and someone to share it with. Who knew what the next day would bring? {*A lifejacket would be good.*}

Chapter Nine

Day 4: Monday Morning- Police - PC Anstey

"I really can't tell you that, officer." Mr Monteray sat solidly behind his desk in his tiny office and stared at Constable Anstey through the thick lenses of his glasses.

"You can't tell me an address?"

"No, I can't. Data protection."

"You can't tell me if you have a pupil here called Jake Sinclair?"

"No, I can't, child protection."

"But this is me asking, a police officer."

"You don't have the paperwork."

Constable Anstey sat back in his chair. What would Sarge say now?

Chapter Ten

Day 5: Tuesday - Jack

"What are you going to get up to today?" Mum asked at breakfast the next day as she sat finishing her coffee while Lu was eating her cereal one grain at a time with chocolatey fingers.

Jack pushed the last of his cereal around the bowl onto his spoon and took his time finishing it off before he answered. "Well, I think I'll look in the shed. Might find something to play with. And I might look around the orchard for a bit."

"Oh, there *is* an orchard then?"

"Yes, it's just down there, over the wall. An orchard next to Orchard Cottage. I wonder what came first?"

"Watch yourself today Jack. You got some nasty scratches yesterday so don't go climbing any trees. And keep away from the river like I said. And be careful in the shed. And watch out for saws or axes or anything sharp. And anything rusty … What?"

Jack was grinning. He nodded towards Lu.

"Oh no! Oh for goodness sake!" Lu had picked up her bowl and was tipping it up to drink the chocolate milk. But, as always with Lu, she hadn't managed to get it quite right and most of the cereal and nearly all of the milk were pouring down her front. She stopped and looked at them.

"Nice," she said as she smiled her lopsided grin.

Mum began to mop her up with a tea towel smiling back at her daughter. "It's a good job you're still in your pyjamas Tallullah Williamson - what a state." She helped Lu drink the last of the milk and got up to get some more cloths to soak up some of the mess.

Jack left her to it and went into the hall put on his trainers and his coat. "See you Mum," he called from the front door.

And as he opened it he heard her call out. "How did you know this was called Orchard Cottage?"

He slipped out and shut the door quietly behind him.

He went round to the generator shed first and looked more carefully in the boxes of tools, choosing a blunt ended flat thing he didn't know the name of, a blunt knife and a screwdriver, all of which he thought might be useful for prising things open. The bushes covering the way to the shed seemed to have more leaves than yesterday. Things grew quickly in the countryside, he thought. He pulled the door as far as it would go and carefully squeezed inside. A torch. He should have brought a torch. He wedged the door open a little bit with a … not sure … something with a metal bit on the end and a wooden handle. He shifted some stuff so he could get across to the window and climbed onto a wooden bench running along the side. He found the handle to open the window and heaved it upwards, breaking off splinters of rusty metal and paint. The frame shuddered. Using the blunt ended flat thing he'd brought with him, he tried to loosen the window by running the blade all round the frame. The frame began to budge. He heaved it outwards and it opened with a bang. It opened upwards so he wedged it open a few centimetres with another wooden handled thing and looked out below. Okay. Hiding place and escape route.

He sat on the bench and took his time looking round. Most of the stuff looked old, dusty and no use to anyone but he thought that if it hadn't been cleared out, it must be useful ... probably ...possibly. Unless whoever had lived here was like Mr Brownlee on the ground floor, who never threw anything away, and the council had had to come and tunnel through the mounds of old newspapers, broken furniture and bags and bags of rubbish to find him and take him somewhere he could be looked after. It took five days and four workmen wearing blue overalls and face-masks to empty the flat. Jack knew because he had watched over the walkway with Milo and Jaye. Well, the shed wasn't as big as a flat so Jack knew it wouldn't need five days but there was only him, not four workmen, so he had better get on with it.

He started with what was on the floor, putting it to one side out of the way when it wasn't useful and by the bench if it might be. He heaved the lawn mower over against one wall and propped up the rake and spade. He didn't mind animals, he had liked the trip to the city farm, but he did feel squeamish clearing the cobwebs off the box of tools so he could look inside. And when he moved a cardboard box and found a dead mouse, he felt his heart jump as he leapt backwards. But then he thought, at least it wasn't alive and running around otherwise he'd be screaming and jumping up on the bench. How shaming would that have been?

He did like, however, the box he found under the bench with a deflated football and some plastic golf clubs and squashed skittles. Not because of those things, which he put in the not-useful-pile, but because there was a wooden cricket bat and stumps and a skipping rope, which he put onto the bench. And at the bottom of the box was a cracked leather case with a metal clasp. He opened it carefully. Inside was set of six silvery metal balls and one small red one. He liked the weight and feel of those as he held them in his palm and as he held them towards the light he could see a pattern etched delicately on the surface of each ball. He traced the pattern with a grimy finger. He liked they way they sat so neatly in the indentations of the case. He didn't know what they were for, a game of some kind as they were in a games box, but he did like them so they definitely went on the useful-things-pile.

Once he'd finished looking at what was on the floor and under the bench he stood on an upturned metal bucket to reach the shelves. There were some jars and tins and containers on one shelf. He prised lids off and peered in, finding dried paint, brown sludge or nothing interesting at all. Except for one. That one he dropped as he pushed himself through the half-open door to get some air into his convulsing lungs. He bent over double, coughing and coughing until he was sick. He fell on his knees, trying to ride the pain of the spasms in his chest. His throat felt raw and scratched and his lungs hurt so badly he thought he would never be able to breathe properly again. It was some time before the coughing slowed enough so he felt able to stand. He turned unsteadily, coughing with every step, and began to walk towards the cottage, picking his way slowly through the undergrowth and clawing bushes, terrified that if he moved too quickly he would cough so much he would be sick again. He wanted so badly to call for Mum but he didn't have enough breath to even make a whispered sound. He held on to the wall as he made a shaky walk to the front door. He banged frantically until Mum came to see who was making so much noise. She looked through the glass inset as she always did before opening the door. He saw the fear on her face as she saw him holding on to the side of the porch. She pulled the door open and grabbed him.

"Jack! What is it? What's happened?"

He fell against her and clung on as she half carried him into the living room. She tried to lay him on the sofa but the coughing was so much worse when he was lying down. Sitting upright and leaning forward the coughing slowed and he was able to breathe better.

"Jack, tell me, are you hurt? What's wrong? Did someone do this? What …"

He held his hand up as if to say 'stop' and 'wait' and managed to calm his coughing to once every four or five breaths. Lu was playing one of her complicated games on the floor with a pile of toys. She watched Jack with a frown creasing her forehead. Mum crouched by his side, looking anxious and scared but she was patient, she gave him time. After a few minutes he croaked, 'Drink."

Mum quickly went to the kitchen and he heard the tap running and water splashing into a glass. Lu came over and took his hand. "Kiss it better," she said and she kissed his fingers and smiled. He tried to smile back between coughs.

Mum brought a glass of water and sat next to him, pressing the glass into his hand. The water was cold and stung as it went down but he sipped between coughs and gradually the pain in his chest subsided.

"Do we need A&E?" she asked.

He shook his head. He hoped not, he really did. The last thing Mum needed now was a hospital trip with Lu in tow.

"Can you talk yet?"

He shook his head again.

"You've been sick?"

He nodded.

They sat for a little while longer, the coughing slowed and if he moved it didn't hurt his chest.

"You sit still. You need a shower to clean you up and we'll sort you out when you're ready. Okay?"

He nodded. Mum went off and he could hear comforting noises as she got the shower and clean clothes ready for him. Rosie had been right when she called him an idiot when he was rocking the boat. He hadn't listened to her when she said to keep still and he hadn't listened to Mum when she said not to touch stuff in the shed.

The bathroom was steamy and warm, and the hot water felt good against all the scratches he'd picked up in the past few days. He felt his breathing getting back to normal as he breathed in the steam. Once he was dried off and dressed in clean clothes he felt better. There was a big squishy (if slightly smelly) armchair in the living room and he sat in amongst the cushions, watching Lu playing. Mum gave him another drink (his fourth so far) and sat on the sofa.

"Well?" was all she said.

He hadn't said anything part from croaking out 'drink' earlier and he was frightened it would hurt when he spoke. He drank another mouthful and tried. His voice was quiet and whispery.

"In the shed, opened a jar."

"What kind of jar? What was in it?"

He shrugged.

"Did you drink it?"

He shook his head.

"Splash it on you?"

He shook his head again. "Looked in."

"Big jar? Small jar? Glass? Coloured glass? Where is it now?"

"Floor."

"Watch Lu. Don't move."

He heard the front door close as Mum went to investigate. He felt tired and closed his eyes, then opened them quickly - watch Lu, he had a job to do.

It didn't take long for Mum to come back and she looked less stressed than when she went.

"I think you'll be okay, pet. It looks like someone mixed up some weedkiller in the jar and left some in it. When you opened the lid you breathed in the fumes. You're not supposed to breath in weedkiller. But there wasn't much, just a tiny bit at the bottom of the jar so you should be okay. But you might not, so if you feel any pains or feel sick or anything different, you must say."

Jack nodded. "Sorry," he whispered.

"Okay. I'm going to get those clothes washed. Goodness knows if the washing machine works, it's ancient, but I'll give it a try. You need to stay in and rest today."

Jack realised he didn't mind; he felt as if a whole day had passed and it wasn't even lunch time. He snuggled down into the cushions with his book and spent the next couple of hours quietly reading about Norfolk - and he found Marsham, bonus.

Later, after some soup for lunch, which he did manage to eat without his throat hurting, he played colouring in with Lu, helped hang washing on the line to dry and emptied a cupboard in the hall which had an assortment of things muddled up inside, from a vacuum cleaner to a dog lead and some cracked wellies in different sizes (nothing worth while, and certainly no lifejacket). He was running out of things to do. There was no internet and TV was limited to a couple of fuzzy channels and some ancient videos, the old tape kind, not even DVDs. He didn't have all the things he'd had at home and playing with Lu was only bearable for ten minutes at a time. Mum was having another cleaning session in the bathroom; bleach wasn't going to make much difference to how it looked but she was waging war on dirt and germs and Jack thought she had a good chance of winning.

"Mum, can I go and get something from the shed?" he asked. His voice was still quiet but he could say whole sentences without feeling panicky about it hurting.

"What is it?"

"I don't know, these ball things."

Mum looked him over, "You feel okay?"

He nodded.

"Go on, but come straight back. And don't touch anything else."

He felt much better being outside. The pile of vomit was drying by the shed door so he skirted round it trying not to look. Mum had opened the door wider to get in and he could see she'd moved a couple of things but his piles were still there and he could come back in a day or two and finish his sorting. The jar was gone - a good thing. He climbed on the bench and pulled the window closed. The leather case was on the bench so he picked it up and took it with him, making sure the door was shut after him.

"Mum, do you know what these are?"

He opened the case and showed her while she was standing in the bath cleaning the curtain rail.

"Boules. French they are. You throw them."

Really? he thought. A bit heavy to throw. You could knock someone out with one of these.

"Give me a few minutes, I've nearly finished and then I'll give you a game."

It was always tricky taking Lu outside because if you didn't watch her every second she'd either disappear or do something she shouldn't, like pick up some broken glass because it was shiny or fall over on the gravel and skin her knees. Mum put her in the buggy with some toys and sweets and they went to a flat-ish area out the back and Mum showed him how to play the game. They each had balls with the same pattern so they'd know whose were whose and they put down a big stone as the throwing marker, and then Mum threw the red ball not too far ahead as the one to aim for. She showed Jack how to throw underarm, stooping down with bent knees, sending a ball as near to the red ball as she could get. It didn't take long for Jack to get the hang of it and they had a good time for half an hour or so. Jack was sure he won overall but he didn't argue when Mum did a victory lap around the lawn. As Jack stowed all the balls back in their case to keep them safe for another day, he thought it was good to hear Mum laughing. It was getting a bit cold now that it was late afternoon and he didn't want to stay out any longer. He clipped the metal catch tightly on the case and went to follow Mum and Lu. He caught the sound of a splat as he stepped under the cottage eaves. Urghh! He twisted his head round to see a trail of gooey stuff stuck to the side of his hoody. "Mum!"

Mum looked over and wrinkled her nose. "It's supposed to be lucky - a bird pooping on you."

"It's gross," he whined.

"It's what you get in the country," she said and disappeared round the side of the cottage to take Lu in by the front door.

"Good grief," Jack muttered as he pulled off his hoody very very carefully. He heard a noise, like some one snorting or sniggering. He looked across to the bushes and thought he saw a movement. He froze. For a few seconds he held his breath and listened. Nothing. Nothing at all. He breathed out slowly and, carrying the leather case, he quickly went into the safety of the cottage.

Chapter Eleven

Day 5: Tuesday - Police - PC Anstey and DC Tizora

"Anstey! Sarge wants you."

Constable Anstey nodded, picked up his notebook and headed to Sarge's office next door. Things were getting interesting. When he'd reported back to Sarge after going to the school yesterday there was a lot of fuss. There was someone with Sarge already.

"Anstey, this is DC Tizora."

Anstey nodded at the plain-clothes detective standing with Sarge.

"Anstey, can you tell me what you found out? About Ms Sinclair?"

"Well, Sarge sent me to the flat to tell her a Mr Harry Moreton was out on parole and we were here if she needed any help. There was no one at the flat and none of the neighbours answered when I knocked but an elderly lady passing by said Ms Sinclair didn't live there. I told Sarge and the next day I went back, and there was still no answer but a boy called Milo said his friend Jack Williamson - not Jake Sinclair - lived there but he hadn't been in all day. I checked council records and Ms Williamson is the resident, not Ms Sinclair. Then I went to the local primary school but the headteacher wouldn't disclose if there was any pupil called Sinclair. So, Sarge let you know."

DC Tizora thought before she asked, "Is anyone at the flat now?"

"No one was there first thing, I checked. A lady ... a few doors down ..." Anstey checked his notebook, "... Vi Jones, said Sal lived there with two children, Jack and Lu. She said they were spring cleaning, clearing out stuff, and there were piles of things being carted down to a car - at the weekend."

"Did you believe that?"

"No, who does spring cleaning these days. It seemed a bit odd to me."

"Did they have a car?"

"No, I checked. But Sal Williamson does have car insurance, took it out last week."

Sarge looked surprised. Anstey wasn't sure if it was the fact Sal Williamson had taken out car insurance or if he was surprised that he, Anstey, had found that out.

DC Tizora nodded. "I think she's skipped before Moreton finds her."

"So, what now?" asked Sarge.

"I'll speak to my boss first but I think we need to do some more footwork here, get a lead on where they've gone."

"What's the story?"

"Witness protection."

Anstey felt his heart skip a beat. A family had had to run - to escape - from what? What had this Harry Moreton done?

"Can I borrow Anstey here for a couple of hours? We'll get things done quicker."

Sarge agreed and after a couple of phone calls, PC Anstey was setting off with DC Tizora.

They went to the flat, checked it was still empty and then knocked on all the neighbours' doors. Taz and Stacey didn't take much persuading when they said they'd helped Sal - but they only knew so much. They had taken stuff to a lock-up, what happened after that they didn't know, Sal wouldn't tell them. She said the less they knew the better it was for her.

The lock-up was empty and when they tracked down the owner at home, she said she had lent it to Taz for a couple of days, she hadn't asked questions, knew it was for nothing illegal - Taz was a good friend.

As they drove back to the station, Anstey asked, "What now?"

"There must have been a car. Someone must have loaded up a car."

"At the lock-up?"

Tizora nodded. "Someone must have seen them - Sal Williamson did it herself? Someone else who's helping her?"

"Cameras? Shall I check cameras?"

Tizora nodded again. "I'll need to liaise so we'll head back to the station. You can make a start on cameras while I do some digging on the original case."

Anstey felt pleased to be at work, on the job for real, for the first time since he walked through the doors of the station a month ago. He set to work trawling through camera footage - feeling as if he was really doing something good for someone.

Chapter Twelve

Day 6: Wednesday - Jack

It was raining when Jack woke up the next morning. He could hear it hitting the window of their bedroom. Not good. He'd be stuck indoors all day.

He went to the kitchen in search of breakfast, hoping there was some cereal left.

No. Lu had got there first and was, like yesterday, eating it one grain at a time with chocolatey fingers.

"Toast?" asked Mum.

He nodded and sat down. Toast? How was that breakfast? Today wasn't shaping up to be a good one. Yesterday wasn't wonderful either, what with nearly coughing himself to death, but it had some good parts to it, and finding the boules set was a definite plus.

He drank some of the juice Mum put in front of him and asked, "Is it going to rain all day?"

"No idea. Perhaps. April showers."

"It's only March."

"Yes, but the clouds don't know that."

He thought for a bit and then asked "How long have we been here? Is it Tuesday?" He usually liked Tuesdays - it was PE all afternoon in school and he went to Milo's after cycling club.

"No, It's Wednesday."

He didn't like all Wednesdays. The ones when he could go to the library while Mum took Lu swimming in the town sports centre next door, were good Wednesdays, because he could be on his own. The ones he had to go to physio for Lu in the medical centre were bad Wednesdays, as they had to get a bus across town and he had to wait in a cold draughty corridor for ages.

He didn't know if this Wednesday was going to be a good one or a bad one. Mum put a plate down in front of him. Eggs on toast. Perhaps it would be a good one.

By lunch time it was shaping up to be a bad one. The rain hadn't stopped and he'd run out of things to do. Lu had been difficult, screaming and demanding, but he knew she was as bored of being indoors as he was so he did try to play with her for a bit. He wasn't hungry as he'd been picking at snacks all morning as he always did when he was bored, so although he was slow getting through his lunch, he wasn't going to waste it.

"After you've finished eating that, get your coat on and go out for a bit," Mum said.

"Can I?"

"Yes, not for too long mind. And find a pair of wellies from the cupboard. There must be some that fit you."

Although he wasn't keen on wearing wellies which someone else had worn, he was prepared to do it if it meant he could get out of the cottage. He found a pair, green and relatively unworn, that were just slightly too big but he put another pair of socks on and they were fine. They clumped as he walked to the front door but wellies always do that.

"Be back in an hour, Jack. We're going into town later," Mum called from the kitchen.

"Okay."

The rain had slowed to a drizzle. Everything was wet and dripping as he clumped to the track to the boathouse and found his way through the bushes, only getting mixed up once. The door was closed. He felt disappointed as he had hoped Rosie might be there but when he thought about it he realised the rain would have kept her at home. It was very dark inside today and it looked like some rain had come in from a couple of gaps in the roof. He supposed it didn't matter as the boat was in the water anyway but he checked to make sure it was dry and then checked Rosie's stuff to make sure it was dry too. All okay.

He found a spot on the platform or decking and sat down. Where could he hide in here? He looked around. If he got into the water he could duck under the platform and hide there. It wasn't perfect but it would do if he needed it. But, what if he had Lu with him? He went to the back where Rosie had stored her stuff. That was the first place anyone would look and the boat was the second. This wasn't going to be very useful.

So he went outside and went around the boathouse as far as the river would let him. There was a storage box round the side but that was obvious too. Still, he looked in and lifted the tangled ropes and canvas to see what was underneath. He could hide at the bottom, so this was a 'maybe' not a definite. He pulled out a couple of things to see what else was in there. What was that? He tugged at it and hauled it out. He didn't know exactly what a lifejacket was but this could be one. It was a coat with no sleeves, just with places for your arms to go through. And it had padding all around and some ties to hold it in place. It looked a bit manky and it smelt musty like so many things round here, and as it was still raining and he was getting wet, he shut the lid to the box and took it into the boathouse. He held it up by the light coming through the open door and judged it to be big enough. It didn't have any holes or tears. It needed a clean to get some dirt and cobwebs off, and those little black bits could be mouse droppings but he hung it on a hook to let it air off and set off back to the cottage. He wondered where Mum was taking them this afternoon.

This time Mum turned right at the end of the road and they set off in the other direction.

"Aren't we going to Stavesey?" he asked.

"Marsham."

That was where Hubbards was. Rosie had said. He could check what a lifejacket was.

The town was bigger than Stavesey. It had a church too, and a war memorial. And a bus stop. There was a carpark behind the main street with a supermarket next to it. They parked in the almost empty carpark and with Mum pushing Lu and Unk in the buggy, all wrapped up and covered against the rain, they walked along the deserted main street, which had several shops on both sides.

As it was quite late on a wet Wednesday afternoon there were very few people about. Mum left Jack minding Lu under an awning while she went into a newsagents. Jack looked over the road for a shop called Hubbards, as the rain dripped off the awning and trickled down his neck. They went to a butchers and to the bakers, where there wasn't much left to choose from but they bought some cakes and the kind of loaf you cut yourself. And then some bananas from the greengrocers. It was different doing the shopping like this instead of going to the supermarket and if it hadn't been raining and he hadn't been left minding

Lu outside, Jack thought he might have enjoyed it. As they came back on the opposite side of the street there was an alley between two shops, a fish and chip shop and a post office which was also a - Jack wasn't sure, as he'd never seen a shop which sold things like buttons and cloth and wool. {*An old kind of shop, called a haberdashery. Good word.*} Down the alley between these two shops Jack caught a sign - Hubbards. Found it.

"Last one, Jack, I'm just popping in here," said Mum. He was disappointed to see her go into the post office not the fish and chip shop, but this was a bonus. He waited until she had gone inside and then swung the buggy round and headed down the alley. It was drier here and he pushed the hood of his coat away from his face so he could see a bit more. The Hubbards' shop window was crammed with all kinds of things to do with boats and fishing. Some of it looked as if it had been there forever and most of it probably had if the faded price stickers were anything to go by. {*You'd half expect them to say 2/6d. Really really really old money.*} On one side against the display wall was something which looked like what he found at the boathouse. This one was bright orange and his was faded yellow but they were pretty much the same. So, job done. Feeling pleased with himself he headed back to wait for Mum.

"All done, fish and chips for tea?" And this time he didn't mind waiting in the rain while Mum went and got the best tea he'd had so far in Norfolk. When they got home, they changed out their wet clothes, Mum put the pretend fire on to warm them up and they sat in the living room eating their fish and chips out of the paper it was wrapped in and watched TV together.

When Jack lay on his bunk thinking about the day before he went to sleep, he decided that this had been an okay Wednesday.

Chapter Thirteen

Day 6: Wednesday - Police - PC Anstey and DC Tizora

Anstey peered in to the conference room and spotted Tizora over on the left side. The room was filled with officers much superior to him so he backed out and listened to the briefing from the corridor. He heard snippets.

'We've got a missing woman' and 'since Saturday' and 'two children.' And then 'violent offender' and 'car' and 'no trace' and then Sarge tapped him on the shoulder.

"Being nosey, Anstey?"

"Yes, Sarge, sorry …"

"Carry on then." And Sarge walked off to find a cup of tea.

Anstey listened again and heard 'break-in at the cricket club' and 'possible arson' and then some mumbling but then there was shuffling and everyone was coming towards the door. He stepped back and waited as people pushed past him, all buzzing with jobs to do.

"Tizora," he called as she went past in the crowd.

"Anstey, found something?"

He nodded and when the last person had moved away he stood next to her.

"Footage."

"Show me," she said.

Anstey lead her through to the work-station he'd been at for several hours yesterday and first thing this morning and pulled up the links to show her a car pulling off the road towards the lock-ups. "No cameras in the lock-ups but …" He pulled up a grainy image of the car, now loaded with stuff, coming back onto the road and disappearing. Tizora sat on the desk chair and looked closely at the screen.

"Who's in it? Williamson?"

Anstey shook his head. "No, you can't see who until …" and he showed her a still of the car at a junction.

"Who is it?"

"Registered owner, Gary Braithwaite."

"So, why are you showing me this?"

"Wait, you'll see." Anstey showed her the car at two other points in the town, with probably Gary Braithwaite at the wheel, and then pulling into the retail park and driving over against the far side - just out of clear vision of the camera. Tizora looked at Anstey. "And … is there a point to this … does Braithwaite know Williamson?"

"I haven't looked for a link yet. But … Look, see this footage …" He showed her a couple of seconds of a woman walking across the car park. "That's her, I know it is. The photos on file are at least four years old but that's her … with two kids, one in a buggy and that lad - right height …"

Tizora peered at the screen. "I don't know, it's not very clear, could be anyone on a busy Friday at a retail park."

"But then … " He showed footage of the car leaving the park. Through the rear window they could see the piles of the stuff in the back and then a face peering briefly at the side.

"Could be Braithwaite with his shopping - it's hours since the car was parked up - he might be re-decorating or going on holiday and had a lot of shopping to do. He might be a shopping fiend."

"He went in on his own, with all the stuff already in it. It's her - look at this one."

The next screen shot was grainy, taken at a set of traffic lights on the outskirts of town. "I tracked the car as far as here, nowhere near Braithwaite's house, wrong side of town, it's a woman - Sal Williamson - it has to be."

Tizora looked closely again and then stepped back. "Do we know where the car went after that?"

"As far as I got."

"We can follow up with a chat to Braithwaite and I'll get someone onto tracing the car - it must have gone somewhere we can follow. Is all this filed on the case notes?"

Anstey nodded.

Tizora swivelled and got up from the chair. Anstey stepped back so she could leave and he felt a bit flat - he had been buzzing, finding the car, and she didn't seem impressed. Oh well, back to checking the neighbourhood complaints list and making some visits to disgruntled residents.

Tizora stuck her head back around the door. "Come on then, get the car round and we'll get over to Braithwaite's and then check the flat - there must be something to say where they went."

Anstey grinned. It was going to be a good day after all.

Chapter Fourteen

Day 7: Thursday - Jack and Rosie

Mum hadn't bought any more cereal when they went out yesterday but she made Jack a bacon sandwich. The bread was a bit thick and the slices were very skewed but it tasted good.

"Here," Mum said, as she pushed a bag across to him.

He wiped his greasy hands on his jeans before looking inside. He slid out a postcard.

"I thought you could send it to Milo, just to say 'Hi'."

The card had a picture of a windmill on the banks of a river, with flat countryside all around.

"You can write it later. And post it next time we're in town."

"Okay. I've never sent anyone a letter before."

"There's always a first time. Your trainers are still damp, so use the wellies today."

As Jack set off to the boathouse he hoped Rosie would be there. He thought it might be the school holidays for Easter but he wasn't sure. If it wasn't, then he would have to wait.

The boathouse was empty. He took down the lifejacket he'd left to air on the hook and shook it to get rid of as many cobwebs and as much dirt as he could. It didn't seem quite so bad as before but he had brought a big brush with him that had been in the hall cupboard and he spent several minutes giving it a really good clean up. He took off his coat and put it on the hook and then shrugged his arms into the lifejacket. It was bigger than he had thought and when he pulled the ties close in front of him it felt loose. He tied it up as tight as it would go so it wouldn't come off.

The boat was tied up close to the platform and moved gently on the water. How did you get in without it rocking? No idea. Rosie said to keep still and balance but he could only do that once he was actually in the boat. He sat on the platform and carefully, slowly, lowered himself down. As soon as his feet reached the bottom he sat onto the seat, holding on to the sides of the boat. The boat did rock but not too much. He held his breath while it slowed and settled. Okay. Now to get out without falling in. He slowly stood straight up and let go of the sides. He waited until the boat stopped rocking and turned to his side. Waited again and then put one foot on the seat. Waited again and put the other foot up on the side of the boat and then pushed upwards, pulling himself onto the platform with both hands. It wasn't very elegant but he made it without getting wet. Excellent.

For the next half an hour he practised getting in and out of the boat, getting used to the rocking as he shifted his weight. He also tried moving from the front to the back of the boat, learning where he needed to put his feet and how to step over the seat without tipping himself - and the boat - over. He had just decided he had got the hang of it when the door opened and Rosie came in. He stood up and smiled at her and she almost smiled back - at least, she didn't scowl.

"I found a lifejacket," he said, pointing at himself. "It was in that box round the back."

She said. "And you haven't fallen in."

"I've been practising. It's wobbly but I think I've got the hang of balancing."

He waited until she came over and showed her the lifejacket.

"I looked in Hubbards and saw one that looked like this. It's a bit big but I've tied it tight."

"It's not bad, it should be okay."

"Can we go out on the river? Only if you want to, I mean if you're not busy, with school and that."

She stepped back saying, "We can go out any time." She pulled her lifejacket out from her stuff and pulled it on. "You have to listen, do what I say." She unhooked the gate at the end and swung it round over the water and hooked it against the wall.

"Yes, of course, I'm good at listening, mostly."

"Budge up, go and sit in the prow … the pointed end." Rosie untied the rope holding the boat at the front and dropped it in to the boat before getting in and reaching over to untie the second rope. She twisted the oars into metal rings at the side. She pushed the boat away from the platform and when it was far enough dipped the oars in the water and gently moved each one to send the boat out of the boathouse and then they were clear. It looked so easy but Jack knew it must be hard to do without knocking the sides of the boat into the sides of the boathouse.

The movement of the boat felt weird, his stomach shifted and his head felt fuzzy but as Rosie pulled out further and turned to row down river he felt more settled. Rosie swung into a rhythm.

"This is awesome," he said. "Where did you learn to do this?"
She shrugged.
"Where did you get the boat?"
She shrugged again.

"I've never been in a boat before," Jack said.

"What, never? Don't they have them where you come from?"

"Yes, but not like this. Only with docks and container ships and big things like that. A small boat like this would be flattened. What's that?!"

Rosie stopped rowing and looked round to where he was pointing.

"What?"

"It was just there, a furry animal, slid into the river from a hole."

"A water vole," Rosie said as she resumed rowing. "Don't tell me, you don't have those where you come from either."

"I don't know. I haven't spent much time by rivers, just the lake in the park." He turned to face the way they were going, carefully peering over the side. "Are there fish in here, real live ones?"

"What do you think? It's a river, it's water, it's where fish live."

"Could you catch them? Can you eat them?"

"I couldn't, I'm vegetarian. But you could if you were a murdering carnivore."

Harsh, thought Jack. Might have to think about fishing but without Rosie. He watched the river closely, trying to spot a fish.

"Am I going to do all the work or are you going to learn how to do it?"

"Er, now?"

"Why not?"

"I thought you'd explain first."

"You learn by doing not talking." Rosie slowed the boat to a stop. "Keep low and steady, come over and sit here." She shuffled along the seat and made a space for him. As Jack stood carefully he felt the boat move and he froze. He waited for it to settle, just like he'd done in the boathouse and then took a step forward, then another, and another, until he reached the middle of the boat. Holding the side he swivelled on his feet and lowered himself down onto the wooden seat and slid into place. He looked at Rosie - expecting some praise for doing it so well - but she just took hold of the oar on her side and nodded for him to take the one on his side.

"It can't fall out of this as long as you put it in properly," she touched the metal thing the oar was slotted into, "but you do need to watch what you do with the oars; you can lose them and then you'll be stuck."

He took hold of the oar, feeling the smoothness of the wood in his hands. He looked to see how Rosie was holding hers and shifted his hands to match what she was doing.

"Like this?"

"And then, lift it up out of the water."

Jack swung it up by pushing down but it shot up too quickly, spraying water and causing him to lurch forward.

"Gently."

Could have said that before, he thought. With his oar matching hers he waited to be told what to do next.

"Swing it forward to about here."

He did.

"Hold it like this."

Jack twisted the handle so the blade was vertical above the water.

"Lower it down and pull."

Water splashed up as the blade went into the water. {*It's called catching a crab - no idea why - because you don't actually catch a crab.*}

The boat rocked a bit and moved at an angle.

"You have to keep the oar in the water, as you pull so push down a bit, not too much. Try again.

Jack swung the oar up, angled it, dipped it into the water and pulled and pushed down at the same time. The boat actually moved, at an angle again because Rosie wasn't pulling too but he actually made the boat move. He grinned at her. She almost smiled back.

"Now we have to do it together to go forward. So, ready?"

He angled his oar.

"One, two, three .. In and Pull."

And the boat moved forward.

Rosie called 'In and Pull' so they both worked together for the first few goes and then she stopped because Jack had got the rhythm. They rowed the boat, both feeling happier than they had for a while, and both feeling a sense of having done well; Rosie for teaching Jack and Jack for learning from Rosie. Jack thought that being on the river might be the best thing he'd done - ever.

"You have to keep a check on where you're going. You keep the bank level with the boat. Get to know the river, where it bends and where you might get snarled up. This one is fine, it's not too tricky."

Jack looked behind him to see where they were going and realised he was rowing facing backwards. *{Awkward to see where you're going.}*

"And where are the brakes?" he asked.

Rosie stared at him. She raised up her oar so he followed suit.

"You just stop rowing."

The boat began to slow. She pushed her oar into the water and moved the opposite way to how they'd been doing it and the boat swung a little to her side and slowed even more.

"And this slows it down more. You have to plan ahead, know where you want to stop and slow it down before you get there."

Jack reversed the pull on his oar and felt the resistance of the water.

"If you want to go left, lift this oar and just use this one," and she showed him, "And right ..." and she showed him. "Now you do it."

Jack copied what she had done and felt the boat move left, then right. He could feel the pull and push of the oars in the water and could feel the change as he pushed or pulled at different strengths. The boat swung about in whichever direction he chose.

"If you want to turn round, just use one oar," and Rosie showed him that too, so they were now facing the way they had come.

They set off again, Jack feeling the rhythm and the power as they headed back towards the boathouse. As they got closer Jack said, "We can't go that way, past the boathouse, in case my mum sees me." Although Jack was getting used to Rosie's stare it still did what it was supposed to - made him feel uncomfortable. "She doesn't know."

"Did she say not to go out on the river?"

"No, not really, she just said to mind the river, be careful."

"Does she know about the boat? The boathouse?"

"No, not really."

"Does she know about me?"

"No."

"Does she know I go to the boathouse, keep my stuff there?"

"No."

They slowed by the boathouse drifting gently towards the entrance. Rosie navigated the boat back in and moored it securely. They sat side by side on the seat, thinking.

"Well, you don't want her to know about the boat, and I don't want her to know about me, so ..."

"Let's just keep it to us then?"

"That's good for me."

Rosie climbed onto the platform and untied her lifejacket.

"Are you going?" Jack was disappointed. He wanted to go out again.

"Have to but I can come back later, half two."

"Okay, I'll be here."

Jack watched her squeeze through the door and listened as she unchained her bike and set off, the wheels sloshing through some puddles on the track. He sat in the boat for a bit. He definitely liked rowing, he decided. But what was he going to do now - it was only late morning and he had time to kill before Rosie could come back.

He hung up his lifejacket and went round the side to look again in the big wooden storage box where he had found it. He emptied everything out onto the grass and looked at what was there. It all looked like boat stuff but he wasn't sure. He put it all back except for another lifejacket, smaller than the one he had used but too small for him. It might fit Lu. So, a possible escape route if he could get Lu to sit in a boat. No, not really going to happen as he couldn't strap her in - but he hung the lifejacket on a hook with some rope - just in case.

It was nearly lunchtime so he went back to the cottage to find Mum in the garden at the back, hanging washing out and kicking a ball to Lu. He joined in for a while, making Lu scream - but with excitement - so that was okay.

After lunch Mum gave him the postcard again and he sat trying to decide what to write. Mum said, traditionally, people wrote "Having a lovely time, wish you were here." But he was only having an okay time considering they had had to go into hiding again and they were in the middle of nowhere and hundreds of miles from home. But he did wish Milo could be here. He wrote; *Staying in a cottage with an orchard by a river, wish you were here. See you soon, Jack.* He had to check a spelling with Mum because he forgot to put the second 'r' in orchard and it didn't look right. Mum wrote the address and stuck on a stamp.

"All ready to post," she said. "Next time we're in town you can put it in the box."

Job done.   And he was bored again. So he found the book about Norfolk and read through the pages about wildlife so he would know what to look out for. The picture of a water vole looked like the creature he had seen, so he knew what they were now. There seemed to be lots of birds, far too many for him to look out for so he settled on crows, herons and mallard ducks, think three would be enough to be going on with.

Rosie was coming along the road on her bike as he went to see if she was coming. It felt good to be with someone, he thought. He missed his mates. They'd be out and about on the rec if he'd been at home. But he didn't mind being out and about with Rosie on the river either.

They took the boat out and headed downstream again. They went much further this time. Jack tried to remember to help keep the boat in a straight line between the banks and he learned how to move the boat gently round a small bend in the river. He practised turning the boat around in a circle and then back the other way. Rosie moved the boat into some rushes and pulled at them until the boat was bobbing in amongst them, hidden from sight. Jack sat looking at the reeds and rushes towering over them and down into the water below.

"Won't we get stuck?" he asked.

"No, the water is still deep enough, but go too much further in though, as it gets shallow and muddy, that's when you get stuck." She began to push with her oar and they drifted back onto the river.

They rowed until Rosie slowed to a stop.

"That's Leas Farm."

The farm was near to the river and Jack could see there were several parts to it. There was a house and some lower buildings, and a barn, and an open sort of shed with equipment in.

"Is that like your farm, the one where you live?"

Rosie shook her head.

"What's different?"

"That one is looked after." Rosie began to turn the boat around. "Come on, we need to head back."

It didn't seem to take long to get back to the boathouse but the day was nearly over and it was beginning to get dark. As Jack hung up his lifejacket he asked, "Is it safe for you to bike your way home? Have you got lights?"

"Of course. There's not much traffic on these roads, even when the holidaymakers start to flood in."

As Jack watched her cycle home along their road he wondered if he was ruining everything. Was he a holidaymaker? He didn't know. But, he knew it didn't feel like a holiday as he headed back to the cottage with a very long evening stretching ahead and nothing to fill it.

Chapter Fifteen

Day 7: Thursday - Police - PC Anstey

Today was a weird one. Anstey had been allowed to sit in on the briefing this morning so he heard all the evidence coming together. No one knew where Sal Williamson/Sal Sinclair had gone. But they did know why. When Anstey had read the files on Harry Moreton, he realised Harry was an unpredictable, angry, violent man and he could see why Sal Williamson/Sal Sinclair would want to disappear.

That morning he had worked his way back along the balcony chatting to Sal Williamson's neighbours. Sal seemed to be well-liked, she took good care of the two children, especially the little girl who had some problems and needed a lot of help. No-one knew about her past so the witness protection scheme had worked in giving her a new identity.

This afternoon he had written up his notes and delved into the footage around town, trying to find the route the car had taken. He'd been staring at the grainy images for ages when Sarge called him to go to a local garage and follow-up on a recent break-in. Two days ago, when Anstey had first gone along in answer to the owner's phone call, there wasn't much to see. A padlock had been opened, someone had gone in but the owner was resigned to the fact that the police were busy and as he couldn't really see what had been taken, he didn't really see what anyone could do about it. But today, he'd discovered what had been taken and he called at the station to let them know - in case it was important. So, Anstey walked down to the garage and found the owner, Dave.

"I didn't see it at first, but when I looked today - they were gone, both of them, back and front. I was supposed to put them on a car coming in today, personalised like."

Anstey looked at the sheet, it was all there, legal and proper, car indexes - number plates - to be transferred to a vehicle today. But, they weren't there. The locked metal cabinet where they had been stored was still locked when Dave had gone to get them. Whoever had broken in must have taken them.

"Who has keys to the cabinet?"

"One set, in the drawer over there."

Anstey looked at the desk drawer Dave nodded at.

"And who has keys to the drawer?"

Dave shrugged. "Never locked, anyone can get in."

Anstey thought. "Can I take a copy of this?" He held up the sheet with the details of the indexes and the car. Dave nodded so Anstey took a photo and left to walk back to the station, thinking, when suddenly he turned back and went to find Dave.

"Solved it then?" Dave asked hopefully as he was going to have to explain to an owner his special number plates had been stolen - not good for business.

"Who else works here?"

"Larry, Bruno and sometimes Kerry, she's part time."

"Kerry? Part time?"

"Saturdays mostly, sometimes Sundays when someone can look after her kids."

"What's her address?"

And Anstey had gone back to the station, found Tizora and told her he thought someone called Kerry had stolen some number plates from a garage a couple of weeks ago and that Sal Williamson had swapped them over - so it was harder to find her.

"Really? Address?"

Anstey told her and they set off to interview Kerry, who turned out to be a friend of Sal who also had a son at the cycling club and who had 'borrowed' the plates temporarily so Sal could get away - she didn't know exactly why Sal had to get away but she did know it was important and Sal was a good friend. And she hadn't broken in, really she hadn't, someone else had done that. She'd just taken the plates. And she really did mean to return them when Sal was safe but she didn't know they were going to be missed at the garage so soon. Tizora didn't arrest Kerry, she said it was too soon to know where all this was leading but she did say Dave might not be happy.

So, a bit weird, thought Anstey, a dead-end break-in was helping with a missing-persons case. He decided he needed to take all cases a bit more seriously - he needed to find the links - he didn't know where they would lead.

Chapter Sixteen

Day 8: Friday - Jack

The next morning was Friday, and at breakfast Mum decided they would go out, as it was going to be good weather and they had not been anywhere yet and Lu could do with somewhere to stretch her legs and run around. Jack was half interested and half not - interested because they were going to a nature reserve and not interested because he had hoped to get out on the river with Rosie again. He had no way of letting Rosie know he wouldn't be there - he didn't have a phone and Rosie didn't have a phone either, only in her house. He couldn't get Rosie's landline number and ask to use Mum's phone because he would have to tell her about Rosie, and probably about the boathouse and the boat and Rosie staying at the boathouse sometimes and … well, it would just go on. So for now, while Mum was getting Lu ready, Jack dashed round to the boathouse and left a message on a piece of paper torn from Lu's drawing book - '*Out today, back later, Jack.*'

Once they were ready, they drove off through the flat countryside onto a bigger road than they'd been on so far, even to Marsham. Mum pulled off the road at one of the villages and Jack hopped out to post his card to Milo. They soon arrived at the place they were going to. It had parking with trees and flowerbeds around, a low building with a cafe and a shop and a toilet, and it was free - a volunteer said it was free but if they wanted to give a donation that would be nice as it was all run by a charity. Mum dropped some coins in the box and was given a map so they could find their way around.

It was a very big place. The biggest open space at home was the park - and the park would fit in here several times. They set off with Jack using the map to follow the 'accessible' route so that they could push Lu's buggy more easily, although she got out and happily walked some of the way, with her hood flying backwards and and her hair fluffing up in the breeze as she scuttled along, jumping in puddles in the wellies they'd found for her in the hall cupboard.

Jack led them around the site, along some winding paths, through gates and over a stile. He was stunned by the openness of it all. He could see for miles, he thought. If he looked carefully he could see there was some colour to it, not just greyish sky, not just dull marshes. Some trees and bushes were beginning to open leaves. The rushes were so many different shades of brown and gold and even red. The water flashed silver in the bursts of sunlight coming through the clouds. And the birds - well, what could he think about those. There were so many, always flocking and whirling and calling.

When they were half way round the route, they stopped at a big hexagonal shed with open windows all around. On the map these were marked as hides and were for watching birds. The birds didn't know you were there and you could watch them for as long as you liked and they didn't fly away. They went inside. Lu was playing a game tracing the floorboards, walking back and forth. Mum was sitting on a bench with her coffee. Jack was watching through the window. And then someone came in. The first person they'd seen apart from a distant dog walker. Jack felt Mum stiffen next to him.

"Good morning, lovely day. Mind if I join you?"

Yes, we do, thought Jack as he turned to see an older man cross to another window.

"My favourite spot," he continued as he sat down and rummaged in his backpack. "Herons are beginning to nest just along there." He pulled out some binoculars and began to scan the reserve. Lu was still playing her game and Mum sat undecided but she put the cap on her drinks bottle and stowed it in the bag on the back of the buggy.

"Oh my goodness, there they are. There must be seven nests on that tree now." He turned to Jack. "Have you seen them? Do you want to look?"

Jack looked at Mum, she nodded and he said, "Yes, please." And he went over and the man helped him get the binoculars set right and helped him to focus on the herons. He could see great big long birds in the trees and all along one stretch of river. They flew in and out with great sweeps of their wings, landing gracefully and precisely each time. He even saw one with a fish in its mouth.

"I come every week if I can, watching them and hoping to see the young ones fly off when the time comes."

Jack could have watched all day but he remembered he had to be polite and said thank you very much and handed back the binoculars. Lu decided she was being left out and went over to them saying, "Lu's turn."

"Of course, here, stand there," and the man helped Lu to stand in the right place by the window and held the binoculars to her eyes so she could see. He carefully turned her head in the direction of the birds and said, "Can you see the birds now, in the trees?"

Lu reached out her hand as if to touch what she could see and groped around, before turning to say, "Big birds."

To Jack's surprise and Mum's relief the man just said, "Yes, big birds. And what else can you see?"

He let Lu hold the binoculars but he supported them underneath as they were too heavy for her to hold alone. She scanned across the landscape slowly.

"Lots of big birds. Tree. Cloud." Her attention was held for a few minutes before she handed the binoculars back and said, "Big glasses."

"Very big glasses," he said.

"We'd better move on," said Mum, gathering their coats and moving to the doorway. "Thank you," she said to the man.

"Any time," he replied as he waved at Lu and nodded at Jack.

Jack and Mum were quietly happy as they walked along the next part of the route. It wasn't often someone didn't react to Lu's face so today was a good day.

And it carried on being a good day. When they came back round to the visitors' centre they stopped for some lunch and they sat at a picnic table watching the little birds hoping for a crust to be thrown their way. There was a play area where Lu was able to climb and run around. There was a massive climbing frame with a rope bridge Jack was able to swing around on.

Eventually Mum said it was time to go and they headed back to the car. Lu fell asleep on the way back, clutching Unk, and Jack realised it was beginning to get dark. It was already past four, so no rowing today. Shame but he had a good day and there was always tomorrow.

When they got home Lu woke up grumpy but cheered up when she sat in front of some cartoons on TV and munched on an apple.

"I'm just going out for a while Mum, just around the garden."

"I'd have thought you'd have had enough of being outside. We must have walked for miles today."

"I won't be long."

"Okay, tea will be in half an hour so be back by then."

Jack ran around to the track and went straight to the boathouse. It was empty, as he suspected, but he checked to see if his note was still there. It was where he had left it but it had been turned over and 'Tomorrow afternoon' was written on the back. Oh well, at least she'd written something, she hadn't torn the note up or been angry. There was nothing he could do about missing Rosie today but he hoped to see her tomorrow. And while he had the chance, he went all the way across to the shed and checked the part he hadn't quite got into before the accident with the jar, hoping there might be some fishing gear. There wasn't, just some old ropes and and a rusty bucket. Not even a game like the boules set. He made his way back to the cottage in the half light of early evening.

How long had they been here? It seemed ages but by tomorrow it would be a week since they'd arrived. When he was at home he didn't have to think too much about things happening because they happened so often, every week and every day. Here he'd settled into a different house, with a garden, an orchard, a shed and a boathouse. He'd met someone new. He'd been to two new towns and a nature reserve. And he'd learned to row. And he'd almost choked to death on some poisonous weedkiller fumes. Alright, it may not be the stuff of adventure stories but it was okay for seven days.

Chapter Seventeen

Day 8: Friday - Police - PC Anstey and DC Tizora

Anstey was out checking on some stolen bikes from a school when Tizora messaged and told him to get back as soon as he could - the Boss wanted to see him.

"What's this about?" he asked when he got back to the station.

"No idea - I'm just a constable, like you."

"You're a detective."

She shrugged. "You wear a uniform - I don't - apart from that we're the same."

The Boss was not a patient man.

"About time, Tizora. How long does it take to find one Constable?"

"Sorry, Sir. He was off site."

The Inspector looked blankly at Tizora. "Phone?"

She shifted from one foot to the other and looked down.

"My fault, Sir, I was some distance away when the DC rang, and walking back took a while."

The Inspector looked blankly at Anstey. "Walking?"

"Sir, it's your new initiative, on the beat so to speak, coppers on the ground, being seen - I ...well, it was uphill on the way back so I ... er ... well ..."

"Stop."

"Sir."

"Number plates."

"Sir?"

"Traced?"

"Er … I'm not sure - I'm not on the team, Sir."

"Tizora - traced?"

"Not sure, Sir," Tizora looked as confused as Anstey felt.

"On the team?"

"Me? Yes, Sir."

"Well?"

"Er…"

"Check. Both of you, today, trace the car. It went somewhere." He began to read a file.

Tizora pulled at Anstey's sleeve and they backed out.

Back in the main office Anstey sat at an empty desk and Tizora sat next to him.

"So, what did that mean?"

Tizora shrugged. "No idea. He gets things done but I don't know how."

"So, what am I doing now? Do I forget the bikes for now?"

"Yes, we're looking for the car." She logged in and reached for her notebook. "Bring coffee, lots of it, we'll need it."

An hour later Anstey found what they were looking for.

"Right, where's the next service station?" she asked.

A few calls later Tizora spoke to the night manager of a coffee shop at a service station who remembered seeing a mum and two children coming in and using the toilets. He remembered because the little girl was crying and had been sick and, well, she looked a bit different, and it was very late for them to be driving still. They used the toilets and the little girl had changed clothes and off they went.

"Well, what now?" asked Anstey.

"I just don't know where they were going. We don't know when or if she changed the plates. What are we looking for?"

Anstey flicked to a programme and pulled up a feed onto the screen. "It's the make and either plate. I'll take the original index and you take the stolen one. This road, this direction, until we find it."

Half an hour later Tizora found the car, new plates, but still on the same road, heading across the country now.

"When did she change them?"

"No idea. There is a junction just before this set of cameras, so she might have pulled off and then rejoined with the new plates. But that's it, that's the make, those are the plates."

"It's a long way from here."

"Not even near her mum or anywhere else they ever lived."

Sarge came in and came to see what they were doing. "It's past your shift and you're still here. No overtime Anstey, not unless you're a detective."

"I know but the Boss said to find the car and - we have. Well, Tizora here has."

"We both did. I'll let the Boss know."

"You're not on shift tomorrow. Have a slow day, Anstey."

"Sarge."

Anstey headed out and walked slowly home, his head buzzing. He wouldn't be able to sleep. It was Friday evening and he thought he might like to go out, meet some friends and be sociable - but he was new here, so he didn't have any friends, not yet. He sighed. Another quiet night in with a take-away and some TV. Later, as he sat alone in his tiny flat, he thought about Sal Williamson. It must have been really lonely when she moved here, new name and new place to live, no contact with anyone she knew, not even her mum. But she'd made friends - they'd helped her, they'd done some very suspect things for her like stealing number plates. There was hope for him then.

Chapter Eighteen

Day 9: Saturday - Jack

As soon as he'd finished breakfast Jack went to the boathouse and spent a little while practising getting in and out of the boat, and moving from one end to the other. He also tried practising tying it up to the moorings but he couldn't get the knots as neat as Rosie so he just tied it as best he could until he could ask her to show him how to do it.

There was nothing else to do until Rosie came later, so he headed back to the cottage. As he came through the bushes onto their garden proper, he could hear Mum's voice. Who was she talking to? No one knew they were here. But then he saw she was on a phone, the one she'd been using since they left home. He drew back into the cover of the bushes and listened.

"I can't tell you. I don't know … if she comes back just tell her I'm on holiday … and I forgot to cancel, last minute thing … if he comes … of course he'll find it … you don't know him … he will find it … if he comes, let me know … I'll need to move again … the police won't be any help … no they won't, they weren't last time and look what happened to Lu … we're fine Stacey, really."

She switched off the phone, took out the sim card and put them both into a plastic bag in her pocket.

Jack held back and crouched down in the bushes, memories of four years ago crashing in his head. He closed his eyes and crammed his hands against his ears, trying to block the sights and sounds of a door being flung open while he lay hiding, shaking under a bed, of screams and Mum's voice pleading and furniture crashing, and, worst of all, of fists hitting flesh and blood spattering onto the carpet. He breathed slowly and concentrated on calming down.

He hadn't had a panic attack for two years but he hadn't forgotten the terror they caused. It was several minutes before he was able to retrace his route back to the boathouse and head for the road. He couldn't go back yet, he didn't want to see Mum until he could control his panic.

He set off down the road and walked past the cottage and the orchard and headed quickly along their road. He carried on past the place he'd stopped before, determined to walk the panic away. The pacing calmed him down so that soon he walked more slowly as he felt his mind slow and relax. He breathed slowly and imagined he was rowing with Rosie, a good memory. He thought about playing boules with Mum. Another good memory. And about the nature reserve and its quiet openness. There was a bend in the road and off to one side he could see the river through a gap in the hedgerow, so he pushed through and stood on the river bank watching the water move slowly past, carrying broken reed and leaves on the swirling surface, taking them … to the sea? Isn't that where rivers went? How easy would it be to row the boat all the way to the sea? Could he do it?

Feeling calmer but not quite ready to face Mum, he decided to carry on along the road just to see where it lead. It felt as if he was walking for a long time. At home he could tell how long he'd been walking because he knew how long it took to get from one place to another, like the library to the bus stop, or from the flats to school. There were markers to let you know where you had reached on the route. Here, he couldn't identify which bit of hedge was which. The fields looked pretty much the same and the trees were just trees - he didn't even know what kind they were. Perhaps when the leaves really came out he could tell the different kinds of trees from their size and shape. And perhaps when the crops started growing in the fields he would know which one was which. But then, he didn't know how long they would be here. Listening to Mum speaking on the phone, it seemed that they might need to move on quite soon. He wondered what Rosie would think if he disappeared suddenly. Would she tell someone?

Just as he decided to turn back, he saw a clump of trees on the next bend and what might be a gate. This was the first sign of human life along this road so he headed towards it to check it out. It was wooden, old and rickety and unpainted, with a track leading into a copse. Checking there was no one around - by habit rather than needing to as there hadn't been a single person on this road since they had arrived - he climbed the gate, hoping it wouldn't fall apart under his weight, and lowered himself onto the other side. Was this trespassing? Opening the boathouse and the shed at the cottage was one thing, he'd thought they were part of the cottage when he'd done it, but there was no way this was part of the cottage. It was too far away. Cautiously he crept along the track. It was overgrown and muddy where the sun didn't get to dry out the puddles under the trees. He looked behind him. Was he leaving footprints? Would someone know he'd been here?

A little way down the track he could see glimpses of the river through the trees. And soon he saw a building but he couldn't see exactly what it was. He crept nearer and crouched down and listened. Nothing. No sounds of anyone around. So, he moved nearer and crouched down again, watching and listening. He moved again and saw that there was a caravan in a clearing by the riverside. The windows were closed and there was grass growing up the sides covering the wheels and base. He walked around it, keeping his distance and being as quiet as he could. When he was sure there was no one outside and when he didn't think anyone was inside, he stood on one of the wheels and peered in through a very grimy window. It was dark inside and he couldn't see much.

He stood down and edged to the door. He turned the handle. It squeaked but it swung outwards letting out a stale, nasty smell. He stepped back, holding his sleeve across his face. He waited for a minute or so before climbing on the first step and looking inside. The smell was stronger but he held his breath and stood on the second step so he could see more of the inside. It was not so dark that he couldn't see much but the curtains drawn inside the windows and the grime on the outside both blocked the light.

He stepped inside and moved left. There was a kitchen, with a metal kettle on a two-ringed hob and some cupboards above, and there was a living area with some seating around the sides with a table in front. He moved further in, He opened a door on the right side and there was a shower room, tiny and mouldy. There were two doors at this end. The first was a small bedroom with bunkbeds, narrow and uncomfortable-looking. The smell was worse here and he almost didn't want to open the last door. He held his breath and opened it. Another bedroom. Bigger, with a double bed against one wall under the window and some cupboards above. In the half light it looked empty. There was a heap of bedding in the middle of the bed … and a bare foot sticking out.

He froze. He began to back out slowly and quietly. He felt his way backwards along to the door, stepped out and ran for it, running through the muddy track, not caring about his trainers. He jumped onto the gate and scrambled over it. He was pounding his way back along the road before he dared look back. When he flung himself over the orchard wall he thought his lungs were going to explode. He rolled over and crept further into the orchard and propped himself up next to a tree. He sat panting, feeling his heart thumping against his ribs. That was so close! He thought he had been so careful, creeping about and listening. An actual person, asleep in bed! He couldn't wait to tell Rosie.

Chapter Nineteen

Day 9: Saturday Afternoon - Jack and Rosie

"You're lying," she said, giving him one of her stares.

"No, really. It was so scary I nearly wet myself," he admitted. "And I've never run that fast. It was so quiet and there was nothing there, and then - there he was."

"How do you know it was a 'he'?"

"I don't know. It just looked like a man's foot, sort of … well … big."

"Women have big feet."

"I know but it was … sort of dark and …"

"Like someone with dirty feet or someone with a sun tan?"

"What, at this time of year? Who's been out in the sun in March? But I don't think it was all dark, just some of it, sort of patchy."

Rosie stared at him. He wished it was Milo he was telling. He wouldn't have stared like that or asked all these questions.

"Why did you go down the road then?"

Because I had a panic attack and didn't want Mum to know, he thought. But he said, "There's not exactly a lot to do round here." He offered her a sweet from the bag he had brought with him.

She looked at them before saying, "Absolutely not, they're not vegetarian and they're in a plastic bag that can't even be recycled."

Really?! *{I love using this - a question mark with an exclamation mark. An interrobang}*

"And you smell," she said, as if she was doing him a favour by telling him.

He stared at her this time, indignantly. "Rude or what!"

"You do, it's worse than the cow shed, sort of musty and ..." she sniffed towards him, " ... rotten."

"It smelt in the caravan, alright," he snarled and half turned away from her, munching on his sweets.

"What, like a dead badger?"

"How do I know what a dead badger smells like?"

"Depends on how long it's been dead. At first it's just like when you walk past a butcher's, a bit bloody but not too bad and then it gets really strong and clingy... and ..."

"You know what a dead badger smells like? What are you? CSI?"

"What's CSI?"

"On TV. You know, crimes, bodies, science."

"No TV on the farm."

Jack stared at her again. "You must watch on a tablet then? Or a laptop?"

She looked away, not meeting his eye. "No, nothing like that. There's a desktop in the office but I don't use it. Not allowed."

Jack was dumbfounded. Life without TV? Impossible. "So, is it something to do with signals, being out in the country then?"

"No."

"But ..."

"Just drop it." Rosie stood up. "Are we going out or not?"

Jack stuffed his sweets in his pocket and slid into the boat, his practice paying off as he kept perfect balance. He sat down without rocking the boat.

Rosie took off the moorings and tutted at Jack's knots. "I suppose you did this?"

"Couldn't get it right. Will you teach me? Please?"

"I'll have to. Can't have you losing the boat for me." She slid onto the seat and took up her oar.

He did the same and they gently moved out of the boathouse onto the river.

It was early afternoon. It was warm enough to leave their coats off and rely on their lifejackets.

Rosie began to turn the boat to where they had gone on Thursday.

"Can we go this way today?"

"I thought you said you didn't want your mum to see you?"

"I did … I don't … but I do want to see this side of the river too. I can duck down if she's anywhere near the bank."

"Okay, but I might need to duck too."

"Don't you want your mum to know either?" He pulled his oar round to shift the boat's direction.

"No mum."

Jack paused. Tricky. What should he say? He followed her lead and they rowed in rhythm as they had done before.

"So, who do you live with then? On the farm?" He felt his shoulder twinge as he used his rowing muscles again after a break.

"Step-dad."

"Oh. I had one of those too." Jack looked towards the bank, trying to spot the cottage.

"He's not here, is he. Just your mum and sister?"

"Half-sister."

"Watched you a couple of days ago, in the garden."

So that explains the sniggering after they had played boules. She had laughed at him when the bird pooped on him.

Rosie was looking over the other side as if she was looking out for something too.

"Do we pass your farm?"

"No, it's up there. But the fields come all the way down so he might be working along here."

"Doesn't he like you being out on the river?"

"He doesn't know about the boat."

"Where does he think you're going then? What do you tell him?"

"He doesn't care."

Jack tried to make sense of this. "If he doesn't care, why would he mind about the boat?"

"Because it's something that is mine, that I like doing, and he would take it away from me."

They rowed on, each thinking about the other.

"The cottage - just through there." Rosie slowed and nodded to the bank. Jack slowed too and ducked behind Rosie.

"Can you see anyone?"

"No, the bushes get in the way. I don't think they can see the river. But let's get away from here." She began to row again and Jack joined in. He kept a check on the bank until he thought they had passed the orchard, and then he relaxed.

"Have you been down this way before?" he asked.

"Only once, but just as far as this, I kept to the downstream."

"What does that mean - downstream?"

"Upstream means going to where the river starts and downstream to where it finishes."

Jack thought about that. "So if we went downstream would we get to the sea?"

Rosie snorted. She was good at that, thought Jack. "Not on this stretch, it goes into Heron Broad, that's where it finishes."

"Broad? That's like a lake, isn't it?"

"You could call it that. There are lots of them here, lots of rivers and water everywhere. You could probably get around the whole county by boat."

"Have you tried?"

She snorted again. "Too much like hard work. We're rowing together, how hard do you think it is if you're on your own? I told you, I go downstream. It's easier and I can get to the village on my own but it'd be too hard to row back upstream any further than that."

"Why is it harder to row upstream?" He waited for the snort. It came, along with one of her stares.

"The current, you're going against the current, the way the water's going. Like now. Can't you feel how it's harder and slower to move forward than last time?"

It didn't seem any different to Jack, but then this was only his second time out on the water.

They rounded a slow bend and he cranked round to see what was up ahead. How far to the caravan? Could you see it from the river? Had someone seen him there earlier?

"How far should we go then?" he asked. "If it's hard to get back?"

She didn't even snort this time. "Don't you listen? We'll be rowing back *downstream* so it will be *easier* and so we can go *further*!"

Good grief! Jack rowed on keeping rhythm, keeping his shouting in his head. {*It's easy, you shout exactly what you want to but just inside your head so nobody hears you and you don't get into trouble.*} He turned every so many metres and checked where they were. As they reached another slight bend he thought he recognised the trees where the caravan was parked. He stopped rowing.

"That's it, that's where the caravan is."

Rosie stopped too and they looked ahead as they floated midstream. They sat for a minute or two. Jack felt the boat drifting slowly the way they had come, the current taking them downstream.

"We could just row past, and look. See what's there," Rosie suggested,

He wasn't sure but then, why not?

They rowed until the trees were thinning and stopped again. They both looked really hard as they drifted past.

Jack pointed at a gap in some trees, "I can see the caravan. It's white, just there."

"Got it." Rosie manoeuvred the boat so they were facing the copse and held it steady in the water.

"Whose is it? Who lives there?"

"I don't know."

They watched carefully, hoping to see someone but also hoping not to.

"Let's moor up and have a look."

Jack gave Rosie a stare this time.

"Are you serious! I went in someone's caravan! They might not be too happy about that!"

"They won't know it was you. They didn't even see you. And we'll creep in and out before they even know we're there." Rosie began moving across and downstream to find somewhere safe to moor out of sight.

"No, we can't, we'll get caught."

"Yes, we can, and no, we won't."

"Just stop! We can't, really can't."

Rosie ignored Jack. "Yes, we can. OR - there's no one there - you made it up." She caught hold of some rushes and pulled the boat towards the bank.

"What!"

"Only one way to find out." She crossed to the stern and picked up the mooring rope. "If we look, we'll know, won't we." She hooked the rope over a stumpy bush and tied it round the base.

"But there *was* someone, I saw their foot sticking out."

"Could have been anything." She climbed out. "Coming?"

He watched her walking away along the bank towards the caravan. Milo would never have behaved like this.

He followed her, several steps behind until she squatted down just inside the trees where he joined her. They could just see the caravan. There didn't seem to be anyone around so Rosie crept forward, keeping low.

"Can't see anyone," she whispered.

"I told you, I didn't see anyone until I got inside!"

They watched for another minute or two and then Rosie moved to go round the back of the caravan, near the river side. Jack followed and they ducked behind a storage box Jack hadn't seen earlier.

"I think it's for fishing," whispered Rosie, "Someone uses this for fishing. They come up, stay for a weekend and then go home." Quietly she half stood up and pushed the lid of the box upwards. They both peered in. Yes, there was some fishing gear in there, and hundreds of dead flies and wormy things. It smelt terrible so she dropped the lid shut and they both sat down holding their sleeves over their nose.

"What was that?!" gasped Jack.

"Maggots. Someone left bait in there and it's turned."

Maggots? Jack thought you used a worm for fishing. He wasn't so keen on trying it out now.

Rosie peered around the side of the box. She pointed to a window and indicated she was going to look. Jack sat tight, ready to run if someone saw her. He heard her shuffle through the long grass and after a few seconds, shuffle back.

"Definitely no one inside," she whispered.

"Yes, but that's what I thought and there was, in bed!" he whispered back.

"They can't still be asleep, it's the afternoon. They must have gone out."

Jack peered round the side of the box, then began to crawl towards the caravan. He edged all round the side and the back until he reached the side with the door, then crouched still, by the bedroom window. Rosie crouched with him. Still no noise from inside.

Very slowly they inched together to the door and stepped onto the first step, and then waited before stepping onto the second step. The door was open, just a little bit. Rosie held her sleeve across her face and grimaced but he didn't think the smell was as bad as it had been. Jack opened the door enough to peer in and looked left and right. No one. They moved off the step and stood inside, listening, both covering their noses. Jack led the way to the bedroom, past the kitchen and bathroom and little bedroom. Nothing had changed, nothing had been moved. The bedroom door was ajar, as Jack had left it. The smell was worse here and even stronger as he opened the door. The heap of bedclothes hadn't changed, the foot still stuck out at one side.

"See," Jack whispered close to her ear. "I told you."

Rosie stared, wide eyed. She whispered so quietly he could hardly hear. "The smell - dead badger."

"What, in here? A dead badger?"

"No, it's a person. A dead person."

Jack looked at her, gave her back one of those stares.

She nodded at him. "Definitely dead badger."

Jack felt his heart thump against his chest for the third time today. That couldn't be good.

They gazed at the heap of bedding and the foot.

"You look," she whispered, nudging him in the side.

"NO!" His voice came out loud and they both froze, waiting for the person to wake up.

Nothing.

In such a small space he could almost reach out and touch the bed but he moved a few centimetres into the room, took hold of a corner of the blanket and looked at Rosie. She nodded, to say 'do it.' He lifted it slowly and they both peered underneath.

As they rowed feverishly back downstream, silent, shaking, sweating too, Jack knew he would never forget that smell - or the mottled flesh - or the oozing mess on the sheets below the body.

In the boathouse Rosie moored the boat, hung up her lifejacket, picked up her backpack and went to get her bike.

"Wait, what do we do?" Jack pulled her back.

She shrugged.

"We can't leave it."

She began to cycle down the track.

"Rosie, stop," he held on to the bike, "We have to tell someone."

She shook her head. "I can't, he can't know I was there."

"Who? Who can't know?"

"Frank." She jerked the bike away and cycled off.

He stood watching her until she turned onto the road. What was he supposed to do now?

Chapter Twenty

Day 9: Saturday Late Afternoon - Jack

Mum was in the kitchen, Lu was playing with some saucepans and empty boxes on the floor.

"Had a good time? You might as well have some crisps if you're hungry - tea won't be for a while. The gas ran out and ... what's wrong? Have you hurt yourself again? What is it?"

She turned him to the light of the window and looked at him.

"I found a dead body."

"What?"

"I found a dead body."

"Where?"

"Caravan down the road."

"Are you sure?"

He nodded. Mum looked at him, sat down so she was level with him and asked him again, "Really, you're sure?"

He nodded. "Sorry Mum."

"Don't be sorry."

She sat him on the chair next to hers and asked him loads of questions. Where is this caravan? How far down the road? Was anyone else there? Did anyone see him there? How did he find the body? Where was it? How did he know it was a dead body? Did he touch anything?

He didn't actually lie, not really, but he didn't tell the whole truth either. He missed out Rosie's part. Mum sat thinking for what seemed ages, then she said, "Show me." She got Lu into her buggy, put some gloves and cleaning stuff in a bag, put on a pair of the wellies from the hall cupboard and they set off down the road looking like a family going for a walk in the last of the day's light.

At the gate, Mum told Jack to wait with Lu just inside the hedgerow in a field, out of sight, while she went over the gate clutching the bag and wearing disposable gloves. Lu was fretful; she had been enjoying her game and wasn't happy at being strapped into her buggy and wheeled down the road. Jack tried to distract her but she wanted to get out of the buggy and was heading towards a full-blown screaming session. He found the bag of sweets he had put in his pocket earlier and gave her one. She was quiet for as long as it took her to eat it. He gave her another one and checked the bag to see how many were left. He reckoned there were enough for possibly five minutes - he hoped Mum wouldn't be long.

The light was going and he was very unnerved by the changing shadows in amongst the trees. His feet were beginning to feel cold and although he zipped up his jacket he was soon shivering. The shadows grew longer as the spring sun sank below the fields. The sky was a pinkish colour, though, which he thought meant tomorrow would be a nice day. A nice day? What was he thinking? He'd found a dead body!

The shadow of a person came through the copse and Jack was relieved to see Mum coming through the trees at last. She checked the ground where Jack had been standing and ruffled over the grass with her hand and scuffed up the soil just a bit and picked up a tissue that he'd dropped from his pocket. She pulled the buggy round to face home and they set off to the cottage. She walked so quickly Jack almost had to run to keep up. At the cottage, she put the wellies into a bag and left them at the front door. Lu was howling now so Mum gave her a bag of crisps and sat her in front of a cartoon on TV while she got Jack to strip off and get in the shower. All the clothes he had been wearing today, including his coat, went into the washing machine along with Mum's and they sat eating tea wearing pyjamas.

Later, when Lu was in bed and it was quiet, Mum sat with Jack in the living room watching a fuzzy TV programme about penguins. He knew she would say something when she was ready, and when she thought he was ready. He knew how to be patient.

"So, it *was* a dead body you found, Jack. A shock for anyone. How do you feel?"

He shrugged. "I didn't know the person and I only saw a bit, so okay."

"It's serious, finding a body, but it's complicated too. We can't be involved, no one can know we are here. And you went into the caravan when you shouldn't. There would be all sorts of questions which we just can't have right now."

Jack nodded, he understood. He remembered the long hours in police waiting rooms with endless questions and everything dragging on, and having to stay with people he didn't know until Gran came and drove him to her house until Mum came out of hospital. And the press, waiting in their street, outside school, pestering them all the time.

"So, I've cleaned anything that you might have touched. Your fingerprints shouldn't be on record any more but I don't trust the police to have deleted them. We'll get some new trainers tomorrow and get rid of the ones you were wearing. You might have left footprints and I couldn't clean the floor, it was too much. It's Sunday so we'll go to a big town, buy some things and get ourselves straight." He nodded again. He knew she was trying to protect him but he also knew it would be hard to cover up the fact that he'd been in the caravan. And Rosie - how could that work when Mum didn't even know she'd been there too.

"Not yet, but in few days, when I'm sure about a couple of things, I'll let the police know somehow, but keep us out of it. We're safe here but I don't know how long for. I don't want to move until we have to. We need more time, Jack. Do you understand what I'm saying?"

Of course he did. He remembered the phone call that morning. He knew it was only a matter of time before they had to move again. And if they were involved in a murder case they would be exposed, but stuck here - where Harry could find them straight away. It would be no use asking for police protection; they didn't get it last time, you only had to look at Lu's face to see the consequences of that.

Day 10: Sunday - Jack

The next morning they went to a big town a longish drive away. Nowhere near as long as the drive to get here but long enough for Lu to start whingeing. They pulled up in a retail park outside the town as soon as it opened but was still empty, and with Lu in her buggy with her hood pulled up, they set off to a clothes shop running along one side. Mum sorted out Jack's new trainers, which he kept on, and also bought him a new coat (in the sale as the winter was over and they were getting rid of left-over stock.)

Before he knew it, they were back on the road and heading homewards. In a smaller town, they stopped at a supermarket and stocked up, moving quickly as usual. Mum dropped the wellies she had worn yesterday in the clothes bank in the carpark. In another smaller town, they stopped at a park and Lu had fun climbing and running for a while, while Jack sat on a bench with Mum eating a hot sausage roll and drinking a can of something sweet and fizzy. Mum dropped his old trainers and coat in one of the recycling units by the car park as they went back to the car.

By the time they got home it was past lunch time. Jack helped unpack the shopping before running across to the boathouse to see if Rosie was there or if she'd left him a note. She hadn't. He needed to talk to her, let her know it was all sorted.

Mum had made him a sandwich which he ate in front of the TV. Polar bears today. And then he didn't know what to do with himself for the rest of the day.

By bedtime, Jack knew he wouldn't be able to sleep. He hadn't done enough today to burn off his energy. He read with a little torch until he knew Mum had gone to bed and was asleep - she snored, but always said she didn't. Then he got up, crept out into the hall in the dark and wondered what he could find to do. He went into the kitchen, closed the door and turned on the light. Sitting with a bowl of cereal he looked through the Norfolk book. He opened the map and found the places they had gone to today. He looked for Marsham and thought he knew roughly where they were staying. He followed the lines showing the rivers and wondered if he could really row all the way across the county. He found the wildlife centre and thought they were not too far from that, so if he followed this river to that broad, he could cross into that river and out to the coast. An adventure. But not one that was likely to happen. He washed his bowl and spoon, dried them and put them away. He turned off the light and turned on his torch so he could find his way back to bed, bumping his way across the room, stubbing his toes on Lu's toys. He stood at the window looking out into the darkness. It was so dark here. No street lamps or houses to brighten up the horizon. You could get lost in the darkness.

Chapter Twenty-One

Day 9: Saturday - Police - DC Tizora

Tizora pulled over and looked up at the street name. Lost again. She needed Anstey. He knew where to go - he didn't get lost and he'd only been here for a month. She was back to see Gary Braithwaite. Just in case he remembered something. She reset the satnav and turned the car around. It was going to be a long Saturday, going over things, just in case.

Day 10: Sunday - Police

In a quiet town, somewhere in the west of England, a man was stopped by a local police officer because he had dropped a piece of litter in the high street. The man apologised, said it must have fallen out of his pocket and he picked it up and dropped it in a nearby litter bin. They both moved on with their day. Later, much later, the police officer wished he had known who the man was on that day - it would have saved so much trouble all round.

Chapter Twenty-Two

Day 11: Monday - Jack

First thing after breakfast Jack went over to the boathouse, and each hour after that. And that afternoon after lunch he went over to the boathouse, and each hour after that. And that evening after tea he went over to the boat house. No Rosie. He had left a note on his first check that morning saying 'All okay.' She hadn't replied.

Day 11: Monday - Police - PC Anstey and DC Tizora

Tizora was getting frustrated - not with anyone - just herself. She had spent hours trying to track that car - in between the other jobs the Boss had her dealing with - and she just couldn't find a trace. She really wanted to find this Sal Williamson or Sinclair or whatever she was calling herself. She had read the files, she knew why Sal had disappeared but she wanted to know where she was hiding so that someone, anyone, could help her when she needed help - and Tizora knew that sooner or later, Sal Williamson would really need their help.

"Anything happening with that missing family case?" Anstey had just come into the office for his late shift.

Tizora shook her head. "Slow. Tracing the car has got us no where - all that work - and it's vanished."

Anstey was disappointed. They had found the car with its new number plates but - they were no further forward. Back to checking for those missing bikes - in a town full of students and kids and cycling clubs. He's much rather be looking for missing persons - well, no, not really, he didn't want anyone to be missing but if they were, well he'd rather be looking for people than bikes.

Later that day, an alert came through the system about a man who had missed his appointment with his parole officer and who had somehow removed his electronic tag before disappearing. The alert hadn't been sent to anyone in particular, just anyone linked in some way to a few names and cases. No-one read it that day, they were all too busy doing other things but if they had, they would have got straight back to looking for Sal Williamson and her children.

Chapter Twenty-Three

Day12: Tuesday Morning - Jack and Rosie

There was no denying it, by mid-Tuesday morning he was bored. He'd already exhausted the shed, and the boathouse, and there was nothing to do in the orchard. He already had some hiding places sorted. He'd been as far as the bridge and then down their road as far as - well, the caravan, and he certainly wasn't going in there again. Every so often the sight - and the smell - of that dead body came into his head. It was hard to stop. He was glad Mum had washed all his clothes and that he had new trainers and a new coat as the smell was only a memory now but every morning, when he saw their bedding heaped up, the sight of that dishevelled bed in that cramped caravan popped into his head. He got into the habit of straightening his and Lu's bed as soon as he got up.

So, it was Tuesday. And what was there to do?

He wandered to the boathouse. The door was closed. He sighed and pushed it open anyway … and he knew someone was there.

"Rosie?"

There was a rustling sound over in the corner, Rosie stuck her head up out of her sleeping bag.

"Rosie! You're here!"

Rosie propped herself up on one elbow and yawned.

"Did you sleep there last night?"

"What's it look like?"

Rude as ever. He dropped his backpack and went over. "Where have you been? I've been waiting for you to come over."

She didn't answer but hauled herself up so she was sitting up in her sleeping bag.

"Are you okay?"

"Are you?" She reached over for her water bottle and drank.

He sat down next to her. "Sort of."

"Well, I'm not."

There was a long silence. Jack didn't know where to begin. How do you start talking about a dead body?

"I wanted to tell you it was alright. I told my mum ..."

"What! Why?"

"It was a dead body!"

She began to disentangle herself from the sleeping bag and scramble over to her bags.

"What are you doing?"

"Leaving." She began pushing things into bags.

"What? Why? You can't go yet - we have to talk."

"I can't stay now everyone knows, he'll kill me."

Jack stood up in front of her. "Just listen, you have to listen."

She became so agitated she emptied a bag she'd just half-filled, screwed up clothes tumbling onto the decking. "No, I have to get away. Leave me alone. It's your fault."

"I didn't kill anyone ..."

"No, you went nosing around and found him. Why did you do that? Why couldn't you just stay at home and mind your own business."

She had a point. He shouldn't have been poking about in someone else's caravan.

"What are you even doing here? No one comes on holiday here in winter. You turn up and swank around like you own the place and ruin everything."

Unfair, thought Jack. If only we *were* on holiday.

"But my mum sorted it out. It's all right."

"How is it all right? I've been waiting for the police to turn up at the farm. I was terrified, you don't know how that feels."

Oh yes, I do, he thought. But he said, "I didn't tell her about you. She doesn't know you were there."

Rosie stopped shoving things into her backpack and for the first time looked directly at him. "So, you lied. To your mum. How do I know you're telling me the truth if you can lie to your own mum?"

"Listen," he pleaded, 'I told my mum, she thinks I went alone, she doesn't know about you and the boat. We went back, she went and checked and she cleaned off finger prints and …"

"Told the police."

"No, she didn't."

Rosie stopped. "She has to, it's what you have to do."

"She will, but not yet."

"So, when will she tell them? The police?"

Jack shrugged.

"It was a dead body! What's more complicated than that?! Are you covering it up?"

"No! Course not! I just found it."

"Did your mum do it? Did she kill him?"

"No! My mum wouldn't kill anyone."

"Your dad then?"

"No, he's not here."

"Did he do it? Where is he? In hiding?"

"He was never here, we're on our own, just us, it's only ever just us."

"You turn up and …"

"I know, you said that already, I swank around like I own the place - but I don't swank around … "

"Yes, you do, you came in here and you didn't ask me if you could."

"You don't own it either. You shouldn't be here, you're squatting in someone's boathouse. Did they say you could be in here? Did they? Do you know who owns it? Well? *You* don't own it, do you? It's not my fault this has happened."

"It is your fault. You found it!"

"I didn't mean to."

"But you did, so it's your fault. I was doing okay until you came."

"What, hanging about in here? How is that doing okay?"

"I managed."

They stood glaring at each other.

"I'm sorry," Jack said as he reached across and put his hand on her shoulder. She pulled back and winced.

"Get off. I'm going, I have get away."

"You don't have to go. No one knows you were there, Mum hasn't told the police. You can go home."

She snorted.

"Why not, no one knows. You're safe."

"No, I'm not. It's never safe." She pulled her hoody up over her head and pulled down one shoulder of her tee-shirt. Then the hem on one side and then the back.

Jack looked at the bruises, which were swelling and beginning to turn blue.

"Who did that? ... Not Frank?"

She nodded.

"Why?"

"I stayed on the farm because I was too scared to go out in case the police were here."

"I don't get it."

"I was around too much. If he doesn't see me, it's mostly okay, sort of okay."

"But what did you do to make him hurt you?"

"I said - I was just there. He doesn't need a reason. I keep out of his way as much as I can. If he sees me he just ... loses it." She shrugged. "That's why I come here. And sometimes, when it's warm enough, I just stay over. It's ... nicer."

Before, well, just before all that stuff happened four years ago, Jack sometimes stayed at Gran's and that was nicer, too.

"As soon as the police know I'll have to run away. They'll be all over the place, asking questions, and he'll stop me from going out and then ... it'll keep happening. He'll kill me, I know he will, just for being there."

"Stay here, it's safer. Don't leave yet. Let's see how it goes. At least if you're here you're out of his way and safe."

Rosie nodded slowly. Where could she go? It was easier to stay. "Just for now. But I'll be ready to go when I have to," and she began to pack her backpack more carefully.

Jack looked over at his backpack. He was all ready and set to go too. He knew what he needed to do when the time came.

"Have you had any breakfast?" he asked.

Rosie shook her head.

"I'll see what I can bring. Don't go, promise. Stay right here."

Jack went back to the cottage. Mum was with Lu, in the back garden, so he sneaked in and raided the kitchen for portable food he hoped Mum wouldn't miss. He found a tube of Arnica cream in the grab bag by the door and took it too, telling himself to remember to put it back later.

Back at the boathouse, Rosie had put most of things into her backpack and her sleeping bag was rolled and fastened neatly. He handed her a bag of crisps, a banana and two biscuits.

"It's all I could take but I'll see what I can get later. There was a sausage but you don't eat those." Rosie almost gave him one of her stares but not quite. "And there's some cream for bruising. Lu's always falling over."

"Lu? Is that your sister?"

"Yes, half-sister."

She took the food and started on the crisps. They sat on the platform together in silence for a while. Jack wondered how much he should tell her but before he could decide, once she had finished the crisps and was opening the banana, she spoke first.

"Have you seen a dead body before?"

"No. Have you?"

"Lots, not a human though, just animals."

Badgers, he thought but he said, "On the farm?"

"Only chickens on the farm, but they don't really count, they're just too stupid to stay alive. And the cows we had once went off to to the slaughterhouse so I didn't see them when they were dead."

"So what then?"

"There's always dead things in the fields and along the river. Mice, foxes, birds, ducks … and I saw a dead horse in Jones's paddock once, before it was taken away. What?"

He was looking at her suspiciously. She was very matter-of-fact about all those dead things. He'd be as freaked out by seeing a dead duck as he was a dead person. You didn't get to see dead ducks at home, not even in the park.

"What?" she repeated. "Haven't you ever seen a dead fox? Or badger? Or at least a bird?"

"No, I don't think so. Sometimes there's road kill out of town but not really on the estate."

She snorted. He really wished she wouldn't do that. He changed the subject. "You'd better put some of that cream on. It'll help with the bruising."

She picked up the tube and read the label.

"It's just Arnica, I'm not trying to poison you."

"I don't know that, you might be trying to get rid of a witness for all I know."

Jack snorted this time and she stared at him and said, "Go on."

"What?"

"Outside, I'm not having you in here while I do it."

He stood up and went outside. He breathed slowly and rubbed his new trainers with his hand to clean some dirt off the top. He thought again about what he should tell Rosie. She'd told him stuff about her dad, or step-dad. Should he tell her about his? And should he tell Mum about Rosie? Mum would know what to do about all those bruises. By the time Rosie came out a few minutes later he had some questions to ask her.

"Shall we row for a bit?" he asked.

She frowned. "It hurts too much but … you could try on your own, if you like. Practice."

So Rosie sat in the prow, Jack untied the moorings, and sat on the seat. He cautiously manoeuvred the boat out onto the river, making her snort again when he bumped against the jetty. He turned it to head downstream - there was no way they wanted to go past that caravan today. He began to row, trying to remember the rhythm Rosie set when they did it together. It had been a while since they had been out on the water and he felt his muscles tighten and ache and it was so much harder than when they did it together. The river was a little more choppy today and he felt the resistance as he pulled the oars through the water, but he soon got into a good rhythm and it felt good to be away from the cottage.

They had moved quite a way, not as far as Leas Farm but almost, before Rosie asked, "What are you doing here? You townies."

Right, Jack thought to himself. Tell her a bit and see how it goes.

"We came to get away from ... my sort-of step-dad ... he's Lu's dad. We're in hiding."

"Why?"

"He's looking for us."

"Don't you want to see him?"

"I haven't seem him since I was seven. He hurt my mum and then we didn't see him for a long time, but he's looking for us now. So we came here."

Rosie thought about that before she asked, "How does that help though, you can't just stay here forever. Why doesn't your mum tell the police about him?"

Because, thought Jack, it's so complicated I don't know how to explain it all. "He hurt my mum and I went to live with my gran while Mum was in hospital. And when she came home, she had to go to the hospital every day to see Lu. She'd been born too early so she had to stay there for weeks. When Lu came home we moved somewhere different, a long way from home, with different names. But he's looking for us now so we're moving again."

"Why doesn't your mum tell the police so they can stop him?"

"They didn't last time."

They rowed for a few minutes before Rosie asked her next question. "Why is he looking for you?"

Jack shrugged.

"Where's your real dad then?"

"Don't know."

"Could you find him and get him to help?"

"No, I don't know who he is. It was just Mum and me, then Harry came along. What about you, where are your real mum and dad?"

"My real dad died, he was a soldier."

"In a war?"

"No, after he'd been away. He was ill when he came back."

Jack didn't know what to say. He thought that perhaps he was lucky, he'd never known his own dad so he couldn't miss him. He rowed on for a while before saying, "How far are we going down this river?"

Rosie looked around in surprise. "We're nearly in the village, slow down, we'd better go back in case someone sees us."

"Have you got any money?"

"Why?"

"We can get you some food in the shop. I've got …" he pulled some coins from the zipped up pocket in his coat. " … four pounds."

"I have got some but it's in my bag in the boathouse."

"You can have this." He offered her the coins.

"I don't know, should we? Won't someone ask questions?"

"Why would they?"

"Everyone does round here."

Jack wondered why that would be a problem. They wouldn't ask, 'Seen any dead bodies lately?' would they?

"I'll go then. Where's the shop?"

"In the street."

"Which street?"

"THE street, there's only one. The shop is in the middle, next to the bus stop."

They found a place to moor and where Jack could get out on to the bank without getting wet. He dropped his lifejacket into the boat and set off along a rough track on the riverbank. He found his way to a pathway, then onto a road and then into the start of the village. A sign at the side of the road announced that he was now entering Freeling. Rosie was right, it was just one long street with houses set back on each side, some allotments and a tiny church. There was no one walking and only two cars passed through the village as he walked in. He eyed the shop as he walked slowly towards it. It was small so anyone in there would probably see him easily and, if Rosie was right, talk to him. He'd better get his story right.

He pushed open the door and found himself in a very small space in front of a counter next to a glass partition. He was the only customer. He looked around the packed shelves covering all four walls and most of the window. So much was crammed in. How would he find what he was looking for?

"Can I help you?"

He looked around to see a lady behind the counter. He was sure she hadn't been there when he came in. She looked ancient to Jack, with grey wispy hair and hundreds of wrinkles on her face. He could only see the top half of her body and she was wearing a baggy vomit green cardigan which cast a strange pallor on her skin. Did they still have witches in Norfolk?

He reluctantly moved nearer to the counter. "Hello," he croaked, his voice suddenly squeaky. "I need some things but don't know where they are?"

She bent down and disappeared from view. He stood tall and peered over. She was putting some knitting down on to a comfy chair behind the counter. So that's why he hadn't seen her. She must sit knitting waiting for someone to come in. Made sense, she was hardly going to be rushed off her feet, was she? And her next cardigan was going to be sludge brown, nice.

"So, what to do you want to find, young man?"

"Bananas, please."

She pointed to a basket on the floor by the door and he helped himself to five yellow ones, ten pence each the sticker said, avoiding the green unripe ones and the brown bruised ones. He put them onto the counter.

"Anything else for you? Did your mum give you a list?"

"It's all in here," he said, pointing to his head. "And some bread, please."

She indicated a shelf on the right and he looked for something small for Rosie that didn't seem stale. He didn't want to squeeze it as that would look rude but he didn't know how long some of this stuff had been in the shop - it could have been years judging by the faded packaging. He put a small wrapped loaf next to the bananas, mentally adding its price to the one for the bananas.

"You on holiday, then?" the lady asked.

"Yes, a cottage by the river. And some jam." He went to the shelf she pointed at.

"That's nice."

He wondered if her name was Queenie too. Perhaps that's what everyone said here, 'that's nice'. He imagined the police saying 'that's nice' when Mum told them there was a dead body in a caravan along their road. He chose strawberry jam, everyone liked strawberry, didn't they?

"You allowed out on your own, are you?"

"Oh yes, it's only a little way down the road and it's very safe here. It's lovely, isn't it?" He smiled at her, trying to look as if he was having the best holiday ever.

"Oh, it is nice. Very quiet. All those stabbings and murders you read about, we don't get that here."

Jack kept the smile on his face as he thought of the stench and sights in that caravan.

"Biscuits?" he said brightly.

"You'll have a lovely time. There's so much to do here. There's a museum and an old railway museum. It's not far to the coast either. It's busier in the warmer weather mind, lots of visitors then."

He chose a pack of chocolate chip cookies and added the price to tally the total. He had enough for some crisps and put those on the counter.

"That's all for now," he said politely.

She added it up and to his relief it came to what he had thought it would and he had enough to pay.

He put some of the shopping in his pockets and waited for his change.

"You come back with your mum next time, we're open every day."

"Thank you, we will," he said and he left holding the bread and bananas. As the door clanged behind him he breathed in the fresh air. Why was it he always seemed to feel shut in? It sometimes felt as if he couldn't breathe when he was inside.

He went back along the road, saying 'hello' to a lone dog walker and passing the quiet houses. He wondered if they were lived in, or if they were holiday houses, like Orchard Cottage. It must be very lonely for any villagers if no one lived in all these houses, a bit like living in a ghost town.

He reached the boat but it was empty. Oh no, Rosie must have run for it! Then she came out from some bushes and crept back into the boat.

"Dog walker, saw him coming and had to hide in case he saw me."

Jack handed the shopping to her. She inspected the label on the jam and tutted but she did say thank you and he was pleased that he wouldn't have to steal food from the cottage. Mum was always careful with shopping and money and she would miss things if he took too much.

Jack slowly got the boat turned and Rosie joined him on the seat to help with rowing home.

"Are you sure, won't it hurt?" he asked.

"No, it's not so bad."

They set off, pulling together.

When they got back to boathouse it was late morning. Jack went over to the cottage for lunch and said he would be back, leaving Rosie to settle herself back into what would be her home for a while.

Chapter Twenty-Four

Day 12: Tuesday afternoon - Jack, Rosie and Lu

"Jack, could you take Lu to play hiding this afternoon? She has to practice."

"I can't, Mum, not today."

"Why not? What else are you doing all day?"

"I'm just messing around, you know."

"Doing what?"

"Nothing, not much."

"Then you can take her, can't you."

And that's why Rosie met Lu that afternoon. She stared - nothing unusual for anyone seeing Lu for the first time - but at Jack, not Lu.

"What's she doing here? She'll tell."

"No, she won't." Jack looked at Lu. "This is Rosie, she's our friend."

"Rosie."

"Yes, Rosie."

Lu hugged Rosie round her waist and said, "Friend, Lu's friend."

Rosie held her arms stiffly and stood still, and looked at Jack as if to say, 'What do I do now?'

Jack just shrugged.

Lu turned and ran over to the boat. Jack caught her just before she fell off the platform into the water.

"Lu! Watch out." He held her back and looked directly into her eyes. "Water Lu, wet."

She looked down at the water and repeated, "Wet."

"Yes, wet."

"Wellies." She held up one foot to show him.

"Yes, wellies for the puddles, not the water. Too much water for wellies. Sit here." He sat her down and sat next to her. Rosie came and sat to one side and Lu reached out and held her hand.

"Lu's friend," she said.

"So, what's she doing here?" Rosie asked Jack.

"Hide-and-seek," said Lu.

"We play hide-and-seek," Jack wondered how to explain. "We need places to hide if … someone … comes. So we play hide-and-seek … practice for when … if … we have to get away."

Rosie looked at Lu. "And how's that going?"

"Not too good. She's a bit young to understand how it works, the game - not the running away bit, she really can't understand that."

"How old is she?"

"Four - nearly five - but she's a bit slow at picking things up."

"Is she supposed to be this small if she's four? She seems very little."

"How many four year olds do you know?"

"None but …"

"Well, she's just small, okay?"

Rosie looked down to see Lu was gently kissing her knee.

"She likes you."

"Oh." Rosie wasn't sure what to make of that but stopped frowning, so she probably thought it was a good thing, Jack decided.

"So, hide-and-seek. We need to look around and see what works here. I've done the garden, orchard, shed and the fields opposite. I'm not sure if here will work out."

Rosie looked around the boathouse before saying, "I don't think this is a good place, too obvious. Once you've opened the door, you can see mostly everywhere."

"And there's no escape route." Jack stood up. "Come on Lu, let's explore."

They went outside and Jack led around the far side and pushed through the bushes to see what was beyond. More bushes. And then some more bushes. They stopped before they reached the river bank and stood still, surrounded by half-budding shrubbery.

"If you got to here," Rosie said, "You could crouch down. No one would see you."

"And then what, where could we get to from here?"

"Where do you need to get to? Don't you just need to wait until they've gone?"

"All this leads to the road, the one by the bridge?"

Rosie nodded.

"And there's nothing else here, no cottages or … caravans?"

Rosie glared. "You're not going to start that again! I'm not coming if you are."

"No, but I went to the other one because it might have been a hideout. I didn't know what was there, did I! I wouldn't have gone anywhere near it if I'd known. And I wouldn't have taken you. And anyway, you're the one who went in just because you didn't believe me."

Rosie snorted. He so wished she'd stop doing that.

Lu plucked at Jack's arm.

He looked around and saw she had something in her mouth, half-hanging out.

"Blurgh," she said, trying to spit it out.

"Lu! What is is? Where did you get it from?" Jack frantically tried to wipe it away with his hand.

"That's a slug!" Rosie shrieked. "She's eating a slug!"

Jack looked at his hand, covered in slime and yelled. Lu began to cry - she didn't like shouting and she didn't like the taste in her mouth.

"Lu, it's okay," he knelt down, wiping his hand on some grass before tackling the slime let on her face.

Rosie looked on horrified. "Really! That's disgusting!"

He cleared as much as he could and found a shredded tissue in a pocket to wipe the rest off.

"There Lu, all clean now." He gave her a sweet from some he had in his pocket for emergencies, because although this may not be a real emergency, like a road accident or a house on fire, if you don't stop Lu before she gets too stressed there could be a real emergency.

Lu took the sweet and began to chew, her face still wet with some tears. "Thank you," reminded Jack.

"Thank you," she said.

Rosie looked at him. "How is this going to work?"

He shrugged. No idea, he thought. It worked for him that time before, because it was just him, they were at home and he hid because he was seven and terrified. How could it work with Lu as well and in this place? He sighed. "It has to."

"It's not going to, is it? She can't hide. She's too … well, she's not …"

"Go home, then. Rosie, go home to your farm and leave us to get on with it." Jack took Lu's hand and pushed his way further into the bushes, finding a way to the road by the bridge.

"I can't go home." She glared after him.

"Why not?"

"You know why!"

"Why don't you tell someone?" Jack was out of sight now.

"Who?" She began to follow.

"What about your mum?"

"Dead."

Jack stopped. Tricky. He couldn't imagine life without Mum. Just imagine, what if he had had to live with Harry? He turned to face Rosie as she caught up with him.

"I'm sorry, I didn't know."

Rosie shrugged. "Where did you think she was?"

"Didn't really think … you said it was just you and your dad …"

"Step-dad. He's not my real dad."

"Right, you did say that." Lu tugged on his sleeve and he gave her another sweet. "So, how long …"

"Last summer."

Jack turned and continued walking through to the road, helping Lu through the brambles. He was thinking. How could he help someone who had no one to help them?

It didn't take long to get to the road. He looked up and down. "Lots of places to get to from here, if you go on the other side of the hedges."

Rosie nodded. "There's an old bunker across that field," she pointed across the road. "And there's a fishing lodge if you follow the river that way," she pointed again, " No one's there most of the time."

Jack crossed the road and went into the field, looking in the direction Rosie had indicated.

"That might work. You can't see it from here, so it could be a hiding place."

Lu was wandering down the middle of the road towards the bridge so he went and grabbed her hand and led her across to the bank so he could look down the river. "How far down is the lodge? By road."

"Ten - fifteen minutes?"

"Can you see it from the road? Can you get to it by boat?"

"It's down a track, a bit like … you know … the other place. And you can get to it from the river."

Jack nodded happily. Options - you need options.

"Let's get back," he began walking down what he thought of as 'their' road.

It was safer here so he let Lu walk on her own. She clumped along in her wellies, squashing anything in her path. They made slow process as she stopped to look at anything interesting: a leaf, a stone, an acorn, an ant scurrying in the dirt (which Jack made sure she didn't eat.)

"So, you live with your step-dad, no one else?"

Rosie nodded.

"What about a teacher? Could you tell a teacher?"

"Home schooled."

"What does that mean?"

Rosie gave him a stare.

Jack stared back, saying, "I'm asking because I don't know what it is is."

She stared harder. "It means I go to school at home."

"Do teachers come to you then?"

"No. He's supposed to do the teaching."

"I don't get it. He's a farmer, not a teacher. And what about PE? And science? Have you got all the stuff, equipment? And clubs, how do you go to clubs? And friends - where are your friends?"

"That's the point. I haven't got any. I'm on my own. No one can see the bruises."

Jack thought for a minute or two. "Did you go to school, before … you know … your mum …"

"Died? You can say it. Yes, I went to school until last summer. I didn't go back after the holidays."

"But you have to go to school. Makes sure everyone gets a chance."

"Some kids don't go to a real school. They get taught at home by parents and tutors. They meet other kids like them and do different things."

"But you don't - meet other kids?"

"No, it's just to keep me away from everyone. And he doesn't have to take me to the school bus everyday, or organise anything."

"Doesn't anyone check? Come and see what you're doing?"

She shook her head.

Jack wondered if he would have to be home schooled, if they were always on the run. He liked being with Mum but he knew he would miss school for the noise and bustle, and for his friends.

"Gran, do you have a gran?"

Rosie shook her head. "He stopped us seeing them when Mum married him."

"Who's them?"

"I had a gran and a granddad. And some aunts and uncles and some cousins."

"But you haven't seen them?"

"Not for a long time."

"Phone numbers? Email?"

She shook her head.

"Can you remember where they lived?"

"My mum's family lived in Lowestoft. My dad … my real dad … came from London."

"If you got to Lowestoft, could you find them."

Rosie frowned, thinking. "I went there a lot, I stayed there when Dad … was ill. And after he died … while Mum was sorting stuff out."

"So we can find it. But it would be easier if you knew where to go. Did your mum have a phone?"

Rosie shrugged. "She did but he took it I think, when we came to live here. I don't remember her using it here."

"Do you think he kept it? Where does he keep important stuff? A box? A filing cabinet?"

"I don't know. I'm not allowed in the farm office, or near his room, or the barn, or …"

They were level with the track to the boathouse now. They stood in the lane, both thinking about what to do next.

"I think I'll have to look," said Rosie. "If he kept it, it will be somewhere. He never throws anything away, too mean."

Jack nodded.

"I'll go back this evening."

"No, you can't! You can't go back there after … you know."

"It's not the first time. I can deal with it."

"No, wait until he's out doing - whatever he does in the fields. You can sneak in and look then."

Rosie thought before saying, "He'll be in the top fields, probably. I could go first thing, watch and go in when he's gone."

"I'll come after breakfast and go with you."

"After breakfast?"

"Yes, first thing, like you said."

Rosie snorted. "First thing on a farm is really first thing - he'll be gone as soon as it's light enough to see what he's doing."

Jack thought about that. "I can't get out that early, Mum will ask questions. Will he be out all morning? Couldn't we go later?"

"We could," Rosie frowned, "But he always comes back by lunchtime, even if he hasn't finished. And he might not be out tomorrow, he might be working around the farm."

"Doing what?"

"Stuff. I don't know."

Lu was sitting in the middle of the lane, gathering some dry, dead leaves into a pile, murmuring to herself.

"Okay. Then I'll come after breakfast. We'll go over and watch. If he's there, we'll come away and try again the next day. If he's not, you can go in and look. I could keep watch."

Rosie nodded slowly. It would be better to go early, but she would rather have Jack there so it would have to be later.

"It's tea time," Jack helped Lu stand up. "We'd better go in." There was a wet patch on the road.

"Lu's wet," she said helpfully. "Oops."

Jack sighed. Rosie looked horrified.

"Let's go see Mum, Lu, get dry and have tea."

"Biscuit?"

"We'll see."

Rosie went down the track to the boathouse and Jack led Lu to the cottage gate.

Later, after tea, Jack got the Norfolk book and opened the folding-out map page. He found the village Freeling, a tiny dot with tiny writing on a very small road. He traced back along the river and found roughly where they were. Then he followed the river back past Freeling, tracing it until it joined another river, and then followed that river until it joined a lake and he could see there were ways to cross the lake and join another river. It's a bit like roads, he thought, you could go along to anywhere if you followed the rivers. He found Lowestoft sitting on the Suffolk coast and traced the nearest river back through the network until he could see there were ways to get there by boat. Rosie could row herself to Lowestoft. She could set off, stop overnight, sleep in the boat, and then get to … he traced the river and found a village just outside Lowestoft … about there, and walk into town. How long would it take? How long did it take to row to Freeling? Half an hour? An hour? He didn't know. And Freeling was only a little way away but Lowestoft was along way. It might take more than a day and a night. She'd need food.

"What are you looking at? Planning an adventure?"

Jack looked up. He'd forgotten Mum was there.

"Oh, this map of Norfolk. Just seeing where we are. How much is an inch?"

"An inch? Why do you want to know?"

"It says one inch to three miles. How much is that?"

Mum came over and sat next to him on the saggy sofa. "So where are we?" she asked.

Jack pointed to the place he thought they were. Mum looked closely. She pointed to where the nature reserve was. "That's where we went, to see the birds, and it's about five inches."

Jack looked - and saw the distance. Lowestoft was miles away. Rosie could never row that far. They had to find that phone.

Chapter Twenty-Five

Day 12: Tuesday - Police - PC Anstey

On Tuesday afternoon the first thing Anstey did when he got into the station for his shift was to read all the files he could access on the missing family case. Not much progress had been made. Tizora was out with the Boss on a public relations exercise at the local community centre so he couldn't ask her what was happening. For a couple of hours he logged some data and chased up on the missing bikes and just as he had started checking the whereabouts of an ice cream van that had disappeared from its owner's drive, he got a call from the front desk to say someone had come in to tell him something.

"Who is it?" he asked.

He heard a muffled conversation and then, "Milo, his name is Milo."

Anstey set off through the station and found Milo sitting on a bench in the reception. He opened the access door and went out.

"Got this," said Milo. He held up a postcard. "It came this morning when I was at school."

The postcard had a picture of a windmill on the front. Anstey checked with Milo that he could read it. Milo nodded. Anstey turned it over and read the short message.

This was definitely a lead. "Can I borrow this?"

Milo nodded. "It will help, won't it? Find Jack, I mean."

"Oh yes, it really will."

Milo stood up to leave.

"Hang on, your name, Milo what? You never told me before."

"Milo Usman."

"And you live at the flats?"

"Number 42."

"Thanks, Milo. This is going to make a difference. We may need to talk to you again. Is that alright?"

Milo nodded and then opened the door and set off home.

Anstey headed straight up to find Tizora, hoping she was back. She wasn't. She was still out with the Boss. He hesitated before approaching the DS but he knew he had to tell someone and DS Clifton was usually as helpful as anyone in a busy workplace.

"Sir, I've just been given this."

DS Clifton looked up. "Really? Your gran on holiday is she?"

"No, Milo Usman brought it. He's Jake Sinclair's or Jack Williamson's friend."

DS Clifton stood up and reached for the card. He looked at the front and read the back. He smiled.

"Norfolk! They're in Norfolk." He reached for his phone and Anstey backed out of the door, his job done. Milo had brought the card to him, personally, yet someone else would deal with it. He hoped it was Tizora. He knew she would take it seriously.

Just before the end of his shift Anstey had to go to see the Boss with DC Tizora and give them the details in person, even though he'd put them on file.

The Boss said very little but Anstey was told that tomorrow, he was to go to the school and get a sample of Jack's handwriting to check against the card and at the same time, in school, talk to Milo with an appropriate adult present, in case he had any other information. The detectives were now liaising with Norfolk police.

Anstey went home after his shift, to his lonely flat and another takeaway, but feeling happier about tomorrow.

Chapter Twenty-Six

Day 13: Wednesday - Jack and Rosie

Jack clung on to Rosie's shoulders as they sped through the lanes leading to the farm. He felt every bump and crack in the road as the worn tyres on her ancient bike spun across the tarmac. He was trying not to hold on too tightly, worrying about the bruises she had shown him, but he was terrified he'd fall off, and he was relieved when she spun them into a gap in the hedgerow and they stopped at the edge of a field just before the farmhouse. He slid off the back of the bike onto the ground and bent double, trying to stop the dizziness and nausea.

"What's wrong with you? Never ridden a bike before?" asked Rosie as she propped the bike against the hedgerow, out of sight.

Jack took another deep breath before straightening up. "Never like that one. Where did you get it? A museum?"

"Found it in a shed," she nodded towards the farm. "It's all I've got."

"I'd rather walk."

"No, you wouldn't. It takes forever to get anywhere."

"Buses?"

"Only one a day and that's on a good day. And they stop so many times it's quicker to bike it." She crept along the hedgerow and Jack crouched and followed her closely. They reached a gap near the farmhouse and ducked down to look.

"Is he there?"

"SSSHHH!"

They listened, although Jack didn't know what he was listening for - what noises did a farmer make? Rosie edged forward, watching the buildings while she listened intently. They moved across into the open yard and went into a shed or barn - Jack didn't know what it was - and stood just inside the door. It was full of machinery, some rusting and some in parts on the dusty floor, and Jack could also see some boxes, barrels and sacks stacked against the walls.

"He's out, the tractor's gone."

She led Jack to a door at the side of the house and gently opened it, listening again. They moved inside. Jack looked around at the mess in the kitchen. Every surface was covered in plates and cups, empty bags and packaging. The cupboard doors were half open, the sink was full of - he didn't want to look. The floor felt sticky and his trainers squeaked on it as they crossed to another door.

"Right, you wait outside and keep watch."

"No, if we both look we have more chance of finding it."

"What if he comes back early?!"

"Tell me where to look," Jack insisted. "We've got twice the time if we both look. In here?" He opened a door.

Rosie snatched his hand and shut the door with a bang. They both froze in the echoing silence.

"Tell me where to look, we're wasting time."

Rosie glared but lead him down the hallway and to a closed door. "This is the office - and his room is upstairs, first door."

Jack tried the handle but the door was firmly locked. He frowned. "Where's the key?"

"He always carries them with him."

"You could have said! We can't get in. What was the point of coming if we can't get in?"

Rosie glared at him - again - and turned to another door. She lead him through what was supposed to be a dining room but which was filled with piles of stuff. You'd never be able to eat at the table without filling a skip with all the rubbish first. She pulled a chair away from the wall in one corner and behind it was a small door, the sort you sometimes get in halls leading to a cupboard you can only fit the vacuum cleaner in. She crouched down and pulled it open. It was empty, but then, thought Jack, what would be the point of tidying your stuff away in a cupboard if you lived in a mess like this. She ducked through and he heard her open another door and he saw some light come through to his side. He ducked in behind her and through to the office on the other side.

Well, this was tidier than those rooms he'd seen so far and was almost uncluttered. They both began to open drawers and cupboards and rummage through all kinds of paperwork and bits and pieces, searching for a phone. Jack moved on to look through some cardboard boxes stacked on a book shelf in the alcove by the fireplace. Rosie looked through every inch of the wooden desk and then began to go through the drawers of the filing cabinet. Nothing.

Jack stood looking around. Where would he hide something small in this room? He felt under the desk, hoping for a lever to a secret drawer or a ledge or - anything really. Rosie lifted a section of the mangy rug looking for a loose floorboard and Jack felt up the chimney. Nothing.

They stood, hopes dashed.

"Upstairs?"

Jack nodded and they ducked back through the cupboard to the room next door. Rosie lead the way to the hall but Jack stopped by the chair she'd moved to get through. "Hey, we have to put it back, so he won't know we've been here. Cover our tracks."

Rosie turned and left the room. She called over her shoulder, "It doesn't matter. I'm never coming back, I'm going to Lowestoft."

Jack followed her, his heart thumping. Really? He began to wish he'd never talked about her relatives yesterday, not if she was taking these risks. She had made up her mind, he knew that from the glare she gave him as they went upstairs, as if to say - just dare me.

At the top of the stairs she went to a room at the end and opened the door into a very clean and tidy room, her room. "I'm picking up some things," she said as she began pulling open drawers and pulling clothes out. "You go in the room at the other end and start looking." She started stuffing things into a backpack and nudged him towards the door.

Jack crept quietly along to the room at the end. He held his breath and opened the door so he could peer in - it was empty, no step-dad and definitely no dead body. He stepped as silently as he could into the room and looked around. It wasn't as untidy as the rooms downstairs. It looked as if it had once had a couple sharing it but he couldn't imagine Rosie's step-dad sitting at the stool in front of the dressing table mirror combing his hair. He felt odd opening these drawers; they seemed personal, not like the ones in the office. How would he feel if someone rummaged through his stuff? He opened the drawers and felt around. He opened the wardrobe and moved the clothes so he could see between and above and below. He opened a suitcase under the bed and rifled through the papers stored there.

Rosie came to the door. "Well?"

"Nothing."

"Sure?"

Jack shrugged. "There's so much stuff everywhere. It could be anywhere, that's if he kept it.

"Right, there's somewhere else to look, come on." She headed back downstairs with Jack trailing after her again.

"Where?"

She didn't answer, just headed back through to the kitchen and outside. She crossed the yard and went around the side of a long, low brick building. "This was the stables, a long time ago, and he keeps them locked. We need to get in." She began tugging at the doors. Jack looked around the side and back of the building. He found a small window above a door, not a horse-sized door, a human- sized door. It was old and wooden and rotten. He went back and beckoned to Rosie, and pointed upwards, not daring to call out in case her step-dad might hear.

She came round and looked up at the window. "You help me and I'll get in."

"I'll do it."

"I'm smaller, I'll fit." She indicated he should help her up, dropping her rucksack on the ground, and so she stood on his clasped hands and reached up to the window. She balanced carefully and pulled at the frame. It budged straight away and with a couple more tugs it fell away from the wall and crashed onto the floor. Jack ducked, with his hands over his head and Rosie fell on top of him. They lay in a heap, surrounded by bits of rotten wood and shards of glass. *{This is where I'm supposed to say 'don't try this at home' but you're not daft, you're reading this book, so you know not to try to climb through a window.}* Very carefully they stood up.

"That's the easy part," said Rosie. "Now I have to crawl in."

Jack clasped his hands again and Rosie reached up to see inside the window. She indicated he should get her down. "We need a ladder. Barn." Off they went to the barn and rummaged until they found a ladder, which Jack found himself carrying back to the window and propping up ready for her to climb.

"I'll open the door for you."

"I hope you can open it from the inside - you'll be stuck in there if you can't unlock it."

She snorted and climbed the ladder, hauled herself over and, if Jack heard right, fell onto something hard on the other side.

"I'm alright," she called. He heard some clunking noises and then the door creaked open.

It was dark inside, only a fragment of light was coming in through the door and the hole where the window should have been. Jack could see some sectioned off spaces, which he supposed was where the horses might have been. And there was some dusty looking equipment hanging on hooks placed high up on the posts. And there was so much stuff stored all along as far as Jack could see. Boxes and boxes. All sizes.

"What is all this?"

Rosie didn't reply. She made her way through the gap between all the crates on either side towards a section further down. Here was a desk, a chair and a bin full of empty bottles. In the gloom she groped for the desk drawer handle and pulled it towards her. It was difficult to see but she peered in and felt around towards the back. She held up a phone.

"Is that it, your mum's phone?"

She looked at it. "I think don't so. I … I don't know. Why would he have two phones for himself?"

Jack looked around. He had seen enough crime dramas on TV to know all this was definitely dodgy. "Anything else in the other drawers?"

Rosie opened them and - there were three more phones. She looked at Jack.

"How do I know which one was hers?" she asked.

"What kind of phone did she have?"

"I don't know. I never noticed. It was just a phone."

"Did it have a cover?"

"I think so, blue?"

None of the phones had a cover. They stared at them on the desk in the gloomy light. Jack looked around. He went over to a pile of boxes and picked at the tape on the top one.

"Stop! He'll find out!"

"And? There's a broken window. He'll think someone broke in."

Rosie grabbed at his hand. "No! It's too …"

Jack pushed her away and pulled hard at the tape and the cardboard. "What's he up to?"

Rosie stepped back and groaned.

"What?" Jack ripped the tape. "You're not coming back. He won't even know it was you."

He peered into the box and pulled out some plastic bags. Inside each one were different sized boxes of what looked like tablets, like paracetamol or hay fever tablets.

Rosie went closer. "I've seen those before."

"Where?"

Rosie shook her head.

Jack pushed them back in the box and folded the flap, partly covering the ripped cardboard and tape. He picked up the phones. "Well, let's just take these and try them."

"He'll know some one has taken them."

"What does it matter if we take them. He won't know it's us." Jack felt in the drawer trying to find the chargers. "Here," he said, pulling the leads out, "We'll take these and see what we can find."

Rosie pulled at Jack. "He's back!" she whispered. "I can hear the tractor!"

They stood still.

"It can't be!" Jack whispered. "We haven't been here that long."

Rosie moved nearer to the open door and peered out. "He's still on the tractor, we need to get away before he gets to the shed and while the engine's running so he can't hear us." She edged out and slid around the side of the stable. Jack could hear the chugging of the engine. He clutched the phones and chargers to his chest as he crept behind Rosie. She scanned the yard before crossing to the kitchen door. "We can go through the front," she whispered. Jack dropped a phone and as he stooped to pick it up, dropped another one.

"My bag!" said Rosie. She retreated to fetch it from back round the side of the stables.

"Rosie!" hissed Jack. "Rosie, leave it." He fumbled for the phones on the ground as Rosie disappeared from sight.

Then, the engine stopped. Jack froze. He heard the crunch of boots coming in his direction. He opened the kitchen door and slipped inside, shoving the phones and leads into his pockets. Where to go? Where was the front door? Escape routes? Hiding places? He had nothing planned!

He went along the hall. The dining room had places to hide but no escape route. The office was locked from the hall and he didn't have enough time to get through that little door, and there were no escape routes from the office anyway. Upstairs? There were hiding places but no escape routes. He was panicking, he knew he was panicking. He had no time to think.

He crept upstairs, hoping the wooden stairs didn't creak, and slipped into the first door, closing it silently behind him. He leaned against the door, holding his breath, listening. When no sound of pursuit came, he breathed out slowly and looked to find he was in Rosie's step-dad's room, the one he'd searched only minutes ago and the one he really didn't want to be in right now.

He stepped carefully over to the window and looked out. The room faced out to the front of the house, a side of the house he hadn't seen yet so he wasn't sure what it looked like. He felt for the window catch, which was metal, rusty and seemed to have been painted over at some point, and gently eased it upwards. It didn't budge so he tried harder, this time feeling the catch move a fraction under pressure. He grasped it with both hands and yanked at it. It lifted, breaking off some of the wood from the frame as it lifted from its screws and came away in his hands. He froze as the wood cracked and then placed it silently on the floor. He held his breath as he pushed at the window, hoping it wouldn't fall out, like the stable window had done. It was also painted over but the paint was so old it flaked as he pushed and the window swung open - probably for the first time in many years.

He leaned out to see what he could use to get down. There was a porch over the front door but it was too far to his left to reach. The ground floor windows either side of the door each had a ledge or shelf of some kind above them. They looked like little roofs, triangular in shape, so not ideal for standing on, but he climbed onto the window sill and edged out, gripping the the window frame, feeling its rough surface scrape his hands, and he lowered himself down to the one just below. He wasn't sure that it would hold his weight so he gently rested one foot onto it. It creaked but it held. He lowered himself so he was standing on it, clutching the wall at his back.

Now what? It was still a long way down. He lowered himself down until he was sitting, then turned over so he could slide over the edge and drop down. He felt his knees jar as he hit the ground and rolled over, laying still and listening in case he'd been heard. He reached over and picked up a phone which had fallen out of his pocket and shoved it back with the others. Then he heard a voice. He dropped down closer to the ground, froze and held his breath.

"… A break in. No, I don't … anything … I'll have to check … take a while … You'll have to move it … someone knows it's here … let me know when … use 2."

It went quiet. He couldn't tell if the person, Rosie's step-dad he supposed, was still in there. There were some bushes on this side, where someone who had once loved this home had planted out a garden of sorts, so he crept over, got himself into the middle of the bushes and sank to the ground. He crawled away from the house, through a hedge and onto a road. He stood and still ducking down, half-ran in the direction he hoped they'd come along. He felt exposed on the road so he found a gap and went into the field. It was slower progress as the rutted ground was difficult to walk over and brambles and nettles caught at his legs and scratched at his hands but he felt safer. He crossed into another field and made his way towards where he thought the bridge road was. How were you supposed to know where you were - it all looked the same. He realised he'd thought this before because he was a townie, like Rosie had said.

When he was on his third field and beginning to worry that he was lost in the wilds of Norfolk, he saw a road sign ahead. Which way? None of the places were ones he had heard of. He looked for the river. But how would he know it was *his* river? And how would he know whether he was going upstream or downstream? He looked up and down the road, looking for clues.

Think, Jack, he told himself. I know you had your eyes shut when you were on the back of that bike, but where did you go? He thought about their route to the farm. They'd gone over the bridge, along for a little bit then turned left down the lane leading to the farm. So, if he turned right now, he might get to the bridge. He turned right and walked for several minutes, still feeling lost. Then, as he rounded a slight bend, he could see the sign and the bridge. He almost cried but he reminded himself he had been through so much worse than being lost in Norfolk. He walked quickly, turned into his road and almost ran down to the boathouse.

Rosie's bike was outside. He opened the door and went in, slamming it behind him. No Rosie. But she must have made it because her bike was here. He pulled the phones and charger from his pockets and put them on a ledge together. He really hoped it had been worth the adventure - if they couldn't get the phones to work, if none of them were Rosie's Mum's, they had gone through all that for nothing. He checked the time, it was past lunch time, he'd better get back to the cottage. And he'd thought that living in the countryside would be boring!

After lunch, which Mum had set aside for him, they went out. It was time to top up on food, Mum said. Jack pleaded to be allowed to stay at the cottage but Mum was not happy with that.

"You're only 11, it's a strange place, there's no phone, no neighbours - so, no, you can't stay."

Jack knew she wouldn't change her mind. They set off and Mum drove them to a different town, a different supermarket and then a different park, so Lu could have a play on the swings and climbing frame. Hardly anyone was around in the late afternoon on a dull March day, and they stayed longer than they would have if the park had been busy. Jack tried not to show he was anxious to get back but he found himself fidgeting on the park bench as they sat watching Lu, while eating sugary warm doughnuts from the bakery. When they got home it was almost dark and it was tea time, so Mum wouldn't let him out. He tried to persuade her but, again, it was no use and he didn't want to make her suspicious by arguing too much, so he gave in for now.

Later, when Mum had gone to bed, Lu was snuffling in the bunk below his, Jack, still fully dressed, crept down the ladder and crossed to the window. What was it about windows today? he thought as he quietly opened this one. Good job he'd freed it when they first came, in case they needed to use it as an escape route. He slid to the ground and crossed to the bushes. It all looked so different in the dark. It was definitely creepy for a town boy used to street lamps and houses brightening the night. He stumbled his way through the bushes and undergrowth to the boathouse track. He stood outside the door and listened.

"Rosie," he hissed. Nothing. "Rosie, are you there?"

There was a rustling and he turned to find her behind him. His heart jolted and he bent over to catch his breath.

She pushed past him and pulled the door open. "Get in!" She shoved him in the back and bundled them both into the dark boathouse. She shut the door and leant against it.

"What happened? Where have you been? I've been terrified he'd caught you! Why didn't you come to find me? I've been hiding all day. Whose idea was it? Yours! And look where it got us! I nearly got caught. And I felt sick, not knowing where you were. I went to find your mum but the car was gone. And it's been so …"

"Have you eaten?" Jack asked.

"What! Is that all you can say?"

"Have you eaten? You need to eat and then we can talk." He found his way in the dark to her shelf, and felt around for something rustling and took a bag of crisps and opened it before giving it to her.

"Really! Food! Is that all you can think about?"

He pulled a torch from his pocket and in its light began to put together some bread and the jam while she shoved a crisp into her mouth. "I thought your mum had gone to report you missing. Or you'd come back and needed to go to the police station. Or to the hospital because he'd caught you." She pushed in a handful of crisps, spraying crumbs everywhere as she continued. "I've been in those bushes all day, all day!" She shoved some more crisps in and chewed this time before saying, "Why did I listen? I should have known after that … that … caravan. I knew you were trouble, poking about." She emptied the last crumbs from the bag into her palm and scooped them into her mouth. He handed her her water bottle. She swigged a mouthful and then gulped down the whole bottle. He handed her a jam sandwich and took the bottle and refilled it while she started on the sandwich.

They sat on the platform, legs dangling over the black water, speckled with a dash of moonlight coming in from the opening. He put the bottle next to her. After a few minutes of chewing, Rosie drank some more. Food and water, that was what people needed sometimes.

"I did come here when I got back. Your bike was there but you weren't."

"I was hiding, back in the bushes, like we did with Lu. And I was so scared I stayed there all day."

It wasn't all day, Jack thought, you didn't get back until after lunch time, but he said, "It was sort of fun though, wasn't it?"

"FUN! Are you mad?!"

"Not fun then — different?"

She glared at him, snorted and got up to fetch some biscuits.

"What else would you have been doing? Sitting in here? We got the phones," he reminded her as she back down next to him.

"We don't even know if they're any use!" She didn't offer him a biscuit, he noticed, even though he'd paid for them and liked those ones.

"Not yet, but if they are, well - it was worth it."

She ate and drank and thought for a bit. "So, what happened to you? You were gone."

"He was coming, I didn't know where to go."

"I said he'd be back, didn't I? You don't listen! If I'd gone early like I said I wouldn't have been there when he came back."

"And you wouldn't have got the phones. You needed me to get you in the window."

"I'd have found a way, I don't need you. I could have got the ladder myself."

He stared at her this time. She stared back. "I'm fine on my own, I don't need you."

"Okay," he said standing up. "I'll go then."

And he did. Back through the moonlit bushes to the bedroom window, climbed in and back up the ladder to his bunk.

Chapter Twenty-Seven

Day 13: Wednesday - Police - PC Anstey

The headteacher was a bit more co-operative this time. He gave Anstey a cup of coffee while someone photocopied a page of Jack's Literacy book and then he sat in when Milo came to have a chat.

"The postcard was very useful, Milo," Anstey said. "We now know where they were only last Friday, when the card was posted, so we're closer to finding them."

Milo shifted in his chair but he looked pleased he had been able to help.

"Did Jack ever talk about knowing someone in Norfolk? A relative? Aunt or Uncle?"

Milo shook his head. "He never said - I didn't think he had any relatives - just a gran but he didn't see her, just spoke to her."

"Did he ever tell you about where he used to live?"

Milo shook his head again.

"What about a holiday? Did he talk about a holiday in Norfolk?"

Milo shook his head again.

"Any ideas at all?"

Milo shook his head. "Sorry. I don't know anything. I wish I did."

"It's okay. We're all trying to help. That postcard was the best thing we've had so far so it's down to you if we find them in Norfolk."

Milo nodded. A postcard, he thought. That was all the police had to go on - not much but he hoped it would help, Jack was his friend and he missed hanging out with him. He hesitated before he said it, wondering if it would sound - make *him* sound - scared or stupid. But he said it anyway. "There was a man asking questions. I don't think he was one of your lot though."

"Why's that?"

"He wasn't in uniform. I know some police don't wear uniform but he was too scruffy, not like plain clothes on TV."

"So what did he say? Did he talk just to you? When was this?"

"It was on the balcony, Jack's floor. Yesterday afternoon. I was just going down. Some of us were going for a kick-about."

"Did you see him knock at the door? How long had he been there?"

Milo shook his head. "He was standing by the flat."

"And what did he say?"

"He said, 'Hey lad, anyone been here lately? There's no one in. Is Jake one of your mates? He likes a bit of a kick-about.' "

Anstey felt his heart thump. Jake. Not Jack. But Jake was a name he'd seen on file …

Chapter Twenty-Eight

Day 14: Thursday - Jack, Rosie and Lu

When Mum woke Jack the next morning she laughed to see he was fully dressed.

"Did you fall sleep reading again?" she asked, as she pulled the curtains back. "It's nine already, late for you to get up. Lu's been up for ages. Breakfast first? Then you can get washed and changed."

Jack peered at the window, and yes, it was already very light out there, way past his usual getting up time. He lay back and thought about last night. He'd been awake for hours, after that fuss with Rosie. He hadn't been able to think straight about what to do next but if she didn't want him, then he was going to stay away. No more boathouse (he'd miss that) and no more Rosie (he'd miss her - possibly.)

After breakfast, a change of clothes and a check on the generator with Mum to remind him what they had to do to keep it going, they set off for a town with a market. Mum usually avoided crowds, especially now they were hiding themselves away, but she said it would be far enough from the cottage not to bump into anyone twice. The problem was Lu, everyone remembered her so Mum didn't want anyone local to see her who might know where they were living. The town wasn't too far, but over half an hour away from the cottage, just about as long as Jack could entertain Lu in the car and keep himself from getting bored.

The car park was almost full but they found a spot and set off with Lu in the buggy, her hood pulled up and her hands clutching a battered doll.

It felt good to be in a town with traffic and traffic lights and zebra crossings. And there were so many shops, on both sides of the high street and down some side streets too. And there was more than one bakery and two butchers and two greengrocers and clothes shops and a book shop and … and Jack felt pleased to be back in his kind of place. So much to look at and listen to. Mum went into the post office while he stood outside with Lu, watching the people go about their lives. This was normal. He felt happy for the first time in ages.

The market was in a square with a church on one side and a police station and a library on another. The stall covers were multi-striped and set in rows around the square. They wandered up and down. Mum bought some fruit and vegetables and stowed them in the tray under Lu's seat. They spent time at a secondhand book stall and Jack found two he thought he'd like, which Mum paid for and which weighed comfortably against his chest when he put them in the inside pockets of his jacket. The flower stall was colourful and spilled out onto the walkway so that Jack had to steer the buggy right in the middle to stop Lu from grabbing at the flowers. Mum bent to smell some yellow flowers.

"These roses smell lovely," she said.

"Rosie, " called Lu. "Where's Rosie?"

"Roses, Lu, roses. Pretty," said Mum.

They headed away from the market to a bridge crossing a river and wandered along for a while, with Lu running ahead in her wellies, exploring happily before they sat on a bench and ate some lunch while they watched the ducks swim busily across the water.

"They're trying to find places to build nests," said Mum.

"It looks too hard," Jack said. "Why don't they just use one from before?"

"They don't last, they're made of sticks and grass so they just disintegrate."

"So why don't they make better ones, that last?"

"The eggs hatch out in a few weeks so the nests don't have to last long."

Jack was a bit confused. He thought birds lived in nests, all the time. "Don't they sleep in their nests, then?"

"No, they just make them to keep eggs in, and then when the baby birds can fly, that's it, no need for nests."

"Where do they all live?"

"Trees, hedges, anywhere really."

I really am a townie, Jack thought.

Later that day, mid-afternoon, Jack made his way to the boathouse, with Lu in tow. There was no reason why he shouldn't, he thought. It belonged to the cottage he was living in and he had as much right to be there as anyone else - more than anyone else. And Lu needed some practice at hiding around here, just in case, as you never knew where you might need to go, so he'd better cover all bases. And also, he needed to get the Arnica back, put it back in the grab bag.

The bike wasn't by the door. He called out "Rosie" and Lu called out too, "Roses! Roses! Pretty."

The door opened and Rosie glared at them both. "What do you want?"

Lu grabbed her around her legs and squeezed. "Roses. Friend."

Rosie did not look down at Lu. She glared at Jack. "Well?"

"Er, have you got the Arnica? I need to put it back."

Rosie took Lu's hands away from her legs and went inside, closing the door shut behind her. Awkward, thought Jack, wondering what to do next. Then she came back and handed over the tube of Arnica. He took it and before he could say 'thanks' she went back inside and shut the door.

Lu looked up at Jack, frowning. "Where Roses?"

Right, he thought, let's get it over. He pulled the door open and went in with Lu. "Let me take the phones, I'll check them out."

Rosie glared again. "I told you - I don't need you."

"Yes, you do. No electricity here."

"They're charged. I don't need electricity."

"Is one your mum's?"

Rosie snorted. "As if I'd tell you."

"If you'd found it, you'd have phoned someone by now, your gran, whoever. You haven't found anything have you?"

Rosie didn't answer.

He tried again. "I can look …"

"No, you can't, what do you know that I don't?"

"You haven't got a phone. Do you even know how they work?"

"You haven't got one either. What makes you the expert?"

"We can try together."

Rosie snorted. "Like that works out."

Lu looked up between them. "Wee."

Jack sighed. Really? Now? "Where's the bathroom?" he asked.

Rosie stared hard. "It's a boathouse, not a hotel."

Jack wasn't sure how to say it. "So, where do you … you know …?"

"Bucket, round the back."

Jack took Lu and the bucket outside and came back five minutes later with a smiling Lu.

"Wee. Bucket!" she said happily.

"Did you empty it?" Rosie snapped.

Jack nodded. "I saw your bike back there?"

"Hiding it."

"Crisps?" asked Lu.

Rosie glowered but she fetched a bag of crisps, her last one, and opened them for Lu.

"Thanks," said Jack.

"You paid for them, I can't say no."

"Let's sit down and work things out." Jack said as he sat down on the platform, keeping Lu on his side furthest from the water.

Rosie hesitated but she sat opposite him and at least looked as if she might make an effort this time.

"So, did you look at the phones? Is one your mum's?"

Rosie shook her head. "I'll show you."

She fetched the four phones and put them on the wooden floor in front of her. "They are all the same, they don't look like the one's most people seem to have. Too small, basic."

Jack looked. She was right. They were all the same. Why would this Frank have four phones all the same?

"He doesn't use these, does he, not every day?"

"Who? Frank? No, he has a smart phone."

Jack picked one up carefully. He'd already dropped a couple when he was getting away and he didn't know if it was easy to break a phone like this. He pressed the power button and the small screen lit up. He looked up at Rosie. "There's no password."

She nodded. "I thought it would be easy if it opened but … look in the contacts."

Jack pressed the button, and one number was listed, just one.

"They're all the same. One number."

Jack tried another phone. She was right; one number. "It's a different number?"

Rosie nodded. "Each one has a different number, that's all. Nothing else."

"And you don't think any of these are your mum's?"

Rosie shook her head. "On the back, there's a number, in some kind of pen."

Jack looked. Faintly he could see traces of black ink, darker than the black of the phones: 1, 2, 3, 4. He lined them up in order.

"Does a farmer need four phones?" He thought it sounded daft as he said it out loud but what did he know about farming.

Rosie shook her head.

"And, what was all that stuff in the stable? Was it farm stuff? Seeds? Or …"

"No, the farm stuff is in the outhouses or barn."

"Didn't you look?"

"He stopped us - kept it locked. Ask no questions."

Lu gave Jack the empty crisp bag and wiped her hands on his jeans. Jack put the wrapper in his pocket and gave Lu a sweet.

"What do you think it is?"

She shrugged. "Nothing good."

"Why not?"

"It comes at night, goes at night, the vans don't have any writing on them, all different ones, usually white though."

Definitely dodgy, though Jack.

As they sat staring at the phones, one of the screens began to glow and a quiet buzz began. They both sat back a few centimetres and froze.

Rosie looked at him in panic. "Answer it!"

"No!"

"Quick, before it stops."

"What shall I say?"

"Frank, say it's Frank."

Jack picked up the phone and pressed a button.

A voice said, "Eleven." And it went dead.

They looked at each other. The phone lay lifeless in Jack'd hand. He placed it down next to the others carefully and sat back.

"What's eleven?"

Rosie shrugged.

"Got it!" Jack picked up the phone and turned it over. "Phone 2! He said to call on phone 2. This one."

"Who did?"

"Frank."

Rosie looked puzzled.

"I was under the window …"

"What window?"

"The front window…"

"Why?"

"I climbed out of the window…"

"The office window?"

"No, the bedroom window …"

"At the front?"

"Yes, upstairs …"

"The bedroom window upstairs?"

"Just stop and listen." Jack glared at Rosie this time. "I went in, he was coming, and I went upstairs and the first room is his room, right? So I climbed out onto that ledge - roof thing - and slid down and was on the ground when I heard him talking. He was on a phone. He said there was break-in, that's us, and they'd have to shift the stuff and to phone on 2."

Rosie thought about that. "Did he know it was us?"

"No, can't have done. He must have seen the broken stable window when he crossed the yard."

And he will have found the open bedroom window, and the broken latch, Jack thought. Fingerprints? Do the police still have mine? That's not good. They could trace him to both the caravan and the farm. Murder and burglary.

"So, they're getting the stuff out at eleven? Before the thieves come back? Is that it?"

"Or before they tell the police."

Rosie sniggered. It was probably worse than being snorted at, thought Jack. "Thieves are not likely to go to the police and say they found stuff when they broke in, are they?"

She was right. And Frank would hardly call them in about a break in when he had something going on he didn't want anyone to know about.

Lu began to snuffle. She was bored now.

"Just put these back on the shelf for now," Jack said, "And we'll get Lu used to the boat."

"What? You're joking!"

"No, it's an escape route. We have to practice."

Jack fetched the lifejackets hanging on the walls and began to fit the smaller one onto Lu. She was interested enough not to complain.

"Lu, we're going on the boat! You have to sit still and be very very careful." He pulled his lifejacket on and tied the tapes.

She nodded and let Jack help her onto the boat. It rocked quite a bit as he tried and failed to get the balance right but as soon as it settled he sat her on the prow seat and sat next to her. Lu felt the boat swell gently under her and didn't seem too worried.

"See, it's nice. Floating on the water."

Lu looked over the side and the boat rocked. She held on, seemingly still unworried by the motion.

Rosie got in and took the rowing seat.

"Let's go out a bit, get her used to it."

Jack nodded and held onto Lu as Rosie navigated out onto the river.

"Wet," Lu said as she leaned further over. Jack held on tight and pulled her back a bit.

Rosie rowed a very little way, stopped and held the boat steady in mid-stream.

"More!" cried Lu.

"How far down is that fishing lodge?"

"Ten minutes?"

Jack nodded to her and Rosie rowed downstream with Jack holding Lu, until he could see she was slowing near some wooden posts along the bank.

"Up there."

Jack looked into the undergrowth. If there had been a track or path it was now overgrown. You could push the boat into the reeds and it would be harder to see. No one would know they were there. Good hiding place, he thought, with good escape routes all along the road, the river and the banks.

Rosie rowed them back to the boathouse and moored up.

Lu seemed to like the boat, but Jack wasn't sure he could keep her safe. She couldn't swim yet and as he hung up their ancient lifejackets he wondered if they would actually save a life. He began to doubt that the lodge would be a good place to hide. He might not be able to manage Lu in the boat and row at the same time. He filed the fishing lodge as a hiding place if they had to go by river, but one he would prefer to get to by road because it would be easier with Lu.

Rosie opened the door and let Jack and Lu out into the fading light. It was getting late, they needed to get back before Mum came looking for Lu.

"I saw you go out this morning, with your mum. Is that why you didn't come?"

"No ... sort of ... I had to think."

She nodded. "Will you come tomorrow?"

Jack nodded.

"With her?"

Jack looked at Lu. He shrugged. "Maybe. I'm going to look at the maps again later. I think you could get to Lowestoft by boat."

"It's miles!"

"I'll show you, tomorrow. And, I think we need to see what happens at eleven tonight. At the farm."

"No, I'm not going back."

"I'll go on my own. I'll just go the bridge and see what goes down your lane. Anyone else live down that road?"

"Not for miles, we're usually the only ones who use it. And tourists who get lost."

That was good, he thought, he would know who went to the farm.

Jack and Lu went back through the bushes. Lu was humming her happy song as she ambled along behind him. This quiet place seemed to suit her, she hadn't had a tantrum for days.

Chapter Twenty-Nine

Day 14: Very late Thursday night - Jack and Rosie

Jack lay in bed, fully dressed for the bottom half and wearing his pyjama top on that half, so when Mum came to say goodnight he looked like he was in bed properly.

"Read for a while, then light out," she said. "Is it a good book?"

He nodded. Mum looked pleased.

"I know there's not much to do here, and you must miss Milo and Jaye but it won't be for long, we'll move soon."

"Home?"

"Not yet, just somewhere else for a while."

Mum pulled the door to and Jack sat up in the half light of the little lamp he'd rigged on his shelf. He didn't want to go yet. He'd miss the boathouse - and Rosie. And he had stuff to do.

He sat reading until he was sure Mum was in bed. He couldn't wait until she was asleep, he had to be there for eleven, so very quietly he crept down the ladder, pulled a hoody on, and picked up his coat from under the bunk beds where he had left it. Gently, he opened the window. Climbing out was easy on the ground floor and in a minute or two he was crossing the grass to the front of the cottage. His trainers crunched on the gravel and he swerved back onto the grass verge. A shape popped out from the boathouse track and nearly made him yell.

"I changed my mind. I'm coming," Rosie hissed.

They jogged along the dark and shadowy lane and up onto the bigger road. Without street lights the road was eerie with moonlit shadows dancing across the surface as the skeletal trees and bushes moved in the gentle breeze. They ran down to the bridge, crossed over and ducked behind the road sign.

Rosie nudged him and they half crawled to the side and crossed into the field. In the dark they made their way nearer to the farm buildings, keeping low, stumbling and tripping, until Rosie stopped and pulled him closer to the hedge.

"Here will be good. We can see if anyone comes."

Jack fished some paper and a pencil from his pocket. "Number plates, make of vehicle."

He could feel Rosie stare at him in the semi-darkness.

"What? Evidence."

"You watch too much TV." she muttered.

They had at least ten minutes before anything was due to be at the farm and their legs began to cramp under them as they squatted down, waiting. It was cold and damp and the ground was squelchy - Jack hoped it was just mud he was standing in. Rosie kept fidgeting and once, almost knocked him over.

"You'd be no good on a stakeout," he said.

She snorted. But Jack was glad she was there. He really didn't like being in all this open space. Weird because he didn't like being shut in either. Perhaps there was a name for that, like there is for not liking being shut in. And he was surprised at how much noise there was. Rustling and clicking and trickling, and a sort of buzzing or droning.

"What's that noise?" he asked Rosie.

"What noise?"

"That one, the one that doesn't stop."

They listened.

"The main road, over that way." Rosie nodded over the far fields. "Traffic goes by nearly all night."

Jack listened again. It was a hum really. He could imagine traffic zooming along day and night, everyone going somewhere for work or on holiday or going home, hoping there would be no hold-ups so they got there quicker. He wondered how long it would be before Mum drove them along that road, taking them somewhere - anywhere - hoping to get there quickly.

They heard a closer hum and saw a sweep of headlights come towards the bridge. They both ducked down closer to the ground. A small van slowed as it crossed the bridge and began to turn into the lane leading to the farm. The headlights went off. The car went past in darkness, screened now from the road by the hedgerows.

"What do we do now?" Rosie asked.

"Wait, I suppose," Jack said. "See if it goes to the farm."

Rosie half stood up, scanning the distance between them and the farm. She could see the fields in the moonlight but not the lane or the van driving along it. There were some lights up at the farm but not in the house. Jack stood behind her and watched too. After a few minutes, they saw a light come on as a door opened. It was so far away Jack couldn't see where it was but Rosie whispered, "The stables, it's that door we broke into, the locked one."

"Is the van there yet?"

"Don't know."

They watched the dark patch on the fields until suddenly two red lights glowed.

"Brake lights. He's there." said Jack.

"How do you know it's a 'he'?"

"What?"

"How do you know it's a "he'?"

"Who do you think it is?"

"I don't know, but it doesn't have to be a 'he.'"

No, it doesn't, thought Jack. But he said, "The voice on the phone was a 'he'."

"Doesn't mean *he* is in that van. Could be anyone."

"Just watch. Can you see anyone - 'he' or 'she' or 'them' ?"

Rosie peered intently. "No, I think they are in the stable."

It seemed a long time before they saw anything at all. Then in the light framing what Rosie had said was the stable door it looked like a bulky shadow was passing.

"Is that someone carrying a box? One of those big ones from the stables?" Jack asked.

"I think so."

And as they watched, they were sure they saw some movement back and forth, as if someone was loading the van.

"They won't get it all in that van. It's too small. They need a big one."

Jack nodded. "You're right. They can only take some. Do you think someone else is coming? Did another phone ring with a message?"

Rosie shook her head. "Just that one, number 2, when you were there."

"Let's wait for it to come back past here," Jack suggested and so they crossed back and hid in the hedgerow again. Jack pulled the paper flat and held the pencil ready. Rosie snorted but he ignored her.

A quiet hum grew closer and the van pulled level with them, as it waited to turn right onto the bridge road. Jack scribbled down the number plate, GB, and 'white' and 'missing hub cap' before it turned and disappeared. They stood up and walked onto the bridge road as the van's headlights came on and it sped off.

"Do we wait and see if another one comes?"

Jack shrugged. "We don't know if one is coming. We could wait for ages."

Rosie began walking back to their lane and Jack followed.

"What do you think is in the boxes? Do you know?"

Rosie shook her head, "Different all the time."

"So, you've seen vans before?"

She nodded. "Evenings, later sometimes, but not in the day time."

"And the stables are always locked?"

"I said, didn't I?"

They stopped and looked over the bridge down to the silvery water flowing below. It looked different at night. Deeper and scarier than in the day time.

"Didn't you ask?"

"You mad!"

"Ask no questions, you said. But didn't you ask your mum?"

Rosie paused. "She didn't ask questions either." She walked over the bridge and set off quickly. "I'm tired, let's get back."

Jack left Rosie at the track to the boathouse and crossed the garden as quietly as he could. He opened the window just enough to slide back inside and pulled it to behind him. It was dark even with the curtains open and he felt his way across to the ladder, stepping on one of Lu's toys and crunching it underfoot. Lu was snuffling, as usual, and she didn't wake up as he climbed the ladder. He pulled off his hoody and trainers, and slid down into his sleeping bag still wearing his jeans. He lay in the darkness, thinking about the farm. He wished he could find out what was going on - but he thought it would be better to get Rosie somewhere safe before doing that.

Chapter Thirty

Day 14: Thursday - Police - PC Anstey and DC Tizora

Anstey sat at his desk transferring notes onto files and linking them to the central system used to co-ordinate investigations. It was tedious but without this system, no-one would be able to join all the dots, link all the evidence. He'd been out tracking stolen bikes, the stolen ice cream van and a spate of graffiti on some garage doors at the back of the high street shops. He typed in the last details and sat back and stretched his arms.

"Anstey," a voice hissed nearby. "Anstey!"

He looked around and saw the top of Tizora's head behind a large old-style computer screen on the other side of the room. Picking up his coffee mug, he stood up and crossed the room slowly, trying to look as if he was just going out to the kitchen - via that particular work station. He squatted down out of sight as he reached the desk.

"There's been a lot of fuss upstairs," she whispered. "The Boss is chasing everyone."

"Why?"

"He says we should have got to Sal Williamson before she ran."

"But I went as soon as we knew Moreton might be a problem but she'd already gone."

"How did she know he was out before we did? And now he's out and free and he knows her address. How? No one knows where she was re-located to, not even her own mother."

Anstey rocked back and forth as he squatted trying to keep his balance.

"Did I go too late because someone messed up?"

Tizora shook her head. "Someone is going through all the channels to see if there is a leak but it's causing a real problem. I'm keeping away from the top floor today."

Anstey nodded. "Good plan. We did our bit, found out what she'd been up to and where she went. What else can we do from here? It's over to Norfolk now. They have to find her."

Tizora nodded. "Yes, you're right. We've done our bit."

Except the Boss thought otherwise …

Chapter Thirty-One

Day 15: Friday - Jack, Rosie and Lu

Two weeks. Two weeks since they had left home. And Jack didn't know how much more time they would have here. The grab bag was ready. The car had some things stored in the boot already, like a change of clothes, some snacks and water, just in case they didn't have time to pack up. Jack had hiding places and escape routes in his head. But he wasn't ready to go yet. He needed to help Rosie first and he didn't know how to do that.

Mum decided it would be nice to go to the wild life place again. As much as Jack had enjoyed it last time, he really didn't want to go today. He tried saying he had stomach ache. And he felt hot. And he felt tired. But off they went, and he did have a good time, and so did Lu, but he really wanted to see Rosie not birds. The man with the binoculars wasn't there in the hide this time, but Jack knew where the nests were and sat watching them while he thought about how to help Rosie.

When he finally went to the boathouse it was late afternoon. It was still light, the clocks hadn't changed yet, so he knew they had time to meet up without Mum saying he had to be back soon. He took his backpack, with the book about Norfolk stowed inside and and some food he had sneaked when Mum was hanging washing out to dry that morning. He also had Lu's backpack with some toys to keep her busy while he and Rosie talked.

Lu was happy to see Rosie and was keen to sit in the boat and play. Jack put on their lifejackets to get Lu used to wearing hers and he sat with Rosie staring at the notes he made last night.

"Why does it help?" Rosie asked. "We can't do anything with that."

Jack thought so too, but he didn't want Rosie to know that. "It might be useful later. Let's see what we can do with these phones." He put them on the bottom of the boat and they both stared at them, hoping for some inspiration.

"Try phoning one," Rosie suggested.

"What? I don't know who would answer."

"You might."

"What? How would I know who it was. I don't know anyone here? You live here, you do it."

"NO!"

"Why not? You might know who answers, then we'd have a name."

"I don't know any of them, I never saw anyone, I stayed away. And, anyway, I'm a girl, they'd know I wasn't Frank. If you did it you could make your voice deeper, sound like him."

"I could send a text."

Rosie looked at the phones. "Do they do those?"

Jack picked one up and turned it over. Number 2. He looked at the buttons and pressed the one he thought might be right. Nothing. He tried a few more but then said, "I don't think they do anything but go to those numbers. These are not like real phones, not like my mum's anyway."

He thought about how Mum was using phones now. Was she up to something? Rosie said the 'he' could be 'she' but ... no, not Mum, she wouldn't do anything to put him and Lu in danger.

"Well," said Rosie, "We have to try something."

"If we call on this one, someone will expect Frank. They will know it's this phone. Is there somewhere we could phone from around here?"

"Not really. There might be somewhere in Freeling but not out here."

Jack scooped the phones and put them in his backpack. "Let's find a phone. Row to a phone."

It sounded silly as he said it but he was stuck for ideas.

"Too far …" she stopped. "What's that?"

"What?"

"Sssshhh."

They sat in the gently rocking boat and listened.

"Is it Frank? Does he know about the boathouse?" whispered Jack. Rosie shook her head.

There was definitely some noise outside, different noise.

Jack thought he could hear shouting. He climbed up to the jetty and went to the door. He opened it a crack and put his ear close to the gap. Rosie came behind him and listened too. Definitely shouting.

He turned to Rosie. "We have to go. Now!"

"Who is it? Frank?"

"Not Frank. Harry!"

He got back in the boat to get Lu. "We have to hide. Hide and seek Lu."

"Wait! Get everything in the boat." Rosie dropped his backpack into the boat. "It's easier on the river."

She grabbed her sleeping bag and threw it in, followed by her backpack and jacket. She swept the shelves of food and picked up the water bottles. In seconds she had cleared everything into the boat, including some rope and her lifejacket, and sat down ready to row. The bottom of the boat was covered with a muddle of things but Jack cast off and they rowed out onto the river, both pulling hard to make good speed. Jack had to keep looking at Lu to make sure she was holding on but they pulled and pulled on the oars until they were out of sight of the boathouse and then carried on as fast as they could downriver.

"The lodge," Jack said, "Can we get to the lodge?"

Rosie nodded. Of course, they could.

Within ten minutes they pulled into the reeds, Rosie pulled on a mooring post and tucked the boat in as far as she could before tying up.

They sat, catching their breath and listening hard. No sounds of anyone coming after them. No shouting. Jack felt relief as his breathing slowed and his heart stopped punching his chest. But then he felt panic. Mum. What could he do to help Mum? She had told him to get Lu away, find hiding places, be ready. Well, he had done that - got Lu away and to a hiding place. What now?

Rosie was standing up and looking into the undergrowth. "It's up there."

"What?"

"The lodge, it's just through there."

She reached out to Lu and began to help her out of the boat.

"I have to go back," Jack said.

"What? Why? You got away. You have to hide, like you said." Rosie stood on the bank holding Lu's hand.

"Mum."

Rosie stared - not quite a full 'are you mad' stare but not far off.

"Not yet, get to the lodge first. Then we can see what to do."

Jack was undecided, but he knew he had get Lu somewhere safe and he also knew he couldn't take her back with him. He needed Rosie to stay with her.

He got out of the boat and they walked warily up to the lodge. They stood behind some bushes and checked it over.

"It's empty," Rosie said. "No one's been here since last summer."

"How do you know?"

"I know."

"Sure?"

"Sure."

She went over to a door and lifted a plant pot by the side of the porch and retrieved a key. She held it up smugly and opened the door with it. They went in to a single roomed building. The curtains and trees blocked the fading light but Jack could see it was basic. A sofa against one wall which was also a bed, a chair, a table and some cupboards above.

He wrinkled his nose at the musty smell. It wasn't as bad as … well, the caravan … but it wasn't good either.

"I stay here sometimes, when it's cold, it's warmer than the boathouse."

Jack looked at Lu. Could he let her sleep here? Would it be safe?

"It's alright. There's a little heater. And there's a standpipe outside. And a bucket."

She looked at him. She wanted him to like it.

"Let's stop for now, and think about it."

"I'll get the stuff from the boat, you see to Lu."

Rosie left Jack to explore the cupboards and see what was outside. Lu used the bucket - lovely - and he checked the tap was working. By the time Rosie had done several trips to collect everything, he'd found a heater and a camping stove and the fuel for both. Rosie set up the heater on the table to warm the place and dry it out a bit, while Lu sat emptying her backpack on the floor. It wasn't very clean and Jack knew Mum would go ballistic if she saw Lu down there but then he thought this wasn't the time to worry about cleaning a floor just so Lu could play.

"So, what does he want, Lu's dad? Why is he here?"

Jack shrugged. "I think ... before ... he wanted to see Lu. Mum wouldn't let him. After the trial ..."

"Trial? What trial? In court? With judges and all that?"

Jack nodded. "But he's out now. He wasn't supposed to find us. We moved, changed names. But he's found us now. And he hurt Mum." Images flashed in his head. "He will again if I don't do something." Shouting. Screaming. The smell of blood. Jack's head pounded as he remembered the past.

"I'll go back, along the road, and check it out."

Rosie frowned. "I'll come too."

"We can't both go, you stay here with Lu. I can do it, I'll be careful." That's what Mum always said, be careful. Well, he would this time. It was no use if he got caught too. What would happen to Lu?

"If you don't come back in, say an hour, I'll go down to the village and tell someone."

"Are you sure?"

Rosie shrugged.

"Okay," Jack agreed. An hour.

Chapter Thirty-Two

Day 15: Friday Evening - Jack

Jack found his way out onto the road and then ducked to the other side of the hedge into the field so he could follow the road but keep out of sight. It was getting darker now, and it was difficult to see exactly where he was treading, what with all the ruts and holes and brambles but he reached their lane and hopped across and made his way along, still hiding from sight. When he was level with the boathouse he waited, watched and listened. Ducking down and keeping low under the trees, he got to the shed and stood listening again. It was quiet. He needed to be nearer.

He stood by the generator shed at the side, knowing he was out of sight, and listened again. He couldn't hear anything: no shouting or yelling or even talking. The car was still parked behind the bushes so … was she still in there? With him?

He made his way to the back and lifted himself up to peer in through his bedroom window. The door was partly open and he could see a little way down the hall. A light was on, in the kitchen. There was a murmur of voices, quiet and low. He climbed in and lowered himself gently to the floor. Reaching over he picked up Lu's pillow and took off the pillow case. Then, moving as silently as he could, he went to the shelves and put some of their clothes inside. He dropped the pillowcase out of the window and climbed outside, picking it up and moving slowly around to duck under the kitchen window. The light shone out across the garden. The voices were clearer here.

"Let them roam, do you? What kind of mother are you?"

It was a voice he recognised. Definitely Harry.

He raised himself up so he could see inside. Mum was sitting at the kitchen table. Harry was standing over her, too close, his hands spread on the table in front of her. Jack froze. He heard the echoes of the past, saw flashing images and began to panic. He couldn't breathe. He felt his head buzz. His heart thumped. Slow down. Slow down. Close your eyes. Breathe. There was a sheen of sweat all over his body and he was trembling but … he lifted himself up and peered in again. Mum looked up at that point and she saw him, and he knew she had because her eyes dropped straight away and she turned to the side on her chair, as if to draw Harry's eyes away from the window.

"I told you. They'll be back soon."

"You said that half an hour ago!"

"It's a big garden. They come back when they're hungry, they can play out for hours."

"They're not in the garden, are they?"

"Tell you what, they'll be in the orchard. We'll go and look."

He banged the table with the flat of his hand making Jack jump.

Mum stood up, forcing him to step back. "Let's find them. We'll go to the orchard. I'll get my boots."

Harry followed her, pushing her along the hall. Jack watched them disappear and realised he had to get around the other side before Mum led Harry out to the orchard. He made his way all around the cottage and crouched by the living room wall. He heard Mum open the front door and the crunch on the patchy path as they walked out and round to where he had just been hiding. She was buying him some time. He had to use it. When he thought they were clear, he moved to the porch, to the open front door, and picked up the grab bag. Clutching that and the pillowcase he headed to the boathouse, through the bushes and along to the river bank.

He stumbled his way through the undergrowth, cursing the darkness. He reached the road feeling frustrated at how slow it had been and worried that the hour was up. What if Rosie had already left? How would he find her? Would she walk? Take the boat? He began to jog down the road, not taking care to hide this time. He just had to get back to the lodge as quickly as he could. He couldn't remember exactly where he'd come out onto the road. Was it that tree? Or that one? He slowed and looked more carefully as he jogged along, the grab bag bouncing on one shoulder and the pillowcase on the other. He began to think he was on the wrong road. Nothing looked familiar. He couldn't have gone wrong, could he? He slowed again, now half-running, half-jogging. Should he turn back, look again. Surely he hadn't run this far?

He stopped. Catching his breath he looked in both directions. Where was he? Then as he looked further down the road he saw a flash of blue and one of red. He squinted. He moved slowly, cautiously towards it. The blue shape moved upwards and he realised it was someone waving their arm, someone wearing something blue. Rosie. She was wearing a blue jacket. And Lu was wearing red. He began to jog and as he got nearer he could see it really was Rosie and Lu. He was so relieved he thought he would cry … but he knew Rosie would snort at him so he held it back … and he ran down to meet them.

Chapter Thirty-Three

Day 15: Friday Night - Jack, Rosie and Lu

"Quick! Out of sight."

He scooted past them and down where he thought they would get to the lodge. Rosie caught him and pulled him to the side. "This way." And she led them back to the lodge.

Inside, he dropped the grab bag and pillowcase and flopped onto the sofa. Rosie lit the candle and pulled the thin curtains across the dirty window.

"I thought you … had … weren't coming back!" Rosie actually looked as if she cared about him.

"It was further than I thought. Had to run!"

Rosie handed him a water bottle and he drank most of it before he told her what had happened. She didn't interrupt, for once.

Lu was happily emptying the pillowcase, which she knew was hers, and was trying to put on a different jumper but over her coat so she was struggling.

"So he's there, with your mum?"

Jack nodded.

"What do we do?" Rosie asked.

Jack shrugged. His chest hurt. He thought it was from running but it hurt more every time he thought about Mum being alone with Harry.

"We have to tell someone. Someone who can rescue her."

It should be me, thought Jack, I should rescue her. He hadn't done it last time, but he was bigger now, he should find a way.

"Did you get her phone? In that bag?"

Jack checked the grab bag. No phone.

"We can get to a phone tomorrow …" Rosie suggested.

"Too late! It has to be now."

"It's dark, we can't row in the dark."

"I'll walk. Leas Farm? Isn't that near?"

Rosie nodded.

"I'll run …"

"You'll have to take Lu."

"I can't - it's too far, she's slow."

"I can't stay here with her. They'll come and take me back. To the farm, to Frank."

"No, they won't. We can explain, about the stables, the van. I wrote it down."

Rosie shook her head. "NO! He'll lie. He always does. And they took the stuff, in that van."

"Not all of it. You said it wouldn't all fit."

"You don't get it. He … he made my mum … he didn't help her, and he made Rob leave …"

"Rob?"

Rosie shook her head.

Jack didn't know what to say. He couldn't get anywhere with Lu in tow. Could he row in the dark on his own to that village and keep Lu safe in the boat at the same time? It wasn't too far to the cottage, could he walk her back and try to get Mum's phone? Or stand in the road and wait for a car? That might be the thing to do - stop a car and ask for help.

Rosie held up a phone.

"They don't work," Jack reminded her.

"I think they have to, you know, for 999."

She stared at the buttons. She pushed the button to switch it on. The screen lit up. Jack looked over. She pressed 999 and send. It rang.

Rosie stared at Jack. The voice asked again. What service did they require? Jack nodded at her, to say go on, do it.

Rosie's voice was quiet and thin as she said, "Police."

As the responder asked Rosie questions she dried up, she couldn't even squeak an answer. The responder asked different questions, was kind and careful, but still Rosie held the phone tightly in her hand without answering.

Jack leant nearer and said, "Orchard Cottage, Norfolk, he's got my mum ..." The phone died; what little charge it had, faded away.

"Try another one!" He frantically searched for another of the four phones. He switched it on, it had some charge and he dialled 999. The responder was different and this time he got as far as "Orchard Cottage, Norfolk, near Stavesey... he's got my mum ...you have to help her ... Harry Moreton ... Sal Williamson ..." before it faded away.

Rosie handed him the third phone. It was the same responder, so she knew what he'd already said but she seemed more concerned about him than Mum, and he didn't want to answer questions about himself. He talked over her. "Orchard Cottage, please get to her. He's there, you have to stop him before he hurts her..." And that left one phone. And this last time the responder said it was fine, they'd got his message, someone would go and check, but who was he, could he speak, could he tell her where he was ... and that was it.

He stared at the dead phone in despair. "The charger, where's the charger?"

"No electricity," Rosie reminded him. "But they understood, they're sending someone."

Jack wasn't convinced. He fretted over the phones, checking each of them and finding each was dead.

"You did it, you sent help."

Jack still doubted her. Should he go and check? He'd have to take Lu. It was too dark now, too far.

Rosie said, "Leave it for a bit, we'll know if they've gone to get her."

"How?"

"Outside, we'll see the lights from here."

Jack bundled Lu back into her coat and shrugged into his. "Come on," he said to Rosie, "Let's watch. Where do we go?"

Rosie lead them back down to the river and they stood shivering in the damp air while they watched in the direction she pointed to. It was a very flat, dark landscape. The sky filled most of it. It wasn't very different from where they had watched last night, Rowley's farm, but it was difficult to see much beyond the bend in the river. After a few minutes, Lu began to fret. She was beginning to get to that dangerous whining stage. She was cold and tired. Come on, thought Jack. Hurry up.

"How far is the nearest police station?" he asked. "How long would it take to get here?"

Rosie thought. She didn't know. And how could she say the police would need to find 'Orchard Cottage, Norfolk.' And there might be several Orchard Cottages and Norfolk was big county. And the roads were winding and the nearest town with a police station must be … miles away ... so, they might not be here for ages yet. But what Rosie didn't know was that an alert was out for Harry Moreton and Sal Williamson/Sinclair and as soon as their names popped up at the emergency call centre, a search found there were four Orchard Cottages in a small radius around Stavesey and so four police vehicles were sent out.

"I'll take Lu in. You watch," she said.

Jack nodded and sat down on an almost dry patch to wait. It was a clear evening. He could see birds flitting around ... or bats ... he wasn't sure which, and a moth kept fluttering towards him. He could see the river flowing past, silvery in the moonlight forcing its way between the clouds. He could hear the hum of that distant road again if he really listened. Twice, he heard a car driving along the bridge road but they didn't seem to have turned into their lane. He wasn't sure what he was supposed to see but he thought he would know when he saw it.

It seemed ages before he knew something was happening. There was a clear sound of a siren passing at speed along the road he'd run down only minutes before. He stood up. In the darkness he could see blue flashing lights whizz past between the bushes and trees blocking the lodge from the road. Then through some hedges across the fields he thought he saw some more blue lights and then red lights. Brake lights? He watched the lights flashing in the darkness and listened but all he could hear was the siren. And then there were more sirens and more lights and ... and ... yes, that was it. They'd got to the cottage. He'd rescued Mum. And Rosie too, she'd helped. He watched for several minutes to be sure that someone was there, someone who could help, and then went to tell Rosie.

The lodge was warmer and he was grateful to be inside but he kept his coat on while he warmed up. Rosie had pulled the bed out and it filled the floor space. Lu was asleep on one side with Rosie's sleeping bag covering her.

"They got there," he whispered.

Rosie smiled.

"What do you want to do now?" she whispered back.

Jack thought. "I'll take Lu and find someone to help."

"Can you wait, until it's light? I can row you to the village, you can ask there and I can go on … I can't stay."

"But Mum will …"

"Please, you can't give me away! Frank … he's so … angry. I have to get to Lowestoft."

"If we tell the police they'll take you there."

"No, they won't."

Rosie sat on the end of the bed and Jack sat on the chair at the table.

"I can't talk about it. I can't. But it's bad, and he lied and it was … just … and it'll be the same. I can't do it, I can't."

What difference would a few hours make? thought Jack. Mum would worry but she'd know he'd found a good hiding place and would come out when he knew it was safe. He could go to that shop in the village and tell the lady with the vomit green cardigan and it would be sorted. All before breakfast.

"Ok, we'll sleep here and go in the morning."

Rosie looked as if she was going to cry so he took off his trainers and lay down next to Lu.

One sleeping bag just about covered them when it was opened out but the three of them lay in a row and while Lu slept, Jack and Rosie drifted in and out of sleep, both dealing with memories neither of them ever wanted to remember.

Chapter Thirty-Four

Day 15: Friday - Police - PC Anstey and DC Tizora

"Didn't expect this," said Tizora. She put her case in the boot next to Anstey's.

Anstey nodded and closed the boot. When they were seated inside he fed some co-ordinates into the satnav. "It should take around five and a half hours - six with a break half way, and nearer seven if there's a problem on the roads."

"Or a problem getting out of town - it's the worst time to be leaving - Friday rush hour. We'll get there late and report in the morning, like the Boss said."

Tizora drove slowly out of the station car park and headed out of town. Neither of them was entirely sure why the Boss had chosen them to go to Norfolk. It could be they had been on the case already and knew enough to be helpful. Or because he felt he had to prove he was fostering co-operative policing. Or that Tizora and Anstey were officers he could afford to lose for a few days when they were so short staffed. But whatever the reason, that Friday morning he had confirmed that they would be re-assigned temporarily to Norfolk to help track down Sal Williamson before Harry Moreton found her, which is why, on Friday afternoon they were on their way south ... too late to find Sal Williamson before Harry Moreton did.

Chapter Thirty - Five

Day 16: Saturday Morning - Jack, Rosie and Lu

By six the next morning, they were almost ready to leave the lodge. They had tidied up, put things away and stowed everything they had brought with them back in the boat. Jack had given Rosie all the food they had left and while they ate some breakfast he showed her the map.

He opened it out on the table and she looked carefully. She found the spot where the farm would be and traced the river to the village.

"That's where we'll head to. I'll drop you and Lu off and you can walk into the village and then I'll carry on. Where do you think I need to go?"

Jack pointed at Lowestoft. "There," he pointed along the river. "You go here and then across here and then, down there and … "

Rosie held his hand still. "Stop!"

"What?"

"It's not that easy. There are currents and shallows and …"

"If you get so far, you can get a bus, can't you?"

Rosie gave him a stare. "A bus?"

He nodded. What was wrong with that?

"Do you know how many buses it would take to get …" she stabbed at the map, "… from here … to here?"

He shook his head.

"Too many. And how often does a bus come along around here?"

He shrugged. How was he supposed to know that? At home buses came every ten minutes and could take you anywhere across town and anywhere out of town too.

"And I've only got £1.75p."

Jack thought for a moment. He needed to get Rosie on her way so he could get back to Mum. He needed to make sure she was safe and he knew she would be worried about him and Lu. And, most importantly, they would be able to go home and he really missed home.

"There's money in the grab bag. I'll give you some and then you can get some more food and when you get somewhere…" he scanned the map and pointed " … like here, you can get a bus to say … here and then you're almost there."

She looked doubtful. "I can't row across that broad by myself, it's too big."

"Then, stop here." He pointed. "You can keep this book and then you can find your way."

She stared. "It's an old map, I'll get lost."

He stared at her, just like she did at him.

"It's only Norfolk, it's not the Amazon. There's always a village or a farm or a bus."

She snorted.

"You'll have to get me some food. I can't risk anyone seeing me."

"Easy. We'll get to the village. I'll go to the shop, and then I'll come back for Lu and you can row on."

She nodded. He wanted to help her but he wanted to get back to Mum more.

Once Lu had been cleaned up (jam makes a mess on your face when you're only four) they put on their lifejackets and cast off. Lu was interested enough in the boat not to be difficult so Jack and Rosie rowed together until they were just outside the village. Jack took off his lifejacket and dropped it into the boat. He left Lu with Rosie and set off to the shop with some of Mum's emergency money in his pocket. Rosie had been quite insistent about what he had to get. Bread (but not white) and jam (apricot or raspberry) and biscuits (with chocolate) and apples (not hard green ones) and … at that point he had left her in the boat and walked off quickly before it got too tricky to remember it all.

The road was as deserted as it had been before but it occurred to him that it still very early. What time did the shop open? A van (a red one he was relieved to see, not a white one like at the farm) was parked outside the shop and the driver opened the back and took out a bundle which she dropped on the step before driving off. He walked across and looked in at the window. It wasn't open. He sat on the step and looked down at the parcel. It was a bundle of newspapers. He wondered what kind of news made the headlines here. Someone crossing the road badly? A lost budgerigar? A bus being late?

The door clanged behind him and he turned to see the lady (vomit green cardigan firmly buttoned up) opening the catch. She looked at him in surprise.

"Well, you're an early bird," she said. "Bring those in and I'll serve you."

He stood off the step and picked up the newspapers by the string, then followed her in and put the parcel on the counter. She disappeared in a narrow gap and re-emerged in front of him.

"What would you like today? We've got most things."

Jack began to collect what Rosie wanted and put the items onto the counter. It was bit of a squash as the newspapers took up so much room but when she had undone the string and rolled it into a ball to be used again, she asked him to to put them on the window sill by the door. He heaved them over and carried on collecting.

"Having a good holiday, are you?"

"Oh, yes, thank you."

"That's nice. The weather's been quite good, no rain, and warm for this time of year."

"Yes, it's lovely."

"Did you go to the museum?"

"Not yet."

"Oh, you should. It's very interesting."

I'll bet, he thought. "Peanut butter?"

She pointed to a shelf.

"Your mum didn't come then?"

Jack paused. "No, not today. She's just getting a picnic ready, wild life park."

"That's nice."

Yes, thought Jack, it is nice but it's not true.

He put bananas on the counter with the last pack of cookies from the shelf, and pulled out the money he'd brought and a bag to put the things in.

"You'd better get back quick, to your mum, there's a madman out there."

That's nice, Jack thought as he put the shopping into the bag as she tallied it up.

"Not safe to be out, a young man like you when there's a madman running amok."

Jack pushed a note across to pay and waited for his change.

"Last night, he attacked some woman over Fretton way. Got away, he did. Some townie, no doubt. Don't want people like that here. It's not how we do things."

Jack took his change and smiled goodbye.

"Take care, and make sure you go to the museum. It's very interesting."

Jack pulled the door shut and set off. He'd be so glad to get home and go to a normal shop, one where you didn't have to search for things and listen to somebody drivel on about madmen. And what did it mean, running amok? What was an amok? And how did you do it? Run about in circles waving your arms about?

Rosie was on the path with Lu, who ran up to him and grabbed him around the hips and squeezed tight.

"Jack," she said.

"Yes, I'm Jack. And you're Lu."

He handed Rosie the bag and she peered in. Go on, he thought, start snorting. It was all I could find in that shop.

"No apples?"

"Not unless you wanted hard green ones."

She sniffed but that was it ... no complaints. Jack felt quite pleased - at last he'd got something right.

"Say good bye to Rosie," he said to Lu.

Lu scrunched up her face and he saw a whinge coming on. "She's going on the boat for now and we're going to see Mum." Lu wasn't sure what to do. She wanted to be with Rosie and in the boat but she wanted Mum more. She settled for a low grizzle.

Rosie put the food in the boat and fetched the map over. She pointed, "We're here, and I'm going along to here."

Jack looked. Seemed sensible. The route along the rivers seemed to link together, and there were some villages so there would be some bus stops.

"Where's Fretton?" he asked.

"Fretton? Why are you asking?"

He shook his head and shrugged. If he told her there was a madman running amok she might panic and if she didn't know where Fretton was it couldn't be local.

"Fretton is our farm, Frank's farm."

"You said it was Rowley's farm."

"It is ... now. He changed its name."

Jack took the book from her and frantically searched the map. It was an old map so it would have old names. He searched until he found a tiny dot, on a crease on the page so the name was broken up. Fretton.

He held it out to her. "The woman in the shop, she said a madman attacked a woman over Fretton way. That's my mum. And he got away. What shall I do! Rosie, what can I do?"

Jack was panicking and Rosie didn't know how to help. Lu put her hand into Rosie's and clung close to her side. "Jack sad," she said.

"He is," said Rosie.

"She'll be alright, if they found her. Won't she?"

Rosie nodded. "They were there really quick and you saw blue lights so they must have helped her. I bet she's safe in hospital right now."

Jack nodded slowly. So, what now. He had to keep Lu safe. How could he do that? If he told the woman in the shop, where would they take him and Lu? They wouldn't be with Mum if she was in hospital. They couldn't go home if Mum wasn't there. And Harry knew where they lived. He also knew where Gran lived. Nowhere would be safe.

"Come with me."

"What?"

"Come with me," Rosie repeated. "My gran will sort it out, I know she will."

"She didn't sort you out - why would she help me?"

Rosie flinched. "It's complicated."

I heard that before, Jack thought.

In the distance along the path, he could see a man walking towards them. He absently looked out for a dog, running along too. That's what people did here, didn't they. Take their dog for a walk. As he stared he felt a cold sweat break out.

Chapter Thirty-Six

Day 16: Saturday Morning - Jack, Rosie and Lu

"It's him!"

"Who?"

"Harry."

"But the police went to the cottage."

"He got away. And he's coming."

"How do you know it's him?"

"The cap, he was wearing it last night. Red."

"Lots of people wear red hats."

"In the boat, quick!"

He jumped in and held his arms out to Lu. She climbed in with him and he sat her down on the bottom of the boat between some bags. Rosie cast off before joining Jack on the middle seat.

"Row!"

And they both pulled as hard and fast as they could, hoping they could row faster than Harry could walk. Lu sat in the bottom of the boat happily exploring the shopping bag.

"Crisps," she said and held them out to be opened.

"Not now Lu," Jack growled.

Lu screwed her face and Jack knew there would be trouble. "Stop," he said to Rosie. He opened the crisps and gave them to Lu.

"She choses her times to be difficult," said Rosie.

"Just row," he snapped.

The boat pulled into midstream and they heaved as hard as they could. They passed the edge of the village and the river swung away and out across open country. There was a pathway next to the river all along as far as they could see.

"We have to get away from this bit of river, he might be walking this way, keeping away from the houses and roads."

Rosie nodded. "I think we can turn off but it's a long way. I don't know if we can get that far, even with both of us rowing."

"Doesn't anyone else use the river? It's always empty."

"It's busier in the summer time. But these aren't really like proper rivers, they're not even like canals. Just backwaters."

Jack kept looking for a red hat, any red splurge in the landscape. He wouldn't feel safe until they were miles from here.

Apart from a short stop for Jack to put his lifejacket back on, they rowed and rowed along a narrow, lonely stretch of water. Lu fell asleep and for a short time they could row without having to stop. He felt as if they had been rowing for hours but when he looked, it was only ten o'clock. They'd never make it. No wonder Rosie had been so reluctant to take this trip. He'd really underestimated how far they had to go and how hard it would be.

Lu woke up and began a low whine.

"Can we stop for a break?" he asked. Rosie slowed and the boat slowed to a gentle halt.

Having Lu in the boat made his nerves jangle but at least she'd float if she fell in. He helped her sit up, gave her Unk to hold and and a sweet from his pocket.

"You shouldn't give her sweets, bad for her teeth," said Rosie.

Jack frowned. "You keep her happy then. Last thing I'm thinking about is teeth."

He looked all around. "Nobody lives here," he said. "What's the point of it?"

"It's nice," Rosie said. "I like empty places, no one to get on to you. You can do what you like."

Jack wasn't sure about that. He liked people around him. Like living in the flats. Here they'd only passed a couple of hikers striding along the pathway. It was lonely, he thought.

"We're about half way to here," Rosie pointed at the map. "Then we can turn off."

Jack looked. He sighed. "And then?"

"Then, we do the next bit."

They pulled away and rowed on steadily. Jack's shoulders hurt. His legs hurt. His hands hurt. The seat was hard and the oars were rough. The weak sun was making him squint. He was not feeling very well either, a bit dizzy and tired. Rosie slowed.

"I need a drink", she said. They bobbed gently on the river as Rosie handed round their bottles. For a few minutes they drifted. Jack felt so much better after drinking all the water in his bottle.

"We need to refill the bottles soon," said Rosie.

Jack shook his empty bottle and sighed. Another problem to solve. Who'd have thought he'd be looking for water.

They rowed as steadily as they could but Lu was bored now and every few minutes they had to stop so she could use the bucket or retrieve a toy she'd dropped overboard. Getting Unk back when she threw him overboard was a very tricky moment. Jack got so wet he had to take off his hoody and try to dry it over the prow. He got out with Lu and walked with her on the path while Rosie rowed alongside but it was slow, and they weren't making enough headway. Some walkers went past with a cheery 'hello' and 'lovely day." Some canoeists passed them and a drone came over. There was a windmill too, a derelict one with one sail hanging at an angle and slats missing on the others. It was just as they went under a bridge that a police car sped past with its lights flashing and its siren splitting the air. They couldn't have been seen yet both felt jittery as they rowed away in plain sight. They didn't talk, only to Lu, and kept on swapping places between rowing and dealing with Lu. Sometimes there was a small shed or a cabin nestling in the reeds. Did anyone live there? Jack wondered if these were lodges, like the one from last night. Could they find one to stay in?

Rosie slowed while Jack gave Lu another sweet to keep her still.

"We can't do much more. We need somewhere to stop."

Jack nodded. "What about one of those shacks, like the lodge?"

Rosie looked around. "Might find one empty - up there, there's a backwater. We could look."

They set off again, weary and sore, and, in Lu's case, bored and fretful.

Rosie turned into a gap Jack probably wouldn't have noticed. She steered carefully midstream. It was open but narrow and they felt the displaced water lapping at the sides of the boat. After a few minutes they passed a shack, Jack didn't know what else to call it, as it it looked more tatty than the lodge from last night, but he pointed at it to show Rosie. She wrinkled her nose and he was pleased when she rejected it. They carried on to a point at which Jack was beginning to think they'd be lost in the reeds forever.

Rosie slowed and pointed. There was a roof in the reeds. They pulled the boat through the reeds, which closed behind them, until they reached a wooden building, single storey, facing out to the water. She moored the boat to the post on the tiny jetty and climbed out. She indicated Jack should wait, holding on to Lu who was trying to get out, squirming and whining. She went to peer in at the windows and listen for signs of anyone being there. When she waved Jack was so relieved - he couldn't go on any more, he had to stop. He helped Lu onto the bank and climbed after her. It felt so good to stand up and stretch. Lu stamped her feet and jumped up and down.

Rosie felt under the door mat, along the porch ledge, in the gutter. She frowned.

"No key?"

She shook her head.

Jack looked in at the window. "It looks good, too."

"I'm not giving in."

"We can't break in!"

"You didn't care in the lodge."

"You had a key."

"It wasn't my key."

"But you didn't break in! That was different."

"How is it different?"

"It's someone's house. We shouldn't be in there. How would you it like if someone stayed in your house?"

"I don't have a house, do I?" She glared at him. "What do you want to do then? Carry on rowing all day? Or find a way in?"

Sighing, he went along with her and they searched and prodded and pulled until he found a loose window. Another window, he thought. Why am I always climbing in and out of windows?

He fell into a bedroom and made his way to the front door. Rosie and Lu were waiting to be let in and Lu ran in, excited to be somewhere new. She bounced happily onto a sofa and rolled onto the floor.

"See, we needed to stop," said Rosie. She began opening cupboards, searching for useful things. In minutes she had some candles, a lamp and a sleeping bag on the table. "It looks like someone comes here often, there's some good stuff. The cooker doesn't work though. No gas probably."

Jack went to fetch everything from the boat, as Rosie had done it yesterday. It took several trips again and he thought they needed to be a bit more organised now they had a new plan. There was one bedroom, a tiny bathroom and a room which was both a living room and a kitchen. Rosie had set up a heater, to take the chill off. Jack wondered if it was being near the river or not being lived in that made these places feel damp.

"TV," said Lu.

"No, Lu. No TV."

"TV." She tugged at his arm insistently.

"There isn't one, so no TV."

Lu threw herself flat on the floor and howled.

Rosie frowned. "She can't keep doing that."

Jack sat down on the floor with Lu and cuddled her. She couldn't help being the way she was. And she really was getting better, she didn't scream like she used to, not often anyway. But the good news was - Jack saw - that they would eat something hot. Rosie had found some tinned soup in a cupboard and set up a camping stove on the table. She was rummaging under the sink to find a saucepan.

"She can't do that when she goes to school." She thumped the saucepan down and looked in a drawer for an opener. "It's like someone presses a switch - happy - screaming - happy - screaming - on - off." She opened the tins and emptied them into the saucepan.

Ignoring Rosie, Jack searched in the grab bag and found Lu's medication. He hadn't given her any last night, he'd been so distracted and worried about Mum that he'd forgotten. He sat her up and cuddled her. "Drink, Lu?" She stopped howling and drank from her water bottle. "Medicine? All better soon?" She opened her mouth and he popped in a tablet and held the bottle up for her take another drink.

"Wee," she said.

They stood up and he went to take her outside to the bucket.

"Toilet," Rosie said, "In there."

"Does it work?"

She shrugged.

Jack took Lu into the tiny bathroom and she happily got on to the seat. This was easier than a bucket, less fuss. The toilet flushed when he pressed the handle. It clunked and splattered but it worked.

He sat with Lu on the floor and emptied her bag out. He helped her find a page in her colouring book and she lay on her stomach scrawling a green crayon across what was supposed to be blue sea and sandy beach.

"How does that work?" he asked, pointing at the stove.

Rosie connected a gas bottle and lit the flame.

Easy enough, he thought. "How did you learn to do it?"

She put the saucepan on the grid over the frame and looked to see how high it was. "My dad - my real dad - showed me. We went camping before … before he was ill."

"Around here?"

"No, in Germany."

"Did you live there?"

Rosie nodded and stirred the soup. "Some of the time."

"So, do you speak German?"

She shook her head.

"Why not? That would be good."

"Why would it be good?" she frowned.

"You could speak it, if you went on a holiday to Germany. And Switzerland - they speak German too."

She snorted. "As if that's going to happen. Holiday? I haven't even got anywhere to live! Remember?"

"Nor do we. Remember?"

"You've got a mum. Remember?"

"In hospital. Remember?"

Rosie stirred harder and glared at the soup. "Find some mugs," she snapped.

Jack looked in the cupboards and found mugs for him and Rosie and small bowl for Lu, because he knew what a mess she would make eating soup from a mug.

"Put some in here for Lu." He held out the bowl.

"It's not ready."

"It will be too hot for her, just put some in."

Rosie sniffed (not snorted, he noticed) but she spooned some into the bowl and then continued stirring the rest.

Jack called Lu over and they sat at one end of the table while Lu spooned her soup into her mouth, without making too many splashes on her jumper, and chewed on some bread. She was hungry and ate every bit. Jack gave her a biscuit and she got down and went back to play on the floor while Jack and Rosie sat and ate.

The soup was good - hot and quite tasty considering the tins may have been in the cupboard for a very long time. And Mum would have been happy to see them eating something with vegetables, even if it was just old soup. Jack felt so much better. They hadn't eaten much so far today and it was afternoon now. He drank some more water and reached for some more bread to wipe the bowl with.

"I need something else, " he said. "I'm really hungry."

Rosie tutted. "You only bought food for me, now there's three of us."

Jack looked through what they had. He began to make a banana sandwich. "We'll have to get some more."

"Where?"

"There must be a shop near the river somewhere."

Rosie finished her soup and, taking the last banana, went to find the book with the map in the pile of things Jack had dumped by the door.

She sat on the sofa and found the map page and opened it out. She traced their route, or what she thought was their route - she would never admit she wasn't sure to Jack - and looked across to see where they could go tomorrow. Jack came and sat down beside her, sandwich already half eaten.

"Where are we?"

She pointed. "This is where I thought I'd go."

Jack looked to see where she indicated. He saw that her nails were filthy. How long had it been since she had had a shower? She'd been at the boathouse for days, and now they were all the way out there. He looked down at his own hands and sniffed at his hoody. She stared at him.

"I need a shower," he muttered. "And clean clothes."

She raised an eyebrow, the way that some people can. {*Try it. Tricky to do. Just don't do it if anyone can see you - they'll think you're weird - and not in a good way.*}

"What?" he asked. "I like clean clothes."

She tutted and dropped the banana skin on the floor.

"Don't do that! Put it in the bin."

"Why? Who's going to empty it?"

"We can't leave a mess, it's not right."

"No one will know it was us. What's the problem."

You are, thought Jack, you're the problem. "We tidy up when we go. Take rubbish with us. And leave money for the soup."

She snorted.

"I mean it."

"Really?"

Mum would say it's what they have to do. So, he would do it even if Rosie didn't. He rinsed their mugs and bowls clean and left them to dry. It wasn't perfect but it would do. He put the banana skins and some wrappers in the paper bag the bananas had been in and left it on the table ready to take with them. He stared at the camping stove.

"Where did this come from?" he asked.

"The lodge."

"You took it?"

Rosie shrugged. "Borrowed it."

"You stole it!"

"I needed it! How was I supposed to live on a boat for days with nothing? I could have died!"

"How? Starvation?"

"Probably. You need things to survive. I needed it - they didn't."

Jack struggled. It was stealing, he knew it was. It wasn't her fault she was homeless but stealing was still wrong.

"You can take it back, when you get to your gran's, can't you."

She snorted. That's a no, then, he thought. What did Mum say? Pick your battles. Was this a battle worth fighting? Probably not, not now anyway.

It was now late afternoon and the light was fading. Rosie lit some candles and put them where Lu couldn't easily get to them. She wondered how people used to manage with candles and small children. It must have been a nightmare keeping them safe.

Jack found a change of clothes and shut himself in the bathroom while Rosie looked through the Norfolk book. He found some shower gel to wash with and a thin towel to dry himself. It wasn't a proper shower but he did feel cleaner afterwards. He put the dirty clothes in a bag in the grab bag and took Lu in the bathroom to clean her up as much as he could. She made a bit of fuss but she was happy to put on her unicorn tee-shirt and a different pink jumper, so it was worth the effort.

As he put Lu's dirty clothes in the bag with his, he saw there were some envelopes at the bottom of the bag. He pulled them out and read the addresses on two of them. No idea where one was but he recognised Gran's address. He hadn't been there for a long time but he remembered the street and the house number because Gran had made him remember it, in case he had ever got lost. There was a stamp on it. Did Mum mean to post it? The other letter was for an address in London. He didn't recognise the name. That had a stamp too.

He put them to one side and looked at the bigger envelopes. He looked inside one with Mum's name and their address on the front and slid out another with a different address on it. Strange. He opened and slid out some sheets of paper. He could read names and addresses crowding the top part of the pages and saw that these were from a solicitor. He read the first paragraph, struggling a bit with the long sentences, but he understood that Harry was demanding access to Lu. The solicitor said it was Harry's right to have access to Lu. The date was four months ago. No wonder Mum had the plan ready - she knew Harry would be coming. The car, the cottage, all their stuff … she had planned it … she had known they would have to disappear. And they only managed two weeks before he found them. Jack felt heavy and sick inside. Harry wasn't supposed to know where they were, what they were called now but he was out there, looking for Lu. The police hadn't caught him, even though Jack had told them about him last night. He had got away and he would be looking for them. If he had seen them today, in the boat, he would follow them. Had he seen them? Jack wasn't sure. How could he keep Lu safe if Mum couldn't?

"What is it?" Rosie asked.

Jack shrugged and put the pages back in the envelopes and back in the bottom of the bag. He didn't want to tell her.

Chapter Thirty-Seven

Day 16: Saturday - Police - PC Anstey and DC Tizora

"How did we miss that? How did he find her when we couldn't? A child - a child - called it in! As if he hadn't been through enough when it all started!"

Tizora glanced across at Anstey as she drove them to the scene from the station after the morning briefing. "It's not our fault."

"It is - it's down to all of us. Witness protection. The solicitor. The social team. The parole people. I mean - who let him out! Look what he's done. He was a risk."

Tizora didn't have any answers. She'd been listening to him since they grabbed a coffee and pastry at the hotel and left for the station. She knew that she couldn't say anything to make him feel better about this case because she felt the same as he did, and she knew nothing anyone could say would make her feel anything other than angry and guilty.

"We can't change what has happened but we can get the next bit right."

He shrugged as she accelerated across an amber light.

In the lane leading to the crime scene access had been shut off and an officer checked ID before Tizora could drive slowly down the rutted lane to the cottage where teams were trying to find out what had happened. The senior officer at the scene spoke to them briefly and went back to the team in the orchard.

So, having failed to find Sal Williamson their job now was to help find the children. They stood and looked at the busy scene. Where to start?

Anstey and Tizora split up and after ten minutes met back at the cottage gate.

"Moreton was definitely here - prints in the cottage. No weapon but Williamson's blood is on the bark of a tree in the orchard, so it looks like he bashed her against it."

"Does it match head wounds?"

"It seems likely - checks on that are happening already. And there is some scuffling where she was found so it looks like she struggled. She's stable now, but unconscious still so she can't help us."

"Do you think the children were there? Or was she leading him away from the cottage? Funny place to be - in an orchard."

"What about the boathouse? What was there?"

Tizora showed Anstey a photo of a handwritten note.

"This matches Jack Williamson's handwriting, you remember the sample you got from the school? But this message is on the back," she showed him another photo. "It's not Jack's handwriting. It looks like a reply and there are signs of someone staying in the place. Was Jack was meeting someone there? If so, who? And where are they now?"

"Who does the boathouse belong to?" he asked.

"It goes with the cottage. And the owner is being tracked. We don't know if Williamson broke in or if the owner rented it to her or if they know each other."

"She's planned all this. She knew she would have to leave and she got the neighbours to help, and the lock-up owner, and the car owner and that friend who worked in the garage. She would have organised this place too. And I wouldn't be surprised if she hadn't got somewhere else planned to move on to." Anstey sounded impressed at Sal Williamson's planning. "But we let her down."

"And now we'll put some of it right." Tizora reminded him. "What else did you find out?"

"There's a shed back over that way. Someone's been in there recently. And no one uses this lane to get to anywhere so no one will have been passing by - it's almost perfect as a hide-away." Anstey looked along the hedgerows. "Where would he take two kids late evening? How would he get them away?"

"The car's still here, round the side behind the bushes." Tizora pointed back along the lane.

"Is there any evidence of another car? How did he get here?"

"Forensics are checking for other tyre marks. And there's a bike at the boat house - but it's old and looks small, too small for an adult to ride."

"They might have gone through the bushes and it's still wet enough to make footprints in the mud." Anstey set off to do a search and Tizora went to the door of the cottage to talk to whoever was working in there, to see if anything else had turned up.

As many of the team as could be pulled off their jobs were gathered in the lane by eight o'clock and asked what had been found. A briefing in the road wasn't ideal but they were the only ones around so they couldn't be overheard. The Boss [this one, here and now] was keen to get things done.

"Where are we? Anything to report back?"

One of the uniformed officers spoke up. "Definitely movement in the bushes around the cottage, and in the cottage gardens, and by the river. Mostly small, matches the Williamson kids' ages but there is another set too. Just as small, so a child."

"This other child then. We need to find out who that was. Someone who lives around here? Someone on holiday? Not likely in March but who knows. What else?"

This time the officer was one of those going through the cottage. "Sir, there were some phones in what we think is Sal Williamson's bag. They are all disabled but there are SIM cards."

"So she was off-grid. Does this place have wifi?"

"Not very likely. The owner can confirm."

"And - what else - that can't be it?" But it was - not much else yet. Too much to examine, too much to sift through. "Time is short. You know what Moreton can do. We have to find the children - especially if they're with him."

Anstey and Tizora leant on the bonnet of the car with a breakfast sandwich and coffee, waiting to be told what to do next.

"No signs of the kids in the area?"

"No," replied Tizora. "Local checks don't show any children about last night or this morning. No one on the only late bus noticed either a man and two kids, or two kids on their own. Someone checked the shop in the village downriver but the woman said she hadn't seen anything. Oh, and a dog walker said he'd heard the noise last night but hadn't seen anyone."

Anstey ate through his sandwich, thinking. Where to look?

Just as they were finishing, an officer came running back from along the road.

"Sir!"

They stood up hoping for good news.

The officer doubled over and wheezed. "Dead body!"

Anstey felt a sickening rush of adrenalin. Not the children?

"Who? Where?" asked the Boss.

"Caravan. Not the kids, at least I don't think so."

Ten minutes later the scene was secure but ... The Boss was not happy. He glared at his officers as they gathered in the road again.

"Does anyone know what is actually happening here? It's taken how many hours to discover a dead body only yards away from a crime scene you've all been working on? A crime scene you are all responsible for."

Tizora ducked her head down and slid to one side, behind a PC carrying a box to a van. Anstey looked at his shoes and scuffed at the patchy grass. This wasn't going well.

"Any ideas?"

"Sir, it's getting complicated."

"I can see that."

"But I don't think this body is linked - not to the attack," said the officer who'd found the body.

"How do you know?"

"It's probably been here for some time, several days ..."

"After Sal Williamson arrived?"

"Er, possibly ..."

The Boss stared stared at the DS who'd spoken. "So it could be linked then? Try not to let 'thinking' get in the way of facts."

"Er, no sir."

"Any identification yet?"

"Robin Bushey. A university student, a London college, final year."

"What's he doing dead in a caravan in Norfolk in March?"
"Er, not sure yet, sir."

Later, at the hotel, Anstey and Tizora sat in the empty lounge and talked about the day. It had plodded on with evidence being collected, files being updated and leads being followed. The incident room had been busy, very busy. And they were unsure how much they'd helped. They'd been sent to interview the neighbours - all of them too far away from the cottage to have seen or heard anything. They'd uploaded their notes onto the system with a reminder that Rowley Farm needed to be re-visited because no one had been home when they called. They took time to read all the files as they were put onto the system so they did learn some information.

They had learned that the cottage owner did know Sal Williamson, that Sal had met her many years before and they had kept in touch even when Sal had moved, and that Sal had asked if she could borrow the cottage, left to her by a relative. She had said yes, of course. She knew that if Sal had asked, she must really need it, because there was no wifi and the phone signal was sporadic and the cottage needed a lot of work doing on it. And, yes, she thought there was a boat but she wasn't sure if it would still be there.

They had learned that Robin Bushey hadn't been in college since February Reading Week. {*A bit like school half-term.*} He hadn't been to any lectures or seminars and his house-mates hadn't seen him. His mother was dead and his father was in New Zealand. There may have been a step-father but he was being traced.

They learned that Sal Williamson was still critical but her recovery was more likely now. Her mother was coming up to be with her.

"So, what do you think will happen tomorrow? Will we be sent home?" Anstey didn't want to go home. He wanted to finish this case.

Tizora shrugged. "I think we know too much," she said. "We could be useful, we're up to speed with the case."

"Sal Williamson deserves us to pick up where she left it. She was trying to protect her children from Moreton so we have to do that for her."

Tizora nodded. "But it's complicated."

{It is very complicated, putting all the clues together. Like Anstey said a few days ago, you have to join the links. Have you worked out who Robin Bushey might be linked to yet? I gave you a clue earlier.}

Chapter Thirty-Eight

Day 17: Sunday Morning - Jack, Rosie and Lu

The next morning after breakfast Jack packed up their bags more carefully than they had yesterday. He tidied up the cabin and made sure Rosie saw him put some coins next the empty (and rinsed clean) soup tins. As they closed the door behind them he felt a bit better about squatting in someone's cabin. And, although he was grateful for being inside during the night, where it felt safer than being in the boat in open country, he did feel better being back outside, where he could see places to run to, to hide in. There had only been one door in the cabin, and a couple of small windows, not enough escape routes.

As he sat on the middle seat ready to row, Jack felt his muscles twitch. The seat was just as hard as yesterday, the oar still felt rough in his hands and as they pulled out into the stream he felt his shoulders scream a protest. How long could they row today?

Lu was fretful; she didn't like being in the boat again. She began a low grizzle which Jack knew well. After ten minutes, just as they pulled back into the bigger river from yesterday, she was moving about the boat too much. Jack couldn't concentrate on keeping a steady rhythm as he had to check her constantly. The boat was rocking and progress was slow.

"No point," Rosie said, as she stopped.

"You sit with her, read, draw, whatever. I'll row," Jack said. "We'll take turns."

Rosie shuffled down to sit with Lu and for ten minutes Jack rowed slowly, mostly because his shoulders and arms were hurting so much, but also because it was so much harder to row without someone sitting next to you, keeping you to a rhythm. They passed reeds, ducks and more reeds. Jack and Rosie didn't talk, not to each other, only to Lu. They hadn't really talked since last evening apart from a couple of short sentences, like 'I'll pack the boat.'

Rosie swapped and Jack sat with Lu, who was getting difficult to keep still.

"We'll have to stop somewhere," he said. "I can't get her settled."

Rosie didn't glare this time. She pulled at the oars without looking up.

Jack reached for the grab bag and found the Arnica. He didn't know if it would help - it was for bruises not aching muscles but he wanted to try. He pulled off his lifejacket, hoody and teeshirt and managed to get some rubbed into his arms and shoulders, where it hurt the most. He pulled his clothes on and swapped with Rosie. She looked at the tube for a few seconds. How much did she really need this? She settled for taking off her lifejacket and jumper and managed to rub some in under her teeshirt. Lu climbed over and held up her hand. Rosie stared at her but when Lu moved nearer and thrust her hand out, she put a blob on it so Lu didn't feel left out, before putting the tube back in the bag.

Jack managed another ten minutes before swapping with Rosie. The river, backwater, whatever it was - Jack didn't know and really didn't care as he just wanted to be somewhere less watery - was definitely heading somewhere busier. Some hikers walked past, the same ones as yesterday? A motor boat chugged past, the owner waving as she squeezed past on one side. A dead feathery something brushed the side of the boat as Rosie pulled them out onto a wider stretch. A couple of ducks stared at them as they rowed past, the swell making them bob about, disturbing the peace. The footpath was wider here and Jack could hear that hum which he now knew was a road nearby.

"Let's stop and walk," he suggested. "It'll be quicker."

"Too far," Rosie disagreed.

"Buses?"

She snorted. "Only if you want to catch one next Wednesday."

He found the book and opened it at the map page. He had no idea where they were. There was nothing along the waterways to show you where you were, not like in towns where there were street names and road signs. Rosie stopped rowing and pulled the map out of his hands.

"Here, we're here, or near enough here."

Jack looked at the map. How did she know? He thought they could be anywhere along any of those blue lines. And if she was right - they hadn't come very far. He slumped down. They wouldn't be able to get to Rosie's family by rowing the boat. It would take too long - especially for Lu. They needed another plan.

Rosie traced her finger across the map.

"It's too far, I knew it would be, even with two of us," she said in a very quiet voice. "I'll have to go back."

Jack grabbed Lu as she leant over the side of the boat, laughing as she made it rock.

"No, we can find a way." He sat holding Lu as she wriggled and rocked the boat. "Where's the nearest village or town? How long will it take us to row there?" He found a sweet in his backpack and gave it to Lu.

Rosie looked back at the map. "There's somewhere not too far. We could get there by late morning, if we took it in turns to row, and if we moored up and checked it out, we could decide what to do. We need more food anyway and there'll be a shop."

Jack nodded. "Let's get there and decide."

Rosie set off again while Jack tried to keep Lu still. It was slow with just one person rowing and it was tiring and stressful keeping Lu still. But there were more boats out on the stretch they were travelling down and there was a footpath again so they felt they were making some progress towards getting somewhere. Jack walked with Lu on the path part of the way and swapped with Rosie every so often but he felt exposed on the path, so he kept looking around in case that red hat came in sight. The morning passed very slowly and he was weary by the time they rowed under a bridge and moored just outside the village, Rosie tying up at a small jetty.

"Can we do that?" he asked.

"What?"

"Moor here? It's someone's house."

"It's someone's holiday place, and they're not here now, they won't know."

Jack looked around. He could see another cottage, lodge or whatever, next door, shielded by some trees and bushes, and he went across and peered through. It looked empty too. He checked the other side and it looked as if Rosie was right, no one was here now. Out at the front there was a road of sorts, narrow and full of potholes. It wound along through some trees and bushes following the line of the river as far as he could tell. It all looked deserted.

Rosie was opening the door to the cottage when he went back.

"What are you doing?"

"We need to check it out."

"Why? We're not stopping here. We can't just break into every house you feel like."

Rosie ignored him and went in. He fetched Lu and tentatively went in too. He felt like he was intruding somehow as he looked around at the main room, at the little cupboards and the table and chairs and the bookcase.

"TV," announced Lu. She climbed onto the sofa and was aiming the remote at the screen sitting on a small table in the corner.

"No, Lu," he said and he took the remote from her. She screwed up her face and opened her mouth wide.

"Ice cream, Lu," said Jack. "Shops and ice cream."

Lu stopped. Her face contorted even more as she struggled with two things she liked - TV and ice cream - she didn't know which one she wanted more.

"Lu," Jack said, holding out his hand to her, " We'll go to the shops and get some ice cream and then come back for TV."

Lu thought about it. She slid off the sofa, took his hand and headed to the door. "Choc ice cream?"

"Choc ice cream," Jack agreed, hoping the village shop sold ice cream - any sort with chocolate would do.

They put their bags in the cottage just by the front door, locked it up with Rosie pocketing the key she'd found, and set off down the road. Lu happily ran on in front of them and soon they reached a proper road, still small but one which cars could actually drive along and pass each other - just about. By the time they'd reached the next road they saw they were almost in the village. Houses lined one side of the road and there was even a sign announcing they were welcome in Branksome - please drive carefully. Jack held Lu's hand now and they walked more closely together. Jack still found it strange that there was no one walking about. At home, he always found someone to hang about with when he went down to the streets, but here, there wasn't anyone at all. He thought it must be very lonely growing up here. Where could you go? Who could you hang out with? He wondered how Rosie managed living on the farm, especially as she didn't go to school.

This village seemed a bit bigger than the last one they'd shopped at - that he'd shopped at. There was a shop but it didn't open until 10 as it was Sunday.

"How long before they open?" Jack asked. Lu was pushing at the door.

Rosie shrugged. Helpful, as ever, he thought. He looked around. The church had a tower and a clock.

"Is that right do you think?" he asked, nodding up to the clock. He took Lu's hand and pulled her off the shop's step and back on to the pavement.

Rosie squinted - and shrugged.

"Then let's work on it being right so we've got five minutes. Hide-and-seek Lu."

Lu let herself be lead away and Jack headed to a side street. He had no idea if there was a park but needed to get them away from the main road where there was more chance of them being seen. Jack watched Lu and kept his eye on a dog walker - another one - crossing the road. So, after they had been to the shop and then back to the cottage, what next?

Lu hid happily until Jack thought the shop would be open and they set off back to the main street. A car passed them, and a cat stared at them, and someone on a bike flashed past wearing fluorescent lycra and a crash hat, but there didn't seem to be anyone else as Jack scanned the street.

They pushed open the door of the shop and went inside. This was bigger than Jack expected and Lu ran off to the freezer set against a far wall. The lady behind the till looked up from her book and frowned.

"What do you all want?"

Jack smiled. "Good morning, we're just picking up some shopping. Do you have chocolate ice cream? It's my sister's favourite."

The lady frowned harder. "Are you here on your own? We don't like too many children at once - never know what they'll get up to."

Jack gripped Rosie's arm as he felt her move forward to snap at the woman. "We're here on holiday, we're having a lovely time."

The woman sniffed. "That's nice. Ice cream is in the freezer. Don't mess it up."

"Thank you," Jack smiled and lead Rosie down to the freezer where Lu was trying to push up the lid. Even if she'd opened it, she wasn't tall enough to look inside. Jack opened it and pulled Rosie close. He could whispered, "Get what we want and get out quick."

"Why?"

"Newspaper."

He found a tub of chocolate ice cream, and they picked up some bread, bananas, apples, biscuits and crisps - again - and piled it in a heap onto the counter.

"I'll just be outside," Rosie said and she took Lu out onto the street.

Jack filled the bag he'd brought as the woman, Dot her name badge said, still frowning at him, scanned the items through the till.

"I heard there's a train museum nearby," Jack said brightly. "My dad is thinking of taking us there tomorrow. Is it good?"

Dot stared at him suspiciously. "It's very interesting." The frown was definitely intense.

Jack handed over some money. "That's good to know. We like interesting places."

Dot handed him some change and sniffed again. As he left he saw she was already back to her book. He breathed out slowly. She didn't seem to have taken much notice of them. Queenie, in that first supermarket, would have done, and the knitting lady in the last little shop.

He swung past Rosie and walked quickly back along the road.

Rosie half ran to keep up, pulling Lu behind her.

"What is it? What happened?"

"Nothing. Just get off this road quick."

They found their way back to the lane leading to the cottage and then Jack slowed down.

"The newspaper, on the counter. It had about my mum. And a picture of Harry."

"Why didn't you buy one?"

"Didn't want her to see the picture near me."

Rosie thought about that. She nodded. "How much was a paper?"

He shrugged.

"Give me some money, I'll go and get one. We need to know."

"But she'll get suspicious."

"Not if it's me. I'll say we forgot to get one."

"Say it's for our dad."

He dug into his coat pocket and found some coins. He handed some over and she handed him the cottage key and he watched briefly as she ran off back to the shop before turning and taking Lu back to the cottage.

He'd only just settled Lu with some ice cream when Rosie came back and put the paper flat on the table.

"Here. Your mum's okay." She almost smiled.

Jack looked at the front page. The images and words swam around so he sat next to Lu and carefully read the article. He learned that Mum was safe, in hospital with some injuries, but safe. He had felt a heavy feeling in his stomach since they'd left the fishing lodge but now he felt so much lighter inside. She was safe, being cared for. Lu dripped some ice cream onto the paper as she leaned over to join in with whatever game she thought Jack was playing. She spooned more ice cream into her sticky mouth and smiled happily. Jack read the front page and turned to the inside to read the several related articles that had made the news today.

Rosie made a jam sandwich and put it in front of him, with a bag of crisps. She sat and ate on the other side of the table and gave Lu some crisps as a healthier alternative to more ice cream.

Jack folded the paper and began to eat.

"Well?" Rosie asked.

He slid the paper over and she read through as he had just done. He carefully looked away as she read the page with Harry's face glaring from a double page spread, detailing the events of four years ago and warning people not to approach him - he's dangerous. The photo must have been recent because Harry's face looked more wrinkled than Jack remembered. Perhaps it was from prison, Jack thought. And he knew he had also changed. He wasn't seven anymore so he looked different too. There wasn't a proper photo of Mum, just an old one from before Lu was born. Mum had been really careful to avoid having her photo taken, especially when they were out with a group of people. She didn't want anyone posting a photo with her in the background - she needed to have disappeared.

They sat eating in silence until Lu needed cleaning up and once she was watching a DVD on the TV Jack and Rosie sat back at the table together.

"I'm sorry," Rosie said.

"Why?"

"I don't know, but I'm sorry - your mum and — him …"

Jack shrugged. "It happened, can't change it."

"Is Lu like she is because…?"

Jack nodded.

"Can't they do anything?"

"When she's older. They can straighten her face when she's stopped growing, so a long time away. I need to keep her safe," Jack said. "Away from him while Mum is in hospital. She'll know what to do."

Rosie flipped back through the paper. "If they catch him, that would be okay wouldn't it? He'd be locked up, back in prison?"

"Probably," Jack nodded, "But how long for? He might get bail and then he'd back looking for us."

"If you go to the police, they'll keep you safe."

"But where would they put us while Mum is in hospital? In care? Together? We can't go to anyone he knows about. I can't risk her being taken away."

Rosie flipped through the articles again. "They don't say anything about you and Lu. Do they know you were there?"

"They must. The police must know, our stuff was in the cottage but perhaps they haven't said yet. It's only been …" Jack thought. How long had it been? One day? Two nights and one day … and now today. So, how long would it be before the news papers had his school photo plastered all over the front pages? Once that had happened he wouldn't be able to go anywhere where there were people. He pulled his fingers through his hair and stretched up and outwards. He felt tired and achy. And he didn't know what to do. He got up and began washing up the kitchen things they'd used. There wasn't a tea towel so he stacked the plates and cutlery on the draining board to dry.

Rosie was re-reading the articles. "I don't think the police have told the news people about you yet. If they had there would be photos and everyone would be out searching for you; they always do when kids go missing. If they know Harry's out there, they'd want you found before he gets hold of you. All this just says is that Harry attacked your mum, she's stable - whatever that means - and they're looking for him."

Jack sat down again and thought about that. Rosie was right. Why hadn't the police started a search for him and Lu? Or had they - and the newspapers just hadn't written about it yet. He sighed. He needed the internet. He needed a phone and a connection. Or he needed a TV that actually showed live TV so he could watch the news channels.

"I think we need to find out what everyone actually knows now," said Rosie, "Not what a paper says that was written yesterday."

Jack nodded. "I was thinking the same thing. Internet. Where can we get internet. Or TV that works."

"There are other places, like this one. Some must have a connection. It's not good around here, you lose the signal every time you move from one road to another one but there must be a place near here with something that works. Or we have to steal a phone that works."

Jack had always thought criminals were adults who lived in towns but Rosie stole and broke into places and used what she wanted to, and didn't seem to feel guilty.

"I'll check out this road," she said. "You stay here with Lu while she's quiet."

She slipped out and Jack sat with Lu on the sofa and watched the cartoon characters fling themselves across the screen. Lu sat as close to him as she could squeeze herself and held his hand tightly. He knew she was beginning to feel anxious and he didn't have much medication left. Mum would have brought what they had had in the flat but it was time to get some more. Another problem he didn't know what to do about. He pulled the Norfolk book from his backpack and opened out the map page. Lu looked at it and pointed at the blue patches.

"Blue," she said.

"Yes, blue. Rivers and lakes."

She traced some with her fingers. "Not wet."

"No, it's a picture, a drawing, not real."

Lu frowned but she looked back at the TV and sank closer to Jack's side.

Jack found the tiny dot that was Branksome and checked the route to Lowestoft if they carried on by river. As a plan it had made sense. Get Rosie to people who would care for her. But now he knew it was just too far, even with both of them rowing and she wouldn't get anywhere near it on her own. If he stayed with her they might get a bit further on. If he left her she wouldn't get very far alone. He checked how far they'd come so far and measured it roughly with his hand. That far in a couple of days, well - almost a couple of days, there was still time today to move on. They could get to - he found a point on the map - here by the end of tomorrow. Rosie could get a bus from that town or village. He and Lu would have to find somewhere to hide. A place like this one, but on its own, empty.

Rosie came back in and closed the door quietly. She held her finger to her lips and pointed to the plot next door.

"Gardener!" she hissed.

Jack groped for the remote and turned the sound down on the TV. Lu stared at him and opened her mouth to complain. He put his hand over her mouth and sank down to the floor with her. "Game Lu. As quiet as mice." She giggled and lay flat and still. Rosie joined them and they lay in a line on a musty rug, listening. Then, just as Jack knew Lu's patience would be wearing out, the noisy chug of a petrol mower split the quiet.

"Now," said Rosie. She got up, grabbed a bag by the door and headed to the kitchen area. Jack joined her and they crammed in everything they could before collecting the other bags from the front door and creeping out. Keeping low they made their way to the road, Jack following Rosie's lead. Lu thought it was a game still and she hopped along happily at the side of the road, pretending she was hiding. A little way along Rosie turned onto a drive of sorts and they went to the back of yet another holiday cottage. They squatted down out of sight behind a little shed.

"What are we going to do now?" Jack hissed. "The boat? How do we get it back?"

Rosie shrugged.

"Why couldn't we have stayed there, being quiet? He would have left."

She shook her head. "Sometimes, usually, they do lots of places, a whole row, and the cleaners come along like that too, getting the places ready for people."

Jack peered round the shed. "He might come here then?"

They looked at the garden surrounding the wooden lodge facing the road. It was definitely in need of some serious grass cutting.

"What about the boat?" Jack asked. "He'll see it."

"Did we leave anything in it?"

"Lifejackets? The bucket?"

Lu had found a little spade and she was digging in the soil next to a dried out bush.

Rosie sat down and piled the bags in a heap. Jack made sure the grab bag and his backpack were there - anything else was a bonus.

"So, how do we get the boat back? Wait until he's gone?"

Rosie shook her head. "I've got an idea. Where's the map?"

Jack shook his head. "Must be on the sofa. I was looking at it when you came in."

"No worries. I'll be back."

Jack caught her arm as she stood up. "Where are you going? Not to get the map?"

She shook her head. "Wait here." She scuttled off in a crouch leaving Jack sitting behind a shed on someone's property. He sat with his back against the shed wall and looked at Lu as she got happily dirty. How did they get here - like this - hiding behind a shed in the middle of nowhere?

"Wee," announced Lu. Oh - really? He stood and looked over to the lodge. It was empty. It had a bathroom. How could he get in? He was beginning to think like Rosie. What would Mum say?

Chapter Thirty-Nine

Day 17: Sunday Morning - Police - PC Anstey and DC Tizora

Anstey and Tizora hadn't been sent home - there was so much to do and The Boss here wanted everyone he could get to help with the search.

"It's in the paper already." Tizora said. She shook open more pages in the paper she'd picked up at the hotel when they left very early on Sunday morning.

Anstey nodded, concentrating on finding his way from the hotel to the cottage. "Could help but there will be so much time wasted dealing with all the idiots who just want to be involved, who don't know anything but say they do - you know, they saw the kids or Moreton in a Sainsbury's {*Other supermarkets conveniently available*} when they didn't, or there's someone hiding in the next-door-neighbour's shed just so the police turn up and search just because they don't like the neighbour."

"That's a bit harsh."

"True though."

Anstey pulled up and showed the officer his ID so they could drive down to the cottage. He had to park close to the hedgerow and Tizora had to squeeze out. She looked through a gap in the hedge.

"It's all fields - what does anyone do around here?"

"What? Too quiet for you? A murder? An assault? Two missing kids?" She grimaced. "See what you mean."

They checked in with the remaining teams and were disappointed to find not much more than had been already put on the files they read before briefing at the station first thing this morning.

Their job today was to continue interviewing anyone living in the area. The map had to be expanded to get any idea of anywhere that someone might live. Farms were often just a dot with no name. They headed back to the biggest dot, Rowley farm, hoping someone would be in today. The lane wove towards some buildings and it did look as if it had been thriving once. It was run down from the outside and there didn't seem to be much going on. Tizora expected to see cows and chickens and tractors and bales of hay - the yard was empty, and there was no one home. They peered through a window into a cluttered kitchen.

"Who lives here?"

Anstey checked a file on his phone. "Frank Rowley."

"Call back later?"

"Yes, there's too much ground to cover to worry about this one … but, while we're here, let's have a look around. Moreton might have have found his way here, or the children."

They split up. Anstey found his way round to the front and saw a partly open bedroom window and some squashed bushes by the front door, which looked as if it hadn't been opened for a long time if the spiders' webs were anything to go by. He peered in through the window into what looked like an office. It was tidier than the kitchen but it looked like someone had left in a rush.

"**Anstey! Get round here!**" He made his way back and found Tizora hanging on to a broken window frame with a ladder lying flat on the ground beneath her.

He grabbed her legs and held onto her. "I've got you!"

She swivelled and began to fall backwards. "Anstey! **Let go!**"

"I've got you! " he shouted as they both fell back onto the yard in a a heap.

Slowly they untangled themselves and sat up on the ground.

"What did you do that for?"

"What? I saved you!"

"You pulled me down."

"And … you're okay … so … ?"

Tizora glared at him as she pulled herself to her feet and brushed the dirt off her clothes. "You just needed to put the ladder back where I could reach it!"

Anstey looked at the ladder and then at the broken window. "Oh."

"Anstey, it's going to be a long day if you don't start thinking."

"Sorry. I didn't sleep very well. Strange bed and all that. And it was noisy. People were coming in late."

"It's a hotel."

"Yes, but …" He stopped himself in case Tizora thought he was whining as an excuse for not thinking. "Round the front there's a window cracked open upstairs and some crushed bushes and an office which looks as if someone has emptied all the files and boxes."

Tizora pulled out her phone. "We need to check who this Rowley is. You check the other buildings - but be careful in case Moreton is around."

While Anstey checked out the farm Tizora called the incident room and asked about the farm. When he got back she was still talking to someone. She stared at Anstey as she ended the call. "The Boss is on his way. Rowley is Robin Bushey's step-dad."

Anstey stared back. "No! The dead body? In the caravan?"

Tizora nodded.

"But," Anstey asked, "Why was he in the caravan if his step-dad lived here?"

"That's what detecting is all about Anstey. Finding out. And finding this Frank Rowley?"

"Do you think … Moreton …?"

Tizora shook her head. "Robin Bushey was dead long before Moreton got here. It's just a coincidence that we have two crimes scenes next to each other. I can't see anything linking Rowley and the Williamsons."

{*Did you make a link? It's still a mystery but keep reading and you'll find the answer.*}

An hour later, once The Boss and a team had turned up to investigate the farm, Tizora and Anstey set off to continue with their search in the area. Tizora drove them back to the road to find the next place they were supposed to be checking out that morning.

As they crossed the bridge near the lane to the cottage Anstey said, "Pull over."

They looked across the field from the car. "Over there, a bunker."

Tizora looked where he was pointing. "Too obvious. Someone will have done that already."

"Yes, I suppose so."

They drove only a very short way before Anstey told her to pull over again. "Down there." He pointed back across the road.

"What?"

"A track."

They parked and got out, and then walked in single file along the track until it opened out onto a clearing. There was a wooden building, single storey and with peeling paint. They went round to the front and looked out across the river.

"If you look that way, you can almost see the cottage - or nearly as far as there."

Anstey looked back at the lodge. "This must be it. They must have been here - watching. Someone could have phoned from here."

Tizora pulled at the door and was surprised when it opened a crack. It had been opened recently.

"There's a key somewhere," said Tizora.

They began to search the area. Anstey noticed a pot that had been moved. Under it was a key. They let themselves in and saw that someone had been in not long ago. Things weren't straight.

"Who was here? Could have been anyone."

Anstey bent down and pulled a one armed doll from under a cushion on the sofa bed. He held it up for Tizora to see and raised one eyebrow. {*Tried it yet?.*}

While Tizora waited by the side of the road to direct the team down the half-hidden track, Anstey was by the lodge. He stared at the river, looking back along as far as he could see before the bend. He looked at a lone duck as its paddled its way past. Then he phoned Tizora.

"The reeds are bent, a boat came in here."

Tizora paused before she said, "The boathouse - they came by boat." She phoned it in straight away. The rivers needed searching as well as the roads. It was getting even more complicated.

A couple of hours later one of the team came out of the lodge to tell them what had been found so far.

"Lots of fingerprints but definitely those of the Williamson boy and some smaller ones that might belong to the girl. There are some additional prints that seem recent, possibly linked, but we don't have those on file."

"So, not Moreton?"

"No, nothing to say he was here."

Good news, the children weren't with Moreton. Not so good news, they weren't here now and they probably came by boat.

"How do you find someone who's using a boat?" Anstey asked. "There are so many rivers and ... whatever these are." He enlarged the map on his phone and pointed to some blue lines. "They could be anywhere."

"What kind of boat was it, do you think?"

Anstey shrugged. "What kind of boat could an eleven year old manage? Did Jack know how to row? Or sail?"

"I don't think it's easy to sail, and you need wind. And he had Lu to think about. Imagine a four year old on a boat! Nightmare."

Anstey pointed at the map again. "If we drive along here, it's running parallel with the river. There's a farm, we can check there, and then along here there's a village, we can check there, too."

Tizora nodded. They went back to the car and as she drove Anstey up-dated those who needed to know by phone. A team was looking for Moreton, and one place had been eliminated, and it looked as if he wasn't with the children.

The farmer was helpful. He hadn't seen anyone but he wanted to show them something. In a barn there was a corner where things had been moved, he thought someone had stayed there overnight.

"Don't you have dogs? No barking?"

"No, not anymore. Too expensive to keep and no use for them here. And I think - or at least my wife thinks - someone got into the henhouse. The latch was loose, not tight shut and she always shuts it tight, foxes get in otherwise."

"Thanks, that's helpful."

"Is it to do with that attack? Down the road?"

"Possibly - too early to say. Someone will be here shortly to check this out. Please don't touch anything or move anything."

The farmer nodded. "Things like that don't happen round here. Too quiet - just how I like it."

In the village the shop was open and as Tizora pushed open the door the lady behind the glass partition stood up quickly. Then she looked disappointed.

"Oh! I thought you might be police again. They came yesterday and after the news I thought they might come back. Such a thing to happen here."

"I am the police, madam." Tizora showed her ID and the lady put down her knitting and came round to talk to her. Once Anstey had squeezed in behind her, it was so cramped Tizora felt like suggesting they moved into the street.

"Oh what a shock. Nothing like that happens round here, it's not like in towns with stabbings and fights and attacks. At least they weren't locals - we don't behave like that. I hope it doesn't put the visitors off, terrible for trade and we need it, you know, to keep going …"

"And have you thought of anything that might be useful, since you spoke to the officer before?" interrupted Anstey.

"Oh no. It's been quiet, it always as is. The holiday makers haven't started yet. Except, there was a lad, shopping for his mum."

"When? What day?"

"A few days ago. And then yesterday. I told him about the museum, he said they would go along."

"Was he alone? No one with him? Parent? Another child?"

She shook her head. "No, he said he knew what to get. He could add up too, knew what it would cost."

Tizora found a photo of Jack Williamson/Jake Sinclair. "Is this him, the boy you saw?

"Yes, - well, he was older, scruffier. Could have done with a tidy up. But yes, that was him."

Tizora found a photo of Moreton. "What about this man?"

"Is that him? That madman?"

"Have you seen him?"

The lady looked hard at the photo. "I don't think so. A man came in yesterday, just after that boy was in here. He had a red hat on, pulled low over his eyes. And glasses, dark lenses, sort of sunglasses - in March!"

"What did he want?"

"Crisps, a bottle of water. Nothing very much. He was very polite. He said he used to come on holiday here and was in the area and thought he'd check it out. Happy memories."

"Is there a camera?"

"In here? There's one for the post-office." She pointed behind the partition. "Up there."

Tizora was almost ready to burst but she held it in until they got outside and then punched Anstey on his arm. "Result!"

"Not yet. The kids are still missing."

"But we're on their trail."

"And so is Moreton."

Tizora stopped dancing about on the shop step.

"Shall we wait for the team to check the footage?"

Anstey checked the time. "There's still some light left. Let's move on."

"Where? Down river?"

"The next dot on the map?" Anstey looked it up. And off they went.

The river and the road parted company. They drove on and then doubled back and set off up tracks and even walked across a field to a hut but there was nothing. They came back to the village and knocked at all the doors. Some places were empty and those that were lived in, didn't give up anymore clues, as there was no-one home. It was obvious the children had disappeared up a waterway and hidden away. They were not going to find them until they emerged from the rivers to somewhere where there were people or cameras. The only positive in the last couple of hours was confirmation from the camera footage that Moreton had stopped at the shop.

It was early afternoon when they headed back to the station to update files.

So close - only a step away, thought Tizora.

So close - only a step behind, thought Anstey.

Chapter Forty

Day 17: Sunday Afternoon - Jack, Rosie and Lu

Jack and Lu were sitting on the step by the back door when Rosie came back. Lu was playing with a box of toys Jack had found in the lodge and he was eating an apple, one they'd bought not stolen.

Rosie gestured for him to wait and she went inside. He could hear some thumps and creaks and guessed she was using the bathroom. She came out holding a glass of water and sat next to him. She drained the glass before she spoke.

"Right, I went back nearer the village, where the proper houses are. There's one that looks empty now so we can get in and …"

"What? Break in?"

"Why not? You broke in here?"

"But this isn't a proper house!" Jack grimaced as he thought about the key safe he'd wrenched from the wall to get at the key to get into the lodge.

"It's still not yours to break into, is it? What's the difference?"

"It's not right."

"Who's to say? You broke into that caravan …"

"Didn't." The memory of the stench made Jack look grimly at the apple before he threw it across the garden into the bushes. "It was open. I didn't break in."

"You weren't asked in … you just went in. And you broke in at the farm. You broke into the stable."

"So did you."

"I live there, remember."

Jack stood up and walked away. He shoved his hands in his pockets and pulled up his hood so Rosie couldn't see his face. He stood scuffing the ground with one foot. He wanted to say 'My mum wouldn't like it' but he didn't think Rosie would understand. He went further away and sat on a half-broken garden chair so he could think. He could hear some distant humming, probably from a road, and he concentrated on emptying everything from his head and focussed on the sound of the humming. Gradually he felt the stress lift and he focussed on his breathing. He thought of some good things; Mum smiling, Lu laughing, running across the park with Milo … in a couple of minutes he felt calm and ready to think. He'd been doing this for four years, since … well, since it all happened. It was supposed to help him cope with stress and panic. It did. And he was good at doing it because he'd had lots of practice. Not so much in the past year or so, but lots of practice anyway. He could sit almost anywhere now and calm himself down. He got up and went to sit back on the step.

"We have to do two things," he said. "First, get you to your gran. Second, keep me and Lu safe until Mum can say what to do. We just have to find a way of doing them both."

Rosie nodded. "We can't row anymore, it's just too hard and too far. So, we need a different way to get there. And we need to know who's looking for you. Just Harry, or Harry and the police."

"Won't your dad …"

"Step-dad."

"... Step-dad, then ... be looking for you? Won't he have reported you missing? You've been gone for days."

Rosie snorted. That's no, then, thought Jack.

"Let's go to the place I found, check the news and ... There's a bus stop, and a bus at 2 ..."

"Not next Wednesday then?"

Rosie paused and said, "At 2."

"How much time have we got?"

"Just over an hour."

"Let's get on with it then."

They shut the lodge, putting the key back in the broken key safe.

The road was quiet but they moved quickly, as Rosie led them to a bungalow just at the edge of town near the welcome sign. They went down the side of the building, through an unlocked gate and into a well-kept garden. There was some washing hanging on the line, a fish pond (as if there wasn't enough water everywhere around, thought Jack) and a greenhouse with some tidy rows of trays lined up on the benches.

"Someone lives here!"

"That's the point. They'll have internet."

"Aren't they here? They'll see us."

Rosie stared at him. "It's *empty*, that's why I chose it. They must be at work, no car."

"They might not have one."

"There's a mark on the drive, oil probably, so they must have one."

Jack still wasn't sure but he crept to the back door, shushing Lu and dragging the bags behind him. Rosie reached up and pushed a window open. She climbed onto the sill and slid inside. Jack tensed, not breathing, waiting for a scream as someone saw her in their house. The kitchen door opened and Rosie peered out.

"Come on."

It was too easy, Jack thought as he led Lu inside and closed the door. Didn't anyone around here think about security? Where were the cameras? The alarms?

Lu climbed on a chair at the kitchen table and pulled a round tin towards her.

"Cake," she said. Jack took it from her and opened it.

"Biscuits," he said. Lu took one in each hand and slid off the chair and headed into the hallway.

They found the living room and switched on the TV. Rosie scanned down until they found a news channel. It was coming up to the hour and while Jack waited for the headlines and Lu sat munching on her biscuits, Rosie checked out the other rooms.

"It's started," Jack called and she came back and sat on the sofa.

The newsreader began by listing what was going to be on this news programme - and the story about Mum and Harry was top of the list. Jack didn't hear the rest, his head was buzzing and he felt as if he couldn't breathe. Lu wiped a sticky hand on the sofa as she slipped off and ran to the TV as Mum's picture filled the screen.

"MUM!" she called excitedly. The screen changed as she got there and she stood in front of the TV screwing her face into a howl. Jack went to her and sat down, pulling her next to him on the floor. "Let's watch, Lu, she'll be back."

They sat together, with Rosie still on the sofa, Lu snuffling and trying to touch the screen.

Jack listened as the newsreader said that a massive police search was underway locating the whereabouts of dangerous convicted criminal Harry Moreton, also known as Harry Bates and Harry Debden, following a frenzied attack on a former partner Sal Williamson.

Lu smacked a hand against the screen as a photo of Mum reappeared. "MUM!" she whined.

"Watch, Lu," Jack said as he pulled her hand away. "Listen."

Jack watched closely as the newsreader told him that an anonymous call had tipped off the police who had found Ms Williamson seriously injured and the suspected perpetrator fled from the scene. Forensics established the identity of the suspect and police urged the public not to approach him. as he was known to be violent and to report any sightings. The whereabouts of two children, thought to have been at the cottage at some point, was unknown. There was to be a statement from the police later today, updating the situation. The news then moved on to a fishing accident at sea.

Jack sat back from the TV while Lu kissed the screen and whined "Where's Mum?"

Well, what next?

Rosie sat next to him and muted the sound with the remote. "So, they haven't said exactly who they're looking for yet. We can get further on before they put you all over the news."

"But where can we go, me and Lu?"

"My gran, she'll know what to do."

Jack wasn't so sure. This gran hadn't tried to do anything for Rosie - why would she help him?

"They'll be looking for a boy and a girl."

"So?"

"Not three boys, brothers, on holiday."

Jack looked at Rosie. "Plan?"

She nodded. "Come and look."

They went out into the hall and crossed into a bedroom. It was a boy's room, with bunkbeds and dinosaur bedding, with blue curtains and khaki plastic toys - and mess.

"We dress Lu as a boy." She opened the cupboard and pulled out a drawer. "And … me too." She held up a dark hoody against her. "See?"

"So, we're stealing clothes now, as well as breaking in."

"Have you got any better ideas? Hand yourself in and lose Lu? Get caught by Harry? Hide in a ditch somewhere?"

Jack sighed. He didn't have another idea. There was realistically, no way he could get to his own gran, on his own (but with Lu of course) and anyway Harry knew who Gran was and where she lived so until the police caught him it wouldn't be safe to go there. Or to Stacey and Taz's or to Milo's. And it was too far anyway, a whole night's drive away so too far to walk. And they couldn't go back to the cottage as the police would still be around. Or to the farm as Frank was there. He already knew all this; he was going round in circles trying to find a way out of this mess.

Rosie was pulling clothes out and checking sizes. "Look, there's some smaller stuff, it's a bit big for Lu but it will do. A disguise." She almost smiled.

They found enough clothes for the both of them and Jack left Rosie in the bedroom to change and went back to the living room. Lu wasn't there. He called out and went into the kitchen. The back door was open. He felt panic rising. "Lu!"

"Lu," she said, crawling out from under the table clutching the round tin. "Biscuits." She held the tin up to him.

He breathed out slowly. He took off the lid, gave her a biscuit and led her back into the living room.

"New clothes, Lu. Clean and fluffy."

He took off what she had been dressed in, wondering what Mum would say at the grubbiness and stickiness of them all, and re-dressed her in slightly too large grey and black clothes. With a beanie on, her hair hidden, she passed as a boy. The trainers were a giveaway though, pink and sparkly. He went to the hall and found a cupboard - yes, this was where the family kept coats and shoes. He rummaged and found some smallish trainers and a coat. Both were too big but he pulled the velcro strips as tight as they would go to keep them on Lu's feet and pulled the hood of the coat up to hide Lu's face, just as Mum often did when they were out. Not bad. She definitely looked like a boy now.

Rosie came out, looked at Lu and said, "Well, that works." And then held her arms out at the sides and turned in a circle as if to say 'look at me.'

Jack nodded. "It's good. You don't even need to find trainers, yours will do. You need a hat to cover your hair." She pulled one from the pocket of the hoody she was wearing and put it on, stuffing her long hair underneath the rim.

"Coat?" He pulled a couple from the cupboard and Rosie found one that fitted more-or-less.

"Three boys." She almost smiled. "We need to sort out the bags, we can't carry them all now we haven't got the boat."

Jack took Lu's coat off and sat her in front of the TV while they sorted through their bags. They stuffed some of Lu's and Rosie's clothes into a rubbish bag Rosie got from the kitchen and packed a change of boy's clothes into their backpacks. Jack checked the grab bag and repacked it with some clean underwear from the bedroom drawers, the food from their shopping trip and … some batteries, another torch and some sweets he found in a kitchen drawer. Stealing again, but what was it Gran used to say - might as well be hanged for a sheep as a lamb. {*In the bad old days, poor people could be hanged for stealing anything, even a loaf of bread. So, they might as well steal something big if they were going to steal at all.*}

The hall clock chimed and they realised it was now getting on for two o'clock when the bus was due.

Rosie turned off the television. They closed the drawers and shut the doors so it looked more or less as they had found it. Hopefully, it would be some time before the family discovered what was missing and by then the 'brothers' should be miles away.

As they walked quickly along the road towards the bus stop Jack dropped the rubbish bag of unwanted clothes into a recycling skip at the side of the post office. If the police searched the area they would find it easily but then again, by the time that had happened, they should be miles away.

At the bus stop Lu perched on the little seat at the back of the shelter while Rosie peered at the timetables displayed on the wall. Jack looked over her shoulder and tried to make sense of it. At home it was easy, the displays were digital and you could download an app to tell you when your bus was coming. Here, it was printed with grids and lines and it was - well - confusing.

"Where are we going?" he asked.

Rosie shrugged. "We can go anywhere on this route. Have you got enough money?"

Jack nodded. He pointed to a place on the timetable. "I know that one, it's a train line, or it was once. Now it's a museum."

"So?"

"It will be empty at night, somewhere to stay, and we can walk the railway lines to that place - can't remember the name - nearer to Lowestoft."

Rosie nodded. "I think I've been there. It had a museum, very boring, and a cafe - good cakes - and there were big sheds with trains in, not real ones, well, they had been real ones but ... you know what I mean."

Jack did. "How long to get there? On the bus."

Rosie checked. "About an hour to that stop. I think it'll be a walk to the museum. But it will have signs so we should be able to find it."

Jack worked it out. "So, we get there about half three. It'll be closed?"

"It will close early - four at the latest at this time of year, that's if it's been open today. Some places don't open until the tourists come later in the year. And some only open on some days."

"What day is it?" asked Jack, suddenly confused.

"Sunday."

Really? Sunday? It seemed he'd been here forever. Jack couldn't think when he'd slept in his own bed in the flat.

Rosie looked along the road.

"It's coming."

The bus slowed and stopped and the doors swished open. She climbed in and asked for two to Easterly. The driver looked at Lu, bundled up in her borrowed coat.

"My brother is only four."

"It's quiet - on you get - no charge."

Rosie smiled at the driver, and Jack nodded thanks as they climbed on and found seats towards the back. Lu knelt on her seat and looked out of the window.

"Red," she said.

Jack glanced at where she was looking - and then looked again. A red hat, just dropping out of sight across the road by the shop. His heart thudded. It couldn't be. He craned around as the bus pulled away and kept watching the hedge where the red flashed from. As they pulled further away he saw someone step out, a man, Harry's height and shape, wearing a red hat.

Chapter Forty-One

Day 17: Sunday Afternoon - Police - Pc Anstey and DC Tizora

Tizora checked for updates on the files back in the incident room at the station while Anstey finished filing their report from the morning.

"You were right," she said, looking across to Anstey. "There have been so many sightings of Harry Moreton but only one that might be a lead."

"The children?"

"Hundreds. But as descriptions haven't gone out none are likely to be useful, just time-wasters."

Anstey signed off and swivelled round to face Tizora. "So, what's next?"

Before she could answer a voice from behind Anstey made him jump.

"You two, a few matching reports have come in of three children rowing along the Lugdon, near Highbridge. One boy about eleven or twelve, one girl about the same age and a smaller girl. They could be our kids. Check it out."

"Yes, Boss," said Tizora reaching for her bag.

"On it," said Anstey.

The Boss stared at Anstey.

"Yes, Boss," said Anstey, reaching for his bag.

Anstey pulled up next to the river and turned the engine off. They both looked across the flat landscape and pondered. How do you check out a river? The car couldn't follow its course from here, it was all reeds and winding streams and confusing when you didn't know the area.

"How does anyone know where they are? Where are the signs?"

Tizora pointed to a footpath sign. "Just that I suppose. Are there maps for rivers?"

Anstey shrugged. "River police? Are they on the case?"

Five minutes later, after a series of calls to and from the incident room, Tizora spoke to the right person, who was someone out on the river nearby. In five minutes a small motor boat rounded a bend and the officer waved at them before gently coming alongside the path.

Tizora and Anstey went over to the river bank.

"PC Weng. Can I help?"

"We're on the Moreton/Williamson team," explained Tizora. "There have been reports of three children rowing somewhere around here yesterday. How do we check that out?"

"Three children? I thought we were looking for two. In a rowing boat? Do you know what time yesterday."

Anstey checked the files for the reports on his phone while PC Weng turned the boat around.

"Last one was late morning. Any ideas where they might go from here?"

PC Weng looked across the area. She knew the rivers, it was her job after all, but where would children go? "Any of the sightings around Branksome?"

Anstey checked and shook his head. "There's one right here, and - then 'the shallows'? Is that a place? Some canoeists reported that one."

PC Weng nodded. "It's small, canoeists would know it. How long had the children been rowing, do you know?"

"Probably a few hours when they were seen."

PC Weng nodded again. "They'll have been tired and it's too far to Branksome. I'll check the backwaters, you head to Branksome by road. I'll see you there in say half an hour." She turned the engine on and set off back around the bend in the river.

"Branksome then," said Tizora. "I hope there's a coffee shop."

There wasn't. There wasn't much of anything as far as Tizora could see. The shop was still open though so they went in to stock up with some snacks and cold drinks. The shop assistant had been reading when they went in but she put down her book and watched them with a glint in her eye.

She smiled a crooked, tight smile as they put everything down on the counter.

"Dreadful business, over Fretton way," she said directly to Anstey as she began to check their shopping.

Anstey dug out a bag from his pocket and began to put things in as the woman rang them through the till.

"I expect a young officer like you is right in the thick of it all."

Anstey glanced at Tizora. She shook her head.

"Any news? Have you found him, that maniac?" She paused, looking at Anstey again.

"We can't say, madam, ongoing investigation," he said.

The woman bristled and said, "Of course." But Anstey knew she was angling for some gossip to pass on.

As Tizora was paying, the shop door bell clanged as someone pushed it open.

"Oh, you're quick!"

They turned to see a youngish man standing at the door.

"I'll grab something and take you to the place."

They turned and watched him go to the shelves as he said, "Didn't think anyone would come out with that Freeling business going on."

He chose a tired looking pasty and a can of something and went to the counter. "I phoned the owner and she said she'd deal with it, never thought you'd turn up straight away."

They all looked at him.

"What?" He looked back at them. "You're here for the break in?"

"We are now," said Tizora as she held out her hand for their receipt. "I'm Detective Constable Tizora and this," she turned to indicate Anstey, "Is Police Constable Anstey." She could see Dot's mouth narrow to a slit in her face as she struggled to link the word Detective with the young woman next to the man in uniform. "Now, why don't we wait for you outside."

Outside the shop away from nosey Dot, Sean told them he was a gardener, and earlier he had found a place he was working at had been broken into and had phoned the owner.

"There's a boat there too," he said as opened the pasty and began to eat.

"A rowing boat?" asked Anstey.

Sean nodded. "They don't keep a boat so I knew something was up. And someone had been inside."

Tizora checked the time. "We need to be here for PC Weng."

"I'll stay, you go with Sean here." Anstey fished a bag of crisps and a drink from the bag before giving it to Tizora.

As she drove off with Sean he moved away from the shop, out of sight of the inquisitive Dot, and sat on a bench facing the river to wait. It was good to sit and enjoy the scene for a while. He thought he might like to come back at some point, for a break - to enjoy the countryside - without the stress of the job. He'd only just finished his crisps when he heard the chug of her boat. He stood up and waved as soon as she came into sight. Like before she drew the boat gently to the shore and this time threw rope over a bollard and climbed out.

"Well?"

"Found something but I'm not sure if it's linked." Weng sat next to him.

"Go on."

"One of the chalets, a holiday place, has been broken into. Probably in the past day judging by the state of the broken reeds and the things left. Strange though, it's tidy - plates clean and stacked, and some money left by some cleaned out soup cans. And this ..." She pulled an evidence bag from her pocket and held it up for him to see. It was a pink tee shirt, very small and grubby. "It was under a cushion and there's no sign of any children normally being there, no toys or books."

"It must be them." Anstey was excited. "If they left this morning could they have rowed here?"

PC Weng thought about that. "Possibly, but it's hard work against the currents. They would be doing well if they got this far."

Anstey rang Tizora and told her what PC Weng had found. And Tizora told him what she had found, including a rowing boat, some small lifejackets and a bucket moored at the cottage. It sounded like they had found the trail.

It was late afternoon by now, the light would be going soon. Tizora called the station and arrangements were made for teams to come out to both sites.

As Dot shut up the shop for the day she looked over at the police river boat, at the two officers she had been watching for the past half an hour and at the police car which had pulled up with more four officers. How she wished it was any day but Sunday as then the shop would be open until six and she could see some more of what was going on. It would give her so much more to say the next time she saw her sister Queenie at Stavesey.

Chapter Forty-Two

Day 17: Sunday Late Afternoon - Jack, Rosie and Lu

The walk along the lanes took longer than Jack had thought it would, even allowing for Lu ambling slowly and getting distracted every few metres, so it was past five o'clock by the time they reached the isolated museum. The weak March sun had disappeared and it was getting darker.

They stood nearby, huddled against a hedgerow, checking the tiny car park for signs of people still hanging around. It looked deserted. There were no cars, no noises, no open doors or windows. Jack nudged Rosie and pointed up towards the roof of what he thought of as a big shed. She looked up and saw a camera fixed to the guttering. They backed into the hedge further and crouched down, pulling Lu with them.

"Hide and seek, Lu."

She giggled and sat down in the ditch as far as she could and pulled her hood over her eyes so she couldn't see.

"It might be the only one," Rosie hissed.

Jack peered out again. The road was narrow, not a proper road, just one leading to the museum. There were no houses along here so it wasn't likely that anyone would be walking home or walking a dog. He pulled back into the hedge and turned to see what was on the other side. A field. Of course it was. What else would it be?

"Let's go round the back and check."

They pushed through and keeping close to the hedge on the other side, made their way to the rear of the museum. Peering through a gap Jack could see some more car parking, a door into what he later found out was the actual museum part of the whole site and also some sheds - or hangers, he wasn't sure what they were called - with big doors, padlocked shut. He scanned the roof lines and saw there were no cameras along this side of the place.

"It looks okay," he whispered, "Let's try that door."

Rosie felt her way through the hedge, her backpack catching on a stubborn branch and her trainers slipping on the damp ground. She helped Lu through and began to walk across the open space towards the small door to one side. Jack followed and caught up with them half way across.

The door was locked when Rosie tried it. She began to search around.

"There won't be a key under a plant pot, not here," Jack said.

Rosie stopped. She knew he was right but didn't want to admit it, so she moved away from the door and to a window along the wall. She pushed on the under side, it didn't budge. She moved further along and checked a corner before she turned to the side of the museum. There were no cameras here either but there was another window, which also didn't budge when she pushed it.

"Those big sheds," Jack said, "What are they?"

"The trains are kept in them, the older ones that don't go anywhere anymore."

Jack pointed to a train carriage, set to one side, with a little white fence around it and some steps leading up to the door at the back - or front - he wasn't sure which.

"What's that?"

"The cafe."

"Where is the station then?"

"There isn't one. Well, this building here was a station once when the trains ran, it's the museum and shop now."

Jack looked around. Where could they break into?

Rosie pointed at the cafe carriage. "That might be a good place. It's got food, toilets and somewhere to sit - and sleep."

They went over and Jack went up the steps and tried the door. He looked in at the frilly curtained windows. "No one here. If we make a noise getting in it won't matter."

Lu sat on the step and began to pull some straggly half-dead plants from the planter next to the railing.

"Lu help tidy."

Rosie went to the side and then disappeared round the back while Jack tried the other way. They met at the back. There was an open window, just one, at the back by the bins. Someone had forgotten to close it when they locked up. Rosie pulled a low square bin over to the window and stood on it. She pushed the window and it opened out far enough for Jack to help her climb in. By the time he got back to the front Rosie was opening the door. He scooped up Lu and their bags and went in.

It was a cafe, as Rosie had said. There was a little counter on one end and a whole run of train carriage seats at the other, with several tables and wooden chairs with colourful cushions placed in groups around the carriage. It was crammed but it was homely with little signs and pictures on the walls and bunting strung along the ceiling.

Lu ran to the counter and stood as tall as she could to look at what was there.

"Cake," she called to Jack.

"Soon, Lu." Jack said as he dumped their bags on a table. "Clean first." He took off her coat - well, not *her* coat but the coat she was wearing - and the hat.

Rosie went behind the counter and looked to see what might be edible. There was a fridge and a freezer squeezed into a corner. She opened them both and turned aside to show Jack that there was some milk, some butter and some ham and cheese, lettuce and tomatoes, and in the freezer, ice cream.

"Oh well, sandwiches again," sighed Jack as he lead Lu towards the door marked toilet.

This was where Rosie had climbed in so he pulled the window closed and clicked the first catch - but didn't lock it - escape route. Once he'd cleaned Lu's hands and face and she'd used the toilet, he sent her out. He cleaned himself up and felt a bit less grubby. He almost wished he'd borrowed some clothes for himself. How long had he been wearing this hoody? It seemed days and it was definitely beginning to smell a bit.

In the carriage Rosie had switched on a very small lamp on a table way over against one wall. Lu was sitting on the floor with some paper and crayons. Rosie's voice came from a side room.

"I don't think anyone can see the light - but it's getting dark and we need to see."

Jack went into the room she was calling from. A kitchen, tiny but with an oven, a microwave and lots of food. Rosie had pulled down some tins and packets.

"What do you want?"

Jack looked at the options. "I don't know. What do you think? What can we do in here?"

"Anything. Something hot?"

"These go in a microwave," he held up a packet of frozen jacket potatoes, "and there's beans and cheese. And I think this is chilli."

"Does Lu eat that too? There's some little pizzas in the freezer."

"Potato and beans is fine."

They set to cooking the first proper meal they had both had for some days now, especially Rosie who hadn't been at the farm for over a week. They worked together in the cramped space and soon the microwave was pinging and a saucepan of beans was bubbling.

Jack found cutlery and set the table with the lamp. They chose some cans of drink and some straws and Rosie carried out Lu's and Jack's plates before bringing out her own. They sat at the table, on soft cushions and in gentle lamplight, and ate together.

It's like being with Mum, thought Jack, sitting at table together with plates and knives and forks.

It's like being with Mum, thought Rosie, sitting at a table together with plates and knives and forks.

Cake next, thought Lu.

And there was cake. From the covered stands at the counter they chose from plates with big cakes on them. One was covered in icing and a yellowy colour but Rosie said it was carrot cake and it had nuts in it so Jack thought it might not be good for Lu, who basically just swallowed cake without chewing. So they choose a sandwich cake, filled with red jam and buttercream. It was divided up into neat triangles so Jack used a special cake slice to slide a triangle each onto a plate and they ate politely, using a fork. Lu tried a fork but she couldn't eat quickly enough so she shovelled in most of it with her hands. Then they tried some lemon drizzle cake but Jack cut a slice in half so he and Lu didn't eat too much sugar. They hadn't been eating properly for a couple of days and Jack knew Mum would want him to try to manage better. Lu needed another clean up and once that was done they sat on some squishy chairs by the window and left the mess on the table. It wasn't late but it was almost dark. It had been a very long and difficult day and the food made them drowsy. Lu was the first asleep. Jack carried her over to the carriage seats and set her down, covering her with a coat and propping a chair next to her to stop her from rolling off.

"Let's clear up in the morning," Rosie said.

Jack was too tired to argue that she never cleared up anyway and he really was too tired to do it himself, so they made themselves somewhere to sleep and drifted off.

Chapter Forty-Three

Day 17: Sunday Night - Police - PC Anstey and DC Tizora

By the time the different teams had done their jobs it was late, very late. Tizora and Anstey had filed all their reports, they had spoken to just about everyone who had some part in the investigation and had read all the information coming in from all the other officers tracking down Moreton and the children. They were the only ones with any kind of break-through.

We're almost there, thought Tizora. Perhaps tomorrow.

We're not quite there, thought Anstey. Perhaps tomorrow.

Chapter Forty-Four

Day 18: Monday Morning- Jack, Rosie and Lu

It was light when Jack woke. He lifted himself up from a tangle of coats and cushions and peered across at the old station clock on the wall. He struggled to focus but thought it said 7. He sank back down and waited until he felt more awake before getting up and going to the toilet. Rosie was stirring when he came back but she lay still while he began clearing the table and taking the dirty dishes to the kitchen. There was a dishwasher so he loaded it as best as he could and washed up a couple of things in the sink. Lu was still snuffling in her sleep so he quietly collected their things together and made sure their backpacks and the grab bag were all set.

Rosie sat up. "Oh, you've already tidied up then." She pulled herself up and stretched and wandered in to the toilet. Jack found his and Lu's toothbrushes and gently woke Lu. "Breakfast, Lu.

He sat her at the table and gave her a banana and some milk from the cafe supplies. He started on a cereal bar from the counter and a can of something far too fizzy.

Rosie came in and helped herself to a can and a bar too and sat with them.

"What time does this place open?" asked Jack. "We need to be away before anyone arrives."

"It won't be for ages. It won't open until ten probably."

"So, someone will be here to get it opened before then. So, we have to leave by nine, say."

Rosie nodded. "Probably."

As Jack was standing at the little basin in the toilet cleaning his teeth and helping Lu clean hers, he heard Rosie calling. It was muffled and he thought she was probably making a fuss about clearing up the breakfast things which he'd left her to do. He heard her calling again. Still muffled but insistent. He stuck his head around the door, toothbrush still brushing methodically and mumbled, "What?"

Rosie thrust a backpack at him. In a loud whisper she said, "Quick. They're here."

"Who?"

"I don't know!"

"But it's too early."

She shoved another bag at him. "I heard a car. Someone's parking."

Jack pulled the bags into the tiny space in the toilet and quickly cleaned Lu's face. Rosie shoved the other bags in at the door.

"He's going to a shed thing."

Good, thought Jack. It gives us more time. "Where is he now?"

Rosie scuttled away, keeping low.

He pushed their toothbrushes into the backpack and pulled Lu's coat on. "Game, Lu. Hide-and-seek."

Rosie came back. "At the one at the front, over that side. Another car's come in."

Jack lowered the backpack out of the window and climbed out, checking around before he dropped to the floor. Rosie handed him some bags and helped Lu stand on the sink and climb through the window. She threw the last bag out and climbed out herself, pushing the window closed behind her.

They crouched down, listening. The car door slammed. Whoever it was, they weren't coming to park round the back. Jack slid on his backpack, wincing as the straps rubbed his sore arms. He hooked the grab bag on one shoulder, took a food bag in one hand and Lu's hand in the other.

"Quiet as mice, Lu."

Rosie gathered up the remaining bags and they crept around the side of the cafe carriage, past the white painted fence, and along to the overgrown patch of grass just edging the museum. Jack made his way through the bushes and scratchy undergrowth and led them quietly away from the cafe. When he thought they were far enough away, he hunkered down, out of sight and turned to Rosie.

"You said ten!" He hissed as loudly as he dared.

She shrugged. "I said probably."

"We could have been caught!"

"But we weren't."

"Nearly were. Nearly got arrested for stealing, breaking in …"

"But we weren't."

"Why did you say ten? It's not ten, is it? It's only ten past eight."

"You asked when the museum opens. I said probably ten."

You did say that, thought Jack.

"The museum does probably open at ten," Rosie glared at him. "But those men weren't coming to open up. They were going to the sheds."

Jack stared at her.

"It's a hobby. You know, hobbies - you do them in your spare time."

Jack felt hot inside. His face flushed. He didn't know why he was so angry - with Rosie for being right or with himself for being wrong.

Rosie stood up. "We need to move." And she set off through the bushes.

Lu began to follow her. "Hide and seek?"

"No," Rosie snarled. "Just walking."

Jack stood up and followed, catching Lu's hand to help her.

Rosie led them to an opening and out onto what looked like a path. It ran off in a straight line in one direction as far as Jack could see, and when he looked behind him, it carried on past the museum entrance and veered off slightly to one side, following the line of fields. They walked in a line across the path and gradually got into a rhythm slow enough for Lu to keep up.

So, Jack thought, as they walked along, this is an old railway line - but without the rails. He wondered who used to use it. There wasn't much around here and he couldn't imagine a train being packed with commuters and shoppers like the trains at home. Perhaps it was just the old steam trains taking farmers and villagers to market. Could you get a cow on a train? He remembered seeing some photos of old trains in a war, shipping soldiers to battlefields in cattle trucks, so he supposed there must be special trucks for cows. But there weren't many cows around here. They'd wander off and fall in the rivers and ditches. Could cows swim? Probably not. Their legs didn't seem to bend like his own did. And what about pigs. Could pigs swim?

"COMING THROUGH!"

Jack jumped and dodged sideways, almost stumbling into the hedge. He twisted round quickly to spot where Lu was and to see what was happening. Rosie was grabbing Lu as he saw a line of cyclists heading towards them. The one at the front waved and smiled.

"Good day to be out."

Jack and Rosie stood frozen as the line passed them, two stragglers passing several seconds after the others. The bikes were all the same colour, blue and grey, and everyone wore a matching crash hat, blue and grey with a luminous yellow flash down one side like a lightening bolt to match the one on the chain guard of the bikes.

"What was that?" Jack asked.

"Bike," said Lu pointing.

"Tours, people pay to go out cycling." And Rosie turned and followed the cyclists along the train track.

Right, thought Jack, as he followed her. He watched the trailing couple cycling furiously to keep up with their party. It didn't matter where he was, he had to watch out all the time just to keep Lu safe. If it wasn't cars, it was rivers, or ditches, or nuts in cake, or people on bikes on a footpath.

The surface wasn't like a normal path or road but it was flat and easy to walk on. It felt good to follow a path and seeing where you were going rather than rowing a boat where you faced backwards, only seeing where you came from. And his shoulders still ached from all the rowing so both his backpack and the grab bag hurt. And he had sore patches on his hands from pulling the oars. So, he was really glad just to walk along a flat pathway for as long as it took.

The day was cloudy. It felt damp even though they weren't on a river anymore. Jack was soon feeling hot and sticky. He took his coat off and stuffed it under the straps of the backpack. Lu wanted her coat off too, and once she was free of it, she ran along happily, swinging her arms and singing some nonsense to herself, which meant they could walk faster. As they walked he checked around and about for a splash of red. He liked being out here but if he could spot someone, they could spot him.

He watched Rosie's back as she strode on ahead with her hood pulled up, and her head angled down. He wished she wasn't Rosie, it would be so much easier if he was with Milo. Or Jaye. They never argued or sulked or snorted. They just got on with each other. He always knew what they were thinking and what mood they were in and what they wanted to do. Rosie - well, she was what Mr Brownlee four floors down would call mardy and what Gran would call a misery-guts. *{My gran would have said mizzog. You've probably got your own words for that.}* She was always looking at the bad side of things. Everything was a problem. He couldn't think of a word to explain the knots in his stomach when she snorted or snapped or glared at him. He hoped they would be somewhere safe soon, he was tired of coping with Rosie being moody and he was tired of Lu being, well - Lu.

It was quiet on the train track. A runner passed them. A farmer started up a tractor in a field nearby. A plane went overhead. Their trainers crunched on the drier sections of track. And just when they had settled into a steady rhythm, Lu sat down and refused to go any further.

"Come on, Lu. Get up. Nearly there." Jack helped her to her feet but she sagged down and struggled.

"Tired."

"I know, but not far now." Jack tried to pull her up but she lay flat on the floor and spread her arms and legs out wide.

He crouched next to her and found a sweet in his pocket. "Here. Sweet. You can have it if you walk."

Lu looked at it as if she was deciding whether walking was worth the bribe. She sat up and held out her hand. Jack held on to the sweet. He knew how this had to go. He pointed down the track.

"Big tree, down there, walk to there and you can have this." He held the sweet out. She sighed and got up and trotted along to catch up with Rosie, who had ignored the exchange.

At the tree Jack gave Lu the sweet and she sat down again, chomping happily.

"Really?" snorted Rosie. "And now what do you do? One sweet every hundred metres?"

"She's four!" Jack snapped. "It's a long way to her. She's only got little legs."

"I knew this was a mistake, back in the boathouse when you said about hide-and-seek and she ate that slug."

Lu got up saying, "Hide-and-seek."

"Then, you didn't have to come, or do anything with us." Jack took Lu's hand and began walking quickly away from Rosie.

"Nightmare! Everything is a nightmare. She can't even walk."

"She can, just not far."

Rosie caught up with him and overtook.

"Should have left her at the cottage. Your mum should be looking after her."

"She's in hospital."

"How can I forget with her trailing along with us."

Jack stopped. He pulled Lu close to him and stared at Rosie's back. He crouched down, and looked at Lu. "Not far Lu. Then we can sit and have a picnic." He pulled her hat straight and tucked in her hair.

"Ice cream?"

"Don't know if there's a shop. We'll see."

For the next twenty minutes, Jack and Lu walked several metres behind Rosie. Jack and Lu played 'what colours can we see' and 'can I count my steps up to ten' and 'who can spot the most birds' while Rosie trudged on alone. Just when Jack knew he couldn't keep Lu going much further, they came to a cottage next to the train track. It was fenced off but right next to where they walked. He looked at it as they passed. And as they moved away, he walked quickly, helping Lu along, to catch up with Rosie.

"That place back there - what is it?"Rosie looked back but she didn't answer and carried on walking.

"Does someone live there?"

She shrugged. He caught her arm and stopped her. "Take Lu." He pushed Lu's hand into hers and dropped the backpack, grab bag and food bag he had been lugging along, and he ran back. Rosie and Lu watched him disappear into the hedges and bushes just before he got to the fencing. Rosie stared blankly, wondering what he was doing. Lu sat down, hoping it was picnic time.

Rosie was just beginning to think she would have to pick up what she could carry on her own, without him to help, and with Lu in tow, when there was a crashing in the hedges and some muttering and groaning. Then Jack emerged onto the train track pulling something behind him. On the path he straightened what he'd found and pushed it towards them. He stood in front of them and pointed at it. "A trolley."

Rosie looked at it and then stared at him. "A trolley. Doing some gardening?"

He bent down and turfed out a couple of clumps of mud and a dead plant onto the path. It was flat bedded, with a wheel on each corner and a long handle. "In you get Lu." He helped her in and loaded in the bags, including Rosie's backpack. "Hold tight." Lu giggled as he began to push her along. He felt Rosie stare at his back but it wasn't long before she caught up with them and walked alongside.

Now they were able to move along quicker and with the motion of the trolley Lu soon dropped off to sleep, just as she did when she was in her buggy, so for an hour they made good progress towards somewhere - Jack couldn't remember what it was called on the map but he knew it was at the end of this stretch of track.

When Lu woke up, they parked off the track and let her run about while they made a picnic of sorts. He craved one of those fizzy cans from the cafe he'd had for breakfast but made do with the water bottles he'd filled last night, even though it was warm and tasteless. The ground felt damp as they sat and ate and Jack looked warily up at the clouds. He and Rosie hadn't said anything to each other since he came with the trolley but he broke the silence.

"Is it going to rain?"

Rosie looked up. She nodded.

"Soon."

She nodded, again.

"A lot or just a bit?"

She shrugged.

"How much further?"

She didn't answer, just finished her crisps and stowed the empty packet in the food bag she was carrying.

"A long way? All day?"

She shook her head.

"An hour then?"

She nodded and got up, collecting everything and putting it back on the trolley. Lu climbed in and they set off again.

So far, apart from the cyclists and the runner, they'd only seen a couple of hikers and - yes, a dog walker. They'd passed over a river and by another cottage, which was derelict, and could sometimes hear traffic in the distance, but it felt as if they were cut off from the world - it was just them. And although Jack was fine with that, as the fewer people who saw them the better, it was also unnerving. Jack felt his scalp prickle when the wind rustled the dead leaves in the ditches. He couldn't see clear escape routes or safe hiding places. He still looked for red flashes behind them.

"How much further?" he asked when they had walked for another half an hour.

Rosie shrugged.

"Just say!"

"I DON'T KNOW!"

Okay! She could have just said.

Lu was beginning to fidget so Jack got her out and she ran alongside for a while. It was slower but at least they weren't carrying all the bags.

Jack could see there were some signs of civilisation ahead. He got Lu to sit back in the trolley and they made their way cautiously. As they got closer they passed a couple of cottages close to the track near to a low brick building.

"The old station," said Rosie.

Jack looked at the cottages. They both looked as if people lived there. Windows open, gardens tidy, washing hanging out. The station building was right next to the track. It was higher than the path, and had some steps going up to what would have been the platform and all along it there was a row of bikes. Those cyclists must have stopped here, probably on their way back, Jack thought. Was it a cafe? Or a part of the museum? He felt Rosie tug his sleeve and pull him on quicker. He pushed the trolley faster and they passed by as quickly as they could, heads down. Once they were past the station she pulled them off the track and out of sight behind a thick hedge, just coming into leaf.

They crouched down and she held her finger to her lips.

"Quiet as mice, Lu." Jack hissed. Lu put a hand over her mouth and pulled her coat over her head.

Jack listened. He didn't actually know what he was listening for but he listened anyway. He heard the swish of a bike going past on the track. Just one. The sounds of its tyres on the track faded and then it was quiet again.

He looked at Rosie. Come on, you need to talk, he thought.

"Harry," she whispered.

His heart started that crashing in his chest that seemed to happen every day now. "Where?"

"He was at the side of the station, looking."

"Did he see us?"

"I don't think so. He was looking at the bikes. We were down in the path, the old track, so lower."

"Was it him? Really? How do you know it was him?"

"The paper, the photo. I'm sure."

"Was he wearing a red hat?"

"No. A cap."

"It wasn't him then."

"Why not?"

"He was wearing a red hat when I saw him near that first shop."

"And …"

"What?"

"Is Lu wearing what she wore back then? Are you? He's on the run. He'll change, like we have."

Jack sank back against the trolley. How could he have been so stupid - looking for a red hat. And Rosie had seen him, Harry, when Jack had missed him. The whole of Norfolk and Harry was right there, next to them!

"Wait here," Rosie hissed. "I'll check." She crept through the hedge to the side of the track.

Lu stuck her head up. "Hide-and-seek now?" she asked.

"Not yet," Jack whispered. "Still quiet as mice."

Lu frowned but she hid herself under her coat again and kept still.

It was only a couple of minutes until Rosie came back but it seemed much longer to Jack.

Lu popped her head out and said, "Boo!"

"SSSHHH," hissed Rosie as she crouched down. "He's gone, he stole a bike. They're all fussing up there."

"Where is he then?"

"I think we heard him go by. I only heard one bike, and they're missing one bike."

"So he's up ahead, where we're going?"

Rosie nodded.

"We'll have to go back." Jack really didn't want to go back to the museum, it had taken all morning and a lot of effort walking this far, but he needed to get away from Harry.

"No, we can go on."

"We can't, not if he's up that way. You don't know what he's like."

"I do, I read the paper."

"No, he's violent and nasty and ..." Jack waved a hand at Lu. "You can't understand."

"I lived with Frank. My mum's dead. Yours is only in hospital."

Jack opened his mouth to argue but he didn't say what he was going to, he stopped himself. This needed thinking about, Rosie needed thinking about. But not now, not until they were safe somewhere.

"So, what then?" he asked.

Rosie pointed the way they had been heading. "Just up there is the village, the one the station was for. We can check the bus timetable and see if there's one to ... I can't remember the place but it will be on the timetable. Then we ..."

"What about being seen? What if they're looking for us?"

"Three brothers. We're three brothers."

"And what if he sees us hanging about the bus stop?"

"I'll go and check first. See if there's a bus - what time."

Jack didn't feel right about this. "Where would he have gone? Up the path to where?"

Rosie shrugged. "It's quiet on the path and he can get a long way on a bike. He needs to keep away from everyone, so he won't go into the village incase he's seen."

Lu had found a bag of crisps and held it up to Jack to open. He took it and opened it for her.

"Okay, then you check up ahead, I'll follow with Lu just a bit behind. Shout - as if you're calling a dog - if you see him."

"What's the dog called?"

Really? Jack thought, what does it matter. "Steve," he said.

"You can't call a dog Steve!"

"Why not?"

"It's stupid. It's a people name, not a dog name."

"Just go!" Jack pushed her forward.

Between them they pulled the trolley out of the hedge and back onto the track.

"Should we leave this? Would it be quicker to run without it?" Rosie asked. Jack looked at the trolley and at Lu, eating through the crisps as quickly as she could because she had found another bag for afterwards.

"No, I can run with it much quicker, than she can run on her own."

He put on the backpack and zipped up the grab bag and slung it across his shoulder, wincing as he took the weight. Rosie picked up her stuff before setting off along the path at a slow run. When she had gone a little way ahead Jack pushed the trolley forward. They moved quicker than they had all morning. Lu bounced about a bit but Jack had to risk her falling out to keep up the pace. He saw Rosie up ahead waving him to move into the hedge. He pushed the trolley as far as he could into the bushes with Lu squealing at the game. He lifted her out and put on her coat and pulled up the hood.

"Creeping game," he said, "Quiet and small. Find Rosie. Sssshhh."

Leaving the empty trolley in the hedgerow, he lead her along until he came to the fence of a garden, the start of the houses in the village. He peered round the corner onto the road and saw Rosie walking along a few houses further on. The houses here had quite big spaces around them, with gardens on all sides, not like at home in the flats where you shared everything, even the walls. He watched as she went as far as a signpost - an open bus stop, just a pole at the side of the road - where she stopped and read the timetable. Lu stepped out from behind and waved to Rosie. He pulled her back behind the fence. "SSSHH!"

"Find Rosie."

"Yes, now hide. Ssshh."

Shortly Rosie came and ducked down with them. "Bus in ten minutes, the last one today."

"But it's only just after lunch time!"

Rosie shrugged. "Townie."

"Any sign of …"

She shook her head.

"Do you know where we're going? The name?"

She nodded. "It's about half an hour on the bus. Then we can work out the next bit - might not be another bus from there until tomorrow."

Really? Jack sighed. It was no use getting angry - slow and even slower - that was how you got about here.

As the time came for the bus to arrive Rosie headed to the stop and, when she was sure Harry wasn't in sight, she waved to Jack. He and Lu walked along to the bus stop and stood with Rosie, next to a very old lady with a walking frame and younger person in some kind of shop or fast-food uniform with a black cap. The bus pulled up, the doors swished open and Jack helped the old lady on to the step, before lifting Lu up after her. The lady had a pass ready and she shuffled onto the nearest seat leaving Jack and Rosie at the driver's window.

"Two to Westerbridge please," Rosie asked. "My little brother is only four, so he doesn't usually have to pay, Mum said."

The driver nodded and Jack passed over the coins to pay and Rosie picked up the tickets. They went to the back of the bus near the emergency exit while the last customer was paying. They were already settling onto the back row as the bus pulled out and set off.

The steady movement felt good to Jack, who missed the everyday motion of a bus ride. The rain had started just after they had left the stop and riding the bus was so much better than walking. He looked at the other passengers. There were only three altogether and apart from the lady he'd helped, no one had looked closely at them. He hoped they just remembered seeing three boys getting on at ... wherever it was. The village was very small so they only stopped once more, at the other end before heading along the narrow road to the next stop. One more person got on, fumbling and dropping coins and taking time. Lu was looking out of the back window, kneeling up but Jack was holding on to her in case she fell back as the bus moved.

"Yellow," she said as they pulled away. Jack looked around and through the back window he saw one of the bikes from the tour group earlier, blue and grey, with a yellow streak on the side. And a man riding it, slowing behind the bus as it pulled away. A man not wearing a crash helmet.

Chapter Forty-Five

Day 18: Monday Morning - Police - PC Anstey and DC Tizora

Briefing at the station was at seven o'clock. Everyone crammed in to hear what had been happening and what was going to happen next. Anstey and Tizora were squeezed against a wall at the back of the crowded room but they listened intently, anxious not to miss anything The Boss said.

The search for Moreton was ongoing. There had been no leads yet and it was urgent that he was found. Some officers were assigned to continue the search.

Investigations into Frank Rowley had been stepped up. Firstly in connection with the body of his step-son, Robin Bushey, found in the caravan near Orchard Cottage and only a mile from Rowley's Farm, and secondly in connection to illegal, unlicensed, imported medication linked to discoveries at the farm.

Robin Bushey's finger prints had been found at the farm so he had been there recently. But why he had gone there was unclear, as Rowley had cut off all contact with him over eighteen months ago, when Bushey's mother, formerly known as Jane Bushey, had died suddenly. Some research was being carried out into her death, possibly linked to the death last summer of Rowley's second wife, formerly known as Melissa Hynes. A team was assigned to investigate all three deaths: Robin Bushey and Rowley's two wives.

Another team was already working with other divisions, such as Customs and Excise, and Fraud, and Serious Crime, to investigate what appeared to be a small operation, importing unlicensed and illegal drugs and distributing them via a regional network.

But The Boss was clear. The search for the missing children was a priority. *THE priority.* They knew now there were definitely three children at all locations and that the third child was probably the missing step-daughter of Frank Rowley, Rosie Hynes. Child-sized prints at the farm matched prints at the boat house and at the fishing lodge.

Tizora and Anstey were very happy to be assigned to the missing children team again and they set off to begin house-to-house inquiries in Branksome, along with several other officers. It didn't take long - there weren't many houses and some were empty holiday places. But luckily - and they needed luck - Tizora and Anstey called at a bungalow when someone was in.

"It was very odd. Nothing was damaged, no sign of a break in, but things weren't really right."

Tizora drank the tea Mrs Waterford had made and took a biscuit from the tin on the kitchen table. "How do you mean?"

"This tin, this one here, was under the table. The TV was on a different channel when the boys switched it on when we got home last night. I think some clothes have gone missing - it's difficult to tell what but I'd say a couple of things in both sizes."

Anstey came in from checking out in the garden. He shook his head at Tizora to let her know he'd found nothing important.

"What sizes? Big or small?"

Mrs Waterford indicated Tizora should follow her and led her to her sons' bedroom. She pulled open a drawer and held up a hoody and some joggers, both small. And then another drawer and larger versions. Tizora thought the small ones looked a bit big for a small child like Lu Williamson but it could work. Would the others fit Jack? Or the girl, Rosie Hynes? Not sure.

"And, I think a coat has gone. My youngest couldn't find his school coat this morning, it wasn't in the hall cupboard but he leaves it at school sometimes, always losing stuff too, so I just sent him off without it."

Tizora asked her to write a list of everything she thought was missing and left her with a constable while she and Anstey walked along the road trying to work out where they might have gone.

Anstey looked all along the road in both directions before coming to a halt by the bus stop. "Here, it's a bus stop."

"Yes, it is. But you won't pass any sergeant's exams on knowing what a bus stop is, Anstey. You need some detectoring."

"Detecting, not detectoring - that's something to do with metal detecting - detectorists."

Tizora stared at him.

"It is, really, and - this is a *bus stop.*"

Tizora realised what he was saying. "It is - and they could have got on a bus!"

Anstey was reading the timetable stuck on the wall. "Only one bus yesterday. At two in the afternoon."

"Really?! One bus. How do people manage here?"

"It was Sunday."

"And …?"

"No need for buses to take people to work, and most things are shut here on Sunday - and in the winter months."

Tizora couldn't imagine that kind of life.

"Back to the station. We need the camera footage from the bus."

It was an hour and a half later when the bus company sent over the footage and Anstey identified the three boys as Jack and Lu Williamson and with one unidentified child, possibly Rosie Hynes. Someone was sent to interview the driver while, after a quick lunch break, having exhausted all inquiries in the village, Tizora and Anstey drove along the bus route.

It had started to rain.

Chapter Forty-Six

Day 18: Monday Afternoon - Jack, Rosie and Lu

"Harry!" he whispered. "Out there." He nodded backwards.

Rosie turned and stiffened. She turned back and faced forward quickly. They sat frozen with Lu squirming between them.

"Is he still there?"

Rosie half turned and checked. "He's not going as fast as the bus."

Jack looked round and frantically scanned the road. There he was, a short distance away, pedalling methodically, quite fast for someone Jack knew was lazy. Must have been prison life - didn't they have an exercise yard, or was that just in films? He turned back. "Has he seen us? Is he chasing the bus?"

Rosie shrugged. "Will he recognise you and Lu?"

"He's never seen her, and she's dressed like a boy. He might know me."

"Keep down then."

Just as Jack sank down in his seat the bus stopped at a road junction to turn left. And the bike pulled past them to wait to turn right. Jack kept his face half turned to Rosie and pulled his hood up. As the bus pulled out, he looked up just as Harry turned to scan the road. The moment froze in time. Jack stared at Harry and Harry stared back. Jack knew in that moment that Harry had recognised him. And then Lu popped up and looked out and Jack knew Harry had seen her too.

The bus slowly set off along the road and he looked back to see what Harry was doing now. Following the bus, obviously. What else would he be doing?

Jack was angry. It wasn't fair. He'd tried, really tried, to do what Mum said, to keep Lu safe, but it was just impossible. There were so many things to deal with. Too many things, one after another, not stopping - with only Rosie to help and she was just - Rosie. What was he supposed to do now?

Who on the bus could help if Harry got on? The driver was behind a screen. The old lady was - well, old - but she could probably hit Harry with her walking frame. The lady with the baby would want to protect the baby. The young person was listening to music and Gran would say they looked as if they would fall over in a strong wind.

It was raining harder. Big splashes hit the windows and streamed down.

Rosie looked behind and said, "He's still there, not close though."

Jack looked back. There was no point in trying to hide now, as Harry knew they were there.

"He'll catch us up at the next bus stop."

Rosie looked forward. "No one there." And the bus sailed on.

"I'll tell the driver." Jack started to get up but Rosie pulled him down.

"Ssshh! We can do it."

"How?" Jack lowered his voice as the woman with the baby turned to look at them from her seat a few rows forward. "He'll get on, grab Lu and no one will stop him." He waved his arm to include the other passengers. "Look at them. The driver could get us to a police station, not stop until we get there. I can tell him who we are. He'll have read the news, he'll know us."

"And what then?" Rosie asked.

"It's safer than getting caught by him."

Rosie checked her watch. "Ten minutes before we get there, to Westerbridge. So a couple of stops probably."

"You're good at 'probably.' Look what happened at the museum."

"We got away, didn't we? But if the bus keeps ahead we can get off and disappear before he catches up."

Jack knew he had to keep Lu safe, away from Harry, and surely telling the driver would be the best thing to do. Keep Lu safe. First priority, number one, always. To do that, they'd left the flat and driven a car they didn't own to a cottage a long way from home. They'd hidden. Mum even used a different phone. She would want him to do whatever he could to keep Lu safe. So, that's what he would do.

Jack looked at Rosie. "If something happens, you take Lu to your gran, promise."

"What?"

"If this doesn't work out, you have to get Lu to where it's safe, your gran. Promise or I'll tell the driver."

Rosie stared at him.

"Or," Jack carried on," are you more worried what will happen to you if I tell the driver?"

Rosie shook her head. "No! If we did tell him I'd at least get to police station nearer Lowestoft and they would get Gran, wouldn't they? And … I'd tell them about … well, it would be better for me if you told the driver. But not for you and Lu. What will happen if your mum can't look after you and Harry's out there. My gran will help, if we get there. She'd help you and Lu to stay together, I know she would."

Jack was still unsure. If this gran was so good, he couldn't understand why she hadn't come to take Rosie home, why she'd left her with Frank. He looked back to check where Harry was. Still not too far back but enough, probably.

The woman with the baby got up and rang the bell. They watched in horror as she made her way to the door and waited for the bus to stop. They both looked back and saw the bike coming closer and closer. The bus stopped and the doors opened. The woman got off, fussing with the buggy, the baby and the bags of shopping.

As the doors closed, the bike drew level and Harry grinned at Jack as if to say - got you, it's only a matter of time.

Jack remembered that grin. He'd seen it so often.

Oh no, you broke your arm when I accidentally let go of you on the slide.

Oh dear, was that a school book I just threw out with the rubbish?

Have you been waiting long? I thought your mum said to pick you up at five not three-thirty.

Time after time. Lies. And more lies. He had fooled everyone, even Mum.

"His face is like Frank's."

Jack looked at Rosie. "What do you mean?"

"Frank looked at me like Harry just looked at you."

Jack looked back through the rain streaked glass as the distance between the bus and the bike widened again. "I hate him," he said.

"I hate Frank," Rosie said. "Let's win this one - we can do it."

Jack nodded. And stopped Lu from licking the window.

"Not wet," she said.

"No, Lu, the rain is outside." Jack found her water bottle and gave her a drink. "We need a plan."

"We need time," Rosie said. "Enough time to get away in Westerbridge."

"Do you know what's there?"

She shook her head. "I have been there but it was with Dad, my real dad, so not for a long time. I think there's a shop and a pub and a boat yard."

"I'm not rowing again!"

"It's too wet."

How can it be too wet on a river? thought Jack. He said, "If we can get off and run for it, we can hide, find a place like the others, empty. He can't search every house."

Rosie thought. "There's a caravan park, just outside the town. Some must be empty. Easy to get into."

Jack's thoughts slipped back to that caravan down from the cottage and his stomach heaved at the memory of the smell.

Rosie checked and saw that the bike was still quite a way back. "I think it's here, this side of town but I'm not sure. Don't want to get off too early."

"Well, look out and see if you recognise anywhere. A road or farm. There might be a sign."

Rosie got up. "I've got an idea." She went down to the front where the old lady was sitting and sat on the aisle seat next to her.

"Excuse me, "she said, "Me and my brothers are going to stay with our gran at the caravan park and we're supposed to get off in town but it's raining so if we get off nearer the park Gran won't have to get wet coming to get us. Is it near here?"

"Oh yes, not far, now. There's a stop, not the next one - that's the pub in Hatton - but the one after that." Rosie smiled and thanked the lady and came and sat down.

"So, the stop after the next one. It must be nearly in town. Not long before we have to get off."

They collected their bags and got their coats tightly zipped against the rain, which was still streaming down the windows. As they pulled up at the next stop, Jack and Rosie kept a check on the distance between the bus and the bike. In the time it took for someone to get on and pay, the bike pulled level with the back of the bus. As the bus pulled away they both knew. Not enough time. If they got off, Harry would get to them. They looked at each other and slumped back on the seats. What now?

The bus drove down the last lanes towards the stop they needed. Time ticked by. The rain streamed down. Their stop got closer. And then, the bus slowed, just for a second, and then sped up again. Jack saw a flashing light through the rain spattered window and heard a bell ringing. He looked up ahead to see a level crossing. The bus sped over. He turned round to see where the bike was. The car behind the bus crossed with them but the next car pulled to a stop as the barriers came down. Behind that car Jack could see the blurry shape of the bike. It nudged forward. For a moment, he thought Harry was going to take a risk and skirt round the barrier - but he didn't. The bike stayed just next to the car, ready to cross as soon as the barrier lifted.

Chapter Forty-Seven

Day 18: Monday Late Afternoon - Jack, Rosie and Lu

Jack nudged Rosie. "Get ready." He rang the bell and they stood ready to get off. They moved forward, Jack holding on to Lu tightly. The bus swept further along the road until it slowed and pulled into a lay-by. The doors opened and they got out.

As soon as the bus left Rosie pointed over the road to a sign. "There, over that way."

They crossed and ran down the lane which lead to the caravan park. In seconds they were gone from the sight of the main road but Jack knew he wouldn't be able to breathe properly again until they were further away from the bus route. They walked as quickly as Lu could manage, hoods pulled up and heads facing down, splashing through the gathering puddles until there was a turning with a sign telling them they'd reached the entrance to the park.

"Not this way," Rosie said. "We need to get in somewhere at the back."

They carried on along the road, standing close to the side when a car passed by, until Rosie decided it was time to climb through the hedgerow into the park. They squeezed through the wet branches, slipping in the ditch, and came out next to a row of caravans. Jack looked in each direction. Where now?

"Is there anyone here?" he whispered. "Do people live here?"

"No, not all year. They have to leave for a couple of months in winter but I think some come back about now."

Jack looked out and tried to find some signs of life. It all looked grey and wet and uninviting in the rain. He couldn't see any lights from any of the caravans around them but then, it was only about three in the afternoon.

They walked past the lines of caravans, until they were as far as they could be from the site office. Then they walked along the furthest row of caravans, checking the doors and windows, trying to find one which they could open. They reached the last caravan in the row. Rosie checked it for open windows and Jack rattled the door handle. It was locked.

Rosie dropped her bags on a step and held her hand up to say 'wait here' and she disappeared.

Jack helped Lu up onto a step and they huddled underneath a ragged awning, trying to shelter from the rain. Lu held onto his leg tightly and looked up at him saying, "Lu wet."

"I know."

"Wellies?"

He shook his head. "Not here, but we'll get dry soon." He felt in his pockets and found a sweet for Lu. He unwrapped it and gave it to her. Although she took it - what four year old wouldn't take a sweet when offered one - he could see she wasn't really happy even with a sweet. She looked tired and pale, and the rain was dripping off her hood onto her face. He couldn't remember if he'd given her her medication today.

He needed to check the packs when they got in somewhere, to count what was there.

Rosie came back and held up a rusty screwdriver. "All I could find."

She went to the door and looked for some way of unscrewing the door. And then a window.

Jack tried prising the blade under a window but it was fixed shut.

"What now?"

Rosie shrugged.

"We should have stayed on the bus," Jack said. "More places to hide in a town."

"My fault then?"

"No, no, I didn't … we just …"

"Look, we do what we have to do. Things happen. We just - get on with it."

"But we don't really know where we are or what Harry's doing. We can't plan."

Rosie waved her arm over the site vaguely. "Somewhere must be open, we just have to find it."

They collected the bags and set off down the row of caravans, Jack checking one side and Rosie the other. They were soon back at the entrance. They huddled behind a brick building.

"The gates are locked, I don't think anyone is here."

"No security?"

They looked up at the rooflines of the small group of buildings with the sign 'Westerbridge Holiday Park' above the main doorway. There didn't seem to be any cameras so they made their way around the side of the building and found some container bins, and a back door, which was, of course, shut. But, it had a padlock. Jack held it while Rosie prised it with the screwdriver. The lock inside grated and clicked as she pushed harder and harder, until the clip finally popped open. Rosie slid the padlock off the D-ring and tugged at the door. It swung open. They looked at each other and both grinned at the same time.

Inside was dark but with the door held open by Rosie, Jack made his way past the boxes and shelves lined up in what was a store room and found the door leading to the rest of the site office. He opened it and they went into the next room. It was a shop, stocking things holiday-makers might need. The shelves were half empty but already Jack could see some things they could use. At the back of the shop was another room, an office and a toilet, and from that a door into a laundry room and a shower room that holiday-makers could use. Jack looked at the huge tumble dryer and smiled.

"Right, Lu, off with these wet things, let's get dry." He stood Lu in the office, on the little patch of carpet, and took off her wet coat.

"What are you doing?" Rosie asked.

"In there, the shop, go get some dry clothes." Jack said, as he pulled off Lu's wet trainers. "Lu's size."

Rosie pulled off her own coat - not her own coat, the one they'd taken from the bungalow - and dropped it on the floor before going through to the shop. Jack was right; there was a section of wall with some clothes displayed with some shelves underneath with what was left from last season's stock. She rummaged through and found a green hoody with an orange monkey surfing bright blue waves and a yellow tee-shirt with a teddy bear eating an ice cream. She frowned. Hideous. But, they would fit Lu and they were dry. She found a pair of joggers, probably a bit long but they could tuck them up a bit. She took them through to the office and held them out. "Not amazing but they're dry."

Jack took off Lu's damp tee-shirt and put on the yellow one.

"Ice cream," said Lu. "Yellow."

"Yes," said Jack. "And a monkey." He held up the hoody. Lu laughed and let him put it over her head. The joggers were too long but Jack turned them up and found some dry socks in the grab bag.

"Anything for you and me?"

They went to look. There wasn't much and it really was hideous but they found enough to change into, as well as some packs of adult socks to put on instead of their wet trainers. Back in the laundry room, Jack found the socket and switched on the machines. Some lights flashed on and he checked the tumble dryer. It needed tokens to feed into the slot. They searched through the office and found a stack in a drawer. They loaded all their wet clothes and their trainers into the machine and set it going. It rumbled into action. First job done, thought Jack. We're dry and our clothes will be too.

"Food next?" Rosie asked.

Jack nodded and Lu called, "Cake."

There wasn't cake. There were some cans and packets, some past their 'best before' date and nothing usable without something to cook on. The fridges were empty. Jack went through to the store room. There was a freezer but it was empty too, its lid propped open. The shelves had some cans and packets in half empty cardboard boxes, all a bit damp to the touch. But there were some cans of soup, and some packs of noodles, the kind you add hot water to.

In the office Lu was playing with some toys from the shop - meant for playing on the beach but she seemed happy filling the bucket with things she found in the desk drawers and emptying them into the waste paper bin. Rosie was checking through her own stuff, looking to see what food they had left. Jack looked around and saw the kettle used to make tea or coffee by whoever worked here. He filled it with a bottle of water from the shop and switched it on. He held up the noodles and showed Rosie. She smiled and held up some biscuits which were still dry in their packaging.

Later, once they had eaten and tidied up, they put all the food they had on the desk and worked out what else they might need. They collected a few things from the shop and store room and put everything in a sturdy bag they found in the shop. It was a beach bag but it was waterproof and easy to carry on your shoulder.

Jack emptied his backpack and checked the clothes for both himself and Lu. Once the tumble dryer had slowed to a halt they took out everything and checked it all. A couple of coats went back in along with Unk, who was still damp from being thrown overboard yesterday, but now they had a set of dry clothes as spares. They packed these into their backpacks, squashing it all in as best as they could manage.

While the coats were finishing off they sat on the floor in the office and drank some cans they'd found and ate some crisps - stale but edible. Lu was happily swivelling on the desk chair and pretending to write and draw with some paper and pens Rosie had found in the desk tray.

"What now?" Rosie asked.

Jack thought before answering. Mum sometimes reminded him to 'think before you speak.' He knew she didn't mean all the time, just when you needed to be careful not to upset someone, and this was one of those times.

"Not sure. Still thinking. Where do you think Harry ended up?"

"In Westerbridge. Followed the bus route, trying to find you."

"And when he got there?"

Rosie shrugged. "Looked for you."

"Depends. If he caught up with the bus and saw we weren't on it, he would back track, know we got off at the bus stop here. He'd look. He'd come here."

Rosie emptied the last of her crisps into her hand and tipped them into her mouth. She munched for a bit and swallowed before saying, "What's the time? How long have we been here?"

Jack checked and worked out that since they'd got off the bus it had been nearly an hour and a half. "Enough time for him to get to Westerbridge, ride back and already be looking for us now. So, we need to leave."

Rosie stood up to get ready.

"But I don't want you to come."

Rosie looked at him. "Why not?"

"He's not your problem, Harry, and it's not safe."

She snorted. "You need me."

"No, I can manage."

She snorted again. "No, you can't. You'd never ever have got here without me."

"But you can go on from here and get to your gran."

"Could but you need to get there too."

"It's too hard. Everything goes wrong. You don't want to be with us when he catches us. I have to go to the police, get Lu safe, even if it's not with me." Mum would understand, he thought. He'd tried, he had, but it wasn't good enough.

Rosie shook her head. "Not now, you can't stop now."

"Let's get into town and decide then. We can't be out here in case he has come back."

They took the coats from the dryer and Jack switched it off. The rain had almost stopped so they bundled themselves up and each put on a plastic rain poncho from a pile in the shop. Lu was completely draped by hers and Jack had to find a pair of scissors to cut several centimetres from the bottom so she could walk without tripping up, but he and Rosie liked the way their capes completely covered them and their bags. He peered out the store room door and checked the area. It seemed quiet so they slipped out and crossed the back of the site office and scuttled along the drive leading to the lane and to the road.

"This way," Rosie said and lead them back along the road to where they'd climbed through the hedgerow into the park. They looked along the road in both directions. Where next, Jack thought.

Chapter Forty-Eight

Day 18: Monday Early Afternoon - Police - PC Anstey and DC Tizora

"This is the bus stop where they got off." Anstey pointed and Tizora pulled over and parked.

"No cameras around and this is yet another village, no shop, no river this time either, not much of anything."

Tizora pointed to a sign. "Museum?"

Anstey looked at the map. "Railway museum. Possible. Go down that way and we'll check it out."

It was a short drive to the museum, and it was shut, the sign said, but there were a few cars parked by the side of a big building. It was raining now and they ran over and found a small open door round the side. Tizora went in, astounded by how much was crammed inside. There was a whole steam engine, and a myriad of flags hanging from the rafters, and lots of crammed shelves on the walls, and hundreds of machine parts stacked on the floor.

"Hello!" called Anstey. "Anyone in?"

"We're shut until tomorrow," a voice called back. "Sorry."

"Police. We just need to ask you a couple of questions."

Two men in stained brown overalls emerged from the back of the engine and came over.

"DC Tizora and PC Anstey." They showed their ID.

"Sorry to stop you from working but we're looking for the missing children and a trail lead us to this area. Have you seen anything?"

It seemed not, they were sorry, they would have liked to help. Then another man came in from the rear of the building. He paused when he saw Tizora and Anstey.

"Police," said his fellow enthusiast. "Looking for the missing kids."

"I read about that and it was on the telly last night. No luck then?"

Anstey shook his head. "Thanks anyway. If you notice anything let us know."

The men nodded.

Back outside they dashed to the car and slammed the doors against the rain.

"We're going to have to go from door to door here, just in case. Dog walker. Someone driving home. The team is trying to track the bus passengers but it won't give us much."

As Tizora was turning the car to leave, one of the men came and waved at them. She opened the window and looked out.

"Can you come back? Terry says the cafe has been broken into. While you're here, could you have a look?"

Both Anstey and Tizora grinned. Oh yes, they certainly could.

Ten minutes later Tizora had phoned it in and another team was on its way.

"Right, we're only half a day behind - well, a bit more than that but the gap is closing. Which way did they go?"

They stood in the hangar, looking out at the rain. Terry brought them each a mug of tea in a fairly oil-free mug and stood almost to attention.

"Anything we can do to help?" he asked.

"No, not really," Tizora said, "We have to keep out until the team's been in. Thanks."

"Do you really think they stayed there? On their own? Those two kids all night."

"This is the third - fourth place that we've tracked them to. Seems the same. Using some of the stuff. Tidying up. Forensics will let us know."

"Clever kids. I hope they got away. Have you got the bloke yet? You know, the violent one?"

Anstey shook his head. "We're getting closer. We need to work out where they went next. Good tea, thanks."

The other men strolled over with their mugs and oily hands and stood around.

"If they left when we arrived they'd have been gone for hours," Gerry said.

"Kids don't walk fast," said Gareth. "At least my grandkids don't."

"And one of them was little, wasn't she," Steve remembered. "She'll slow them down. They won't have got far."

"What's that down there?" Tizora pointed through the open side door at the track running past the cafe.

"The railway line. Or what was the railway line. It's a footpath now."

Anstey looked at it hopefully. "So anyone can walk down it? It looks easy walking, straight and flat."

"It goes to what was the next station and then on to the end of the line."

"How far? When does it finish?"

"About five miles," said Gareth.

Tizora and Anstey looked at each other. They just had to get down there.

"Can a car get down?" Tizora asked.

"No, not allowed," Gerry shook his head.

"Can a *police* car get down?" Anstey asked.

"Not really, wreck the suspension, and there might still be walkers and cyclists along it," Steve said.

"I can lend you a bike. One of you can cycle down and the other one can meet them at the end with the car," suggested Terry. "We'll wait for the forensics, however long it takes."

Five minutes later Anstey was perched on an ancient bike, partly lovingly restored by Terry but mostly rust and definitely lacking in comfort, while Tizora was setting off in the car to the end of the track.

"Race you!" she called as she set off.

Anstey wobbled as he kicked off. The four men cheered him as he picked up speed and he hoped none of them was filming him as he veered down the track. Once he got going it was quite fast but puddles were forming in the ruts which splashed upwards and the rain was running down his back where the cape Gerry had leant him was gaping and flapping, so it certainly wasn't fun. He kept an eye out for signs of the children - something dropped, or a track in the hedges, and for anyone coming towards him. It didn't seem long before he got to what had been a station and saw that someone was still inside, a volunteer tidying up.

He parked the bike against the wall and went in.

"Keep your eye on that," she said, "One got stolen only today."

He looked out at the bike. "A bike?"

He pulled his ID from his pocket under the cape and showed her.

"They've sent you out on a bike? To find a stolen bike?"

"No, I've ..."

"Well, with all that business over Freeling way I'd've thought you had more important things to do than come here to ask about a stolen bike."

"I *am* on that case but that bike might be important."

Anstey got the details and phoned it in. Somebody needed to track the bike - he was sure Moreton had taken it. And that meant he was close to the children - who were on foot. He hoped the team tracking Moreton were searching over this way today.

He carried on and got to the end where Tizora was waiting.

"It wasn't a fair race," he said as they forced the bike into the boot. "I had to stop." Anstey was definitely wet, so he emptied the bag they'd used for food at the shop, opened it out and sat on that so he wouldn't have a soggy seat later.

As they drove back to the museum he told her about the stolen bike and passed the information on to the incident team.

The forensics team had just started when they got back. Anstey gave Terry his bike back with thanks and they waited with another mug of not quite oily tea as the team got to work. It only took minutes to confirm the three children had been there. The team was going to carry on and Tizora and Anstey said thanks to the men and set off.

It was still raining and hard to decide where to look. They followed the road back to the end of the railway track and looked out through the rain streaked windscreen.

"Where next?"

Tizora shrugged. "No idea. They'll be wet, if they're out in this. Lu is only four."

Anstey pulled up the map again and looked over the likely places. "Westerbridge? I'd go there. It's big enough to hide in."

"I'd stick to shut places, like the lodge or the holiday places."

"Do they need food?"

"Probably not. They ate at the cafe. They bought stuff at the shop too."

"So, somewhere dry near here."

Tizora spotted a sign. "Bus. They went on a bus."

"Another one?"

She climbed out into the drizzle and went over to the sign at the bus stop.

"Right," she said as she got back in. She uploaded a photo to the file and sent an alert. "If they check CCTV on buses from that stop, from about 2pm onwards, they could pick them up and we'll know where to go next."

"Let's head to where it goes then, at least we can get something to eat. I need to take away the taste of that tea."

Tizora drove them to the town and they parked up. It was mid-afternoon. The rain was slowing and while they were waiting for the researcher to let them know if the children had caught a bus, they sat in a cafe and ate far too much - when you're on a case you have to eat when you can.

Chapter Forty-Nine

Day 18: Monday Early Evening - Jack, Rosie and Lu

They carried on walking, now on a narrow footpath at the side of the road. It was still light but with no street lamps here Jack knew they couldn't go for much longer before it got too dark for Lu to see where she was going. He wished they had the trolley again. The road widened and they saw a church, a line of houses and phone box up ahead. A phone box. Who could he phone? Whose number did he know? Jack didn't know anyone's number. Why would he, no one has to remember phone numbers now. He stopped near the box and tugged at Rosie.

"Do you know your gran's number?"

She shook her head.

"The address? Do you know that?"

"Yes."

Jack thought, desperately trying to think of a way to get a message to someone who could help them.

"No point," Rosie said. She pulled the door open for him to look inside the phone box. It wasn't working. It was used as a library, one of those you find in small villages where the local people put in books to share. Oh well, thought Jack. It was just an idea.

As they passed the church he stopped and looked down the weedy path to the closed doors. What about the vicar? Didn't they help? "The vicar, shall we ask him to help."

"Her."

"What?"

Rosie pointed at the glass - covered display board next to the lych-gate.

"Rev. Precious Gates." Jack read the name. "So can't she help? Doesn't the vicar live next to the church?"

Rosie pointed to the information. "No, not any more, she lives in Westerbridge, just comes here for some days, not even every Sunday."

Oh well, another idea gone. They carried on, as usual just seeing a lone dog-walker and one car.

"Where does this go?"

Rosie pointed up ahead. "Down there, should be a river, going to Westerbridge."

"No rowing in the rain you said," he reminded her.

"But we can't stay on the road, there's no more buses and we need to get away. We need a boat."

"We can't steal a boat!"

"Why not? We already have."

"No, we haven't. Not a boat."

"Yes, we did, you rowed it."

Jack stopped. "I thought ... that wasn't your boat?"

"Why? It wasn't my boathouse, was it?" She carried on walking so Jack had to catch up.

"Why didn't you say?"

Rosie shrugged.

Jack trudged alongside Rosie, holding Lu's wet hand. Actually, he thought, he should have known it wasn't her boat if it was in the boathouse next to Orchard Cottage. Why would she keep a boat in someone else's boathouse? Did people do that? Keep a boat somewhere else. Possibly, he thought, as not everyone who had a boat could keep it next to their house. Not everyone lived by a river but they might live *near* a river and want a boat. He was struggling to think about that. He was tired and feeling fuzzy.

It was just beginning to get dark when the road ran out but widened into a sort of parking area, gravel rather than proper road and full of potholes. It was deserted. But then, thought Jack, it was a late afternoon on a wet Tuesday - or Wednesday - so who would be out here now? There was a jetty, small and only able to moor a few boats. There were some upturned boats at the edge of the car park, and a couple half on the bank and half in the water. Opposite, there were some similar boats, tied up along the bank.

Rosie looked along the line of boats moored on the jetty and further along the bank where the car park ran out. She began walking along the rutted path, checking for something to steal and Jack and Lu followed on behind. She stopped to take an oar from one boat and carried on before she stopped again and untied a rowing boat. It didn't look any different from any of the ones they'd passed but Rosie knew what she was doing. There was an oar in this boat - so now she had two and a boat to use them with. Not again, Jack groaned, he didn't want to row ever again. It was too slow and painful. And they didn't have lifejackets, they'd left those somewhere way back, or possibly not that far back, and probably just yesterday.

He helped Lu onto the seat and dropped the bags in and Rosie climbed in after them. They rearranged the bags, got Lu sitting safely and Rosie began to row. The boat pulled away from the bank and she headed downstream, aiming to stay in the middle of the river. But before she'd gone more than fifty metres she slowed and pulled over to a bigger blue boat, moored on the opposite bank, held by a buoy bobbing in the current and a rope running to a stake on the bank.

"We can't row that," Jack complained. "It's too big."

She snorted and caught hold of the other boat with one hand and pulled them close and then she stood up and held out her hand towards Jack, "Rope." And he passed her the rope to tie up with. The rowing boat moved on the waves but stayed close enough to the bigger boat, clunking into its side as she wrapped the rope around a metal thing - Jack didn't know what it was called - secured to the side. Rosie hauled herself up and over and fell into their next ride.

"Blue," said Lu.

"Blue," said Jack. "And …?"

Lu looked. "Wet."

Jack had to agree but he had expected her to say 'red' as there was a red line along the side of the boat.

"What are you doing?" he called.

"Wait, nearly done it." Rosie called back. He couldn't see where she was but could hear some clunks and crashes.

She looked over at him, smiling. "Get in."

Jack lifted Lu up and Rosie pulled her over the side, into the boat. He passed up their bags.

"Oars," she said, so he passed those up too before he climbed in.

This was bigger than their rowing boat had been, and it also had a little cabin at the front. The door was open and Rosie had ducked back in. He sat Lu on the bench seat at the back, tucking the rain cape over and around her before squeezing behind Rosie to look at the inside.

She was checking through some drawers and under flaps and along ridges.

"Keys. We need the keys."

She held up a rusty key and smiled as she turned to him. Then her smile faded. As Jack turned to see what she had seen, Lu screamed out. He turned and saw Harry picking her up.

Chapter Fifty

Day 18: Monday late afternoon - Police - PC Anstey and DC Tizora

The rain had almost stopped but it was still drizzling when the call came. The children had been on a bus, had got off at a stop by the caravan park outside town. They got back to the car and sped off to the stop. Tizora pulled in and stopped at the closed gates.

"I bet they *are* here," she said. "It's dry and empty."

"So, let's have a look."

They squeezed through a gap in a hedge and walked round to the reception. It was shut up. They walked quietly along the rows of caravans looking for signs of life, a light, a noise, voices. Nothing. Back at reception Tizora went round the back and found the opened door to the stores. "Anstey," she whispered. "Here."

Quietly, they went through the stores, the shop and the office until the laundry room was the last room left. Empty. But someone had been here, just like before.

"We're not going to be very popular - another scene to process," said Tizora as she phoned it in.

"This is still sort of warm," said Anstey as he opened the tumble drier. "It's been used only a little while ago."

Forensics would have to check who had been here. It might not be the three they were looking for. It might have been Moreton.

Two officers arrived after twenty minutes, to secure the scene and wait for forensics, leaving Anstey and Tizora able to move on.

In the car Anstey looked at the map yet again. "Where would Jack go now?"

"What's that dot there?"

"A village - again. Small. Leads down to the river."

"The same one as down by Orchard Cottage?"

Anstey squinted as he followed the blue lines. "Sort of. Actually, probably not. They all link up though."

"Were they heading somewhere? Trying to row somewhere?"

"They're just kids. How could they get even as far as that holiday place? And with Lu."

"They seem pretty good to me. They must have had a plan. Get to somewhere. Boat. Bus. Walk."

"And what now." Anstey looked out along the road. "Where would they go after this?"

His phone rang and he put it on speaker so Tizora could hear the latest from the researcher. The stolen bike had been caught on CCTV at a level crossing, just behind the bus which the children had been on. In Westerbridge it had disappeared down some side roads and then it came back out and was heading out on the road they were parked in. No idea who was on it. But it hadn't crossed the train track again. It was somewhere between Westerbridge and the level crossing.

"It's Moreton. It's got to be."

Tizora pulled out onto the road and took the next left along a quiet road to a village.

Chapter Fifty-One

Day 18: Monday late afternoon - Jack, Rosie and Lu

Lu squirmed and kicked her legs but her arms were pinned by the rain cape and by Harry.

Jack leapt forward and tried to grab Lu back but Harry pushed him hard in the chest so that he fell back and landed painfully against the bench. He slid down, scrabbling at the seat but it was too wet and slippery from the rain and he fell on to the deck. He rolled over on his knees to push himself up.

"You always were a useless kid," Harry smirked. "She's mine. I'm taking what's mine." He stepped onto the edge of the boat to climb off, clutching a screaming Lu.

As Jack frantically hauled himself to his feet Rosie flew past him and thwacked an oar on the side of Harry's head. When Jack thought about that moment later, it really did seem as if time had slowed. He remembered how Harry had half turned to face them, a look of pain and shock replacing that smirk, before he crumpled, sagged or collapsed - Jack couldn't really describe how Harry's body sort of deflated as he sank down, falling sideways onto the path, cracking his head again on the side of the boat as he fell.

Jack dashed forward, shoving past Rosie, to leap onto the footpath and drag Lu away. She clung so tightly to his neck he struggled to breathe. She was okay. Not hurt - just terrified. He thought then, he would never let her go. Rosie was still standing in the boat with the oar in her hand, pale and shaking.

"Is he dead?" she whispered.

Jack shuddered. "There's blood." He stepped round Harry and climbed back into the boat as Lu gulped deep breaths between howling and sobbing onto his shoulder.

Rosie saw she was still clutching the oar and threw it over onto the bank with a shudder. She edged forward. She kept as far away as she could but leaned over and looked at Harry's head.

"It's bashed a lot, there's blood."

"Does he look dead?" Jack asked.

"How do I know!"

"You said you'd seen lots of dead things."

"Not people, badgers and … things like that."

Badgers, you did say that, thought Jack.

They stood looking at the distorted body lying on the footpath.

"Well, we've caught him, so if we go to the police now we'll be okay." Jack said.

Rosie shook her head. However hard she tried not to, she kept looking at the messy red patch that was Harry's head. "You might, if your mum is better but - they might not let you stay together with Lu if she's not. And I won't be okay. Frank. And he'll say … I killed her … and now … I've killed Harry too."

Lu was still whimpering in Jack's aching arms so he sat down on the seat at the back. His knee and right side hurt from the fall when Harry pushed him over but he tried to ignore the throbbing and concentrate. What should they do next? Now that Harry was dead - probably - did that change things? But what if Mum was still in hospital and couldn't look after them? Perhaps he and Lu could go to Gran, because they would be safe there now they didn't have to worry about Harry finding them? He looked at Rosie. She was very pale, still shaking, so miserable sitting hunched up on the bench with the rain dripping steadily from the cabin roof onto her head.

I'm only eleven, thought Jack. I'm in a boat next to a dead body, I'm on the run with somebody who lies and breaks into places and steals things and snorts at me every time she thinks I'm being stupid - and I've lied and I've broken into places and I've stolen - and I'm wet and fed up and … he felt his face flush. Lu had settled into a low but constant crying on to his shoulder, as if his rain cape wasn't already wet enough. He hid his face down and then heard a snuffling over Lu's low whimpering. Rosie was crying.

"I want my mum," she whispered as she cried.

"So do I," Jack said. "I hate him. He nearly killed my mum - twice."

"I hate Frank. He *did* kill my mum." Rosie sobbed into her sleeve.

"HEY! JACK!"

They looked up. What? Who was that?

"JACK? Jack Williamson?"

Across on the other side of the bank a woman and a man in police uniform were running towards them, and calling and waving.

Rosie looked back at Jack startled. "We have to go, now! Untie the boat."

She fumbled with the dashboard while Jack put Lu down and undid the mooring rope attached to the rowing boat and pushed it adrift. In the background Jack knew the police officer and the woman were shouting over to them but he was panicking too much to hear what they were saying.

He climbed out onto the bank to untie the mooring at the back, stepping on Harry's outflanked arm as he scrambled back in.

They heard the officer shout, "**STOP! YOU — STOP!**" as he drew level with them along the opposite bank.

"*NOW* Rosie!"

The engine stuttered into life … and stopped. Rosie was shaking as she tried again. This time she revved the engine and pushed a lever and steered midstream. As the officer caught up level Rosie pushed hard at a lever and the boat moved quickly forward.

"**Stop! STOP!**" He almost stepped into the water to reach them but held back. "**We know who you are. STOP! We'll help you.**"

"**PLEASE!**" the woman shouted. "**WAIT!**"

Rosie concentrated on steering into the mid-stream and then the boat sped up, leaving the police officer and the woman staring after them, still waving and shouting. Jack picked Lu up and sat holding her as Rosie put distance between them. He saw them stare and point at Harry's body on the footpath and then stare back at him.

Murder. That really complicated things.

Chapter Fifty-Two

Day 18: Monday evening - Police - PC Anstey and DC Tizora

Within minutes Tizora notified all the teams who needed to know and she stood in the drizzle keeping the scene secure until support arrived. Anstey clumsily caught and paddled the rowing boat across with one oar to see who was on the far bank. He stood forlornly in the rain, dripping over the body of Harry Moreton.

Anstey's head was spinning and he couldn't even begin to calm down. He blamed himself for losing Jack and Lu. As he stood in the rain he went over all the ways he could have got there earlier, even five minutes earlier. They had spent too much time eating at the cafe. They should have checked out the caravan park quicker. They should have decided to drive to the village sooner. He should have jumped in and swam after the boat. So close - only minutes away but we lost them, he thought.

Tizora stood next to Anstey and thought about what they now knew. Harry was out of the picture, either injured or dead. Jack and Lu were both alive and safe. They had footage of the boat to help to trace where they went next. And, there was definitely someone else with them, driving the boat, who Jack had escaped with, so possibly the missing Rowley girl, Rosie Hynes. So close - we're nearly there, she thought.

Chapter Fifty-Three

Day 18: Monday early evening - Jack, Rosie and Lu

"Nasty man," Lu sobbed, as Rosie drove them away.

"Very nasty." Jack knew the policeman was filming them, and could see the woman talking on her phone and looking over at Harry's body on the far bank. There wasn't much he could do about that but knew now that the police would know what boat they were in, and where they were. He went to the tiny cabin and sat on the little bench with Lu. She was cold and tired so he took off the rain cape and found she was dry enough underneath. He sat her down in a corner, making a little den with a couple of cushions and a hoody he took from the grab bag. He gave her Unk, a drink and a banana, before taking his own rain cape off and putting it with Lu's in a bin so they kept the cabin dry. He stood with Rosie at the steering wheel.

"Where are we going?" he asked. "Do you know?"

"Westerbridge is just here, but we go past and out across the broad."

"And then what?"

She shrugged.

Oh well, Jack thought, we have half a plan then.

He took the steering wheel while Rosie took off her rain cape. He'd never driven a boat before and it was something which he would have found new and exciting only days ago but now just seemed yet another thing he had to do just to make things right.

Rosie navigated into a bigger river and turned them towards Westerbridge. It was busier than anywhere Jack had been on the rivers so far. Although it was late afternoon, almost dark and drizzling with rain, there were several boats out on the water. As a river police boat sped past them the way they'd come from, Jack ducked down with Lu in the cabin. He watched it disappear but then kept close to the cabin walls so he couldn't be seen while they passed through the town. There were a few boats moored up on either side and some houseboats, as well as the cottages and lodges Jack had got used to seeing. There wasn't much to show anyone was living in the places though, as only a few lights were switched on and the windows and doors were tightly shut.

Rosie concentrated as she took them under a bridge and through the other side of the town, carefully choosing which side to take. As they came out the other side a siren blared towards them and as they looked up and back they saw the blue lights of a police car flash over the bridge and along the road. Rosie turned and checked the controls. She couldn't make the boat go any faster so they just had to hope that by the time the police got to Harry they would have got far enough away to hide somewhere.

While Rosie drove them further from town, he sat with Lu while she played with one of the dolls from her backpack. This one did have both arms and legs but its head was on back to front. Lu didn't seem to mind. He hoped that if anyone saw the boat they would see Rosie, still looking a bit like a boy in the hoody they had dried at the caravan park, and they wouldn't see him and Lu sitting on the floor. They must know about them by now. He had that stabbing punch to his stomach when he wondered how Mum was; was she awake and worried or was she still 'stable' but unconscious? He didn't know which one was worse; that she was worrying about him and Lu or so injured from Harry's attack she was still unconscious. His stomach lurched even more when, for the first time, he thought about the worst thing of all - what if Mum didn't get well, what if she …? He couldn't think about that. He had to concentrate on getting somewhere safe with Rosie, Lu and the boat. He stood up and looked through the low window to see where they were going.

"We need to decide," Rosie said, as she slowed the engine. "It's getting dark and there aren't any lights on the boat. If I go down that way," she pointed across the river further up, "There's a cut through to the broad. We can try to get across before it's really dark. We could get a long way before we have to moor up somewhere. But if there are people still out they might stop us because we haven't got any lights and if they know the police are looking for you - that's it, the end, back to Frank for me, whatever for you."

"And …"

"What?"

"You said decide, so what else …"

"Or - we can go that way," she pointed, "Moor up and wait until morning, then go across and hope no one's still out looking around here."

"Let's get as far as we can, leave early in the morning … anything to get there sooner."

Rosie sped up a little bit before turning the boat and taking them down a narrower stretch.

"Is it far?" asked Jack.

She shook her head.

"How do you know where to go?" he asked.

"My granddad took me out. He liked boats and being on the water. We came as far as Westerbridge, so I can remember the way."

"In a boat like this?"

"Smaller but with an engine. We usually stayed nearer to where my gran lives but he took us out to further places, when he could."

Rosie turned the boat slightly and brought it out onto a wide expanse of water; a broad. In the fading light he could just about see the edges, the fields bordering the banks and the little island in the middle, but he could see that it was big and open, so they would be easily seen crossing it.

Rosie edged the boat by the shore and took them around one side, keeping close to the banks - but not too close incase they got stuck in shallow water. The drizzle had stopped, so Jack kept watch from the back of the boat. He could see no other boats out on the water but he constantly checked and wished they could go faster. Rosie steadily circumnavigated the broad and brought them to a waterway on the far side.

It was dark now, but not so dark as it would be on the streets at home. The sky seemed to give them more light than street lamps would, even though the patchy clouds scudded over the moon and blocked its light.

"Can you see enough?" he asked.

"Just. It's safer in the middle, nothing to crash into."

Crash? Could boats crash? Jack thought they sank.

"Wee," said Lu. Jack sighed and picked her up. This was going to be tricky on a boat. But at least it had stopped raining, he thought as he tried to work out how to help her.

It was properly dark when Rosie said, "That's it, we'll have to stop." She edged the boat to an overhanging tree and nudged the front under the branches while Jack grabbed at a branch from the back and pulled it hard, swinging the back end close to the bank. He held the branch while Rosie stopped the engine and came back to him and tied a rope to the branch. She also tied a mooring at the front to keep them safe from floating away. They were now tucked into the bank, partly shielded by the branches and reeds.

Lu was asleep in her nest in the cabin so Jack found a torch and they each rummaged through the bags to find something to eat. When they had eaten what was easy to manage in the cramped space, so a banana squashed between a slice of bread, some crisps and biscuits - again - they turned the torch off in case someone saw the light and settled to sleep.

It was cold and damp, and scary here in the backwater, all alone in the dark. Things rustled and creaked. The overhanging branches hit the boat in the breeze which also made the river slap at the sides, rocking them gently. Jack thought it was noisier than at home. At least when he heard noises at the flats he knew what they were; doors closing, cars parking, someone thudding a ball at the garage doors on the ground floor. Here, he didn't know what that rustle was, or that crack or clunk. The more he listened in the quiet of the night, the more he could hear.

He turned over and wrapped himself more tightly in his coat, pulling the hood up over his face. After a minute he shifted again; the side of the boat was pressing into his leg, the one he'd hurt today, so he had to move on to his other side. He settled again and lay still. He shuffled again, this time because his arm was going dead. He flexed his fingers trying to stop the pins and needles. He settled again, curled in a tight ball but sitting up against the side of the cabin wall. As he began to drop off to sleep, his head lolled forward and jerked him awake. He sat up properly and stretched his legs out, bracing them against the cabin door, trying to get himself stable in the gently rocking boat.

"Stop fidgeting," Rosie snapped.

"Can't help it, can't get comfortable."

"Go out then, more room out there."

"It's cold - and …"

Rosie snorted. "Scared of the dark?"

"Yes, a bit. Not used to it. There's too much water and too many trees and reeds and … nature."

"It's the country, what else would be here."

"It's alright for you, you're used to it, living on a farm."

"Not."

"Not? What's that mean? Not?"

"Not … used to it. Only lived on the farm a while, not even a year."

Jack felt his mouth open in surprise. Gran always said he was catching flies when he did that so he was glad it was too dark for Rosie to see his face properly.

"Where *did* you live, then, before?"

"On an army base in Germany when I was really small. Then on a base here, and then in the house in town, or at my gran's."

"Like me and Mum and Lu, moving around. I liked where I lived last, in the flats. I didn't see my gran anymore, she couldn't know where we were, but we could talk - just on a phone. I liked it all apart from not seeing Gran. I didn't like leaving it and coming here. I really miss school, going to football, sitting in the library, taking Lu swimming, going over to the rec and the park with my mates … I really miss them, my mates."

Rosie sat up and he heard her shuffle to face him.

"You left because of Harry?"

Jack nodded in the dark. "Every time we moved it was because of Harry."

"But he's gone now. You can go home."

Jack wondered about that. Would they go back? Or would they go back to where Gran lived? Or somewhere new? "Where do you think you'll go, when this is all over?"

Rosie shrugged.

"Your gran, she'll help, won't she? Or those cousins, are they around here?"

Rosie leant forward, her shape moving in the darkness.

"It's complicated," she said.

"You said that before."

"Well, it is. It's been so hard."

Jack waited. Mum said sometimes you have to let people take their time. He let Rosie have lots of time. It seemed like minutes but it was probably only seconds before she said, "I'll tell you."

And in the darkness of the cabin, she told her story to Jack.

Chapter Fifty-Four

Last Summer - Rosie

I've told myself this story - which isn't a story, it's true - lots of times, until it's straight in my head. Let me get to the end. Don't stop me, wait until I've finished.

After my dad died, my real dad, I went to live with Gran. Dad had looked after me but - when it was just me and my mum, she couldn't do her job and get me from school and take me to places so I stayed with Gran. Just in the week at first. My mum would take me to school on Mondays and Gran would look after me until after school on Friday when Mum would come and get me and take me home.

Gran is the best gran ever. She let me help her cook tea and took me swimming and Granddad taught me to row and took me out on his boat. I liked being back home with my mum too. She always had jobs to do, like cleaning and shopping, but we watched films together and had take-aways.

Then after a while, I stayed at Gran's some weekends too. Then it was Christmas. We stayed at Gran's, me and my mum, and the house was full because everyone came, except Granddad because - well, because he couldn't remember us anymore and he had to stay in a special place for people like him. That was sad but all the rest, well, it was - good, like Christmases are supposed to be. I slept in the back room with all my cousins with sleeping bags and cushions. We laughed all night. And ... my mum was happy, like she hadn't been for ages.

Then, a couple of days after the proper Christmas when everyone had gone except my mum and me, I met Frank. My mum brought him to Gran's to meet us. I didn't know then they'd been seeing each other, dating, while I was staying at Gran's. We went out for a day together, bowling and the cinema. It was nice, being like a family, the three of us. I hadn't felt that with my dad, my real dad, for a long time, but he couldn't help being sick, being sad, I did know that.

At Easter they got married. My mum was the happiest I ever remembered. It was like something new was happening. We sold our house to one of Frank's friends, so it was quick, and moved to the farm - a new life together, all three of us. My mum wasn't working now and she was excited about the farm.

I started a new school, catching the bus everyday because we only had one car and Frank needed it but I met kids in my class on the bus and I thought, then, that I would make friends. But Frank didn't want anyone coming to the farm. He said it needed things doing before anyone came round and he didn't have time to come and get me from anyone's house.

There was stuff to do on the farm. We still had some cows then, and a milking shed. There were chickens and a couple of cats. And there were lots of buildings to look around and all the fields too. My mum was trying to do things in the house and we were sorting out cupboards and the attic and ... lots of stuff really. Frank was out a lot and when he came back, he didn't say much, never asked about what I was doing or how school had been. Even my dad used to ask about what I'd done at school.

When the school holidays came, I was at home all the time. And that was when it all started to get bad. My mum was always tired. She was sorting stuff all day, as well as cleaning and cooking but there was so much to do, and Frank was always off doing something somewhere. She didn't have enough time to take me out and Frank always had the car so I asked if I could go to stay with Gran for a bit. Frank said no, he needed the car and couldn't take me and anyway, I had to help Mum, earn my keep, he said.

Then, one night, I woke up and heard some cars in the yard. There were lights and voices but I couldn't see what was going on. I asked my mum in the morning but she said I had to ignore it, pretend it never happened. A few nights later, there were noises again, lorries this time, men calling out, not even trying to be quiet. And then a van came in the day time. Frank opened the stable and they loaded some boxes in the van. They were big boxes, different shapes. Not farm stuff, something else.

There wasn't a phone I could use to call Gran, my mum said she didn't have a signal on hers, so I wrote Gran a letter. I thought if I did some jobs to earn my keep, as Frank said, but asked Gran to come and get me, it would be okay. My mum didn't know I had written the letter - I thought it would be a surprise if Gran turned up. I didn't have a stamp but I thought Gran could pay when she got it. I was walking to the post box on the main road when Frank drove back to the farm. He stopped and opened the door. "What's that?" He'd seen the letter in my hand. I know now that I should have hidden it. He got really quiet and scary. He got out of the car and stood right up close so I had to step back. He held my arm so tight it hurt. He said, "You do what I say or or your mum gets it." I didn't know then what that meant. I didn't tell my mum. I kept my arm covered so she wouldn't see the bruises.

The next few days were horrible. He never shouted, never really said anything, but everything we did was always wrong. Mum was so upset. She tried harder to get it right, to make sure everything was done and finished but it was never good enough. I helped but it didn't make any difference.

Then, one day when I went to feed the chickens there wasn't enough food in the store shed, so I went to look in the barn, and then I tried that door at the end of the stable. It opened, it was dark inside but I went in anyway. I bumped into some boxes on the floor and knocked one off the pile. It was heavy so it made a lot of noise when it hit the floor. I was trying to pick it up when he came behind me and grabbed my arm. He did that thing of standing too close, staring at me just a bit too long before he said, "Don't ever come in here again." He didn't shout, which was even more scary.

He pulled me outside and back to the kitchen. He pushed me down onto a chair and grabbed my mum, dragging her by her hair and shoving her against the cooker. I jumped at him, trying to pull him off but he hit me and knocked me over. My mum was screaming but he just held her tight, then he turned the cooker on, holding her arm on the flame.

"If that nosey brat goes near the stable, I'll burn her." He looked at me.

He let my mum go and went out. She was in a state. Her arm was red and blistered. We sat at the table and cried. My mum cried because she was hurt. I cried because it was my fault. I helped her bandage her arm. She had to throw her shirt away, it was burned. She said it would be *alright, we'd soon be like a family, Frank was just busy because there was so much to do ... but I knew it wasn't going to be alright.*

We were stuck on the farm. Frank never let us go anywhere. My mum couldn't even go to the doctor to get her burned arm seen to. The cows had been sold but the chickens were still in their houses so I fed them with the last of the feed from one of the old sheds and collected the eggs. The stables were always locked up so even if I'd dared to look again, I couldn't get in anymore. A lot of the stuff in the sheds, like the milking machines, had been taken away in vans and lorries. Some days Frank went out on the tractor and some of the things growing in the fields were dug up, sold I suppose. But it wasn't a farm anymore, not really.

About a week after Frank had burned her arm, my mum wasn't well. She was in bed all day and hot and sweaty. I took her some water, opened the window, trying to cool her down. I made her some toast but she couldn't eat. I knocked on the office door, and he wouldn't open it so I shouted, 'Mum needs a doctor.' He just shouted back 'No doctors' and then ignored me.

I searched in the kitchen, the bathroom, the hall cupboard, trying to find paracetamol, they're for when you're hot, I knew that. Back in my mum's bedroom I looked through her bag and all the drawers, and then in Frank's too. In one of his drawers there was a package, a big envelope with 'Samples' stamped on the front but no address. It was open so I looked in. There were packs of tablets, all with curly writing on them, like shapes not words. One had a little bit of our kind of writing on and I thought it said they were aspirin. I gave my mum two, that's the usual amount. And three hours later, I gave her two more. She seemed better, quieter, but then she was worse. She was calling out, moving her arms and legs, breathing louder.

Frank had gone out but he wouldn't have done anything even if he'd been there. I needed to get help. I ran up to the main road. The first car coming along was a red van, a postman, so I stood in the road and stopped him. I said could he see my mum, she was ill and I didn't know what to do. He was worried, especially when he knew I was on my own. He went back with me, and when he saw my mum he said he'd help. He was in her bedroom calling an ambulance when Frank came back. I thought he'd be angry but he wasn't, he was so ... nice. He said he'd only gone to get some medicine for her, he said it had been so sudden, thanked the postman for being so helpful ... He said I should take the postman downstairs and he could get back to his job, thank you, all okay now.

I didn't want to leave my mum, but I went down with the postman and took him back out to his van. I wanted him to stay. I wanted to tell him what was happening. But I was scared. I let him drive off.

Frank came down. He stood close to me. "Mouth shut." He let me go back upstairs and I sat waiting for the ambulance. It seemed to be ages before anyone came. I went down as soon as they came. I could hear Frank talking. I could hear things like 'too young to know' and 'panicked' and 'all a mistake.' I went into the kitchen and Frank looked round. I saw his face change before he smiled at me.

"Here she is, she's worried about her mum, bless her."

I was terrified they would just leave but they said they had to see her now they were here - rules they said. I wanted to tell them I'd given her some aspirin, some water, that her arm was burned, but Frank was staring at me, so I didn't.

Frank took them upstairs and I followed but he stopped me at the bedroom door and made me stand outside. It didn't take long before my mum was being carried into the ambulance. She was really sick and had to go to hospital. That was the last time I saw her.

Frank wouldn't take me with him to the hospital. He left me at the farm all night, on my own. When he came back he said I couldn't go and see her at the hospital, because she was in a special ward and they didn't let children in. He went back to the hospital and then, that evening, late, he came back again. He looked - different. Relieved. I knew before he said it ... she had died. He said it was my fault. He said the hospital had done some tests, so they knew she'd had some pills that made her so sick she died. But he said that they didn't know who had given them to her, so if I kept quiet and stayed at the farm, I wouldn't go to prison for murder.

I don't know how many days passed. It got very blurry. I didn't even go to the funeral, I don't know if there was one. I asked if I could go to Gran's but he said she blamed me, she didn't want to see me, I'd killed her daughter. It was just ... bad, really bad. I was so scared the police would come and get me.

Frank went out every day. He seemed happy, not like someone whose wife had died. He had some new clothes and a new phone. I asked him if I could have my mum's phone but he said he didn't know where it was.

The vans kept coming every few days, usually at night. When one came one afternoon I hung around watching from the barn. The driver and Frank went into the stable and came out with some packs of something wrapped in plastic and some boxes and loaded them into the van. The driver shook Frank's hand and he smiled and laughed. I kept out of sight if anyone else came - I didn't feel safe, I didn't trust them.

It got to the time I should be going back to school. I asked Frank when the first day was and about uniform and my bus pass. He said,

"You don't go to school, not anymore, you're home schooled - it's sorted. They don't want you. They can't have you near the other kids."

And that was that. I was stuck at the farm. I didn't see anyone. I couldn't speak to anyone. A lot of the time there wasn't even Frank. He sometimes went out later and sometimes he didn't come back.

One day, when he went out late morning, I walked to the main road and down the lane where Orchard Cottage was. That's where I found the boat. There was no one there, it was out of season. I used the bike to get there when I thought Frank was going to be out. It was getting darker, winter time, so I couldn't be out long and if he didn't go out until the afternoon I couldn't go out at all. But most days, I went to the boathouse, and started rowing, just a little bit then more often and for longer. The weather was okay but when it got wet and cold I stayed in the boathouse. I took some stuff over and could stay all day. Frank didn't miss me, when he came home he never looked for me, but I was careful to hide the bike and I never let him know I'd been away from the farm.

After Christmas, not really Christmas for me, Frank was in more often, staying in the office or the stable. The vans didn't come as much, not even at night. He went out with the tractor, but it made him angry, he didn't want to do it. He's not a farmer and he doesn't care about it. He's just doing some of the things he's supposed to, because people would know if he didn't.

There was an argument one night, lots of shouting from the yard. It was something about the number of boxes and money. Someone was cheating someone else and blaming Frank, I think. The next day he changed again. He stopped ignoring me and it was bad now. Back to how it had been before he burned my mum. Every time we were in the same room he said something or hurt me. He said ... I was bad inside ... I had killed my mum, it was all my fault.

I stayed at the boathouse more and more. I waited until he'd gone out one day and went through the bedroom - trying to find some more clothes - and I searched and searched for those pills I gave my mum. The 'Samples' envelope had gone but I looked everywhere in case he'd hidden them. I found some stuck under the top of my mum's bedside drawer. It must have got jammed. I think it's the pack I used, it has that writing on it and four missing - I gave her four. I've still got the pack and I'll keep it safe, always, so I can prove it wasn't me.

And one day, the stable door was open. Frank was out. So I went in. I found some money in envelopes, and I took some from each envelope, not enough so he'd notice.

I took stuff to the boat house and stayed there overnight for the first time. It was cold, freezing, but I felt safer. The next day I rowed to Freeling and went to the shop to buy food, with the money I'd taken. I'd been hungry all the time, there was never any proper food at the farm. The chickens had all died so there weren't even eggs. It felt good to have something ready to eat, so I went back every few days, rationing the money. I checked out places, like the fishing lodge and some of the holiday places. And I went to the farm too when he was out, left things moved about just to make sure he thought I was still around.

A few weeks ago, Rob came back to the farm when I was there. He came once before, last summer, just after we'd moved there. We didn't know about him, or his mum. He was Frank's step-son, just like I was his step-daughter. They had a really bad row about Rob's mum and some money and I was scared ... really scared. Then Frank started a fight and he hit Rob until he left, ran away. When Rob came back this time, he was *still looking for Frank, but he wasn't there that day. Rob asked about my mum and said he would come back and help me. He said he had sorted some stuff out and he was going to the police. I waited and waited for days but he didn't come back. It was almost worse than before, having hope and then losing it.*

People always let you down. I decided I had to do things for myself. I wouldn't rely on anyone, never ever again.

I had a plan. I was going to get stronger at rowing so when the weather got better, warmer and there was more daytime, I could set off. I would escape. Look after myself. Hide in the waterways. Or go to a town, where nobody knew me.

And then you came - and ruined it all.

Chapter Fifty-Five

Day 18: Monday Late at Night - Jack and Rosie

Jack sat huddled in his coat, head deep inside his hood so Rosie couldn't see his face. If he looked at her he might cry, and he didn't think she would want that. There were so many questions buzzing in his head but he didn't know what to say that wouldn't upset her or make her angry.

He heard her shift and turn to her side.

"I'm not a murderer, you're safe," she muttered.

"I know," he said. "We'll get it sorted, in the morning, together."

Day 19: Tuesday very early morning - Jack, Rosie and Lu

Jack woke just when it was getting lighter. It was very early still but he knew he couldn't sleep anymore. He ached from the hard surfaces and he was cold and stiff. He checked Lu. She hadn't slept well and he'd had to cuddle her several times when she woke up but she was sleeping now. He stood up, wincing at the pains shooting down one side from when Harry had shoved him over, and opened the cabin door to go outside.

It was colder out here but it felt good to be outside, feeling the wind blowing across his face. He sat on the little seat at the back of the boat and watched the ripples on the water. Some ducks, he didn't know what kind, swam alongside the boat, looking as if they expected to be fed. "Sorry," he said to them, "Nothing for you today."

He sat for ages, thinking about what Rosie had said. He still didn't know what to say to her but he knew Rosie hadn't killed her mum, he was sure of that. But you did kill Harry, he thought. And I'm not sorry about that. And I hope you don't go to prison for it.

It was almost light when Rosie came out and stretched and groaned. "Worse than sleeping in the boathouse," she moaned. "So cold." She looked around. "It's early, but we could get going."

Jack nodded. "The further we can get, the sooner we get help."

Lu woke when Rosie started the engine. Jack untied the moorings and went to get her up from the nest she'd slept in. She was definitely heading for a full blown tantrum. She was cross and red faced. He couldn't remember if he'd given her any medication last night. He checked the pack, still three left so probably not. He sat her on the bench outside. He gave her the last of the water from her bottle and then some of his with a tablet from the pack. Both bottles were empty now, they really needed to find a refill. He sat holding her at the back, feeding her some banana and crisps, the last of their food, as Rosie drove them forward.

Another time it would have been a nice trip in the early morning quiet, with the whole river to themselves it seemed. The boat chugged gently, quietly, and very steadily, so it was still peaceful as they headed downstream. Peaceful, that was the word, Jack thought. But Lu was fidgeting and he had to hold her all the time to stop her from leaning over and falling in. And there were people every so often on the banks, staring at them as they went by. As Jack looked back at one dog walker, he saw him take a phone from his pocket and start a call.

"Rosie," he called, "Get a move on. He's on his phone."

She looked back, and saw the man looking down at his phone and shake it and hold it up.

"No signal," she said. "He'll have to move to somewhere else to call someone." She looked at the panel and said, "If I go faster it uses more fuel. We might not get far enough."

"Just go as fast as you can. This … all this … running away and hiding. We have to get to your gran's today."

She nodded and Jack felt the boat shudder as she revved the engine. They soon left the dog walker way back and she headed out onto a wider stretch of river. As they went under a bridge Jack partly covered Lu with their coats, pulling their hoods up, so if anyone was looking down they wouldn't see them clearly. He was sure he could hear a police siren in the distance.

It was almost seven o'clock now. People would be out and about, for work and school. This part of the river had more houses and cottages along each bank. Jack felt exposed after so much time in places which were isolated, empty. Lu moaned as Jack held her close to him. "Not long, Lu," he said. "We'll get off and walk."

She wriggled. "Buggy."

"No buggy Lu, we have to walk."

She pushed him hard, hurting the side where he'd fallen. "No! It hurts, stop." He let her go as he doubled over. Lu scrambled away from him across the bench and leaned over so far she slipped over into the water.

"**STOP!**" he shouted as he tried to grab at her. It was one of those times - again - when everything seemed to be in slow motion, like a film slowed down so you could watch it frame by frame. In seconds she seemed so far behind he had no chance of pulling her back, even though Rosie had slowed the engine as soon as he had called out. He pulled off his coat and trainers, (afterwards he wondered how he'd remembered to do that when he was panicking so much) and he climbed over the side to swim to her. Lu was shouting and flailing her arms. He got to her, held her from behind and looked around for the boat. Rosie was hanging over the back, her arms out to catch them as he swam back. She tried to pull Lu upwards but she was still struggling and she was now so wet and heavy Rosie couldn't do it. Jack got an arm over the side to hold on and pushed up from below, so that between them, they got Lu back in the boat. Rosie helped Jack and he lay on the decking sopping wet, exhausted and shaking. Lu rolled over and grabbed him, sobbing. He held her but couldn't move, his side hurt so much.

Rosie heard someone calling from the bank. "Are you alright? Do you need help?" She looked to see a woman looking anxiously at them, dropping her bag and coming to the water's edge. Rosie left Jack and Lu in a wet puddle, and started the engine.

"**Stop!**" she heard, "**Wait!**" But she set off as quickly as she could and left the woman standing on the bank staring after them. They had to get further to the coast, to where they could get to Lowestoft. They had to go by the quickest route, she decided. Where was it she'd gone with Granddad that day, when they went all the way to Westerbridge? She knew it was along this river, along this stretch, but they had turned off … where was that? She looked back at Jack briefly but needed to concentrate so she faced forward and looked carefully for something that reminded her which way to go.

When Jack and Lu came to the cabin, she still ignored them. He had taken off their wet trainers and socks but they still squelched across the tiny cabin. Lu sat on the floor as Jack looked for some dry clothes in their backpacks. He undressed Lu and dried her off with a tee-shirt before pulling on some dry clothes and wrapping her up in his coat. She was still shaking, possibly with cold, but probably because she was terrified. He sat her on the little bench, out of the wet patch and looked for some clothes for himself. There wasn't much left, and nothing was clean but he pulled on a tee-shirt and hoody and … hesitated, looking at Rosie.

"What?" she said.

He looked at the joggers in his hand. He left the cabin and stood just outside, where Lu could see him but Rosie couldn't so he could change his trousers. This is stupid, he thought to himself. I'm standing on a boat where people can see me half naked just so Rosie can't. What is that about?!

Jack went back inside and gathered up the wet stuff into an empty plastic bag which he dumped outside on the deck. The trainers were a problem as they were wet because he'd dropped them in the puddle the rain had made at the bottom of the boat. He found some socks and the pink trainers for Lu but he had bare feet.

"My bag, socks," said Rosie. He looked and found some slightly small but dry socks and pulled them on.

"Thanks," he said, sitting with Lu and hoping he never had to swim in a river again.

"Now you know why lifejackets are the rule. My granddad said that and he was right."

Jack could only agree. The muddy taste in his mouth made him feel sick and he felt his skin crawl and tingle as he thought about all the dirt and dead things in the water. He sniffed his hand. He needed a shower, really needed a shower. Lu clung to him, hurting his side again, but he held her close, trying to warm them both. "How far?" he asked.

Rosie shrugged.

"I think," she said, "We have to turn. It's been a really long time. I'm trying to remember."

Jack peered up to look where they were going. It all looked pretty much the same as all the other rivers, backwaters, stretches - whatever you want to call them. It was busier than where they'd come from, so he kept down low, with Lu, hoping no one was looking for them here.

He felt the boat turn over to the right and Rosie smiled back at him. "It's here, we turn here."

The boat carried them onwards; Lu snuffling but calmer, Jack aching but drier. Rosie was anxious but happier than she had been for a long time. She was worried about seeing Gran, what might happen. But now she knew she could run away, and so if she had to - she could do it again.

Jack felt the boat slow. "Where are we?"

"Fuel is on empty."

He stood up, still holding on to Lu, and looked out. They were slowly coming to a stop in the middle of the small river they were following. Rosie pointed ahead. "If we get up there, we can walk and see if there's a bus."

Jack groaned. They were too easy to spot on a bus. Everyone was looking for them now.

"They're not looking for you, so you get the bus, go to your gran's. I'll hide with Lu."

"You already said that. We're all going to Gran's."

"But you said she blamed you for … you know … your mum … She won't want to see you."

"No, I said that *Frank said* she blamed me. I don't think that's true, not now. I won't know unless I see her and ask her myself."

She's right, thought Jack. Whatever Frank said was probably a lie. But why didn't she help when Rosie's mum died? Did she even know? Had Frank lied to her too?

Rosie slowed even more and the engine spluttered to a stop.

Chapter Fifty-Six

Day 19: Tuesday Early Morning - Police - PC Anstey and DC Tizora

Before Tizora even got to the station for briefing at seven o'clock, she'd turned the car around and headed off to the location of the latest call from someone claiming to have seen the boat with the children. Anstey kept a check on a map on his phone as they raced down the lanes following the satnav.

"It's not easy to get to," he said, "Too many rivers and not enough bridges."

Tizora stopped at a junction, waiting for a gap so she could pull in to the traffic and join the main road.

"Moreton isn't a threat anymore so everyone can work on finding Jack and Lu," Tizora said. She pulled out into the flow of traffic and sped up.

It has to be today, Anstey thought.

Chapter Fifty-Seven

Day 19: Tuesday Early Morning - Jack, Rosie and Lu

Rosie angled the boat over to the bank. Jack had to let Lu go so he left her in the cabin with Rosie and went to the back of the boat. He leaned out and grabbed at the reeds and pulled them closer to the bank. He held on tight and reached over as far as he could but then ... what next? He pulled at the slippery reeds again, slowly pulling the boat closer to the bank. He lifted one leg over the side of the boat and shakily lowered himself onto the reeds. He felt them sink under his weight but they held enough for him to claw his way over them, until he could stand up at the bank. He would be the first to admit that his exit from the river was clumsy and awkward and ... well, it would have made Milo laugh, but he hauled himself onto the bank and rolled over and stood up. He pulled on the mooring rope, making the boat swing a bit, but it came closer and closer and he found a stumpy bush to tie it to. He wrapped the rope around and around and tied a rough knot to secure it. He tugged at it and stood back and looked at it - Rosie would snort at how badly he'd tied it. He didn't care anymore.

It was quiet here but it was nearly seven o'clock and he knew it wouldn't be long before someone came by and started being nosy. Rosie left him in the cabin to get himself changed (again) and she sat on the seat with Lu, who was no longer howling but whining as she ate their last biscuit. Quickly, they re-organised their bags, leaving out the wet things and empty food packaging, but keeping their last few dry clothes.

Jack checked the grab bag. It had Lu's medication, a torch and the letters and the envelopes of money he'd found back at the lodge, but not much else. He decided to put on the wet trainers to protect his feet from stones and rough paths. Cold and oozing was how he would describe the feeling as he laced them up. Shame, he thought, I've only had these a week and I liked them.

He had almost got used to the squelching as they walked along, carrying their bags and holding Lu's hand, when Rosie pulled him to the side and ducked down. Here we go again, he thought as he crouched down next to her.

She pointed forward and nodded at him. He looked out. "What?' he whispered.

"The van."

He looked again.

He looked back at her. "I can't drive."

"But it says Lowestoft."

Jack looked again. How was this helpful? He'd rather catch a bus than steal a car.

Rosie was excited for once. "We can get to Lowestoft."

"But we can't drive. Stealing a boat is one thing ... but a car."

"No, think. There must be a way to get a lift?"

"It might be out on rounds, not going *to* Lowestoft but *from* it. And the driver will just take us to the police. Or call the police."

Rosie knelt down. "There must be a way."

Jack looked again. He motioned Rosie to stay with Lu and squelched nearer to the van, ducking out of sight. It was parked outside a cottage. There was man coming out of the front door. He put some fishing gear in the back of the van, closed the doors and went back inside the cottage.

Jack waved Rosie forward and they crouched near the van.

"I think he's been fishing, he put stuff in. Quick."

He led them to the side of the van and checked around before opening the back. The front door of the cottage was open so the driver must be coming back out. There was enough space for each of them, amongst some boxes and the fishing gear, so they climbed in and Jack gently pulled the door closed. Rosie sat against one side, wedged in between some boxes, her backpack on her knees. Jack sat Lu down next to him and pulled her close. "Quiet as mice, Lu, hide-and-seek."

She burrowed into his side, hiding her face. He winced as she pushed against his ribs. They settled in and waited. They heard a rattle of keys as the driver climbed in and shut his door and then music came on and a phone buzzed as the engine started. Jack held Lu close and tried to wedge them both in close to the side of the van. The van moved and they all felt the rumble as it edged off the run-in and onto the road. As the van turned they fell sideways, losing their grip and balance. Lu cried out and clung to Jack.

"It's okay, Lu," he whispered.

He sat them both upright and looked at Rosie. She was hanging on to a bracket fixed to the wall of the van as the driver accelerated.

It wasn't a good ride. And it went on forever. Jack didn't know how far they had to go and with no windows to see from he couldn't gauge how far they'd come. They rocked painfully from side-to-side every time the van turned. When it slowed they lurched forward, when it stopped they swung backwards. Jack held tight to Lu but she was panicking.

"Sick," she said, looking at Jack with eyes wide open, her face pale.

Jack felt around with one hand, scrabbling to find something she could be sick in. Rosie picked up a box on her side and emptied it; empty food packaging fell out in a messy pile. She passed the box to Jack and - almost in time - he held it to catch the vomit - well, most of it - there was definitely some splatter. Lu cried between heaving into the box.

"All done?" he asked. She nodded miserably as she continued with a low whine. He put the box away from them when the van stopped and Rosie passed him a dirty tee-shirt from her backpack to clean Lu's face with.

"Drink," Lu said.

There wasn't any. "Not yet, when we stop," Jack said.

Lu cried louder; Jack was glad the music was loud enough to mask their noises in the back but he was happier when the van set off again. This was a mistake, he thought. We should have thought about it before doing it. And what was going to happen when they stopped? The driver would open the back and … they'd be caught. All this way, rowing, walking, stealing, breaking in, killing Harry … and just at the end they would get caught.

It wasn't much longer before the van stopped and the engine was turned off. The driver opened the door and the music went off. The door slammed and clicked.

They froze and listened. They could hear a road and some voices. Where were they? Jack tensed, waiting for the door to open. Nothing. Still nothing. Where had he gone?

Rosie looked at Jack and pointed to the door. He nodded. She shuffled forward and pushed at the door. How did you open it from the inside? She tried a thing that looked like a handle, twisting it both ways. It didn't budge. She looked at Jack in panic.

"We're locked in!"

With Lu clinging to him, Jack moved to try the handle. It still stayed firmly locked in place.

"That can't be right, we can't be locked in." Rosie was pulling hard at the handle. "You must be able to get out. What if there's an accident and you have to get out - why won't it work?" Rosie was on her knees, tugging furiously at the door.

"Make it work," she cried, "Get it open."

"SSSHHH!" Jack hissed. "They'll hear!"

"Good. **Get us out!**" And she started banging on the wall with both fists. Lu cried louder and Rosie banged harder.

The handle turned and a face peered cautiously in. Rosie pushed the door wide and fell out onto the ground, panting and crying. A hand helped her up and she clung to the person's arm.

"What are you doing in there?"

Jack looked at the man looking in at him and Lu. I know you, he thought.

"Let's get you out." He helped Jack slide out, tricky with Lu still clinging on to him, and helped Jack stay upright as he wobbled when he stood on firm ground having been flung around in the back of the van. Rosie was crying quietly and Lu was sobbing into Jack's shoulder.

"I'm sorry," Jack mumbled, "She was sick. I got most of it." He pointed to the box. "I'll clean it up."

The man looked at him. "No need, let's get you sorted first, shall we. I know who you are." The man waved his hand and when Jack looked he saw they were on a drive, leading to a bungalow, in a street full of houses.

Jack stood still, holding Lu tighter, trying to decide if he could run holding her.

"You can't take her, I have to keep her, until my mum is better."

A woman came to the front door and called, "What's going on, Tom?"

The man shrugged - a bit like Rosie but not in an annoying way. "Not sure. Get the kettle on, Mary, pet."

Jack looked at him closely. "I know you - the man at the bird place - binoculars."

The man nodded. "Yes, well remembered. And I remembered you when you popped up on TV. Never thought you'd be in my van though."

TV? Why would he be on TV?

"Let's go in, have a sit down and a think."

Jack hesitated. "Wait! The bags."

"They'll keep for later," said Tom as he began to shut the van door.

"No, I have to have them with me," Jack insisted.

"Okey-dokey," Tom reached in and pulled the backpacks and grab bag out onto the drive before he shut the van door. He helped pick them up and carry them to the bungalow.

"Oh my, it's them isn't it!" Mary cried as they went into the hall.

"It is, Mary, who'd have thought it, ay?" Tom dropped his keys onto the hall table and led them through to a kitchen. It was warm and clean. Jack thought he would never be clean again.

"In here, lovelies, sit down. Oh dear," she looked at Lu, "What a mess. My gran would say you look like you've been dragged through a hedge backwards."

"My gran would say you look like the wreck of the Hesperus."

Mary stared at Tom. "Why would she say that?"

"No idea. She was as mad as a bucket of frogs."

Mary tutted and waved him aside. She helped Rosie sit and said, "Let's get you a drink. Are you all hungry?"

As she bustled (as only some ladies can) Jack sank onto a chair at the table with Lu still clinging on, not quite as tightly now. Rosie sat next to him, rubbing her wet face with her sleeve.

"Is juice alright for the little one?"

Jack nodded.

"And you two, juice or tea?"

"Juice and some water, please," said Jack.

"Same," said Rosie.

Jack loosened Lu's coat and helped her with the juice. She was calming down.

He drank the water in a few gulps, and started on the juice.

Tom sat down at one end of the table, while Mary put some bread in the toaster and got some eggs from the cupboard while Jack watched him - if Tom used his phone, he would take Lu and run - he could get away before the police came.

"Wee," said Lu.

"Oh, okay, er ... where's the ..."

"Down the hall," Mary said, "first door on the right."

Jack picked up the grab bag and carried Lu along to the bathroom. He helped her and afterwards tried to clean her face and hands. He checked the window and loosened it, an escape route. He looked in the mirror. He was very grubby, his hair was ... well, filthy ... and his clothes smelt horrible.

Back in the kitchen he dropped Lu's coat with the grab bag by his chair and took his own coat off. He sat with Lu on his lap and was soon eating a plate of scrambled eggs and toast. It was so good to eat like it was a proper breakfast. Their plates were clear in no time and Mary put a wedge of cake before each of them. Jack felt so much better, and he knew Lu did too. She had let him go and was sitting on a chair next to him, eating her cake without moaning, and playing with a toy truck Mary had given her. Rosie hadn't said a word since they'd got out of the van. She had stopped crying though, and she looked less pale now.

Jack thought how patient Tom and Mary were. They must have had a hundred questions to ask - but they didn't. They waited until Jack, Lu and Rosie had eaten and drunk and had rested enough to feel calmer after their nightmare ride in the back of the van.

"So," said Tom, "Want to tell me what we do next?"

That was different, thought Jack. He's asking what we want to do, not telling us what we have to do. What should he say?

Rosie spoke first. "I have to get to my gran's."

Tom nodded. "And who is your gran?"

"Jean, she's called Jean, she lives in Lowestoft, by the big park, the one with the lake."

"Oaklands?" Mary asked. "The other side of town?"

Rosie nodded.

"And you," Tom looked at Jack, "What do you want to do?"

Jack really didn't know what to do now, he just wanted it all to end.

"The police are looking for you - everyone's worried. Do you want us to take you to them?"

Jack shook his head. "I have to keep Lu, until our mum is better."

Lu looked up at him and smiled in her lopsided way. "Mum," she said. "See Mum."

"It might be time to see your mum," Mary said. "She'll be worried about you both."

"Is she okay, do you know if she's okay?" Jack was scared what the answer would be.

"They said on the telly last night that she's conscious, so that's a good step forward."

Jack felt his face flush. Mum was alright, not - well, not dead. Tom patted his shoulder gently.

"You've done a grand job, getting away and looking after your sister," he said. "But you need some help now. They found that man ... he's ... you're safe."

"Harry," said Jack, "He was called Harry."

"Yes, him. He's been found, he can't get you now."

Rosie whispered. "He took Lu. I hit him with an oar. Will I go to prison?"

"No, of course not, not once the police know what happened. He was a bad man, you were helping your friends." Tom leant forward. "So, why do you need to get to your gran?"

Rosie whispered. "I just need to get to her, before my step-dad gets me back. Ask her something. Tell her things."

"Not the police?" Tom asked.

She shook her head.

Tom and Mary looked at each other. Mary nodded at him and he nodded back.

"Well, let's get you to your gran's and see how that works out then." He stood up and started to put his coat back on.

"What about us?" Jack asked.

"How about we go to the hospital and see your mum, let her know you're okay, and then - you have a gran too, don't you?"

Jack nodded.

"She'll probably want to see you too."

They gathered everything together and they all left the bungalow.

"I can't face that van again, "Rosie whispered to Jack. "*I'll* throw up this time."

Tom had heard her and he laughed as he opened a garage door. He showed them a car, a proper one, with seats and everything.

"I won't go in that old thing," Mary said. "It's Tom's old work van. He hasn't even had the sign painted over now he's retired."

"We only got in it because it said Lowestoft," Rosie told Mary as Tom backed the car out onto the drive. "Where my gran lives."

"Oh, don't tell him that, he'll never get it sorted out!" Mary smiled as she said it and Rosie smiled back. "He's got a place where he goes fishing but it's the end of the season so he was clearing it up. I don't let him put all that smelly gear in this car!"

Mary sat in the front and Rosie, Jack and Lu sat in the back. Lu wasn't in a proper car seat but Mary made sure she was on a booster seat and strapped next to Jack, where he held her hand tightly and clutched the grab bag on his lap. Tom drove away from the bungalow and turned onto a main road. As he drove them through town Rosie kept looking at signs and Tom asked her where to turn once or twice until he pulled up in a little car park at the entrance to a park.

"Is this it?"

Rosie nodded. "I think so. It's down that way." She pointed to a pathway running past the lake.

Tom said. "We'll drive around to the other side. Can't have anyone see you yet."

Minutes later they all got out.

"Down there, it's there!" Rosie began to walk quickly on the footpath, everyone following behind.

Lu could only walk slowly, so Tom kept up with Rosie, and Mary walked with Jack and Lu.

"Will she be alright?" Mary asked.

Jack shook his head. "I don't know. It's complicated."

"Yes, you said."

Jack could feel his heart beginning to thump harder as they walked a little way down a street by the park. What would Rosie's gran say? Did Frank lie to her? Or just to Rosie? Or to them both?

Rosie stopped by a house. As Jack, Lu and Mary caught up she went down the path and stood at the door. They stood at the gate and waited. She looked back at Jack. She shrugged. Jack nodded and held up the grab bag to say - if it goes wrong, we run for it. She rang the doorbell ...

Chapter Fifty-Eight

Day 19: Tuesday Morning - Anstey and Tizora

Anstey and Tizora were trying to get their files updated and onto the system as quickly as possible and also read whatever was coming in at the same time. The station was buzzing. There were calls and messages and far too much coffee and sugar.

The third child had now been identified as Frank Rowley's step-daughter, Rosie Hynes. There were so many unanswered questions around Rosie. There were so many people all pushing the case from one person to another. Her school, social services and even the armed forces were involved in unravelling what had happened to her - and her mother, Melissa Hynes. A little snippet of information here and another there and none of the information together in one place.

And Frank Rowley had been picked up at an airport, trying to leave the country. The passengers on the plane hadn't been too pleased when their flight had been delayed but they would certainly have a story to tell as they had watched armed police board the plane and handcuff the man sitting in seat 25D before leading him away.

And then The Boss had called a briefing. Re-group. Decide what to do next.

"So," he said, "Where have they gone? Where would a child go? Where would they escape to?"

It was very quiet in the room as Anstey raised his hand as if he were in school. The Boss stared at him very hard. Anstey pulled his hand down before anyone laughed at him.

"Well?"

Anstey cleared his throat. "Her gran. Rosie had a gran living in Lowestoft. It's on the file. She'd go to her gran."

The room was silent.

The Boss pointed at Anstey and Tizora. "With me." And he strode out of the office, shrugging his arms into his jacket as he left. Anstey and Tizora dashed after him.

Chapter Fifty-Nine

Day 19: Tuesday Mid-morning - Jack, Rosie, Lu, Tom, Mary and Rosie's gran.

… And that was it. A woman opened the door, looked at Rosie and then grabbed her, hugged her and they both cried. Tom and Mary stood with Jack and Lu at the gate. Lu was trying to lick some paint from the gate post but Mary passed some tissues around because, quite suddenly, they seemed to need them.

Then Rosie's gran noticed them properly and stared hard at Jack and Lu. He got ready to run if they needed to but she waved them all to come in. "I can't believe it!" She said between sobs. "So many questions! Come in, all of you, come in."

Rosie beckoned to them and even as they all went into the hall her gran was asking some of the 'so many' questions.

"Where did you find her? Who are you?" she asked. "Why is she with you? And these two … from the news. Shall I call the police?"

She took them into the living room. "And where have you been all this time?" She hugged Rosie. "Why didn't you come home?"

They found places to sit, Jack by the door with Lu and Tom and Mary on a sofa together. Rosie didn't let go of her gran, she stuck close to her as they stood together.

Tom looked at Jack. "This lad knows about it, we just found them, so … best ask Jack."

Rosie's gran looked at Jack and he looked at Rosie, who nodded to say 'tell her.'

"It will take too long to say it all," he said, "And I need to get to my mum. But we ran away together."

"I think the police know that," said Mary. "There's a long trail from the place you were staying ... every day on the news ... everyone out looking for ... that man ... and for you three."

Rosie's gran's face suddenly went pale as something popped into her head. "Have you been there, at that farm, all the time?"

Rosie nodded.

"Dear Lord, if I'd known ... the police, they came yesterday ... they said your mum ... Why didn't you come home?" She began crying again as she held on to Rosie.

Jack had so much swirling in his head he didn't know where to start.

"I think," he said, "That Rosie can tell you all that. She has the story straight ... she told it to me. Frank has been doing something really bad. The police need to know about him."

Rosie's gran said, "They tracked him down yesterday. Arrested him. He's been up to no good. But he told me ... well, he lied. We can sort that out later too. I can't believe you're here and safe."

Tom spoke up. "As Jack said, these two need to get to their mum. So, we'll take them to the hospital, and then, see what their mum says to do next."

"They can stay here, with Rosie, if they need to. I'll look after them."

"Let's get them to their mum first." Tom said. "The police need to know that they're safe but give us an hour? Do you understand what I mean?"

Rosie's gran understood.

357

Chapter Sixty

Day 19: Tuesday Late Morning - Jack and Lu

As Jack and Lu left Rosie with her gran, he felt a bit empty. They waved at them standing in the doorway as they walked back to the car. Jack trusted Tom and Mary - he realised now that sometimes he had to ask for help to get what he wanted, what he needed - but he was still ready to run.

The hospital carpark was packed full and Tom drove round and around before finding a space. Then it was a long walk to the main part and Lu was struggling to keep up so Tom carried her. Jack knew people were staring as they walked past, looking around, nudging each other, and he was worried that the hour was passing quickly, that the police would be here before he saw Mum, that he and Lu would be taken away and even Tom wouldn't be able to do anything about it.

As they walked through the sliding doors of the reception, Tom said to Mary, "Phone ready?" She took out her phone as they queued to speak to the woman on the desk. Her name badge said she was called Ella, and that she was here to help.

"These two have come here to see their mum," Tom said, when it was their turn. "Which ward is Sal Williamson in?"

"Mum," said Lu. "See mum."

Jack couldn't breathe. And he could feel his toes squelch in his still damp trainers as he rocked gently on his feet, getting ready to grab Lu and run if he had to. The woman looked at them, her face changed many times as she realised who Jack and Lu were.

"We can only give that information to close relatives," she said.

"These are her children," Tom said. "That close enough?"

"Er, I'll have to check," she said, and nodded to the woman sitting next to her, Christine: Assistant Leader Reception who began calling someone from the phone on her desk. "Take a seat and someone will be with you when they can."

"My wife is recording this," Tom said, as Mary gave the woman a little wave with one hand and held the phone up with the other. "Jack, ask which ward your mum is in."

Jack stared at the floor but said, "Which ward is Sal Williamson in. She's my mum. This is my sister."

"That information can only be given to adults."

"I'm asking, on his behalf. I'm an adult," said Tom.

"You are not a close relative. I cannot give you that information." She said, looking worried and glancing at Mary who was still holding her phone. Christine: Assistant Leader Reception finished the call and said someone was coming. Jack could hear some muttering from someone in the queue behind him. A small crowd was gathering around in the area behind them.

"Do you watch the news? Read the papers? You *have* heard about these children?" Tom asked.

Ella nodded, very pink in the face. "Policy. I'm just doing my job."

"Yes, you are, Ella: Here to help."

Another woman came from the office area behind. Her badge said Maureen: Reception Leader. As she looked at them she, like Ella: Here to help recognised Jack and Lu.

"Oh, what seems to be the problem."

"They're asking what ward …"

"Oh, yes, that … might be a problem. You are not a close relative, are you, sir?"

"No, but he is." Tom pointed to Jack.

"But …."

"He's a child, I know, we've done that bit." Tom was patient, Jack knew that, but how long was this going to take? Rosie's gran would have called the police by now, and they would be heading to the hospital.

"I want to see my mum," he said loudly.

"Oh, well, yes, I can see that but it's not visiting hours on any wards right now," said <u>Maureen: Reception Leader</u> as she waved at a man in uniform crossing the reception area.

"Where's Mum?" asked Lu. She reached over for Jack and her face began to screw up. He knew it wouldn't be long before she screamed. Jack looked back and saw the area was filling up with people listening to what was going on and some were recording on their phones, like Mary was.

Someone in the queue behind them pushed forward. "What's wrong with you?! Let them see her!" Then there was a real buzz of voices all around.

"It's so stupid … tell them … take them to her… red-tape … on TV …read about it … jobs-worth … get someone higher up …"

He pulled up Lu's hood and turned her face away from them.

"Soon, Lu," he said, "Soon."

"Can I help?" said <u>George: Security</u> who'd come over to see what was going on and who looked twice when he recognised Jack and Lu.

"Yes," said Tom, Mary, Jack and <u>Maureen: Reception Leader</u> all at once.

"All these people, these children and these two here, need to leave, right now," said Maureen: Reception Leader. "They're asking for information we can't give. We're only doing our job."

"But, it's them, off the telly," said George: Security.

Maureen: Reception leader shrugged.

George: Security said, "Come with me, I'll sort it."

"We're not leaving," said Tom.

"No, you're not, but - as Maureen says, she's doing her job - I can do mine. I'm security, let's see what I can do."

As George:Security lead them away there was a cheer from the crowd. Jack stuck close to Mary and Tom, holding the grab bag tighter as they hurried through a maze of corridors to an office. He opened the door and said, "Look who's here."

Jack could see this was like a proper office, with desks and screens and cabinets. And as they went in the three people working there turned round to see who their visitors were.

"Oh, it's them, oh wow!" said one.

"It really is," said George: Security smiling.

"We don't have much time," said Tom, "I think the police may be here soon and ... they want to see her before then."

"No worries," said David: Security Technical and he clicked away and brought up some information on his screen. "Still in Henry Stapleton. Bed 8."

"I'll call up," said Indira: Security Technical Support as she reached for the giant phone on her desk.

George: Security nodded. He turned and began a call on his mobile.

Lu was beginning a quiet moan and Jack knew she would be crying soon. How much longer?

"Guv," called <u>Joseph: Security Assistant</u>, "They just walked in the front door." He nodded to the bank of screens showing the all the security cameras.

On the screen right in the middle, Jack could see two men (one in police uniform) and one woman walking towards reception. His chest pounded as he recognised two of them from yesterday. He saw one of the men was holding his phone just as he heard <u>George: Security</u> speak.

"It's George, from security. No rush, Inspector, just come down to the office, you know the way."

Jack felt utterly betrayed. George had trapped them here.

"Okay, let's go. Indira, stall them as long as you can."

"Yes, guv."

What? Jack looked at Tom. Tom shrugged but he followed George so Jack did too. Mary held his shoulder as he walked, keeping him close. She was still recording on her phone but she seemed less fierce than she had been in reception. In a couple of minutes, George had brought them to a closed double door that had a sign saying *Henry Stapleton Ward*. He buzzed and someone came to open the door.

"It's them, it really is," <u>Nina: Staff Nurse</u> said to someone behind her. She smiled and opened the door wide.

Tom put Lu down and gave her hand to Jack. "In you go. We'll be outside."

"Just here," Mary nodded at the seats along the wall.

"And me," said George.

And that was that.

Later, after lots of crying and hugging with Mum, and lots of fuss and questions - hundreds of questions - Jack felt like he was somewhere else, not there at all. And it didn't feel like it was him answering either but someone else who'd done such weird un-Jack-like things.

Seeing Gran at the hospital in the ward, sitting with Mum, had been the best bit after actually seeing Mum herself - because it meant that Mum had had Gran with her for the last few days, someone who cared about her when Jack couldn't be there. And although Lu had never known Gran, she loved her right from the start and was happier than she had been for days.

They had stayed there all day. PC Anstey had looked after him. He said he knew Milo and said that Milo had helped by bringing the postcard to the police station. And he seemed very happy now that Jack and Lu were with Mum and safe; he hadn't stopped smiling all day. Jack wondered what Milo would say when he told him about all the things that had happened over the past days.

Jack had had a shower and was wearing some new clothes that the detective had gone out and bought for them. And they'd had burger and chips and pizza that PC Anstey had brought up to the ward, sitting right next to Mum and Gran. And some doctors had checked him over and treated all the cuts and the sore patches and the bruised ribs so he didn't hurt so much.

And now, Gran was going to look after him and Lu because they were going to stay in a special house nearby, with a police officer to help, but with Gran looking after them. It was late evening when PC Anstey and DC Tizora drove them to the house. He sat with Lu between him and Gran on the back seat and he watched the traffic and the shops and the houses go past as they drove back across town in the early evening.

All those people, living their lives as if nothing had happened. And it hadn't, not to them. They might have seen about it on the news and a ripple had spread out and they'd talked about it perhaps. But what did they know about what had happened to Mum, and to Lu and to him? Four years ago? Or these past days? Just headlines for a few days, then the ripples spread out to nothing and it was all forgotten.

But he wouldn't forget, like he hadn't forgotten from before. Like Rosie wouldn't forget. He would see her tomorrow, at the police station, to tell them what had happened. He wondered if she would be pleased to see him? Probably not, he thought. After all, it's been complicated.

Well, that's all done. I hope you liked it, at least some of it.

There are other things I could have added at the end, like all the things that happened the next day and the day after and the day after that. But then the story could have gone on for ages. And how do you know when someone's story actually ends?

And you might be wondering what happened to Jack. Was his mum okay? Where did they go to live - back at the flats or back nearer to his gran? And what about Rosie? Did she go and live with her gran? And what about Anstey and Tizora? And Frank Rowley? You're going to have to work out that for yourself.

And Jack and Rosie did lots of things that were wrong - breaking into places and stealing and lying and killing Harry - so what would the police have to say about that? Were they criminals? What would happen to them?

I just wrote the story - it's up to you to decide.

Acknowledgements

Thank you to everyone from my childhood who fostered my love of a good book: the teachers who taught me to read and the local library for being free and my parents who encouraged me to read whatever and whenever I could.
Thank you to every writer whose good books fired my imagination and took me to places I could believe were real and introduced me to people I could believe I could meet.
Thank you to all those book lovers who have enthused, despaired and laughed with me over a good book. Shared reading is the best of all.

Printed in Great Britain
by Amazon